Unto All Generations is a slight re
Not Wither novel with a Bible study added. These
made about Esther and Emanuel's story:

Norman Rohrer/Founder of Christian Writers Guild/ Author/Mentor: *I found myself growing sentimental... marveling at Esther's practical wisdom...This reads beautifully in quaint, delightful English by one who hails from Mother England...I find myself speaking like a Londoner of Esther's time. Your entire book offers a refreshing glimpse of "times forgot" and Scripture asks us repeatedly to "remember."*

Roger/retired Christian bookstore owner: *I don't usually read fiction, but you hit a homerun!*

Cathey/Masters in Library Science/Educator: *As I read this book I laughed, I cried, and I was amazed at the faith and stamina of Emanuel and Esther.*

Judy/Librarian: *Loved this book. Well written.*

Terri/Elementary Educator/Online comment: *Inspiring to me! The story, the lessons, the history...all of it was AWESOME! Thank you for working so hard to give the world another way to see how God wonderfully works in our lives.*

Pam/Avid Reader: *Fabulous! Would recommend to anyone wanting an inspirational read.*

Marilyn/Nurse/Online comment: *Enjoyed reading it, twice. Very uplifting.*

Carol and Virgil/Retired Educators/Volunteers: *I can't explain what the book meant to us. We're ready for the next.*

1

Jerri/Snowbound one Christmas/Retired Nurse: *I had a wonderful Christmas. Why? I used the day to read "Leaves...."*

Ange/Pastor's wife/Teacher: *I read it almost without stopping ... It really draws you in ... like living life there with Esther.*

Donna W/Author: *...I just finished (your novel). I want you to know that it affected me deeply. I have also lost a child and two husbands. I found myself dissolved into tears many times during the reading of your book. Now I'm not saying your book is negative, just that it spoke to me. I also think it teaches good work ethics, love for family, faith, and trust in God. I'm sure Ester's telling of their hardships during the Civil War was how it was for many families. No, our history classes in school don't tell the whole truth. You did an excellent job of filling in the lines, and your hard work and research are evident in your book. I loved the voice of Ester* telling how it was. I hope you will write another book some day. You have talent.*

*"Ester" is a misspelling in the Civil War letters within the novel. To maintain authenticity with those letters, the author chose to misspell a few words and occasionally use improper grammar throughout the novel.

Donna A*/Activities Director: *Oh, Marge... You should do a Bible study to go along with this novel. I hope we're related because there are Williamses in our family!*

(*This Donna spurred me on to add the Bible study...)

𝔘𝔫𝔱𝔬 𝔄𝔩𝔩 𝔊𝔢𝔫𝔢𝔯𝔞𝔱𝔦𝔬𝔫𝔰*

Plus

𝔄 𝔑𝔬𝔳𝔢𝔩 𝔄𝔭𝔭𝔯𝔬𝔞𝔠𝔥 𝔱𝔬 𝔅𝔦𝔟𝔩𝔢 𝔖𝔱𝔲𝔡𝔶

Entitled

*(Holding onto Faith & Humor
When God Dismantles Our Comfort Zones)*

*Novel portion is a 2015 revision of the 2009
Leaves That Did Not Wither*

Writings by Margery Kisby Warder
(Most on www.amazon.com/Margery-Kisby-Warder)

A Novel Approach to Bible Study©: Holding onto Faith & Humor
When God Dismantles our Comfort Zones (2012)

Christmas Musings (2013): (Includes 3 sections)
Christmas in Our Hearts, Last Christmas, and
Mary, Meet Dr. Luke

Elizabeth's Prodigal (2014/2015)

Leaves That Did Not Wither (2009)

Twelve Times Through (Daily Directions for Life from the Book of
Proverbs) 2014, co-authored by Dr. Paul Warder and Margery
Kisby Warder

Unto All Generations plus *A Novel Approach
to Bible Study*©

And short essays in
Bartlesville Wordweavers' Anthologies
"Wings Against the Storm," *Seasons Remembered* (2013)

"The Scoop on Leadership Development," "Marveling at
Gracious Love," and "My Tribute to a Gracefully Aging Lady"
in *Seasons of Life* (2014)

Unto All

Generations

Plus

A Novel Approach to Bible Study©

Entitled

*Holding onto Faith & Humor
When God Dismantles Our Comfort Zones*

Margery Kisby Warder

Parson's Creek Press©

*Discovering Truth Is A Wise Use Of Time;
Applying Truth To Oneself Is Obedience;
Teaching Truth To Others Is Compassion.©*

Printed in the United States of America, 2015

Parson's Creek Press© Mission Statement

*Bringing Inspirational Characters & Writing
to Readers of All Ages
Because Good Words
Can Lead to Good Works©*

Parson's Creek Press©

*Discovering Truth Is A Wise Use Of Time;
Applying Truth To Oneself Is Obedience;
Teaching Truth To Others Is Compassion.©*

Unto All Generations &
A Novel Approach to Bible Study:
Holding Onto Faith & Humor
When God Dismantles Our Comfort Zones
Margery Kisby Warder

©2015 by Margery Kisby Warder
All rights reserved.

Cover Design/Interior Design: Brandy Walker
www.sistersparrowdesigns.com
Published by Parson's Creek Press©

ISBN-9781514203828
Inspirational/Historical Fiction, Christian

Unless otherwise indicated, Bible quotations in the novel are taken from *The Book of Common Prayer and Administration of The Sacraments, Other Rites and Ceremonies of The Church According to the Use of the United Church of England and Ireland: Together with The Psalter Or Psalms of David, Pointed As They Are to Be Sung Or Said in Churches: And The Form And Manner of Making, Ordaining, And Consecration of Bishops, Priests, and Deacons.* Publisher: "Oxford: Printed at The University Press. Sold by (?) Gardner and Son, Oxford Bible Warehouse, Paternoster Row, London. Minion, 32, 1848, Cum Priviligio or from later versions of the King James Bible.

Military prayers and songs within *Unto All Generations* are quoted from a re-issue, non-copyrighted "The Soldier's Prayer Book," arranged from the Book of Common Prayer; with Additional Collects and Hymns. It is a duplicate of the 1861 Union Soldier's Prayer Book, approved by Alonzo Potter, Bishop of the Diocese of Pennsylvania, June 13, 1861, and published in Philadelphia by the Protestant Episcopal Book Society, 1224 Chestnut Street.

Images/icons are from iStock or Microsoft Word (clipart), used by permission.

Unless otherwise noted, elsewhere and in *A Novel Approach to Bible Study*, scriptures are taken from the New American Standard Bible. Copyright © 1960, 1962, 1963, 1968, 1971, 1972, 1973, 1975, 1977 by The Lockman Foundation. Used by permission.

DEDICATION

Unto All Generations

is dedicated first to our Heavenly Father Who delights in designing earthly lives and distributing gifts He knows will unleash joy and humility and thanksgiving as His children begin rightly using all they receive from Him Who loves them more than can be measured,
and is
also dedicated to those He sends to enrich our lives ~
loved ones, family and friends, gift validators, critics and encouragers, patient and skilled advisors, and the obedient brave ones who remind us we'll all face the day of accounting, when what will matter most is where we'll spend eternity,
and
is further dedicated to Esther, Emanuel, and John, and people like them, whose good and quiet lives are passing unnoticed by descending generations,
and, finally,
to authors who will risk bringing truths from past lives of the unknown to light to enrich present day readers.

NOTE FROM AUTHOR

In 2009, I published *Leaves That Did Not Wither*, based upon family history and nineteenth century documents. More recently, I learned various authors were migrating from traditional publishing venues to more economically get their works to the reading public. Since no one had come begging to turn my "little known novel" into a blockbuster movie, I decided to use CreateSpace for my novel also.

Removing *Leaves That Did Not Wither* from the market meant the same story needed a new ISBN. I opted to give it a new title and cover also. I removed comments made by my precious mother, who is now deceased. I added my "Novel Approach to Bible Study" discussion guide, originally sold separately. This edition is entitled *Holding onto Faith & Humor When God Dismantles Our Comfort Zones.*

Leaves... and *Unto All Generations* are essentially the same novel about Esther, Emanuel, and John, except that the latter includes the study guide.

My other novels' truths will be based upon fictious characters and events. This novel relied heavily upon written and verbal family history and historical documents.

If my writing pleases you, I'm told "reviews" are like "gold," so I thank you in advance. I enjoy Bible study. Occasionally I may be available for discussions or speaking which can be arranged through: author.speaker4Him@gmail.com. Thank you,

Margery Kisby Warder

Margery Kisby Warder

TABLE OF CONTENTS

Unto All Generations & A Novel Approach to Bible Study:

Holding onto Faith & Humor When God Dismantles our Comfort Zones

INTRODUCTION

Welcome to a "novel" approach to do Bible study. You may choose to skip ahead to read the novel, pause here to begin the Bible study, or combine reading the novel with Bible study.

PREPARING TO GET OUR FEET WET

We live in exciting times. One advantage many enjoy is the ability to get behind the scenes after we've watched a DVD that warms our hearts or even one that gives us the willies while we're waiting for the culprit to meet his demise. By spending a few minutes scrolling through the options for listening to writers, directors, actors, and producers, we're offered additional insight into the movie we just watched.

This study guide, *A Novel Approach to Bible Study: Holding onto Faith & Humor When God Removes Our Comfort Zones*, can be beneficial even without reading *Unto All Generations*. Or, you may be one who finds the novel satisfying by itself, without behind the scenes information. I've been told the protagonist, Esther, likes to settle into one's mind as a comfortable houseguest whose friendship readers savor. One method to gain insight into her way of thinking would be to explore questions in the study guide.

This discussion guide is not designed to be a "quick read." It uncovers both novel and Biblical truths, but the questions will likely teach us more about ourselves. Even if you choose not to read the novel, the Bible study has been created to help the participants explore ways to hold onto faith, and humor, even when, as the title says, God dismantles our comfort zones.

In the novel, young Esther tries to find solid footing in her struggles with Victorian conditions as a young wife. In 1858, just a week after arriving in Michigan, unexpected responsibilities fall upon broken-hearted Esther, and a few years later, though she doesn't hear the Civil War's canons, its pain strike her, too. *Unto All Generations* follows Esther's faith journey. Interestingly, her story may parallel ours, too.

When I write, I pray I'll waste neither my time nor any time you would spend on my writings. We'll all answer to God about the use of our time, our mind, our resources, our opportunities, and whatever else God grants to us. God's Word helps us understand how to fulfill God's purpose for our lives.

Thank you for experimenting with this approach for studying the Bible. You'll probably want to record your answers where you can refer to them later, or for discussion with others. If you don't have a Bible, free online versions are at: *https://www.biblegateway.com/*

Your purchase of this book permits you to copy portions of the study guide for others in your discussion groups, but please include copyright information.

May truths within this book bless your life long after you've read the last page.

Margery Kisby Warder,
Esther's Great-granddaughter

A Novel Approach to Bible Study
Lesson One (Questions 1-16)
(Prior to Beginning the Novel)

Would you be excited if someone could guarantee that you were going to leave a legacy? What if you knew your tax-free legacy could impact not only your current family and closest friends, but also coming generations?

Whether we're aware or not, we each are leaving a legacy. Whenever we interact with others, we impart our respect and blessing, or our disapproval, or leave the rude impression that we believe our lives are more important than theirs. Scary, isn't it?

Others notice our actions and reactions. We pass along our legacy in each encounter we have.

By the grace of God, if we are intentional about blessing others, people can benefit from the way we live our lives, even if our encounter is brief and even if our financial resources are minimal.

Our daily lives reveal where our eyes are fixed. If we are focused on eternity, we'll be more often stepping away from our inclination towards selfishness and leave, instead, a positive faith-filled impact.

God longs to spend time rejoicing over us. Imagine that. Remember how that tiny baby or those old familiar friends left us rejoicing? We know what it is to rejoice over someone. Please look up Zephaniah 3:17, and read about God rejoicing over His own.

It is possible, of course, to detract from what God wants to demonstrate through our lives. In the novel, you'll meet people easy to like. You'll also meet a character or two you'd probably not want to move in next door or marry your best friend.

Hmm, maybe today someone is praying about the neighbor he or she hopes to have, or for the perfect match for his or her loved one. Have you considered how intentional God is when it comes to developing neighborhoods? You do bring your legacy with you wherever you settle.

Esther and Emanuel left a legacy that reached past their time, past their children and grandchildren's lives, and on into mine. I've worked to continue their legacy. *Unto All Generations* is one tangible way I'm passing along their legacy.

1) The early version of the novel referenced "leaves" in its title. Read Psalm 1 and Jeremiah 17:7-8 from the Old Testament. Also, read Psalm 92:12-15. Briefly discuss how the Word of God uses trees as pictures of a human's life. (In some other references, God declares the tree shall be cut because of its pride, etc., which ought to cause us to consider our life's impact.) What causes leaves to wither?

2) Using the above references, describe the difference between the blessed and the wicked lives.

3) Read Deuteronomy 7:9, Psalm 89:1 and Psalm 103:17-18. Discuss "faithfulness" and the impact upon lives that come after our last earthly breaths. Part of Esther's purpose in "writing her memoirs," and the author's in this novel, could be summarized in Psalm 78:1-4, Psalm 145, and Proverbs 17:22. Jot down those purposes.

4) What is your style, or the styles of communication you have observed in others, that tell coming generations of the Lord's glorious deeds, His might, and the wonders He has wrought/done during your earth-time? Does humor have a role in sharing faith? What steps will help you become more intentional about leaving a "faith legacy" for those who come after? How and when will you do that?

5) Do you find it difficult to listen to people whose mastery of your language is obviously inferior to yours? When have you been surprised by their impact upon your life? When did you "go to bless others," only to discover you received as much or more than you gave? How willing are you to have a fictional character "coach" you?

Think on this: Early in the novel, you'll realize Emanuel is principled, but illiterate; Esther is quaint but becoming increasingly bold, though her grammar and spelling are sometimes jarring until you make yourself comfortable as they "converse" with you. These rather simple people are hospitable, so relax with your tea as they reveal their hearts. Perhaps you'll decide they make good "life coaches." After all, their "office hours" are perfect for your schedule and their rate is reasonable.

6) If your circumstances have not yet exposed you to people quite different from yourself, think of Moses' stuttering hesitation to obey God's call to become the leader appearing before Pharaoh, or think of others in the Bible who were "unqualified" for their assignments. Why does it make sense that God would use the "unqualified"?

7) Summarize what James writes in the New Testament, chapter 4, verse 6.

8) If you are willing, briefly share the lesson or wisdom you gained from someone you might not have chosen to be your teacher.

READING TIP: This novel mixes history (including personal family history), a fictional "memoirs/ autobiography," inspirational romance, and special literature. It begins with Esther at her writing desk revealing her most recent days in 1880, but flashbacks quickly transport readers back to Esther's childhood and other events and thoughts she wants to include to bring her, and us, back to her writing desk in 1880.

Novels generally let us watch characters' lives change. Some changes are internal, some external. Often change comes through circumstances the character faces. As you read this novel, pay particular attention to what motivates new directions or deepens character or faith for both Esther and Emanuel.

9) Esther's 1912 obituary revealed that on her tenth birthday, her older brother gave her a copy of the scriptures and liturgy commissioned by Queen Victoria. Why might a brother give such a gift and how might it be helpful if a young girl's dreams shatter by life's "real" circumstances? Why are Bibles given, or not given, now?

10) Please read the book's back cover and compare those words with the New Testament passage found in the Biblical book entitled Romans, chapter 8, verses 31-39 (*If you have time, you might enjoy the whole chapter's insight about our own spiritual life*).

11) The same Romans 8 verses can be read by Christ's followers today. How might this passage help you in your circumstances?

12) Which other passages help you remain patient during times when life isn't unfolding as you had hoped or planned?

13) Stress can be unhealthy; sometimes we must alleviate stress for our own health. However, if we're just longing for the "easy life," why might we, or God, permit stress to strike a harsher blow than it warrants?

14) What have you come to understand as the definition and "benefits" of stress? Why would Sovereign God permit stressful situations?

15) How might you improve the author's expression of trusting God's sovereignty and trustworthiness? Her acronym for the purpose of stress is: **Sovereign, Trustworthy, Righteous, Eternal (God) Stretching Saints.**

16) A friend's mother's note in her Bible quoted Mark 7:37a, saying that when we're called aside in Heaven to discuss what transpired here on earth, we will be able to say, like those astonished onlookers, "He hath done all things well..."

Before plunging into Esther's story in *Unto All Generations*, (or *Leaves...*) would you be willing to pray the simple prayer that follows?

Prayer *Father God, as I read this novel or work on questions in this Bible study, may Biblical truths placed within it be an encouragement to me in my daily life, and, though the book is both fact and fiction, may I be enlightened and encouraged to live a life that fulfills Your design for my life.*
In Jesus' Name, Amen.

If you like combining the study and novel idea, please now read the following introduction by "Esther," entitled, "Would You Take a Cup of Tea with Me before We Start?" Questions follow each chapter. You may skip on to the Bible study sections only, but some questions that relate to the novel may be more difficult to answer.

UNTO ALL GENERATIONS
Introduction by Esther
CHAPTER 1

WOULD YOU TAKE A CUP OF TEA WITH ME BEFORE WE START? (Michigan, 1880)

I prayerfully search my heart as I write on these papers. Many, no, most, dreams was shattered.

Even so, God is good. God's faithfulness and His mercy was upon me. God-willing, it shall pass unto all my coming generations.

CHAPTER 1
WOULD YOU TAKE
A CUP OF TEA ...
1880

Many, O LORD my God, are Thy wonderful works which Thou hast done, and Thy thoughts which are to usward: they cannot be reckoned up in order unto thee: if I would declare and speak of them, they are more than can be numbered.

From my 1840's Psalter, Psalm 40:5
King James' Version of the Holy Bible

Tuesday, March 2, 1880
Rural Livingston County Michigan, Reed Farm

If I could live anywhere, I'd live by a rippling stream. My soul finds peace and refreshment as sunlight shimmers across rippling water. In that quietness, I listen for what's important, what's true, and how to finish obligations layed on me. I draw life and peace from water. If I was a tree, I'd beg to be planted streamside so not one leaf would wither 'fore its time.

Nobody knows where a journey's to lead when God plants us on this earth. Mine began on March 20, 1830, in West Head, Norfolk, England, surrounded by kin. It's taken me across the Atlantic, down the St. Lawrence, and bumped me over dusty roads to set me off here near Green Oaks, Michigan, with a husband laying 'neath the sod in an unmarked grave dug in a lonely battlefield during America's Civil War, leaving me to raise children who never layed eyes on the British Empire that once ruled a quarter of the entire globe. 'Tis fair to say I've had times reverently asking Almighty God, 'How can this dare be called good?' I've also knowed joy others likely

18

envy. I'm a woman blest.

After much restlessness, I undertake this accounting, mostly for my children and my children's children, to fulfill promises and set straight records 'bout Emanuel Kisbey. Seems sometimes a task falls to us, not so much 'cause we'd do it best, but 'cause nobody else sees what needs doing. These blank pages, soon to holt words by one not schooled as she'd wish for such an undertaking, stand between me and peace. I've learnt to do whatever's necessary for my inner peace, including risking judgment of those more capable, just so sleep comes peaceful.

Who claims life's fair? Life's life. None gets out alive, except the likes of Enoch and Elijah in God's Book. We'll likely face death ourselves. We'll certainly lose loved ones. Heartaches can steal from our courage supply. Here I sit with 'Civil War' letters from my Manuel, the Union's Pvt. Kisbey, who worked hisself to death for respect from famly and fellowman. Unless I write, how can others know his life's intentions or his hopes of holting together famly, whether 'twas his parents', his own, or even his country's?

In some ways 'tis a wonder Manuel and me became husband and wife, for our early lives differed though we was both of Norfolk. His famly farmed near Stow Bardolph. 'Tis good we never met in Norfolk, for I'd not likely saw then what a good man Manuel was to be.

We quiet Copseys was more proper than his loud Kisbey clan, and 'parently his people's children worked fields more'n lessons. Some was never schooled atall. Most days Emanuel's famly was poor. He was always illiterate. 'Sides all that, Kisbeys never registered with the State Church which we Copseys thought good Englishmen did. No, Manuel's people was Methodist. 'Fore I'd look at Manuel, much had to change.

Mostly me.

'Bout thirty years ago, July 1852, when I married my beloved Manuel, for that's how I called my first husband knowed t'others as Emanuel, I made a promise I'm still keeping. I promised God I'd love and honour Manuel till I

19

died. A bit earlier I'd made a similar promise directly to God, knowing God don't take vows lightly.

I keep promises best I can. If John Reed hadn't respected such vows, I doubt we'd married each other here in Michigan a few years ago, but that comes much later in the story.

Meanwhile, I sit here with but a handful of things belonging to a man who tried to earn respect from famly and fellowman for more'n just hisself. How will others know Manuel's life mattered? When his dreams and plans was trampled by people, circumstance, or the government, did he leave anything for his children and grandchildren or others on life's journey? Not answering those questions has kept me from peaceful sleep.

Lately John's suspicioned only writing will cure my restlessness. With my fiftieth birthday approaching, John and the children gifted me with fixing this upstairs hallway as my writing room. John's even hired Alice to run the householt so I'm free to write. He says to get at it, but in a gentle tone.

I get daylight from two windows. When I look up from these papers, I can keep watch on the lane and fields of this fine farm. I'm trying not to look more'n I should, though.

The stair-doors, which we usually scold children for not closing, is left so heat from downstairs fires in the cook-stove and parlor hearth reach this hallway. I'm dressed so chills won't distract my thinking. I'm comfortable enough. If I call down the stairs or ring this little china bell I'm to keep on the table, I'm tolt Alice will supply more hot English tea to keep my fingers nimble. Woe is me, I'm without excuses!

Still, I hesitate, praying as I sift fifty years down to what's most important to pass on. Truth be tolt, I seldom excuse stalling or stewing, so I'll pray and write.

Words John spoke yesterday won't go away. He reminded me my nature's been that once I felt peace, I could face any circumstance. John figures withholding truths 'bout my journey with Manuel has not only unsettled me, it's kept others from peace as well. Inner peace is my soul's measuring rod. Disobedience shrivels my soul.

But can I do this? Anna's schooled more'n me and she's but ten. 'Duty,' John says, 'often asks us to both sacrifice and risk humiliation.' As I write, I pray it also furthers Truth.

So, how does one measure the worth of a man whose government 'parently doubts existed, a man long buried in an unmarked grave far from we who knowed and loved him? What words might convince an angry son his mother did not send his father off to die in war, or that she's never forgot his father? Who throws troubles and heartaches and trials at us, waiting to see if we'll turn backs on the only One who hears our deepest sighs?

And who am I that I should try to answer such questions?

Yesterday afternoon, I mulled over these thoughts while walking to my favorite spot. Most days the collie and I make our way there. 'Tis beyond the paschure gates, down where our farm's stream curves among stately oaks and wild plum, though now most trees look hopelessly barren. Still, knowing hope's never froze beyond thaw and that one season follows t'other, 'tis a peaceful place to clear the head, letting the mind and heart listen to God and common sense.

Countless times that spot's fed and strengthened my soul. Later this spring, incense for that sanctuary with stumps as pews will drift from wild plum and fruit tree blossoms 'cause John's orchard is just east of the fence. And later still, when apples and peaches burden trees whose roots reach vainly toward the stream, vainly 'cause proud tall oaks stand first in line to drink, that spot will welcome hushed fishermen pondering thoughts, slapping sweat bees, and catching supper. Each summer tries teaching fruit tree roots to depend on the Almighty for rain or the buckets we carry to water them, but don't nature seem reluctant to quit striving and straining? Even ours, sometimes.

On summer mornings, I rise early and after gently starting a little cookstove fire, I take my Psalter, my *Book of Common Prayer,* and walk through dewy grass down to 'my' stump where I sit alone, praying till the sun wakes nature and lights pages I use for meditation.

'Fore long songbirds' twitters is drowned by commotion 'round the pump at the end of a line of bare planks where John put the windmill, or else all the outhouse traipsing bids me take up the common duties of homemaking and motherhood. Don't think I mind them. Fact is I'm guessing I was born to cherish famly responsibilities. But now for a few days, thanks to my understanding famly, I'll sit upstairs and try my hand at writing ~ least 'til that favorite spot beckons too loudly or I despair at thinking I thought I should use up life's hours on this writing task.

On wintry days like yesterday, I take the old brown horse blanket to brush snow from the stump and to cushion and warm me while I sit. I've tolt John the best seat on the farm is my stump by the stream. He claims 'tis his chair near the parlor fire, espeshly after supper. Guess we differ 'cause I spend most hours inside stirring and he spends most hours outside dealing with whatever comes to Michigan farmers throughout the year.

But, anyways, yesterday when I got back to our house I knowed John'd planned something. I s'pose 'twas done to encourage me, and it did, for humour can. John ceremoniously gathered the children still home 'round our kitchen's water bucket. He had each child solemnly put one hand on the pail and raise t'other, as though they was 'fore a judge. I just shook my head, wondering what he was up to, but his brown eyes twinkled as he gestured comic'ly, 'Children, unless there's a fire threatening life, bones poking plum through skin, or bleeding you can't stop, DON'T bother your mother when she's upstairs writing. She's got fifty years to cover and we'll all eat better once that's writ!'

Anna panicked, wondering if I'd be out of sight till she's married. John looked so serious when his low voice teased her, 'Oh, young lassie, I'll be keeping callers away years after your mother finishes writing.'

Right then I knowed 'twas time I cut excuses and just sit up here and start to write.

Michigan's a long ways from the motherland Manuel, me,

22

and our infant Jonathan Levi left in 1858, waving to what was left of our famlys standing 'long England's shore. Tears threaten just thinking of that time. Such mixed feelings was inside, though being English, espeshly like Mother, I tried not to not show them. T'is hard to believe, Manuel and me, cuddling Jonathan, hoping we was right to set off, knowing t'was likely we'd never go back. Ever.

How had I come to love and wed Manuel when much of my childhood was in London and his was not? Lots of people and situations made tracks across our childhoods. Some we hardly noticed back then, but a memory of them flashes like lightning into grown up minds. 'Spose you'd say we brought England with its people and situations over to this new land, for each had shaped our thinking and character.

More came, too.

In general, 'tis safe to say Queen Victoria's England had 'least three enemies surrounding m a n y householts. These snuck on as stowaways when we crossed the Atlantic, eager to serve under 'least one of their new commanders who'd craftily claw its way into our lives.

When attacked either side of the Atlantic, we'd discover we was equipt for each skirmish, though often Courage pled to flee if Doubt got to struggling hard against Triumph. True to form, the most dangerous adversary lurked 'round in disguise, intent on preventing Life or devouring it with little provocation, plotting to shrivel us 'fore our time. 'Tis so even now.

Just to be clear, I'll tell you, no, none of these enemies was Manuel's Aunt Gertrude, though many a time 'twas tempting to think of her as such.

This morning our Reed householt's quiet other'n Alice's stirring downstairs. I see tracks in the snowy field show that the children took the practical shortcut to school where lessons is underway.

Here I sit, a tall stack of blank papers gaping at me, waiting for my setting records straight and keeping promises I made to Manuel and to God.

Most people won't ever learn of Manuel and me.

Perhaps even some famly will keep questioning who we was or why we acted as we did. Such would delight the adversary ~ but I hereby defy his interference as I write of God's faithfulness while Manuel and me stood in the gap waiting for others to take our posts.

Though sometimes my eyes spilt more'n one bottle could holt, when I, Esther Copsey Kisbey Reed, pencil the last page, I hope our children and other generations understand better how we commoners was kept by our good and merciful God, kept as though we was royalty, but with less show.

Seems reasonable I write first of our people and childhoods in England nearly fifty years ago. I'll start with a scripture we Copsey children memorized and go ahet and call it 'Chapter 2.' It'll make John smile when I tell him I got that far!

(You may continue the novel without doing the Bible study or elect to choose questions to complete.)

A NOVEL APPROACH TO BIBLE STUDY
LESSON TWO - QUESTIONS 17-46
(INCLUDES QUESTIONS REFERENCING "WOULD YOU TAKE A CUP OF TEA WITH ME?" CHAPTER ONE)

17) What does Esther think is important to experience and know, and what does she reveal about her faith?

18) Read also John 4:7-14 and John 7:37-39a, John 8:12, Romans 8:28 and Ephesians 2:10 and jot down how these verses add wisdom to the discussion.

19) What are reasons why Esther is going to write her "memoirs"? You can decide at the end of the novel if she accomplished her goals.

20) Explain how important inner peace is to Esther.

21) Think back to times when you lacked inner peace. From your experience or study, what seems to be the cause of that uneasiness within the soul?

22) Consider at least these two references to "peace" from the Old Testament, Isaiah 26, verse 3, and from the New Testament, Philippians chapter 4, verse 7.

23) How important is "inner peace" to you, and how do you cope when you do not have it? See also Matthew, chapter 11, verse 28. (Come unto Me...)

24) We read that Esther habitually seeks the solitude of the stream because it helps her sort out what's important, what's true, it clarifies how to complete her duties, refreshes, and also gives her peace. Compare Psalm 40:5, with the way Esther sees life by the stream. What four things does this verse from the Old Testament reveal about God and His ways?

25) Queen Victoria issued the order for the new printings of the "Book of Common Prayer" during the 1840's. That spiritual guide included lessons given for both morning and evening readings and for special occasions, and presented the Psalms in rhyme. Esther's obituary indicated her brother gave Esther her own "Common Book"

for her 10th birthday. Who gave you your first Bible? Do you still have it? To whom have you given a copy of the Bible?

As you continue reading the novel, consider what Esther seeks and whether or not you think she received what she sought as her life unfolds.

As you consider Romans 8, verses 28 and 29, and the events in your own life, are you at a place yet when you can "bear witness" to its truth, or are you still waiting for that truth to be confirmed in your understanding?

26) What do we know as some of Emanuel's goals?

27) What promises has Esther made and what weight does she give promises?

28) When have you made, or when do you think you would you be willing to make, similar promises?

29) How strong is your desire to have a spiritually healthy, responsive soul?

30) Who are "healthy soul" people you would compare with Esther?

31) What do you think might be the three or four enemies most Victorians faced in England and which crept on board when Esther headed to the young United States?

32) What or who do you suspect is or will be Esther and Emanuel's most dangerous enemy? To understand a bit more about that most dangerous enemy, read these New Testament passages through and briefly jot down what you learn:

   A: 1st book of Peter, chapter 5, verses 6 -11:
   B. 2nd book of Timothy chapter 4, verses 17-18:
   C. Ephesians, chapter 6, verses 11 - 17:
   D. What did Jesus say *about the enemy* when He was talking to the 'religious" leaders? (John 8:44):

33) Esther almost humorously tells readers that Manuel's Aunt Gertrude is not their most dangerous enemy but that it is tempting to think of her as such. Why do you suppose we sometimes

mistakenly identify a cantankerous acquaintance as our enemy? Who would be pleased if we mistakenly saw people in that way?

34) If we recognize our opposition is not the "flesh and blood" person giving us a rough time, but that the opposition is coming from God's enemy (who will be finally defeated by Jesus Christ in judgment), how does/should that change our attitude toward those who attack or offend us? When should we be willing to leave the end results up to God alone?

35) We read that Esther and Emanuel "stood in the gap" during their generation, waiting for others to come in the next generations to also stand in the gap. She also speaks of declaring that a faithful God mercifully cared for her and Emanuel as though they were royalty.

Read Psalm 89, verse 1 and Psalm 100, verse 5. These passages speak of passing stories of God's faithfulness from one generation to another. Why should we be reminded that God does not want to exclude any generation from knowing Him? What does that mean to you? Can you trace the "story-tellers" of truth in your life? Where did you learn of God's love for you?

36) What do you think Esther means by standing in the gap? (We'll look at the "stand" verses in question 36, which also helps with answering this question if you want to peek.) Read 1 Corinthians 15:1-2 and 1 Peter 5:6-12.

37) If followers of Jesus Christ are to stand in the gap during their times on earth, and if you are already a follower of Him, how are you preparing for, or participating in, that responsibility?

38) The Bible uses the word "stand" hundreds of times. Note how "stand" is used in the following passages from the New Testament:
 A. I Corinthians 16:13-14
 B. Ephesians 6: 10-20
 C. Philippians 4:1
 D., Colossians 4: 12
 E. Ezekiel 22: 23-31.
39) Before we end this portion of the study, picture the Body of Christ forming an army to defend the Lord's triumphant reclamation of all that is to be His. Where does reclamation need to happen in your community? How could you help? In our nation?

40) How can Christ's followers help extend the Lord's "territory"? Do you work at this task alone, or in groups? Which do you prefer? Why?

41) Each believer has a responsibility to "hold his place" until relieved of duty. If all believers will stand faithfully in their "assigned" gap, the enemy loses ground during that generation's faithfulness. We may grow "weary in well-doing," but the enemy's intentions are certain; his arsenal is creatively varied. Isn't it sobering to think that the enemy has no plans to leave any generation, any newborn, without seeking to destroy, to devour, to distract from learning about Jesus Christ? How can you go to battle for the eternity of your loved ones, or others near or far from you?

42) Remember the enemy of Jesus Christ is a deceiver. He doesn't want to be detected unless you're ready to enlist with him. Sometimes the enemy of Jesus Christ changes tactics, becoming subtle, even putting believers into what an Arabic Christian calls "the lullaby of satan." The enemy tests for success through skirmishes. He's willing to change tactics so he can take as many to hell with him as he can. He plots in open defiance of God's Son who sacrificed Himself to spare each individual. Which is more likely for you and those around you: to get distracted from accomplishing your service to the Lord or to despair or become fearful because "the world is so evil?" What can you do about it?

43) It's never been easy to follow Jesus, but God knows how all of this plays out and He is VICTOR! In this world, Jesus said, we will have troubles and persecution, misunderstandings. Do you think grudges seek a heart in which to harbor so that "the work" stops?

44) Sometimes love is the toughest choice to make, but it's expected by our Savior, especially within the Body of Christ. See John 13: 34-35. Has "being loving" ever been tough? Have you ever thought "love" was too weak to make the hurdle? Who is the source of love? Prayerfully read 1 John 4:8-9.... There aren't always "pretty answers" to conflicts – but we have the responsibility of having our hearts as clean as they can be. Maybe it's good to ask ourselves, "Is this mess so pitiable that I'd prefer either of us forego eternity with the Lord?"

45) Be wary of joining a "skirmish." Discern who the coach is. In the early days of the "Church," one attraction for non-believers was

"seeing how much they (the church attenders) loved one another." Is this a sign of the church today?

46) Believers have many opportunities to join a fresh battle wherever the Lord's enemy is setting up camp and preparing for attack. Sometimes the Body of Christ stands in the gap on offense and sometimes on defense. How is your generation of believers standing in the gap(s), holding the line until the next believer generation comes to relieve you? Are you on offense or defense? Explain your answer. Where are you preparing to do battle next? What are you wearing? Ephesians 6:10-19.

Prayer:

Lord God, help me to remember there is a war going on even when I cannot see it. Remind me that wherever there is a lack of true peace, there is a place where Your story needs to be offered to the hearts of mankind.

We acknowledge that only You can change hearts, but we also acknowledge that the lost have a better opportunity to be in a personal fellowship with You if we believers let You rule in our hearts and minds, listening for Your "orders".

Stir my soul, Lord, so that I realize it is my highest privilege to worship You, and my highest, most worthwhile accomplishments will be obedience when You ask me to faithfully serve You. Instill wisdom and courage as I spend time in Your Word alone or in fellowship with Your army on earth. I am available to hold the post You assign me until You either move me to another post or relieve me of my duties on earth and carry me into eternity where I can more fully celebrate Your victorious and loving gracious work on earth.

In the days ahead, help me more fully understand both my daily responsibilities within Your kingdom and the various steps I need to take to become even more fully prepared and equipped to faithfully stand "battle ready" in my assigned gap so I honor You in love and truth.

In Jesus' Name, Amen.

CHAPTER 2

ESCAPING

OUR

CHILDHOODS

(1830-1842)

Chapter 2
Escaping Our
Childhoods
(1830-1842)

Remember now thy Creator in the days of thy youth, while the evil days come not, nor the years draw nigh, when thou shalt say, I have no pleasure in them.

My Psalter, Ecclesiastes, Chapter 12, Verse 1
King James' Holy Bible
Green Oaks, Michigan
March, 1880

None save God knows where a journey's to lead when He plants us on this good earth. As I tolt you, mine began March 20, 1830 A.D., in West Head, Norfolk, England and now has set me off here in Livingston County, Michigan with but memories of the motherland that once ruled a quarter of the globe. My journey's seldom been with ease, but I'm a woman blest for I've been led and taught by Triune God's providence. In spite of all that's happened, I say with quiet joy, 'God is trustworthy. He bestows abiding peace.'

'Course I don't remember my birthing day, fifty years ago this month. I was tolt Mother, Hannah, called by some famly Ann or Anna, endured a mother's unpleasantries while waiting a newborn's cry to turn a hard day into a tender wonder.

Except for birthing, my very proper English mother kept most things hid inside till Manuel joined our famly. When Mother learnt to show her feelings more, and she and I grew closer and I knowed I'd miss her when we left for Michigan. Mother's surname was Knight, but if her Knights had spellbinding tales, they was kept from me. Elders made it clear the Almighty intentionally gave children two ears, but

31

only one mouth. I never asked Mother's age, for 'twas not proper to inquire 'bout that or much else regarding elders.

My father, William Henry Copsey, so industrious his ears rarely caught more'n Will-, instilled 'principles' and 'diligence' in us children. Father lived these characteristics whether worshiping in the Church of England, tending Norfolk's fields, steering barges 'long England's eastern shorelines, or considering shipments at London's docks from countries whose behaviors he questioned. Father was practical. James was to one day earn wages proper for the head of a householt. We daughters was to find husbands who'd better our lives. After marriage, we was to dutifully bless him with disciplined grandchildren to enjoy.

Upon hearing my birthing cry, James determined to look out for his little sister. I'll always treasure the *Book of Common Prayer* he gave me for my tenth birthday. I'll copy from it as I write, for its words are precious to me. James was born 'bout 1817 and departed this world the year after I married Manuel, Emanuel, who gave me my Kisbey name.

My beloved sister, Sarah, five years older'n me, spoke words fit for my heart if my heart was fit to house them. No doubt I tried her patience, but she 'parently had ample supply, for she seemed so perfectly good that when we confessed our waywardness in our Cathedral, I suspicioned she was lying. We loved each other dearly. Later she and her Henry worked to see I got a suitable husband. It was they who beckoned us across the bottomless Atlantic in 1858.

Norfolk's fresh air, fragrant fields, and famly ties nourished our early years. I fondly recall two times our famly rode the barge all the way from the Wesbech region through the Wash and chilly North Sea to take in the beauty of the splashing coastline of England's eastern shores when we was headed toward London. The first adventure was for knowledge, the second, for our move.

I suspicion we'd traveled more had Mother been able to keep the Atlantic's strong breezes from blowing 'bout our dresses. I know her protests prevented any consideration of making the barge our home, though some bargemen's famlys did. I smile remembering how quickly Mother pulled washing from the barge's line to keep England's eyes from seeing Copsey undergarments.

Father knowed his next task was to find us suitable housing on London's edge. 'Twas sensible we move closer to Father's work at London's docks, though several Copseys tolt us, 'The closer ye get to London the shorter yer life will be.' I dreamt of leisure and fancy finery, and I blush to say 'twas a hope I kept alive for many years.

London. The destination of world travelers! 'Twas, I think, the world's largest city, and may still be, but 'twas not where most with a nose would choose to live, though over a million had by early 1800. It multiplied each year after, both of people, and t'other things, too.

During our stay, thousands fled poverty and hunger to beg London for a crust of bread. London's survival depended on the repulsive stench and noise. In time we became accustomed to most of what took London visitors' breath away. I'm not saying 'twas good or healthy or preferred, but whatever London gave us 'twas as life was for us those days. 'Least our parents' home was comfortable and a distance from poor districts.

I still recall the fuss when, as a seven-year-old, I heard all 'bout a new queen to be crowned. Soon eighteen-year old Victoria bowed her head for crowning, stepped to her throne to rule her vast kingdom that sprinkled flags like some could sprinkle salt, and scandalously ordered her first cup of tea. Her earlier attendants had forbade the 'child' such beverage. Her Majesty, Queen Victoria, wanted tea. 'Fore long, most of England drank with her.

Though she wobbled a bit when she first stood as Queen, she matured, took court counsel, and endeared herself to nearly all us subjects. 'Fore long she consulted her beloved Albert as well.

We Copseys joined vast throngs in giving approval to one, even two, who set such good examples. Her Majesty was a change from earlier monarchs Englishmen dared not criticize within earshot of Westminster, but from my Michigan hallway, I'll write as I please. Early in Queen Victoria's reign necklines went up, hemlines went down, and pews across the kingdom began filling again.

My famly was in those Church of England pews and proud to be English. Proud. Why would anyone within the Empire not appreciate being English? Anyone free, o'course, I mean. England seemed quiet during my childhood, but its earlier turmoil and confrontations now read 'bout in school, names like Napoleon and t'others, convinced my parents not everyone on the face of the earth had in mind to be content being English.

We Copseys was staunchly Church of England. I loved the rituals and formality and espeshly the breath-taking music, so stately and holy. I suspicion I'd struggled to feel awe for God if I'd been of my grandparents' generation which choose such somber non-melodic hymns. I almost shudder trying to 'magine how they'd protest Michigan, US, worship I've attended! Seems to me 'life' means changes, without discarding reverence o'course, for truth be tolt, that can be a danger.

Father never allowed hisself to be idle except on Sundays, and Sunday afternoons he idled us all without a touch or word. Even our breathing had to be idled. That did us no harm and likely lengthened our days. 'Sides, following Saturday's preparations for Sabbath, we needed rest.

On Saturdays our house was cleaned top to bottom. Mother insisted 'twas not clean 'less it smelled a certain way. I can almost smell it now, clean this far away! Oh the work we did! Even pitchures that'd draw us from holy thoughts was turned to the walls. These was pleasant to view, but scenes of people working fields or children scampering freely or even playful pets conflicted with solemn Sabbath activity. Last thing, when work was done, we bathed for Sabbath, too, 'less we was sick.

In our cathedral, I felt close to God, using my voice and reading our *Common Book of Prayer and Administration of the*

Sacraments to tell Him so. My parents judged me more perfectly good than I deserved, for even in the cathedral my eyes or mind wandered when sermons had big words. Memory is a good trainer for parenthood I 'spose.

I remember Father disciplined me upon discovering not all I enjoyed reading at cathedral was from *The Common Book.*

Still, my 'good' then was likely from awe I felt for Almighty God on Sundays. I figured real worship required grand old cathedrals whose windows tolt Bible lessons. Those painted scenes is still glorious to recall, though I since learnt the beauty I admired was criticized by many as a shameful waste of money. Perhaps that's why some cathedral windows stayed plain. But art moved me. When I stepped into our sanctuary, with streams of colored light filling the place, I longed to be attentive to God. I couldn't 'magine being closer to God anywhere and the feeling was satisfying to me as a child, so I never complained 'bout going. 'Course, wise children did not strive to think contrary thoughts outloud.

Like most children, sometimes I yawned and tuned out church rituals, and truth be tolt, I almost prayed a busy God would overlook my behavior while tending to the desperate or delivering His stern judgment upon someone considerably naughtier'n me.

I wasn't often outwardly naughty, though, for Father and Mother never tolerated that. When my conscience bothered me, I eagerly awaited Sabbath when I'd kneel or stand with the whole congregation confessing in concert our waywardness. I'd of dreaded confessing sins alone, mind you, which relieved me England's Victoria was Protestant.

If I remembered even a slight disobedience, whether 'twas caught or not, I was pretty earnest in group confessions. Sarah, I thought, likely had little to confess, even in private. Talking right and being good seemed to come easy for both her and James. Maybe 'cause of early corrections, good was by then a habit.

For me I'd say during my lifetime, my confessions went from confessing at cathedral 'cause everyone else was likewise confessing, to being grateful Sabbath had come so I could confess with everybody else, to finally openly, sincerely, confessing whenever I knowed I'd offended God or fellowman.

Same for praising God: doing as others did till I knowed my heart got noticed by God. Truth be tolt, God sees a whole congregation, no, His whole creation, heart by heart. Precious ones, I blushed when I learnt that, but 'twas something I needed to know. No applause, though, for I took my time grasping that truth. When 'twas mine, I discovered truth can be uncomfortable. Least at first. I'll write of that awareness later.

Copseys took religion and faith seriously. We looked with suspicion on those who broke from the Church of England, espeshly those non-conformists whose services was without liturgy. We tolerated Low Church people who kept ties to High Church, for they followed the two books, but other sects was, to our way of thinking, a curiosity at best and apostate at worst. I admit now, with Age and perhaps Wisdom on my side, 'twas easy to judge without understanding our God expected England's politics to be tied to church history and we concluded nations fared better when people worshiped in the protestant State Church. Enough blood and taxes had settled that question years 'fore my birth.

Similarly, I can't count the times I heard Father claiming 'twas fools who left England's shores for America. 'Fools,' he'd say, 'risking life and limb from both the wicked and the waves of the Atlantic, and worst of all, those who crosst joined rebel fool cousins who'd turned against kin and king!'

Sometimes, though, Father's dock work gave him pause, espeshly if the shipment was tied to slavery. After I'd left for America, Southern cotton came to London's docks and my father returned to agricultural work. England long knowed enslavement was a terrible sin. Each worker ought to be payed his due, even deciding which work he wanted 'less he'd broken reasonable laws. Some laws need changing and get changed when people wise up or when the Lord breaks down stubborn hearts.

Speaking of history, I was privleeched to go to school, mostly 'fore our move. Most children did not, except for schools helt on Sundays when children wasn't working, for many children laboured like adults. If a child schooled Sundays, he'd 'least hear reading and Christian morals. Wesbech had Sunday school too, but we learnt Bible at our day school and to home, and Father wanted Sabbaths idle except for worship.

My school master, who I nicknamed 'Mr. Spectacles' so often in my head I've forgotten his surname, conducted classes at his home for neighborhood children. He tolerated no inattentiveness and if we was tardy once, the consequences made us determined 'twas our last instance of discipline.

Spectacles' wife had her own brood and tended even others' past suckling in 'most factory fashion if needed. Some mothers worked to pay for children's lessons; others took advantage of quiet mornings to home. Fussing nursery children made students lose interest in lessons, so Mr. Spectacles sent us girls to his wife for 'practical homemaking skills,' even said we'd get a letter grade if we thought of protesting.

Our schooling was better'n the usual Dame Schooling and we was above Ragged School charity. My headmaster was self-educated, so my parents checked to see they got their six pence' worth. One measure had us standing long times giving line upon line recitations. I 'most begged to paint or write more, but Spectacles thought 'twas wasting time and paper when I could be memorizing. Truth be tolt, some lines I still know, but I rarely see a reason why! Oh, maybe for image and rhyming, but who has the time!

I only schooled a few sessions. Once I could figure most words, work basic numbers, and my alphabet was readable, Father thought I'd been properly schooled. Like most young girls, I hoped to become the wife of a handsomely prosperous gentleman and raise a good famly. Or I'd be like Aunt Emma.

Aunt Emma, having plenty o' wealth for travel or tea at leisure, enjoyed culture and preserving dignity. Aunt Emma's good heart couldn't look past what needed changing for London's poorest. No one tolt her to do it. She once tolt me her happiest days was spent on London's poorest streets. Later I tried understanding that when Manuel and me struggled for survival there for nearly six years. I never came to love some parts.

Aunt Emma's husband traveled far and often, leaving Emma to take in London's culture as she desired or work charitable causes. Best I could tell she did as she pleased. Who wouldn't want that? Having one's own way is basic to our nature, truth be tolt. Not that it's good that way, but 'tis that way till we're changed, seems to me. Seems so to others, too, for the 'Articles' Church of England ministers still adhere to, 'fore they can preach, claim 'tis our inclination to do evil and we deserve God's judgment of damnation unless we allow God to change our nature through the merits and grace of His Holy Son, Jesus Christ. So I knowed wanting our own way is common to us all. None exempt. 'Tis our lot. Surely you know we cannot change ourselves. Don't need to live long to know that, seems to me.

So, as I was telling, Aunt Emma liked including us in her life. Father and Mother approved of 'Aunt Emma' times, hoping we'd take to character training and culturing and perhaps through her meet wealthy husbands.

Aunt Emma packed energy throughout her slender frame. I suspicion she was 'bout forty when, after one of her teas, she proposed we join her in tutoring the less fortunate. Tea with Aunt Emma, so full of flair and enthusiasm, had to be like having tea with Queen Victoria. Aunt Emma's enthusiasm could turn a green apple red, the way she could convince people to join her causes. If James had sipped tea with her, he'd likely joined the Royal Navy that very afternoon!

Aunt Emma 'dressed down' a bit to do tutoring, but she never wore common clothes, for she didn't mind poor people knowed someone of means remembered them. I heard a poor soul once asked one of our queens why she dare wear such elegant clothes to visit shabby poor people, and she replied, 'You'd of worn your best to come visit me.' Such was Aunt Emma's thoughts. I doubt she owned real common clothes.

We rode inside Aunt Emma's horse-drawn carriage, watching a sunny day grow threateningly gray the closer we got to poverty. When we stepped from the carriage, if she'd not had her parasol, we'd all been soaked. But people knowed where Aunt Emma stopped to pass out food, her claiming once again friends had misjudged appetites and now worried things would go stale. She did her bartering, too, claiming she couldn't tidy her house without more rags which people traded for good clothes from her baskets. Aunt Emma stretched truth a bit to give another dignity, but she had a good heart. Even Westminster couldn't use as many rags as she bought or traded for, but those rags got used by someone.

Aunt Emma gathered a group to hear Sarah reading from a book or paper, or publications of interest like *The Penny Magazine*. If they asked questions Sarah didn't know, she'd study to bring back answers the next week. Sarah had a group on her own without Aunt Emma's help, she was so slender and pretty, but Sarah didn't understand me when I tolt her so.

Aunt Emma gathered a group for me too, though I was only eight or nine when I first tutored. She'd tolt me how to teach, and I hoped her confidence was not misplaced. She'd writ rhyming words for me and I helt them up and we'd all speak them. I had older people in my group, and I felt I ought not teach elders, but Aunt Emma insisted all non-readers was suited for my group. Elders kept the younger quiet, except o'course those still really hungry.

Alayna was one such adult. Such a pretty name I thought for such an unfortunate woman. Alayna's husband was struggling to keep them out of the workhouse. Workhouses was a last resort except for the occasional charitable ones humane to famlys. London had several, even Wesbech had had a poor house, but I knowed little of them other'n Father's threats we'd better diligently chore or study or we'd end up there or spend nights locked in gaol. Mother'd shush him, claiming he was frightening us, but till I met Alayna his threats raised more questions than fear. Through Alayna I realized some workhouses was indeed dreadful places, sometimes treating people 'most like slaves. Regardless of age or health, few was spared hard work. Famlys was separated, often left wond'ring 'bout loved ones. Children younger'n me was up 'fore dawn. Their routines was at the pleasure of the workhouse operators. Workhouses made arrangements with various men in London, some kind and some downright despickable! Sadly, most workhouses drove people into greater despair.

Workhouse food was often scarce and bad. Work was difficult. Slackness was harshly disciplined. People thought idleness caused poverty. I've learnt of other causes, but at first I judged idleness the culprit. London's homeless and workhouse children was rounded up and put into unspeakable circumstances by wicked men. Other children was 'hired out,' risking their lives doing dangerous work in factories or mines. Sometimes I'd hear grown-ups who'd not stepped foot near a workhouse spouting, 'Workhouses was charitable solutions for London's poor,' espeshly since some places began or ended days with prayers. 'Tis likely 'prayer reports' kept workhouses free from condemnation by England's religious people, and by others who'd spot rotten apples in a barrel. Perhaps a few workhouses rescued victims. Most profited by supplying cheap labour to London's factories or despickable men.

Alayna came to my group to avoid a workhouse 'rescue' and oh, how she struggled to read so her children would be literate. Book reading was her hope for having more say 'bout their futures. She'd eagerly repeat simple words I read. She'd finger letters in her hand, for paper and pencil was not available for those Aunt Emma gathered for tutoring. I s'pose you know 'twas taxed. Alayna's little ones was in tow and she'd take the oldest's hand so he'd write in the air with her. Her children was as well behaved as hungry children can be.

Alayna often arrived after Aunt Emma's food had been gobbled up by t'others and the famly's disappointment broke my heart. The oldest child tried reading, but t'other two was just hungry and I recall Alayna shushing their whimpering with, 'We'll eat again later.' When would be their 'later'?

As we rode home, I tolt Aunt Emma of their hunger, knowing our meals was warm and waiting. She didn't offer solutions. She looked as though she was powerless to change anything for them. As I stepped down from the carriage, Aunt Emma touched my hand so I'd look to her face. Her soft eyes was teary, 'Esther, I don't think feeding Alayna is my responsibility. I'm already bringing all the food I can tote. If I saved food for latecomers, we'd be surrounded by disorder while we're tutoring.'

'But it's not their fault they're hungry!' I protested, watching my tone o'course, but my insides felt things needed saying.

She shrugged her shoulders. 'Someone else will need to help them,' she said, tapping for her coachman to drive away. My heart sank. Aunt Emma calloused? And strangely powerless? Surely she'd organize more donations.

I didn't eat much supper. My parents thought perhaps I was too young to be exposed to Aunt Emma's crusading ways. They wondert, too, if Aunt Emma's charitable ways was too risky for us and I wondert what they knowed I didn't. In bed with my covers pulled up, I wondert what the night would be like for Alayna's hungry family. My night was fitful, dreaming Alayna's family was in the workhouse and, when Mother woke me that I was in a workhouse, too.

I moped a few days 'fore Sarah asked, 'What are you going to do for Alayna's family?'

That angered me. 'Me?' I countered, 'Adults should solve those problems.' But Sarah's question stuck. That afternoon I finished householt cleaning and found Mother working on our evening meal. 'Could I help make those biscuits?'

Mother looked surprised. 'I'll not turn down kind offers,' she smiled, fixing a place for me 'long side her at the counter.

She began teaching me the basics of biscuit making, a scoop of this, a spoon of that, a glob, and a pour of curdled milk. 'Father'll be pleased you're becoming a little homemaker.' My sticky fingers made me question why I liked biscuits so much, but the question of how soured milk was used was answered. As we checked their browning, Mother seemed touched when I admitted I was learning so I could make 'tutoring biscuits.'

My 'tutor biscuits' took years to be as predictably perfect as Mother's, but they was satisfying to Alayna's hungry famly and each batch I make here reminds me of tutoring days in London. I thought Alayna's quick, 'God bless you,' was kind, but I wondert if God would hear such an informal prayer by such an unkempt woman in such a soggy district. I didn't question whether God could love her. Rather, I was quite certain there was appropriate ways to approach God and I doubted Alayna met those standards. Back then I thought man's best prayers passed through stained glass. Alayna's timid prayer must of reached Almighty God though, for I was blest then for 'tutor biscuits,' and many times since, though some might claim I traded Alayna places. Aunt Emma had knowed even a child can improve another's condition if exposed to need.

By the way, one Christmas Aunt Emma gave us small slates to teach reading lessons. What a help they was! I prized that slate and may still find it tucked away here. Books we received from Aunt Emma seemed too good to just be read by us. When the stories was as recitations to us, we carried them to teach reading. Later we left books with people who'd tutor others once the stories was locked in their minds. Some was Bible stories. I've often wondert how many children heard 'bout God's love for them through books and papers we gave away. S'pose one day I'll know.

Though tutoring made me feel good, I liked the safety of our simple but comfortable wood frame home, despite daily chores. Our rooms was sparse compared to those kept by wealthy Englanders. One season I worked for a lady who believed each item proclaimed her wealth. 'Twas difficult moving my skirt 'round in such rooms without breaking expensive things. Breaking expensive things is one less worry for the poor!

Father thought us capable of cleaning our home without spending money on domestic help, though a few door-to-door women was allowed coins for occasional chores 'cause Mother took seriously Boaz's admonition to let the poor glean fields.

Mother patiently trained me to carefully clean chimney lamps twice daily so reading time would be easier, though we had little to read other than our *Common Book*. We kept dust cloths in our pockets, sometimes to our embarrassment if we was out. If I mentioned I had nothing to do, Mother set me to sorting drawers. Till I learnt to hold my tongue, we had orderly drawers! Guess I did it enough to want them sorted.

When we was old enough, we toted personal use water to our rooms and slop buckets from our bedrooms down to the collector bucket near the back hallway. Such buckets smelled foul, o'course, and we argued 'bout whose turn 'twas to empty those. I s'pose my begging off the task got me by a few times, but emptying foul buckets was a pop'lar and simple way to punish disobedience. We added our waste to London's, for 'twas all we knowed to do.

Smelly London was not prepared for the influx of people during the 1830's -1840's, and let's just say none took deep breaths for fresh air. I'm tolt even Prince Albert and Queen Victoria's palace couldn't keep out open sewer smells to which we reluctantly became accustomed. You prob'ly know raw sewage brought on more'n stench. Smallpox killed thousands the year Victoria was crowned. The next year whooping cough and measles was messengers of death, claiming 50,000 or more. Most never lived to the age I now am. Numbers like 20,000 died of this, 30,000 of that. Scarcely a famly from Palace to Poor Street escaped heartaches. Hot weather made death more common and chores inside or out less pleasant.

We had other householt chores like mattresses to turn, clothes to air or mend, surfaces to dust or wash, and always coal dust to wash from window panes. Seemed no matter how diligent we was, homes got layers of coal dust and soot and street dirt from open windows. Floors, too, often needed wiping up 'cause not every muddy shoe stayed put on the rug Mother set out. If shoes wasn't the culprits, our soiled long skirts sometimes lightly smeared mud wherever we walked. Those with shorter attire cleaned floors less perhaps, but they likely payed a price in other ways I need not detail. I hope my heirs know modesty's a virtue.

Though we was learning homemaking, my practical and straight-forward father made Sarah and me understand we was not to think on marrying any fellows still dreaming of what they'd become. Father clearly expected us to only consider a man already doing what needed doing to provide well for a famly. Might as well say, too, Father saw no reason we consider courtship with a man entertaining thoughts of living away from England, and espeshly not in the land of rebels, the United States.

I once saw a red coat with black frogging in Father's wardrobe and wondert if it had stories to tell, but o'course I never asked, and I s'pose it did not, though from somewhere Father got the idea the US was all young upstarts failing to submit to parental authority.

Being young, we never questioned Father's admonitions. His thinking was to guide us to adulthood. Elder respect was instilled by parents and pulpits, and still seems right to me, though o'course, Almighty God can step in when the elder's absent if a heart's teachable. I've seen that happen, and I've knowed where hearts needed Almighty God to speak, but they was closed to Him, 'least for a time. God doesn't barge in on people, though seems to me He could. He bids. Sometimes people try His patience 'fore they come. Seems best to come quickly, for God could stop bidding.

Mother knowed Father's reluctance to acknowledge America's independence would be mirrored when the time came for us children to pursue ours. England and America worked out their new relationship, and we Copsey children would work out the condishions of our release from Father's domination too. He just wanted our best.

Early on Father tolt us we'd not be released for courtship, nor would our marriages get his blessing 'less he was convinced all parties was grounded in the Christian religion and faith, given to sound judgment, and prepared to share work responsibilities within a householt. Suitors with dreams might make interesting parlor conversation, but such would not become a fit candidate for marriage to a Copsey daughter. Till then, we Copsey daughters was to learn what women in householts do, and if our time was not occupied with such, there'd be outside work to build our constitution. We kept busy learning diligence while James became acquainted with duty, sometimes spending summers back in Norfolk.

When Father thought we was closer to knowing how to industriously run a householt, just the furnishings and feasting, mind you, for husbands ran the house, we was among the thousands earning keep by hiring out to famlys as domestics. Didn't hurt us though. Strange how I found doing a task for others, and sometimes for coins, less distasteful than doing it to home. If I'd been really good, I'd not minded either I s'pose. If we'd not knowed famlys wanting domestics, doubt I'd been hired out so quickly, though I looked older than my age. I, like most domestics, lodged with the famly 'cause domestics worked dawn till near midnight and was grateful for room and eats. 'Twas better'n selling Lucifermatch boxes or making mutton fat candles night and day.

Sometimes we all spent a week helping Norfolk kin. We did agricultural labour 'long with t'others, but I liked inside work best. Sarah willingly worked outdoors or in. James o'course didn't do inside work other'n what was required to look after oneself. I certainly admired my big brother who 'parently felt responsible to help shape my character.

I remember my tenth birthday, March 20, 1840. Shortly I'd begin my first placement as a domestic for a busy famly. I don't remember other gifts I received that birthday, for generally we didn't make much over birthdays, but I've carefully treasured James' gift and it sets nearby as I write to you. James gave me *The Book of Common Prayer with the Psalter* which I believe was published that year by order of Queen Victoria. God's often used it to comfort me.

Our famly nearly always read the daily lessons, two in the morning and one in the evening. I can't 'magine life without the *Book of Common Prayer* readings. Even now, with the book nearby but unopened, I feel God's presence longing to speak to me. I've nearly worn it out with my hours of reading it. As you likely know, nearly every life event has a special reading, and while hearing it read by one's vicar or parent brought stillness to the soul, reading it alone dealt even with a child's heart. That I know with certainty.

Perhaps one of you, my dear descendants, will one day carefully thumb through my personal copy of *Common Prayer and Psalter* when I'm unable to use it, but even if you do see mine, I'd encourage you to spend your money and secure a copy for yourself. I believe 'tis worthwhile to quietly read its Holy Words and sing its rhyming Psalms. Test me. See if I speak truth. I hope you'll sense the wonder of its language, but more important, like me, you'll be awed each day by the Giver of Truth.

My understanding of God's truth grew deeper and fuller 'cause of James' gift and I'm forever grateful he gave what his little sister needed more than he could 'magine. The Holy Bible and our *Book of Common Prayer* was fundamental to all that was good in our beloved motherland. Where monarchs or subjects failed, the Book could of spared us much had we let its words be our instruction. I do not, however, worship the Book, just to be clear, and while the words are important, obedience is what brings settling to the soul. Manuel warned against being all talk and no do.

Wednesday, March 3, 1880

Now back to writing of our lives. I apologize I cannot write this in one sitting. Even today I'm not without duties, but if I spoke of them I s'pose my original intent of this letter would not be accomplished, so I press on.

As I writ, Father had ideas 'bout who we children should become, what we should do. Years later, as a mother I cared less 'bout how a body would earn its keep but worked to help God form the man or woman within my children. I studied my children, hoping I was training them for listening to the Lord and for living proper from the inside out. In that way Father and I differed, but I know he intended our good. 'Fore I took on those nearly grown-up responsibilities of a hired mother's helper my tenth year, I was treated to a week with Aunt Emma who'd been invited to a small countryside estate in Essex. What refreshment my lungs felt as I pulled in air from England's hills and dales! As a guest with scarcely a task, I watched estate domestics' clever shortcuts for later use when responsibility for ridding up houses fell to me alone. Shortcuts allowed me more time with little ones since 'twas not my duty to tend little ones to home. I also enjoyed 'high tea' at the estate, though they could of had t'other. High tea was at the famly table and portions served was bigger, which suited me, perhaps a bit too much.

I thought 'Aunt Emmas' and indulgences was due all good children. I can't say how I'd felt if I'd knowed the disadvantages my future husband was facing while Aunt Emma was spoiling me. Later Manuel said 'twas good I'd knowed some middle class comforts as a child for we seldom knowed such as adults. Manuel never dodged hard labour during the fifteen or so years I knowed him. Those was a good but hard fifteen, and I'll treasure them till the day I die. And don't you ever let nobody speak ill of Manuel. He was a good man. A good one. I'm proud I was his wife. Our children should always be proud he was their father. I hope I was as much God's gift to Manuel as he was for me, even though few took notice of that truth. People, me included, tend to judge others too quickly. Not all o'course, but many poor folk work hard and don't get much to show for it. Seems to me, rich people spend more time sitting than poor do. Mind that 'fore you make judgments.

So, beginning the summer of 1840 or 1841, I worked for the Mortons. His name was Robert and hers was Phillis, but I never spoke those names to them. I helped mother eight-year-old Harriett, and Henry, six, but John kept me busiest, not yet in breeches. I rose early and worked late doing whatever I was tolt or saw to do. Wiping bottoms o'course seemed foul to me the first few times, but after a while, wiping bottoms became 'bout the simplest part of my tasks. Occasionally I managed younger children alone, and though prob'ly only ten, I got their respect which was necessary. Older children and Mrs. Morton, too, was often helping Mr. Morton deliver ice or doing agricultural field work, or hurriedly gathering, preparing, and putting on food to eat. I'd be with my famly from time to time, finding we appreciated each other even more after absences.

'Parently my work, or perhaps my rate of pay, was satisfactory to them, and I stayed on a few years as a mother's helper and domestic. I became like famly, gaining confidence by conversing with the older Mortons as though I'd been born there. My work prepared me for managing my own famly later, though o'course Father and Mother chided I was much too young to dwell on such thoughts.

Aunt Emma knowed I was grateful for the gallivanting we did together each spring. Since the fire's dying out now, I must soon be under wool comforters. Let's leave me with Aunt Emma when I'm still quite shy and 'round thirteen or fourteen. I'm 'bout to step into a brougham hetted back to London.

Tomorrow I'll need to let Manuel's childhood catch up with mine lest I age long 'fore he does. Manuel, with his voice low and a bit rough, was a storyteller who kept me and our children stalling sleep many a night, and how I wish you could hear his tales. Most was true, though some was no doubt enlivened without harm.

For Manuel's story, I'll be as faithful to truth as I dare so you can know his life and heart, though o'course you know I cannot get all facts straight without him here. I vowed on our wedding day I'd love and honour Manuel till my death, and I shall. Life's brought changes, but my heart can faithfully love my Manuel while also making room to share my heart with others now helt dear.

I've often tolt my children of their father and they asked me to put on paper the way I tell of him, so I shall. Manuel was born in the same county and 'bout the same year as me, 1831 perhaps, but our paths had not crossed, though we had kin not far from Emanuel's. The house is chilly now so I must stop for tonight, but first I'll put down words we Copseys might of read, but Manuel's likely did not. Here 'tis:

'There is virtue yet in the hoe and the spade, for learned as well as unlearned hands. And labour is everywhere welcome; always we are invited to work."

R. W. Emerson, 1837, the year Queen Victoria ascended to the throne.

Thursday, March 4, 1880
Emanuel's Escape from Childhood (1837-1942)

Ralph Waldo Emerson toured England 'round the time of Victoria's ascent to the throne and his writings and sermons caused no small stir, but Emanuel's famly wouldn't of cared much for Emerson's philosophies, nor for that matter, would they read declarations and laws by their monarchs. This famly, whose surname had survived centuries, turned England's soil. Their hands was far more comfortable holting hoes than writing instruments. Most Kisbeys was still illiterate in 1837

. True, some scattered throughout the Empire, some daringly crossed the vast Atlantic, but when most was to spell their name, they'd requested scribes write it 'just like it sounds.' And scribers did just that, affixing that surname to plots of land, a few certificates of birth, records of baptisms, and bills of sale. Their 'write it like it sounds' request was likely made with the confidence of someone knowing his right to breathe free air and who helt a basic trust in the goodness of fellowman. But how much simpler life would of been had they'd learnt to spell their name and not just master their 'X.'

Even so, those who knowed Emanuel's people would declare, like me, that for the most part the Kisbeys, the Kisbees, the Kisbies, Kisbys, Kesbeys, Keisbeys, Keshby, and assorted spellings thereof, was a good and hardworking lot. Most spent their years ankle deep in agriculture, preparing soil, planting seed, tending crop, and trading excess produce with the closest buyers. Why would Emanuel's people long for the silver spoon when 'twas satisfying and more practical for survival if they learnt to manipulate the hoe or spade?

Of what benefit was schooling when it took children from fields supplying their table? Could not minds mature when occupied with fieldwork, and did not physical labour benefit both health and attitude? The Kisbeys was generally moral, optimistic and industrious, though few tasted wealth and some lived hand-to-mouth. These good citizens gave and, in turn, expected respect and fair treatment from famly and friend. Fathers rooted out tendencies toward laziness. Laziness would disgrace their name and posterity. It'd also left them hungry.

To ensure no offspring went hungry 'cause some Kisbey failed learning to earn a meal, most young at one time or t'other was sent to bed without supper with hopes of instilling the direct connection between work and eats. Somewhere God had declared if a body wouldn't work it didn't eat. One missed supper usually made the future brighter for offspring whose borning cry was still decades away. However, aged or broken bodies was given proper respect and pity.

Sweat produced maturity and Emanuel was maturing. By age seven year, Emanuel's father considered him half a man. Without a school or dictionary, Emanuel figured 'man' meant 'one who worked for the good of kin till wearied by day's end.' Though he'd never darken a school door, Emanuel's ability to grasp facts, create solutions with his hands, and espeshly his way of living, convinced others he'd become a man of wisdom. Not fortune. Not fame. Not without failures. But he'd possess wisdom. If you're lacking possessions, wisdom is one to keep.

If later you'd asked him if people's considering him wise was satisfying to him, he'd likely claimed 'least three other considerations mattered more. He'd spend his life earning and keeping the one, lose his life selflessly doing t'other best he could, and faithfully demonstrating to the end his understanding 'bout the one he considered essential. 'Most of what pushes people in life is just wispy clouds,' he'd say, and I'm convinced he rarely listened for what I'd call 'the applause of man' for he knowed his priorities. 'Fore I finish his story I hope I make clear what mattered to my Manuel.

Like 'bout a hundred thousand other Englishmen, Emanuel's famly was trying to holt onto a small piece of land ancestors had struggled to maintain and keep from a monarch's grasp. Monarchs could, and did, grasp produce, property or even a family's prized pets, should such threaten a monarch's boasts of being the Empire's most skillful hunter on whichever lands he claimed. Subjects either helt goods with open hands or quietly kept them from show.

Kisbey goods sat on 'bout eighty acres, and I s'pose like the Bible's Andrew, you might ask, 'But what is this among so many?' There was several Kisbey mouths to feed and I dare say from experience, it takes a lot of work to feed growing children. Another thing Kisbeys knowed, and I learnt, is that the harder you work to produce food, the hungrier workers is when it comes time to set meager portions on the table. My knowledge of those facts came later for a limited time, but I'm s'posing when Manuel left for his heavenly banquet he could count on one hand the times he'd overeaten, bless his soul.

In contrast to practical, down-to-earth Copseys, the Kisbeys was dreamers. Dreaming, they discovered, was 'bout the only thing without English tax. But in case Parliament figured a way to tax dreams, the Kisbeys kept dreams small: Things'd get better, tomorrow's a new day, and the Almighty supplies necessities. Most dreaming happened outside where a mind thinks clearly. Their small stone cottage's interior was mostly dark. England taxed windows, too.

Few English displayed or spoke affection to children once they slid from a parent's lap to walk independently, but the Kisbeys was different that way. They was loved by homefolk, but as Manuel put it, not 'fussed over.' Siblings since Cain had scuffled, so tumbles and squabbles happened, but disagreements was settled by bedtime, else parents got intent 'bout rooting out bitterness the next day with work requiring companionship. Famly unity was important to all. 'Sides, without companionships, how could they enjoy their loud humor? Humor works best with clear consciences. And the Kisbeys liked humor.

Each September, 'round Emanuel's birthday, he'd hear Almighty God thanked for loaning the famly Emanuel, just as he'd heard similar prayers for his older sister Frances and brother John, and his five younger siblings Ann, Robert, Levi, Sallie and little William. 'Sallie,' by the way, was what her famly called her but lots of Sarahs was Sallies. Manuel tolt me they never expected birthday gifts. But, truth be tolt, what greater gift or benefit could a child own than his parents' prayers to Almighty God?

So, from the highest knoll of the Kisbey place, six-year-old Emanuel took in a deep breath that refreshed him to the soles of his feet. Eyes closed, he identified several different birds. He watched a train travel its long straight track, toting he knowed not what. Shep yapped. Turning slightly Emanuel saw a few sheep and cattle still grazing contentedly. He loved their farm, but he couldn't help wond'ring what places beyond his father's stone fence might holt for him.

During mealtimes he'd heard talk of London, but his parents claimed there was neither time nor need to go there. So far enough work and food was right there on the farm, so why travel to London? Too many questions 'bout London brought a boy more chores. Farming the sloping hills a respectable distance from the noses of those taxing everything but the tall hard chairs on which Kisbeys sat was as close to kings and queens as Pa Kisbey wanted to be.

Even so, London's news reached their ears. Emanuel suspicioned London was an evil place, espeshly for children. Still, hearing nearby hamlets' bells and learning London's cathedrals and shops could stop a brave boy in his tracks,

Emanuel wondert what a day in London would be like. He'd seen horse drawn carriages, sometimes filled with famlys, but most often toting ladies and gentlemen so finely dressed he 'magined they had royal audiences.

Hmm. What would he ask if he was to bow 'fore the new queen? As a child, his was not lofty requests to become a prince and travel Britain's vast kingdom. Though earlier if he'd considered an audience, he'd requested his older siblings be put in dungeons for making him feel too childish, lately he'd been changing what he'd request 'fore Queen Victoria. Manuel knowed if his siblings was in dungeons he'd be expected to also do their work. Best not let them be put there, and 'sides, they didn't really do nothing deserving such severe punishment. No, if Queen Victoria asked him what favor she could grant, he reckoned, with a bow to his new Queen, the best he'd request would be having her servants spread a banquet for his parents and their youngest children, he included o'course, while they watched t'others work the farm without his help. Maybe then they'd find how tired they got doing his part!

Satisfied, he thought of how he hoped one day he'd see up close London's strong locomotive steam engines pulling cars filled with people and freight. Yes, London had adventures waiting to be had by brave young men who went beyond their property lines for something other than a stray animal.

Perhaps someday soon he'd ask permission to go to London. Or, if he had a mind to, and if they'd listen, maybe he'd somehow convince his famly to spend a whole day touring London. If that didn't work, well, maybe he'd just go there alone, and stay as long as he liked. O'course he'd be at least a little older than right now, but he'd go sometime if he wanted to, with or without permission.

'Perhaps when the work's done you'll go one day.' Emanuel jumped. He'd not seen his mother's approach, and in the stillness her voice startled him. He turned to catch her familiar smile. She set down two pails of milk, grateful to relieve her hands momentarily.

'Ma, how'd ye know w'ot I's thinking?'

Many times I heard Manuel claim his mother could read his mind. 'Tis God's gift to mothers I reckon.

Emanuel never lost his boyish admiration and respect for his mother and I never thought him wrong for having it. That's not to say they always thought alike. They didn't go 'bout solving problems the same, and truth is, Mother Kisbey would live with difficult consequences during her lifetime, but somehow she seemed to see beyond her time.

My first visits with her till we left for the United States made me admire her in spite of her simplicity. She made a good Kisbey. I hope future generations will think I did as well, but I continue with their conversation 'fore I interrupted it.

'You're not the first Kisbey standing here thinking of other places to be.' She likely tussled his brown hair 'fore putting her arm 'round his shoulder. 'So you'd rather be in London than on this farm?' She'd been aware of his boyish chatter that followed his many questions.

'Oh, prob'ly not fer long. I'd gist like ta know how it'd be different fer people there than 'tis fer us here. I'd like ta see a city sometime. Might as well be London as any.'

'From all I hear, you've picked the biggest. Emanuel, one day I suspicion you'll go to London and spot a beautiful girl to marry. Perhaps she'll be a princess.' (I know she said that 'cause he tolt me and since I'm in his story, I thought I'd be sure you know 'twas said!)

'Then she'd not marry me. Princesses marry rich princes or kings with lots o' land and power and I'm gist a farm boy.'

'Ah, but you're a good blue-eyed farm boy. I'm reckoning England's had queens who'd rather married a blue-eyed farm boy than some kings or princes buried in Westminster Abbey.'

The Kisbeys would not likely intentionally affect the vast British Empire's political affairs. Maybe a Kisbey or two set foot in a castle somewhere, but most Kisbey faces was far from familiar with monarchs, whether for good or ill. Still, they was generally proud to be English.

True, only days 'fore this misty dusk found mother and son talking of powerful London, Emanuel's parents' sentiments had matched many subjects who heaved a sigh of relief when young Queen Victoria stepped to the throne. An eighteen-year old might better serve her country than the likes of George III or his sons, so fond of rebelling against their father's strict disciplines. The Kisbeys expected elders and rulers to be good and decent examples for offspring and subjects.

If you study our motherland's history, you dear descendants might also conclude right along with King George III's Parliament that he'd been an unfit ruler – so unfit Parliament attempted to replace him on numerous occasions. His bouts of temporary insanity had tragically turned out to be mere bouts, with the king regaining enough reasoning to holt onto his throne till 1820 when finally King George IV was crowned. The previous ten years, while England hoped for sanity from St. James Palace, King George IV served as Prince Regent.

But for many moral British, King George IV was a disappointment. His behavior – unspeakable. His numerous intimacies kept embarrassing his subjects. The Kisbeys was among those who contemplated christening their daughter 'Caroline' if she'd not seemed so much a Sallie. We Copseys chose Bible names, though o'course, some Bible characters was not so good either. I s'pose God included their lives for our benefit, hoping we'd learn who to be like and who to not.

Caroline, King George's estranged wife, was helt in higher regard than the king, though some closer to London and its politics challenged such judgment, for rumors was she was not without her own moral failures. Respect for position and not the man had caused pause at King George's passing. Most of Manuel's famly was listeners, not readers, and I often thought the farther from London, the clearer one's political judgment.

King William IV, also King George III's son, reigned next, and thus he was king for the first years of Manuel's and my lives. Though perhaps even less moral than his deceased brother, during King William IV's reign a few sound changes began rippling through England and in some respects affecting people in continents far from England's shores.

The United Kingdom's destined to always be in flux, and the popular claim that the sun never set on the British Empire 'tis valid. I must confess I 'twas not disappointed my schooling stopped 'bout the time we was to memorize names of all the places people was subjects of our Monarchs. I don't mind recalling history, but I'm not so much in favor of keeping straight names and spellings of places I've not been nor will ever see. I've enough trouble calling my children and pets by their right names, let alone places I cannot pitchure.

Makes me think I best keep busy or I'll grow old doing this and start calling my househoIt by wrong names. Pressing on...

Assuredly, among those most grateful for the seven years of King William's reign was men, women, and children throughout the British Colonies whose freedom from slavery was finally guaranteed. Saying a person's free and allowing their contentedly becoming so takes time, as governments slowly learnt. Their freedom had come after twenty long years of attempting to enforce the Act that affirmed no human should be enslaved by another. The price had been high and lives had been callously disposed of at sea the moment greedy and despickable ship captains spotted authorities who'd heavily fine them for the 'cargo' beneath their hulls.

For years, righteously angry but patient men and women had worked diligently to ensure Monarchs would forsake, and hopefully repent of, this immoral practice. Could the Almighty forgive enslavement without mankind reaping great consequences? How high would be the price? Who would pay the final toll?

If only all mankind learnt lessons from t'other without having to learn things firsthand again, that would be a blessing. But slavery's evil, too, became part of our story.

Slowly Parliament's other reforms recognized human worth and dignity, including abolishment of public punishments and death, though some resisted such 'leniency.' If London represented the cross section of life for those within the United Kingdom, civility was yet to be defined. At least King William IV had walked among the people of his kingdom, though perhaps his ventures was not without shameful motive. Who knowed but that commoners labouring in London's foundries or confined to its poor houses was bumping elbows with semi-royal blood?

Truth be tolt, most of London knowed of his indiscreet 'unroyal' famly and the popular woman who birthed him nearly a dozen children. Poor woman, she must of thought each visit was his last!

Years much earlier, even 'fore our parents' earliest day, some believed young William to be a brave hero whom God had spared. As a Royal Navy youth serving in this far off land from which I now write, William IV survived a kidnapping plot which General Washington approved, whom Providence destined to become the first president of what was then regarded as a rebellious collection of former Englishmen who defiantly asked Mother England to cut loose her apron strings.

I've heard, too, that President Washington might of been on the Royal Navy's side had not his mother bid him step from its ship years 'fore. Makes one ponder how different history might of read had those events not gone as they did.

Young William IV and the Royal Navy returned defeated by the young country carving out their path to independence. 'Tis not so difficult to see why monarchs thought people across the Atlantic was committing treason since 'fore many of the grandparents of those rebels had been England's law abiding subjects. And some, o'course, not so law abiding, for you likely know not all sailing to the New World left of their own accord.

But back to the end of William IV's reign. As he was layed to rest after his heart attack in 1837, the United Kingdom was still far from a blest and internally peaceful nation giving equal worth to fellowman.

'Time to throw the whole lot out,' had at times been Emanuel's father's sentiment, though quietly expressed in a land where kings is kings. Far as I knowed, Kisbeys was not intent on partaking in uprisings to unseat monarchs, even though all knowed a subject's labour often gave powers-that-be far more money and goods than workers kept for themselves.

No, most Kisbeys respected authority 'cause 'twas written somewhere in the Holy Scriptures. When talk 'bout monarchs became too careless during mealtimes, one parent or t'other quieted their brood with the reminder to respect and pray for those in authority over them.

Generations of Kisbeys watched monarchs come and go, and like the powerful eagles occasionally threateningly circling overhead, they'd learnt the British Empire at times grasped and released its prey while a long line of Kisbeys worked its fields. They did, however, speculate God's holiness was possibly responsible for the 1834 fire that mostly destroyed Westminster's Palace where Parliament sat, and they'd wondert if the sweeping epidemics claiming thousands of lives was a consequence of Holy Judgment. They was English subjects, yes, but they'd heard enough scripture from their local parson to know that if it came to choices, only God was worthy of their highest allegiance.

Like millions claiming England as their motherland, the Kisbeys was part of the working masses unable to acquire much more'n necessary for staying alive. Opportunities for education was few, and none had come to most in Emanuel's family. His younger sister, Ann, announced she'd one day become a reader. When Ann begged to write words which till then would of been unreadable, for she'd maybe seen a few words on paper likely from a church book, she was reminded she'd need to use the dirt 'cause paper was taxed. I recall Mrs. Kisbey saying Emanuel tolt Ann three things: write less than she talked, write only really important words, and write those words very small. Ann's parents cautiously approved her dream, knowing she'd leave home to fulfill such lofty goals. 'What,' they wondert, 'would a woman do with such skills?'

No offspring's dreams was discouraged though. Emanuel's parents often said while they didn't know God's exact purpose for each child's life, they was certain hard work prepared them regardless. All offspring learnt to work. The farm and his mother kept the famly clothed, but not clothed in a manner to pass unnoticed at us Copsey's formal Church of England. Their illiteracy, too, would of made participation awkward in such a liturgical setting. Perhaps Low Church fit people like them, but the Kisbeys took a different route.

Emanuel and his siblings was the third generation attending informal, but struckchurt, religious meetings of the increasingly popular Methodist Movement. Earlier Kisbeys found something spiritually cleansing 'bout gathering in God's open fields to learn that regardless of social standing, they was loved by Almighty God. Biblical truth seemed more easily understood in fields than in cold cathedrals with polished marble and gleaming gold where worshipers read from books sunlit through painted glass. Why not, they reasoned, worship the earth's Creator without the hindrance of massive carved stones and stained glass?

As Wesleyan teachings spread, London, lesser cities, and England's countryside became dotted with chapels and simple churches gathering in poor and illiterate worshipers for either Wesleyan or Primitive Methodist instruction. Secluded from those, like us Copseys, who feared such gatherings was too unrestrained to be holy, most Sabbaths Emanuel's famly met in a chapel as simple as they. There they'd listen and respond to a pastor who knowed them well.

Scarcely a soul present would handle pages illogic'ly splattered with strange shapes. But congregational recitations was faithfully given during the hours they met, so hearts of any observant child could learn sacred lessons. The pastor read and expounded from the Holy Bible few others owned. And after a time, prayers would be prayed, more songs was sung or recited, and the service closed.

In the chapel yard congregants enjoyed neighborly conversation with adults likewise anchored to their life's station. Infants would be admired, children and new worshipers greeted, elderly was affirmed, and 'twas likely a young man and woman might begin conversations that'd develop into lifelong interaction.

What teachings was they given? With other farmers and common labourers, the pastor, likely not wearing gloves as our vicar did, spoke deeper than the goodness of God and brotherhood of man. While some 'break away groups' followed the *Book of Common Worship* readings, Emanuel's parson often stood 'fore the people with only his open Bible, teaching whatever he believed God bid him preach. Often he stressed each individual's free will in determining one's submissive relationship to God which could grant believers eternal life with Him.

Owning responsibility for one's thinking and behavior suited most Kisbeys. True, they was tolt that to establish such a sacred and personal relationship with God, each religious participant, following a working accomplished by God's Holy Spirit, was required to humbly admit one's need to claim Jesus Christ, the crucified, buried, and risen Son of God, as one's only Saviour from sin's holt and punishment.

Even though all England's subjects bowed to State Sovereignty out of fear if not genuine devotion, when it came to spiritual matters, many English or other resisted the humiliation that inevitably accompanies personally accounting for one's sinfulness. But for the Kisbeys, bowing to a Sovereign was compatible with their thinking, espeshly to Sovereign God who cared 'bout them more than any earthly ruler could.

Additionally, most Kisbeys was practical folk who readily admitted they was not destined to be rulers of even themselves without Almighty God's help. They knowed they, like all mankind, was sin-filled. But when the Kisbeys knowed God's forgiveness, their grateful lives showed reverence toward God and joy with fellowman. Trusting their eternal destination to God's grace instead of depending upon one's imperfect efforts to earn Heaven seemed reasonable.

One by one, most publicly confessed belief in Jesus Christ's sin-cleansing blood, humbly submitted to God as their Highest Ruler. Then they went 'bout intending to live consistent with their conscience. We'd hear 'twas the inner promptings of God's Holy Spirit. Emanuel's Kisbeys tried living so God would attend to their prayers and they'd sleep peacefully each night.

Our leaders encouraged us in similar ways, but evidence of being Christian for us was knowed as 'lively faith.'

We Copseys read our Prayer books and Bibles twice daily, but the Kisbeys was without readers. Religious questions was shrugged off, 'least till their next worship service. Generally they simply trusted God to be reliable and sought to please Him. When questions rose, they mostly did what seemed right. Resisting the self-humiliation required in the Christian faith baffled Kisbeys.

Daily circumstances often included humility. Why refuse to acknowledge one's sinful tendencies? Had not others felt a temper rise or tried to holt a tongue? Why blame others for one's behavior? Both humility and responsibility fit their understanding of maturity. Methodism's revivals had altered Kisbey minds for generations. Emanuel's parents hoped 'fore long Emanuel'd realize admiration for his parent's faith would not be sufficient to guarantee his eternal destiny without his personal response and commitment to Jesus Christ.

Emanuel respectfully heard his father continuously remind his children that in all things, religious and otherwise, actions brought consequences. More than once Emanuel heard he could choose actions but he could not control actions' far reaching consequences.

Emanuel recollected a time when his father demonstrated the lesson of action-consequence. He was 'bout three when the two had come upon a bridge while walking to a neighbor's farm. His pa's stride broke. He'd bent down, their blue eyes meeting 'fore instructing Emanuel to pick up ten pebbles.

The idea of playing a counting game with Pa delighted Emanuel. Emanuel's little hands grabbed brown ones and white ones, needing to make two trips to the railing where his father helped him line them by size. Holting Emanuel, they dropped pebbles in an orderly fashion, watching as each splashed. After a few splashes, Pa had Emanuel notice the rings each pebble caused.

'No pebble slips into the water without making ripples, Emanuel.' Emanuel's chest pressed flat against the railing, his body balanced by his father's strong hands. Fascinated by the watery circles overlapping one another in their race toward the banks, Emanuel was set upright next to a railing and instructed not to move.

His father found a gray flat rock, thick enough to require considerable strength to tote back to the bridge.

Warning Emanuel to grasp the support, Emanuel's father raised the rock and dropped it to the stream below. He quickly steadied Emanuel whose excitement 'bout the enormous splash and rugged far-reaching ripples caused him delight and carefree gesturing.

'More, Papa, more,' he begged. 'Again, again.' But the lesson was not finished. Instead Emanuel was made to understand that the course of the stream had been changed, though ever so slightly, as water was diverted 'round the rock.

'Actions bring consequences, Son, and I don't want you to ever forget those ripples.' Consequences was a big word, but not unfamiliar.

Within minutes, father and son worked their way down the bank and stood barefoot in the cool stream. Emanuel 'helped' Pa tote the rock out of the stream. 'We had no right to change the stream. If it'd been good to leave it there, we would of.'

After they'd climbed back onto the road, Emanuel's father began creating a tale I'd hear Emanuel tell our children in which a rock changed a stream's course, hung up fallen twigs and branches, changed life for animals dependent upon the stream, and became a dumping site so severely abused that most of London's people died of thirst. Emanuel, who relished tales his father tolt, soon suspected 'their rock' could not do all the damage his father 'magined, but just in case it might, he felt heroic preventing such disasters.

For the rest of his childhood, whenever Emanuel was advised, 'Son, think 'bout what you're doing,' he claimed he thought upon the rock's changing a stream's course and suspected he ought to consider his action's rippling consequences. Most of Manuel's rippling consequences was likely good, though.

What if all fathers taught their children the consequences lessons?

Was the stench of waste that came to their noses from Kisbey's animals or from nearby hamlets and streams, or was London's odors somehow crossing long miles separating them from the ill-kept city? Something had triggered Emanuel's bridge memory. Emanuel knowed London stunk 'cause people was not tending its rivers and streams. His mother smelled it, too.

'Emanuel, when you go looking for your London princess, I hear you'll need to holt your nose the whole time you're there!'

Farming 'bout one hundred miles from London, too far to sniff its smells, Kisbey noses wrinkled less than London's noses. London's rivers, espeshly Thames, was filled with raw waste. Smells turned stomachs, what with swirling waste and animal innards from slaughter houses and, too, the smell of millions of bodies needing baths.

Truth be tolt, there was even unclaimed bodies from epidemics slowly wasting away, and if I think on that, my throat thickens. Somehow as a child when we had to smell it, I knowed I was only temporarily confronted with it.

Later, oh, never mind.

For now, to make the pitchure clearer, let me say though working condishions was being modernized, modernization sometimes gave and sometimes took work from poor people.

Consequences of 19th century industrilization was not entirely positive. Disease often weds with disorder. Cholera, lice, diarrhea, typhus and typhoid fever and influenza, though not all knowed as such, was prevalent throughout London, but espeshly within slum regions. People bent on escaping London's woes sought their escape through indulgences beyond their means and common decency. Low class people was often in poor houses or debtors prisons. Bills and debts must be payed. Work must get done.

To meet demands of bills and trade, employment was expected of children as well as adults. A few employers was conscience driven to provide adequately for their work force;

others chased the pound without regard for humanity. If a body could work, why was it not creating goods demanded by London and the rest of the world? True, William IV's reforms meant the very young could not be employed, and those over nine was finally limited to nine hours per day. What would Queen Victoria change?

'Will the new queen be better fer England, Ma?'

'We can only hope. She's young, Emanuel. Just 'bout ten years older'n you.'

'Can a lady be smart 'nuff ta be as good as a king?'

'Your father thinks so,' his mother smiled, rubbing his shoulder. 'Oh, Emanuel, no doubt many things will change. Only God knows where life will take you 'fore you rest in a grave somewhere.' Tenderly she added, 'May you always deserve His goodness.' Emanuel remembers their brief embrace before she added, 'But tonight, grab that hoe so we can go back to our cottage with chores completed 'fore Sabbath tomorrow. Let's leave young Queen Victoria to tend England.'

She'd spoken for his father as well in giving Emanuel their blessing. This evening on the knoll was one of Manuel's favorite memories of his lifetime.

Many things would change. Queen Victoria would be the United Kingdom's first monarch to occupy the century old Buckingham Palace. Another thing the numerous King Georges never got 'round to doing was moving. Newly remodeled, the massive palace was surrounded by nearly twenty hectares of gardens. Perhaps Her Majesty would enjoy strolling in them while members of Parliament bickered and fought to conform thinking to match their own. She's had decades to cause ripples in the world.

Yes, powerful Queen Victoria would outlive young Emanuel, but he'd make ripples, too.

If you wish to skip the Bible study, please skip ahead.

A NOVEL APPROACH TO BIBLE STUDY
LESSON THREE - QUESTIONS 47-64
(INCLUDES QUESTIONS REFERENCING "ESCAPING OUR
CHILDHOODS"/CHAPTER TWO, 1830-1842)

47) Briefly describe the similarities and differences between the Copseys and the Kisbeys. Is there evidence of outright or subtle humor in these families?

48) The process of having rough edges chipped away is unpleasant, but how else can we become like diamonds reflecting the beauty of Jesus Christ within our "sanctioned" relationships? How can God use "differences" to induce maturity so each person becomes easier to live with and more Christlike?

49) Maybe settling for a "this will do" microwave or mixer or color of a car is something you can live with, but the consequences of settling for a "this will do" spouse or business partner could produce exponentially greater disappointments. God warns believers not to become yoked to unbelievers. That especially means in marriage, but other "yoking" (business, church fellowships, etc.) deserves some thought as well. Why/how could forming a partnership with an unbeliever raise issues in business and other decisions?

50) The indwelling Holy Spirit is to provide counsel to Christ's follower, but the non-Christian cannot be expected to be following the same counsel. The Holy Spirit indwells us by invitation from a humble heart relying upon Jesus Christ alone as God's Son. By contrast, all of us humans begin life with another "internal advisor," one opposed to accomplishing Christ's purposes in a fallen world.

When a Christ-follower and a non-Christian form a partnership in marriage or in business they are "walking on two different roads." God's adopted family members are to be guided toward life and light, continually conforming to the likeness of God's Son, Jesus Christ. God longs to fill His children's lives with love, joy, peace, kindness, patience, goodness, faithfulness, and self-control and those characteristics will affect the believer's life and thinking. How could conflicts arise in fulfilling contracts, fulfilling responsibilities, or executing consequences if the partner's internal advisor is not the Holy Spirit? Summarize John 10:10, Galatians 5:22-23, and Galatians 5:25 for believers.

51) The natural person's internal adviser will direct his followers away from God in both big and little ways, and though those followers can appear "nice" and "generous" or possess other admirable characteristics, they remain tools useful to God's enemy. The enemy's snagging of believers through marriage or business or other entanglements is not without the intention of limiting effectiveness and destroying the victories intended for Christ and His kingdom.

If unmarried, acknowledge how unreliable hearts can be and how easily marriage is romanticized...or ridiculed. Ask yourself if you're at a vulnerable time in which you might easily pursue an unsuitable "match" who could drain the joy from the fulfilling life God designed for you. Whether married or not, God plans for you to be a happily contented person. Trust God, your Creator, to have your best interest as His plan. We all must remember, no one could love us more than He does, and He is the designer of individuals, of marriage, and of family. Trust Him. Set high standards.

Is there a perfect spouse? Could you be one? Probably not. Even godly spouses become tools God can use to expose each person's imperfections so the couple more perfectly exhibits Christ's love for the church (Ephesians 5). So, whether marriage is a part of your life or not, practice Christlikeness by being an encourager, a forgiver, and faithful friend...and healthy ways to be less selfish.

Comment on present and generational consequences when Christ-followers marry Christ-followers. A good man/woman marriage between dedicated Christ-followers can be earthly joy. Pray that if you become/are a spouse, each of you will move into closer fellowship with God through Jesus Christ. The result will be a deeper fellowship with one another.

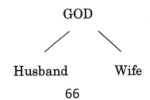

GOD

Husband   Wife

52) Give examples of Esther's progression of her understanding of religion and   faith within these pages. We can sit in church or we can sit at Jesus' feet.

53)   How do those examples compare with or differ from your own progression of religion and faith as a child and youth? (Answers will vary.)

54)   Read Ecclesiastes (Old Testament), chapter 5, verse 13. What wisdom does this passage make available to Esther and other readers? How does Aunt Emma apply that wisdom when she includes Esther in her outings?

55)   What was London like?

56)   Can you identify any of Victorian England's enemies? Which enemies seem timeless?

57)   Compare Esther's parents with Emanuel's parents and briefly describe how each contributes to the emotional and character development of Esther and of Emanuel. Though not overly exposed, which parents likely had humor?

58)   No parent is perfect. Which of the four is the parent you would most like to have had in your home (or present when raising your grandchildren)? Why?

59)   Which parent would you want least to imitate? Why?

60)   What do we learn about Emanuel's goals, his character, and his commitment to family that we had not identified before? Identifying them now will help determine if he meets his goals by the end of the novel.

61)   What is the similarity between the "consequence" lesson taught by Emanuel's father and the comments about ripples made by Queen Victoria and by Emanuel?

62)   What "ripples" have others made that influenced your life?

63)   What ripples do you hope you are making to influence others beyond your lifetime and how intentional are you in your efforts?

64)   Before closing this section in prayer, read James 1 from the New Testament to help summarize what's been read and to prepare for what comes in the rest of "Leaves../Unto All Generations". Jot thoughts/verses that rise to the surface for more concentration with this reading. James 1:

Prayer

Creator God of all and Gracious Father of some through faith in Jesus Christ, we have been surrounded by people who have already impacted our lives, some for good, and some for ill. Though sometimes we incorrectly assign "good" and "bad" to what has happened to us, we know nothing comes to us that has not been allowed by You Who loves us more than we can measure.

In the days ahead, nudge us to become more like Your precious Son, enabling us to release what needs releasing and to cling to what must be kept at all costs.

When we are to speak, open our mouths, but when we are to listen, open our ears and hearts. Much work can keep us busy, sometimes at the expense of fellowship with You. Help us prioritize so we do what matters to You.

Work in and on and through us until our words and our actions are acceptable in Your sight so our "religion" is genuinely pure and undefiled, demonstrating our love for You and Your love for others. In Jesus' name, Amen

Before reading "Cares, Cows, Carriages and Commotion," please read James 2:1-9, 14-20 and James 3:5-10. Jot down some words to help you recall the essence of each passage.

CHAPTER THREE

CARES, COWS,
CARRIAGES, AND
COMMOTION

(1842-1845)

CHAPTER THREE
CARES, COWS, CARRIAGES,
AND COMMOTION
(1842-1845)

These six things doth the LORD hate: yeah, seven are an abomination unto Him: a proud look, a lying tongue, and hands that shed innocent blood, an heart that deviseth wicked imaginations, feet that be swift in running to mischief, a false witness that speaketh lies, and he that soweth discord among brethren. My son, keep thy father's commandment and forsake not the law of thy mother: bind them continually upon thy heart, and tie them about thy neck.

My Psalter, King James' rendering of King Solomon's advice, Book of Proverbs, Chapter Six

Friday, March 5, 1880 A.D.

My dear readers, here I sit once again with my cup of hot tea and a filled teapot, compliments of Anna, who is feeling quite grown up these days and looking forward to staying home from school 'cause of the wintry weather. I shooed her on to house chores with Alice as she was noticing what she called 'odd words' on my pages. Our children may read what's writ, but what's writ is writ and I can't go back and look for 'odd words' or I'll not get this fashionably completed. So, please be charitable with regard to 'odd words' and I'll get on with my accounting. I'll continue with Emanuel's life so you'll learn how our two lives began to cross paths.

'Tis likely Emanuel's life would of been predictable for him had it not been for a set of tragic circumstances over which Emanuel had no control.

One person that cannot be left out of Emanuel's story is his 'Aunt Gertrude.' I had Aunt Emma, and Emanuel had Aunt Gertrude. Aunt Emma had money but she'd been content without it. Aunt Gertrude 'parently needed money to be content. I shudder to think Aunt Gertrude and I likely once had similar desires for our lives.

I never offered to trade Aunts, and though 'tis my habit to not speak ill of others, I think you'd be hard pressed to find someone willing to take Aunt Gertrude in trade. In charity, I suspicion each person has reasons for being as a person is, but seems to me we make some choices 'bout how we'll handle what's difficult, and if we choose to hang on to what's hurting us, we end up letting our hurt be the first thing others has to deal with.

Twas true of Aunt Gertrude. Now, Uncle Ned started out intending to be a likeable man and intelligent enough to get ahet years 'fore Aunt Gertrude knowed him. How he failed to see Aunt Gertrude's ways always puzzled the Kisbeys. Guess if courtship's short enough, anyone can be fooled. Aunt Gertrude saw Ned's money as a short road to higher status and as something she'd like to manage. O'course she couldn't without winning Ned, so she did. In no time she was managing him too, even telling him what to say 'fore they got places, if he was to speak atall. Emanuel and Levi said Uncle Ned had been gray and wrinkled long as they could remember and we came to suspect both features was brought on early 'cause of her. Aunt Gertrude outsized him in every way possible, usually packing her increasingly stout frame into clothing cast off by someone of higher class and less girth than her. She kept Uncle Ned behaving most times like a skittish stray, though she'd 'parently commanded if she turned 'round he best be within her shadow. 'Twas never any doubt who held the scepter in that little kingdom.

Aunt Gertrude and Uncle Ned, these being o'course Emanuel's famly, was childless. If I remember right, Aunt Gertrude's only pregnancy had not gone easy and when time came for the birthing, Uncle Ned needed Emanuel's famly's help in getting a doctor or midwife, them being neighbors and blood. But babies arrive on their particular schedule and farmers' work on theirs, and Emanuel's famly was out working fields when Ned needed their help. Seeing Uncle Ned's waving, they came to him and understood what he wanted, unhitched their team, and took off for help. The doctor was doing country calls and by the time he got to Aunt Gertrude, the situation was dreadful. The doctor delivered a dead baby boy.

Everyone o'course felt heartbroke as the news spread. Famly and neighbors came to sorrow with them. Most was not allowed in the house. Aunt Gertrude only saw callers on the day of burying. Then she went straight home and pretty much stayed shut off from people for a long time. Aunt and Uncle couldn't, or decided against having more children.

For some time they was like lost souls, like a person can be when a child's taken. A few months later, Emanuel was born. He was their reminder of the boy they'd lost. O'course his famly didn't know that at first and Emanuel didn't know that till he was growed. If he'd understood that some of his dealings and feelings might of been different, but 'twas not for a child to think on. 'Sides, for a time, Aunt and Uncle refused dealings with Emanuel's famly, espeshly Aunt. They was neighbors and as years went by Uncle would risk talking to some Kisbeys, but his visits was unreported to Aunt. During this time, naturally, Aunt secretly longed for children. She cut herself off from mingling but kept her critical tongue poised for striking brave visitors who'd be struck by what she'd stored up.

Emanuel's mother was one destined to receive Aunt's venom. Looking back, I think Mrs. Kisbey had nurse-like ways 'bout her. When gradually her attempts to visit improved the situation a bit, what she endured was likely tongue lashings criticizing her mothering ways. Emanuel's much loved mother, (Susan was I believe her Christian name) was a sensible woman, unwilling to sit by without trying to prevent Aunt Gertrude's shriveling up into a bitter woman, making life unbearable for others, and espeshly for Uncle Ned, though he was not kin. Emanuel's mother, always willing to think people could start over, taught her famly to make another's starting over as easy as one could. But she'd not intentionally sacrifice her famly for someone whose starting over wasn't real.

When Emanuel was 'bout ten, his little brother Robert suddenly died, of what I'm not sure, but even those far from London was often caught as epidemics claimed lives. 'Twas a sad time for the close knit brood. Every child was important to the rest. Not long after, with even greater impact, Emanuel's beloved father died, leaving his wife, who'd herself become sickly, with a houseful. I think I can place the houseful correctly in 'bout 1842 as Frances, the oldest, then sixteen-year-old John, Manuel 'bout eleven, Ann would of been ten then, and Levi's two younger, so eight, leaving the two little ones, Sarah/Sallie at four and William coming three.

Maybe don't holt me to those names and ages. There was a batch of Kisbeys like I tolt you and Manuel's not here to set it right. O'course I was never sure Manuel tolt his own age right either, by the way he acted from when we courted, I mean. Makes me think of something else I'll take time to tell you.

I heard Manuel tell a funny story 'bout how the children didn't understand the commotions when William was being born. His older brother, John, didn't either, though John thought he was wise 'bout what was taking place. Anyways, the children was outside while Mrs. Kisbey was carrying on like the Bible warned most women would. John was sure Mrs. Kisbey was dying and he tolt Manuel and t'others how their ma was dying, and they got into such a fight, yelling and all. Manuel thought John was a liar, and even if 'twas true, John was being uncivilized in telling little ones in the manner he was, saying 'Ma's dying, ya know!' and espeshly John sounding like those that didn't agree was just plain dull. Here the kids was fighting 'cause of name calling, name calling was 'cause some thought their Ma was dying or their brother was lying, and Ma Kisbey's not keeping too silent herself until William gave his borning cry, which was not heard by t'others for their carryings on. Out steps Pa Kisbey holting the newborn, startling his whole brood. But they was to be startled more as

Pa Kisbey set the newborn right down on God's good earth, in its wrappings o'course, and proceeded to spank the whole lot from John to youngest! Manuel's Ma said she knowed her whole brood had healthy lungs that day!

Don't know how I got to that but a woman's mind can do that, I guess.

Anyhow, lots of changes happened after the deaths of Robert and Mr. Kisbey. He was a Levi too, if I'm not mistaken. Someone tolt me Manuel's pa was Robert, but Levi seems right to me. Now Manuel would of come closer to having all the names and ages right, but we didn't speak much 'bout that. When people's gone, everyone, me included, thinks of questions we want answered, but can't be, so I'll just go on. Brothers Will and Levi was later helping their mother. I called her Mrs. Kisbey 'til we became famly and then I called her Ma Kisbey. Manuel just called her Ma and talked of his Pa as simply Pa, like our children for us. Never thought I'd need to be certain 'bout Kisbeys since Manuel knowed. But life and death changed things.

For a time, the sad famly limped along adjusting to what Providence and Life handed them, comforted o'course with their strong faith. Emanuel's mother's illness, most likely tuberculosis, made her less fit for hard work. Ann could take over the domestic part but it didn't much suit her, though seems to me a person has to look high and low to find young girls eager to wash and clean once the newness wears off. Ann was mostly hoping to do reading and writing.

Then Aunt Gertrude arrived, having rallied by others' grieving and also having somehow come into more means. She and Ned did the famly and neighborly things like bringing in food, advising 'bout farm work and all. But soon her respect calls lost the respect part. 'Fore the famly knowed much 'bout it, Aunt and Uncle, but likely her mostly, persuaded Emanuel's mother to sell the farm to clear a few obligations and use the rest to live on. Aunt thought John for certain was to be on his own providing income for younger ones. Frances merely needed a husband, but in the meantime, she was to work where she'd be schooled more. Years 'fore her schoolmaster had died I believe or else Frances'd likely taught her siblings schooling. Aunt promised Ann would be in a private girl's school, and that school, Slepe Hall at St. Ives which took Ann from Norfolk to Cambridgeshire, was still standing last I knowed. Some boys, including Emanuel, was to be hired out as agricultural labourers. T'others was to move with Emanuel's mother nearer Norwich or even south to London, supplying costermongers, that's English for street vendors, with home-made goods.

Feigning despair at the strength she'd need to correct child rearing errors, Aunt Gertrude sighed and announced, what with her natural gentleness and child rearing wisdom, she'd help Sallie and Levi reach their neglected potential, providing them with education and more affluence. Truth be tolt, Aunt Gertrude likely desired the attention Sallie drew and Levi was ambitious enough to be good free farm help, and Will was likely not yet in breeches.

Ann's private girls' school was the best part of the plan and it delighted Ann when she learnt of it. O'course payments for Slepe Hall and some of Sallie and Levi's care was to come from Kisbey earnings with also a bit of charity from sacrificing Aunt and Uncle which they noised 'bout.

An ill mother is no match for an Aunt Gertrude. And if I must find something good to say, I can say Aunt Gertrude, to her credit, could organize. But her ideas did not set well with everyone, espeshly not with Emanuel. The boys' hardy fieldwork, done partly to honour their father and their name, had them thinking they'd dutifully keep the farm and famly together. It'd also kept them from hearing Aunt Gertrude urging Mother Kisbey not to discuss plans, saying t'others had enough to worry 'bout and grieve over and too many opinions would only be confusing. Was not Gertrude a 'godsend,' disregarding her own inconvenience? You notice I did not write 'Godsend.' If God should keep me from sleeping soundly tonight, I'll likely strike what I writ. I sent her a letter of contrition years ago. I hope she got it.

Emanuel espeshly wanted their name honoured as they farmed and kept famly together but such was not to be, for the children learnt of the new plans when Aunt Gertrude placed the bill o' sale upon their table one night, along with her charitable shepherd's pie. The meat was from Kisbey's own lamb she'd had Ned slaughter for the famly's convenience.

Questions, discussions, and protests began immediately. Aunt o'course expressed horror that 'children' was permitted such disrespectful manners towards elders. She could not distinguish disbelief from disrespect. Had they no say on matters of such importance? Things was loud and confusing. Emanuel, though young, asked Aunt Gertrude to leave so the family could decide 'bout her arrangements. That stung Aunt Gertrude, him being the reminder of their boy. From that point on, Emanuel would find she was without civility towards him no matter what. Knowing Manuel, standing up to her would of been uncomfortable, but life with his famly was at stake. Aunt Gertrude left in a huff after telling Emanuel something like, 'I can promise ye'll someday see my doings is the best thing that ever happened to the likes of all ye Kisbeys.' Uncle followed, claiming they'd only wanted to help. Poor Mother Kisbey was tearful, wishing she was stronger and saying surely changes was just temporary.

But a bill o' sale is a bill o' sale.

Emanuel tolt me talks that night was somber like planning a funeral for a family wiped out by cholera. 'Fore retiring, they prayed o'course, asking the Lord's care for them, and they tended to think He was, even with those changing circumstances. They was not people scrambling for more than daily needs, espeshly when life was hard.

Once when Manuel was courting me I tried to get him dreaming 'bout big houses and bank accounts, thinking I was pitchuring what he'd like too. I remember Manuel said what he'd like at day's end was to be able to give something to someone needing things worse'n him. I tolt his saying to Aunt Emma 'fore I'd decided 'bout whether to marry him or not, and she, with all her wealth and ease, tolt me she thought Manuel was 'bout the smartest man 'round. That got me thinking.

Back to what I was writing. Emanuel's hopes to undo what was done was judged impossible though Manuel thought Aunt Gertrude's doing things behind their backs gave them right. He reminded siblings 'bout the 'rocks and ripples' lesson and insisted both was bad, but to no avail. Then he argued if they was being torn apart, could not the pieces be fewer? He wanted the famly together much as possible.

That night each gave ideas, but John, being the oldest son, got final say. He looked facts in the face. He'd not been fooled by Aunt Gertrude, but seeing the importance of schooling and claiming 'twas fair costs for rearing and educating Kisbeys fell to Kisbeys, he urged his siblings to work and school so they'd earn good futures. Without older siblings 'round to help, and his mother's health worsening, perhaps like Robert and their father's had, he concluded Sallie, and occasionally Levi, was regrettably best off with Aunt Gertrude. William still needed mothering. They talked long, considering how each could earn meals and pay 'least their own way so Mother Kisbey could get doctoring and, God willing, a place to live with some farm money left for old age.

The outcome? John settled Mother Kisbey, Levi and William in a small place in London. Ann got her private girls' school. John took London foundry work after he, Frances, who I think also did lacework, and Ann, all schooled under a neighbor William Lenton back near Stow Bardolph if I'm not mistaken. I'm quite certain that was close to charity on the master's part.

Schooling was haphazard for most children. A few mission minded religious individuals and institutions took on schooling, espeshly for poor folk, hoping both to teach them of God and reading so they'd understand the Bible. I suspect that's how Aunt Gertrude schooled Sallie and Levi when she had them. Ragged schools popped up for the poor, and workhouses sometimes included a little learning 'sides the hard labour they required. Even so, for most, not nearly as much childhood was spent with schoolmasters as these days.

Mother Kisbey baked breads and sewed and in time, both William and Levi toted goods to costermongers for a coin or two. Another supply needed 'bout then was the piece work for wax dolls with cloth bodies, but I don't think a Kisbey boy ever got close enough to starving to be seen toting dolls. 'Twas humility enough toting kitchen goods.

Sallie went with Aunt Gertrude and, like any child turned loose in a chocolate shop, enjoyed being doted upon. She learnt to avoid Aunt's sharp tongue and even stayed on her good side by acting cleverly so adults would praise Aunt for her sacrificial efforts to raise a poor deprived child. Sallie's ways opened doors otherwise fastened for Aunt Gertrude. 'Fore long, Aunt Gertrude played the reading and numbers card, urging Mother Kisbey not to deprive Levi. He occasionally joined Sallie, doing schooling, and chores for Uncle Ned, too. I think Levi claimed Uncle Ned was good for him. A boy needs a man to guide him.

Ann and Levi, and later Sallie, took to learning. People who take to schooling often get along easier in life than those who don't. That's not talking character mind you. Character has little to do with how well one reads or writes, and you can mark that down in ink. If quills was natural to me I write it in ink now myself. But you can remember it if you just read it again. Or you can find out from life.

So, I think I got all Kisbeys accounted for except Emanuel. When the Kisbeys left the farm, Emanuel was asked to work for the man adding the Kisbey farm to his own. At seven Emanuel's father had called him half a man, and now being near twelve and doing a man's workload, Manuel felt right 'bout staying on.

He'd liked a chance for school, espeshly reading, but time and situations never permitted such, and with that being how life was for him, and knowing some tasks required reading, he figured he'd just earn his way without those skills. 'Sides, not till much later did some mysteries of his illiteracy come to more understanding, but I'll wait with that.

Now there he was. This one who wanted most to be with famly found himself most separated from t'others, not by his or the famly's intentions, but by, I reckon we'd say, Providence, though I say that without approving Aunt Gertrude's ways.

A lot of sadness and hard feelings can be handled with a good measure of hard work, and Emanuel was one to work hard. He'd not seek work where more skills or knowledge than he had was required. Least to start. He had dreams, but he knowed farming.

'Fore long the neighbor's own sons had growed enough to handle Emanuel's part. They shared equipment like the threshing machine with t'other farmers. S'pose you know threshing machines was chastised, too. Life, and new ways, was changing people's ways of doing things.

Emanuel moved on, working other fields. His lodgings was never much, but he'd not knowed how to sleep if they'd been more. Different farming methods expanded Emanuel's knowledge and confidence. He also discovered more strengths and weaknesses in the human race than he'd knowed 'fore.

Emanuel never lost room and board due to shortcomings on his part. The mid-1840's circumstances and taxes changed lives. Few could keep even good hirelings once famly could take over where a stranger collected pay. And a thousand righteous pities on those souls trying to survive without much help or notice from 'neighbors' when they'd lost the husband who'd broke soil and took in harvest.

So Emanuel worked farm to farm, mostly earning meals and a place to sleep, determined to not burden his famly. He figured they likely shuffled a meager food as even as they could to Emanuel broke sweat and sometimes bread with strangers, working a day, sometimes a week, sometimes a season. Further and further south he fled for work and food, 'most like fowls of the air going field to field.

Then one season his good labour got him recommended to a wealthy Essex gentleman farmer, knowed to neighbors as Mr. Roberts, but knowed to Emanuel as simply, 'Sir.'

The landowner's situation proved interesting and not altogether pleasant. Emanuel knowed little 'bout the man when he got hired on but 'twas obvious to Emanuel he'd found a well-kept place with eats to meet his growing appetite. He hoped the work would permit him to acquire means to pass to his family next time he saw them.

Manuel tolt me when he was hired for that season, he ached to think how important family had become to him. He chastised hisself for ever letting dungeons and siblings board in the same thought. Now he longed for his kin by day and drempt by night of Pa and Robert 'bout to banquet, and them looking 'round the long table for t'other Kisbeys to join them.

S'pose if I'd knowed Manuel then, I'd asked if the table had a place set for Aunt Gertrude, but since she wasn't called Kisbey, I'll just let his dream stand. (I must be careful ~ the Lord God may just see fit to put my mansion next to hers so I get a better understanding of that difficult woman.)

Anyhow, if you ever wanted to see Manuel be sentimental, you just brought up famly he'd not seen for a spell. Many times I saw him unable to finish talking 'bout those close to him. To his dying day, Manuel was sentimental 'bout that first famly and us he brought into his life. Separation broke his heart more'n he let on.

I'll miss his ways to my dying day.

I must lay aside my pencil now, bundle up against the wind that whistles against the window's edges, and take a long stroll. Seems like a good time to visit with Almighty God again today.

'Twas a chilly walk. I saw a spry baby lamb we'd warmed inside a few hours last week after its birth. Wonder any survive 'fore their wool untwists. I've warmed my fingers 'round a fresh cup of hot tea to holt the pencil again. Back to Manuel's story.

Emanuel kept a folded paper of his people's London where 'bouts should he someday decide to work or go there. So far his Ag labour gave him only meals and bed, so his means was low indeed. O'course his character was not, and he knowed feeling sorry for hisself did not bring good changes. Manuel, though, believed feelings was fine to feel and know, he just opposed getting stuck in wrong ones after they lose their merit. For being that age, if people'd knowed his head, they'd knowed he was wise already.

At the new place Manuel did chores, but after he proved hisself, the milch cows became his primary job. There was 'bout fourteen cows that was to be milked beginning with the sixth toll as it came rolling over the hillside from a distant belfry. Ready to milk, his bottom on the three leg stool, feet on the ground, and bucket below the udder at six bells. Nothing slipshod. Milked in precise order. Twice daily.

The Devonshire herd had been purchased 'bout two years after the gentleman had experimented with his estate. Though it'd took time 'fore Emanuel was given responsibility for the Devons, it took Manuel no time to know they was the most prized creatures on the farm, even more than the humans who shared life with Sir, and right off, Manuel knowed 'twas a pity. Not till after Manuel showed he was up to scything, stacking wheat for threshers who was hired by Sir, serving as Sir's hayward, doing fence mending and the like, was Manuel ordered to milk the Devons. Manuel figured the man must really hate milking 'cause he knowed the man prized those Devons.

Manuel tolt me those creatures' inborn wit and strength was something to beholt. He earned Sir's commendation for his work with a yoked pair, and those, Manuel swore, though he never tolt Sir, was the only two willing to allow yoking. Manuel got to where he could read their moving back and forth or here and there. He figured when those independent critters agreed to something, like removing Manuel from overseeing them, his yell or soft talk or stick or song might not stop them from placing him wherever they decided.

The bull was another story. He dominated the farm with determination. Many days Manuel tried to keep a fence 'tween him and the bull. We had a bull and cows later and Manuel taught me to keep an eye out when heads and bodies was helt certain ways as it showed the creature's thoughts 'bout you. I was never to turn my back and Manuel's policy was, 'If they's mean, we eat 'em. Beef's good, and more predictable on platters than in pens.'

Emanuel curried those prized Devon's reddish coats often. 'Twas 'bout 1844 and later I tolt him he was likely skilled enough to curry Queen Victoria's gleaming white steeds 'fore Her Majesty's birthday rides through London.

Their barn was to be kept as clean as Sir's garden, and as fresh smelling too. 'Twas good for Manuel, as he slept nearby. Their diet was as precise as their milking schedule. If the amount of milk varied, Emanuel had to explain if he'd milked them off schedule, out of order, changed feedings and the like. Manuel was to see they stayed content.

Another being selected for contentment was Edric Bertwald, which was just his first two names. Slightly less prized than the Devons, hefty Edric was to be content even if others rearranged their lives to make that so. Edric, just a year older than Emanuel, liked comfort. Even at 'bout thirteen Emanuel saw the short-sightedness of Edric's stepfather. O'course Emanuel rarely spoke to Sir 'bout anything and certainly not 'bout spoiling Edric. Some days Emanuel went without hearing a human voice other'n his own when he talked to Devons at milking.

Once Sir inspected Emanuel's handling of the Devons as Emanuel curried them. That was the only time the two had a conversation 'bout their pasts. The man had been orphaned early by one of London's epidemics closer to the beginning of the nineteenth century. Emanuel was reminded of his own fatherlessness, but as he listened, he knowed his life was not as difficult as Sir's had been. Sir's harsh uncle had not hidden his resentment for being obligated to feed and clothe someone he'd not sired. Sir nearly died several times under the abuse from the demanding uncle who was co-partner of a London factory where Sir spent long hours each day. Emanuel's employer experienced the worst 'bout London, early and often.

Then through consequences of disease and quirks of law, suddenly one day Sir found hisself sitting 'fore a judge only to discover he was the rightful and sole heir to a sizeable fortune. He owned the factory he loathed. '

Tis unlikely his uncle had intended such, but the law made it so. With no desire to own or operate what'd taken the sap from young sprigs like hisself, he immediately solt the factory to interested parties and left the lawyer's office with fistfuls of cash and notes to bank, bought several sets of nice clothes, and took his first bath in the fanciest hotel he could find.

He soon found his way to a businessman with whom he negotiated for 'a stone house at least an hour from London but surrounded by sprawling meadows with a stream and a carriage to get there.' Same night he sat alone on the estate he'd bought. He tolt Emanuel he'd bought Buckingham if it'd been on the market. Emanuel worked, listening in awe and approving of the man's ways, but upon hearing 'bout being ready to buy Buckingham, Emanuel concluded the man was given to extreme impulsiveness.

With regard to rearing children, Sir's treatment of Edric indicated the pendulum had swung as far from physical abuse as it could. Though Sir's interactions with his stepson was few and formal, he obviously desired Edric live a life of ease, but, Emanuel observed, without realizing such life brought with it the dangers of boredom and the likely curse of incurable laziness, a condition Emanuel had learnt to avoid at all costs. Here laziness was almost dictated. Idleness was un-English for Emanuel, except o'course on Sabbaths, but Sabbath was not kept at the new place, 'least not for Emanuel.

Emanuel pitied Sir and Edric for their lack of relationship and he never heard how the famly came to be. Edric had to miss being fathered. Was not having a son pleasure to a man? He suspicioned Edric knowed nothing 'bout Sir's past, for such knowing requires times together, walking or the like, and Sir and Edric kept their distances except at mealtimes which Emanuel knowed was as noiseless as a snowfall. Though Emanuel was amply fed and reasonably treated, he knowed he was far from ready for matching wits with this seemingly well-read gentleman whose circumstances out-classed Emanuel, so he kept his thoughts while earning his keep.

Quiet evenings, as London's tolling chimes joined others drifting past cottages and through meadows proclaiming 'twas indeed six o'clock, Emanuel put the Devons in their designated stanchions. Following the farmer's precise instructions, the milk production stayed consistent. All but one milk bucket was dumped into metal cans and placed in the ice house or cold spring near the barn awaiting the milk wagon to take the product to market.

Each day Emanuel was tolt which cow's milking would be the famly's house milk. Sometimes extra milkings was kept for making cheese and specialty foods. For several months, the calluses on Emanuel's hands thickened, as did his fingers. In payment for his work, Emanuel got room and decent eats.

Emanuel's room had been partitioned off from the rest of the barn, and while others might take offense at such, Emanuel knowed the barn was kept in good repair to house the precious Devons. His room was supplied to keep him warm and fit for milking and chores. The herd's body heat likely kept the small room warmer than bedrooms in the nearby stone house after their fireplace's last embers had cooled.

Emanuel'd not spent a night with famly for nigh on to two or more years by now. The more determined he was to keep mind and body busy with work at hand, the more he desired to be with famly. Perhaps 'fore long he'd see them again. But with the daily milking schedule, Emanuel seemed destined to stay close to the barn day and night for a very long time.

His eyes nearly knowed the barn by heart. Most items had a practical use. But he couldn't help wond'ring 'bout a couple pieces hanging on pegs that he'd not seen used. He'd heard tales of London's horrors and he wondert if the strange contrivance near the hay mow had tales to tell. Regardless, each night he rolled over and slept the sleep of one who'd earned his keep.

Some midmornings Edric found Emanuel and tagged along as Emanuel worked. Emanuel never saw Edric 'fore then and he'd still be groggy. Was Emanuel bothered by Edric's laziness? No, Emanuel neither blamed nor envied Edric. And if Edric could keep pace, Emanuel liked his company. Edric was a reader and his reading made the hours fly by.

From old copies of *The Penny Magazine* Emanuel and other working class peoples learnt things they'd not knowed otherwise. Or Edric might bring out crumpled pages of *The Times*. Why in one day, Emanuel, with his hankering for world and history knowledge, might learn of departed kings and queens, dangers lurking in London's muddy streets, or helt his sides as he pitchured an author's descriptions of riding open air trains that left passengers too filthy to continue to important appointments. He descended mines, or learnt of steamboat or other improvements being made to so many inventions that Emanuel was convinced he best keep to simple farm choring.

Something that stuck in Emanuel's head occurred the afternoon Edric read 'bout the young United States that layed across the Atlantic Ocean. The ideas questioned long helt views 'bout Americans being rebellious citizens.

That warm afternoon when Edric finished Mrs. Butler's accounting in the August 15, 1835 copy, Emanuel rested against his scythe and asked Edric to read it again. Was the article true or was it poking fun and stretching facts like he suspicioned other pieces he'd heard did? 'Keep that paper, would ye? I'd like ta hear it agin.'

'Keep it? Why? You thinking you'll travel to America someday?'

'Nah, prob'ly not. I gist like the way it sounds,' Emanuel had said, but even as he spoke he was lying to his soul. But how could someone just earning enough for eats and bed ever think he'd cross the Atlantic?

Still, if Edric's reading was truth, who wouldn't want to travel there?

'Here, you keep the paper. We've 'bout read it out. Put it with your things ...'

'But I caint read—'

'I know, but some day someone 'round you may want in on your dream. I'd wager you go there, Emanuel.' And with that Edric went back to wait for his next meal.

Why, Emanuel would of worked all that day, and maybe the next, just for the piece Edric read, but owning a whole paper? Why, 'twas like gold coins to Manuel. He'd likely never touched paper, it having a heavy tax and all. One newspaper or book might circulate among responsible adults, but young ones like Emanuel only knowed to respect papers. Many times already, this copy in his hands had been folded and refolded. He studied its strange shapes printed on the page. Was the whole page 'bout America, or just part? He'd ask Edric to show him next time Edric was in a friendly mood.

He studied the creases and carefully tucked it inside his shirt 'fore swinging his scythe again. He wasn't quite finished mowing when the bells rang their sixth toll.

Months later a spring day came along and with it came Edric out to the hedgerow Emanuel was tending to ensure Devons stayed put in that meadow. Emanuel'd already learnt their speed and will was too much of a challenge. Mending fence or hedgerow was better'n spending hours chasing stubborn cows, some of whom would be calving any day.

Emanuel was saprized to see Edric coming his way early on this chilly morning. Work was warming Emanuel enough he'd removed his trusty old coat, but unless Edric moved faster 'twas likely he'd soon head back to the stone house where smoke curled slowly from its chimney.

'Manny,' Edric began, adjusting his vest that'd ridden up during his walk.

Emanuel glared at him. His name was Emanuel. Even to famly. He didn't answer, looking directly into Edric's eye.

'Emanuel, yes, Emanuel. My mistake. Emanuel, I was wond'ring if you was up for some adventure.'

Emanuel firmly helt plans, even when I'd try to get him to set aside work years later, espeshly if things was scarce.

The stepson was up to something and if Emanuel'd seen the whole of the day 'fore it happened, this accounting would go far differently. Nowdays we know none of us can a minute from now, let alone see a whole day or what tomorrow holds or a year into the future. The Lord knows more whys, but one is likely that some of us would go into hiding from life. The lesson is to just trust the Holder of Time. Emanuel would say later that we listen for what we want to hear, but to his credit, he spoke to Edric 'bout his need to do the chores given him.

Then Edric said, 'I know that, but if I helped, we'd get done early and there would be time for fun. You're always working.'

Emanuel was intrigued. Edric even had gloves along and extra wire to help mend hedge and fence lines. If Edric helped, he'd do it high fashion, a man's hat o'top his head, striped trousers too fancy for real fieldwork. Emanuel never owned gloves, and his brown canvas pants showed both that he'd worked and growed. Emanuel's cap was weathered, too. Edric'd be the fanciest fence fixer on God's green earth, if indeed he could fix fence.

What's on yer mind?'

Edric donned the gloves and began awkwardly wrapping wire 'round a hedge post. 'I thought after we finish our work here, we'd do something.'

Emanuel heard the 'our work' and the 'we'd do' and it s'prised him. What was Edric up to? He admitted Edric's 'work' 'twas hopeful. 'Course he'd watched work often. 'Such as?'

'Well, I received money for my fifteenth birthday and just look at the way the sun's a shining, inviting us to more than what's here. Today's one of the nicest days we've had so far this year. No telling when the next nice day will come along. If I help you finish up, would you go with me to London?'

'London?' Emanuel had thought skipping rocks on the stream perhaps. 'I've never bean ta London. Un after w'ot ye read ta me 'bout cholera un people's waste smellin' things up, why leave fresh air?'

'But you're always looking at it like she was your mother. I seen you. When a bell chimes, you stop and look at London.'

'We caint see London from 'ere. I stop ta count chimes. I knowed better'n ta be late to milk.'

His moneyed companion tried again. 'We could catch a carriage at the crossing just below the next farm at 'bout eleven o'clock and be in London 'fore noon. I got the coach fare.'

'I don't. I'm not dressed fer London. I work yer stepfather's fields. I milk cows. I'm not a Londoner.'

'But I read more 'bout London last night,' Edric said, sounding like he could sell three-legged heifers.

'From papers like ye give me? Or new ones?' The article 'bout America was safe with Emanuel's meager belongings in his barn room.

'Not from *The Penny* for sure. My stepfather says people who published it spent time in prison and lost their presses. No wonder we only got old copies. If they was still publishing, I think there'd be stacks 'round my ole man's chair.'

Edric's disrespect for 'Sir,' didn't s'prize Emanuel, but imprisonment for writing did. Did Edric know, was he saying facts? Why would papers 'bout animals and laws and sights people enjoyed knowing 'bout be cause for prison? Maybe the whole paper was untrue. He still liked his paper.

If Emanuel had knowed the tempo of change, the contests in Parliament over social issues, perhaps he'd understood the dislike for Hetherington who'd campaigned to change laws. Hetherington's presses built his support base. Children far too young to join Hetherington's reformation efforts perhaps heard employers whisper Hetherington's name. He'd wanted life better for London's youngest factory workers. Those who doubted the fairness of supporting upkeep of churches they'd never attend might also strain to shake Hetherington's hand. But how'd Manuel know any of that?

Wot's going on in London that has ye wantin' ta go?' Manuel thought it right he know 'fore he'd go.

'Nothing particular,' he shrugged. He struggled to twist another piece of wire into a loop on a fencepost he eyed Emanuel, trying to act casual like. 'Doubt we'll see much of anything. Town's likely cleaned up after the flood a few weeks ago, so we might gist get bored right off. I just think two young men others consider adults ought to be able to take a day once in a while and see the world. Such an idea ought to be worth thinking on, espeshly for young men like us.'

'The world? Edric Bertwald, yer gist talkin' London. There's a whole lota world beyond London.'

'So people say. But has you seen any of it?'

'Ye knowed not. I've spent my th'teen years smellin' London and milkin' cows. Well, I've smelt cows, un a few other animals, too, but from all I cain tell, the farm's smells is better'n smells o' London.' Emanuel looked toward the old city as though she might take offense. 'Oh, Edric, why da ye tempt me like this?'

'You're tempted? Well, that's more than I dared hope,' Edric said with obvious enthusiasm. 'I've worked it out. I'll be Stepfather's hayward a few hours just like you so's we can finish sooner. You point to where repair's needed and we can at least pen the cows in while we're gone.'

'Ye mentioned any o' this ta yer stepfather?'

Edric shifted his considerable weight. Edric was 'bout as tall as Emanuel, now approaching his final height two inches short of six feet. Emanuel's meals had been 'bout like Edric's, but Emanuel's work made his body considerably leaner.

'Ye's not, has ye?' Emanuel waited to see Edric's eyes, strangely overly attentive to fence mending.

'Oh, Emanuel, why would you think I'd risk getting us into trouble?' He shrugged as he made his quick glance. 'My stepfather tolt me I could go.' He was not entirely convincing. But then, Emanuel'd not knowed him to be deceitful. Besides,

London... today? If Sir had given approval, then why did Emanuel argue? Maybe something good was going to happen if he'd let it. Permission was key, though, so Emanuel asked again, not wanting to be a fool.

'He approved? You're sure?'

Sometimes 'twas hard to get a word in when talking with Edric, espeshly if Edric was solt on his idea. This was one such idea. What was Edric saying?

'So, you see, it's all worked out. Nothing to worry about. I tolt him I'd spend the day with you.'

'Un tha' met with his 'proval?' He was s'prized but pleased when Edric nodded. He'd worked for Sir for over a year now. Maybe this short day was his reward, a bonus that expressed Sir's trust in him, his appreciation of Emanuel's faithful care of all he had assigned him to do. O'course he'd finish this immediate chore and they'd be back 'fore the six bells chimed. What harm would come of a quick trip to London?

If only he'd knowed.

I hope, dear ones, you don't mind my writing Manuel's part this way. It brings back so many memories of Manuel's story-telling ways and the children asked I sometime put down stories their Pa tolt. I'm not too old to learn from young ones.

The two finished fixing gaps decent enough, hoping the intelligent breed would not investigate repairs too carefully. 'Sides, the cattle was enjoying new grazing and the fresh spring fed pond. What creature would consider leaving what was good?

What creature indeed?

For a moment Emanuel thought how refreshing an easy day right there would be, taking time to consider the big questions that comes to minds when a body's stilled. He never had a day but that he felt 'Sir' judging.

But he'd tolt Edric he'd go. He'd keep his word. He decided he was old enough to know that was important if a person expected to go through life with friends he could count on. 'Sides, truth be tolt, he was excited 'bout it.

After being reassured Edric had no reason to report back to his stepfather and that Edric's new birthday money would pay for both of them, the two fellas soon hurriedly fastened the paschure gate and began trotting down the hill, past trees, clamored over the stone boundary fence line, and strained to get to the crossing 'fore eleven bells. Edric strained more o'course.

Turning 'round while running backward, Emanuel called, 'We'll not make it if ye don't run,' then turned to pick up his own pace. He'd seen coaches pass his farm years 'fore, but he'd been too busy and too cautious to consider passing Sir's fence line 'fore that day. He'd not felt threatened by Sir. Not outright anyways. He'd not been criticized even. But there was something 'bout the man beneath the surface that made Manuel wary of causing Sir's displeasure.

If Edric couldn't catch the carriage, Emanuel certainly would not go alone. First, he had no carriage money, and next, he'd not know where to say he wanted off, 'less he tried to find his famly, but the day would be too short for that, and third, not being a reader, how'd he ever get along in London? 'Someday,' he thought, 'I must master readin' even without going to school. We'd be like blind men if Edric couldn't read.'

Now readers, you recall I'd spent another week with Aunt Emma at her friends' estate where I'd more or less been a favored guest 'fore I'd again be a mother's helper nearer our home just outside London. If our relationship had depended on this first encounter, you'd likely not be reading this story. Our paths would cross but our day would be so different. As Manuel writ later, 'Long would be the road that has no crooks or turns.' But as faithfully as I recall it, here's the accounting.

'Fore stepping into the open carriage to sit across from Aunt Emma for our ride to London, I'd donned my newest outing clothes from Aunt Emma ~ a shiny blue dress that fell to my ankles, a fancy hat with a scarf that wrapped 'round my neck, and even a pair of better shoes. I'd blushed as my hosts commented I looked older than my almost fifteen years. The carriage was adequate, though without footman, so we'd stepped at our own risk. My warm wool shawl kept out the morning chill. The road was bumpy, but I seldom felt upset by such rides. We'd 'do London' together, that's what Aunt Emma called it, for a few hours, then we'd celebrate my birthday with famly. My, that was thirty-five years ago this month!

Edric arrived gasping as the horses obediently slowed the carriage to take on passengers. He payed and Manuel, knowing his place, let Edric step up and in first. Seeing a woman and her supposed young red-headed daughter, Edric boldly sat beside me, opposite Aunt Emma, by whom Emanuel then settled.

He'd say later he was wishing he'd brushed his pants and coat a couple more times 'fore they touched her finery, though we was by now slightly dusty ourselves. Aunt Emma's ruffles and parasol made Emanuel nervous, fearing his field dust mingling with her finery would get him tossed off long 'fore he saw London.

Edric coughed and wheezed to catch his breath as we began jostling along. Aunt Emma noted my blushing, and concluding I was uncomfortable exposed to the young traveler's illness, she decided to rearrange our seating. Sometimes this carriage ran the whole route with scarcely a soul, but here we was sitting near who knowed what!

'Would you gentlemen be so kind as to sit together?' Aunt Emma's voice was barely heard above the pounding horses' hooves. Expecting a favorable response, she lifted my hand to move me to where Emanuel sat.

He stood, seeking to balance his lanky frame as the coach swayed, keeping an eye out for low branches that might swipe us if we didn't settle quickly. 'No Ma'am, not atall,' he said, stepping 'round me and squeezing into the space beside Edric.

'You're not sickly, I hope,' Aunt Emma nodded toward Edric, whose rough coughs gustily escaped. She began opening her parasol, holting it like a shield in front of us, which I didn't mind 'cause, truth be tolt, I figured we sat across from two of the strangest creatures on God's earth. There was, I'll admit, something a bit interesting 'bout Manuel from the beginning, and Edric, too, but I'd never drempt Emanuel would ever be more than a nameless passenger dressed in field clothes hetted by carriage for London. But, mind you, Aunt Emma had invested considerable time training me not to be rude. I had, after all, visited nice places serving fancy teas, but Aunt Emma had seen to it that I'd also worked with London's poor.

'I'm just short of breath, that's all,' Edric managed between coughs.

What the quick pace had started, the dust was finishing. Edric's face and sweat made him look sickly and Emanuel wasn't the only one who thought so.

'Young man, I feel compelled to tell you that I don't like the sound of your cough. Will you be seeing a physician?'

Edric was still wheezing and gasping for air so he was silent. Aunt Emma scrutinized both boys suspiciously.

'Oh, no, Ma'am,' Emanuel began, 'Edric's cough's rare but 'tis not catchin'. I know him and 'tis the one of the few times I ever heard it. I think 'tis caused prob'ly by his not being used ta runnin' fer carriages.' He looked at his red-faced friend. 'Isn't that right, Edric?'

Edric nodded, unable yet to speak again.

'Edric? Edric?' Aunt Emma said, letting the name rummage through her mind. 'Is your stepfather Mr. Aston Roberts?' she asked, but without waiting for the cougher's reply, she turned to Emanuel. "Is he Edric Roberts?"

'I don't rightly know, Ma'am.' What strange truth. From the time Emanuel set foot on Edric's stepfather's farm, it'd been clear the man was to be 'Sir' to Emanuel. Without wages or transactions, 'Sir' it had remained.

'You don't know? Aren't you two together?' With parasol still shielding us, she continued, 'I must warn you, cough's like that in London often mean the beginning of the end. Is Mr. Roberts your stepfather?'

Sheepish at the attention, Edric replied, 'Yes, Ma'am, I'm Edric Roberts, but, to the best of my knowledge, I'm not ill. I'm just not used to running to catch coaches.'

'I'd say Edric's not used ta runnin' fer any reason, Ma'am,' Emanuel chuckled. He brushed his hand on his pants, offering it to us. 'I'm Emanuel Kisbey, and ye is ~'

Aunt Emma was still tallying the thousands whose deaths started with a cough, perhaps like Edric's. 'Well, I'm thinking,' she began, but reminding herself she was not a physician, she stopped, leaving Emanuel with his hand stuck out midair.

Was his handshake offensive to this woman? Had she given her name as t'other carriage had passed?

Seeing his awkwardness, I took pity.

'And I'm Esther,' I smiled, taking his hand to spare him further embarrassment. Aunt Emma's sudden concern 'bout illness had removed her manners. Epidemics was frequent in the 1840's, though I'm not certain London had one just then or not. I've since learnt how hands pass disease, but that late spring morning, I wanted to end a poor young man's uncomfortableness. Turning to Aunt Emma I tried humor by saying, 'And I'd only knowed you as 'Aunt Emma,' but didn't you introduce yourself as 'I'm Thinking'?'

The tension eased as t'others saw my effort. Aunt Emma quickly apologized for her uncomely behavior but reminded me to call her 'Aunt Emma.' Then, releasing the lock on her parasol, she began closing it, though Manuel was certain it'd go up again if Edric coughed. 'Now, let's start again. So, you're Mr. Roberts' Edric?'

'I am. And I don't believe I've had the pleasure of meeting you charming ladies,' Edric replied in a manner so polished Emanuel slumped and groaned. Right then he longed to be tending Devons. 'How do you know my stepfather?'

'His wife, your mother, is my husband's cousin. Unless I'm mistaken, I believe I attended your baptismal gathering. 'Twas a lovely gathering as I recall. It gave us an opportunity to meet relatives and old friends there at your stepfather's new place.' She hesitated, 'Was that in '29?'

'I beg your pardon, Ma'am, but I guess 'tis reasonable I am excused for my lacking a clear recollection of my christening. However I was named 'Edric Bertwald' I'm tolt. The 'Roberts,' as you may know, came later.' Who was this Edric headed to London, Emanuel wondert. 'And today, I'm just a young gentleman headed for a day of leisure.'

Emanuel's well-worn shoe nudged Edric's. If Edric's tone had been more impertinent, Manuel's elbow would likely of silenced this boy now overestimating his manhood. Surely Queen Victoria would be knighting him when she recognized his valiance and finesse.

'I find it saprizingly uncharacteristic that Mr. Roberts sent you off to London alone. Will you meet someone there?' She paused and smiled, realizing Edric had not coughed for a spell. 'I assume you don't need a physician.'

'No, Ma'am. I'm healthy as a,' Edric searched for words, 'I'm healthy as a Devonshire cow. And, in case you don't know, that's healthy!'

Emanuel leaned back, pulling his cap over his eyes, deciding he'd listen as though Edric was reading make believe from an old *Penny Magazine*. He'd ignore the ladies' ruffles. He wondert where such well-dressed ladies was going for 'twas obvious they wasn't just plain country folk.

Whatever happened, life was going a bit out of the routine today for Emanuel. I saw he smiled as he listened, though his face was partially hid by his cap. Aunt Emma had just commented that Mr. Roberts must think Edric quite mature to let him set off to explore London without him. Edric's response made Emanuel's bolt upright.

'Well, Ma'am,' Edric said, leaning forward, 'Can you keep a little secret? He doesn't know that's where we're spending the day.'

'What?!' Emanuel demanded, standing to his feet. 'Driver, Sir, please stop this thing! I need to get off!'

Isn't it a mysterious thing how people laugh at other's fixes? I couldn't help it and later Manuel remembered that and teased me about it.

'We're almost to London, boys,' Aunt Emma tolt them. 'You might as well enjoy your visit.'

Emanuel leaned toward Edric. 'Edric Bertwald, w'ot do ye mean yer stepfather don't know we's gone? Ye sed ye tolt him! Ye sed he sed I could go with ye!'

For Emanuel, this was no childish prank.

'Manny,' Edric started, as though years wiser than Emanuel whose countenance convinced him otherwise. 'Excuse me,' he began again, bowing slightly for emphasis, 'Emanuel, if I may, let me refresh your memory. I did not lie to you.'

Emanuel was not amused but I'm ashamed to say he was the only one. I helt my hand over my giggles. Edric appreciated his audience. Emanuel was not a fool. He'd likely be the only one paying for Edric's performance.

'Ye did lie, Edric Bertwald.' His tone removed the name's upper class sound. 'Ye either lied then or ye lied now. Either way, 'tis wrong as wrong can be. Which is it?'

'Emanuel,' Edric said with exaggerated patience that nearly made Emanuel lose his, 'you must calm down. Let's review our situation. If you will recall, I said, 'My stepfather tolt me I could go' and I also said, 'I tolt my father I'd spend the day with you. Do you comprehend what I'm telling you?

'And did he?'

'Emanuel, you worry too much.'

'And ye don't worry 'nuff! Wot kind o' shenanigan ye tryin' ta pull? We's goin' ta be in such trouble!'

'Father won't know we're gone. Anyway, why'd he care? This morning I said I was bored. He said, like always if he speaks to me atall, 'Find something interesting to make you content.' When I thought 'bout it, going to London would make me content. Could it not be argued he gave his approval?'

Emanuel slumped back down in his seat. 'He has no idee whar we's going, does he?'

'Prob'ly not.'

Aunt Emma eyed Edric. 'If Ashton learns you're gone, I reckon your 'it could be argued' will need London's most skilled lawyers.' She spoke more softly to Emanuel. 'But in truth, not that I condone this young man's ways, Emanuel, Mr. Roberts won't likely check on you two till the evening meal, right?'

'But 'tis wrong to go if 'Sir' didn't know and 'tis not like we was slipping off to fish fer an hour. He might not check, but that don't make it right.'

'See? We all agree we won't even be missed.' Edric smiled, 'That's what I'm counting on. Emanuel, he prob'ly thinks we'll work t'other end of the meadow and he'll not likely go there. He's taking the carriage to meet someone today anyway. 'Sides, we'll not stay long here, just a couple hours and we'll go back.'

'In time fer milking, understood?'

'O'course, we'll be back 'fore that. 'Sides, what's the worst thing that could happen?'

Wise Aunt Emma tilted her head, looking over her eyeglasses at the three of us. Emanuel and me watched her come up with a multitude of answers, but she kept silent. Edric just shrugged and smiled.

Emanuel thought the carriage stopped at the dismissal of the Tower of Babel. Emanuel helped us step from the carriage. Aunt Emma smiled, 'Now, boys, don't catch London's illnesses. And, Edric, if you figure out how to do it, greet your parents for me. My name is Emma.'

Then we was swept into a milling crowd.

Aunt Emma bent over so I'd hear her. 'The quiet one has character worth admiring.'

I looked back where we'd left them. I'd thought entertaining Edric had made the better impression, perhaps because of my age. He seemed more daring than Emanuel and my glances 'parently was noticed by Aunt Emma. 'Character, Esther, is genuine. If the opportunity came, I'd invest in Emanuel's future. I pray others look long enough to see his character. I think they shall.' Then we was off.

I scarcely remember what Aunt Emma and I did as we strolled through London. For the brave boys, their afternoon adventures helt listeners attention whenever they tolt of it in the years ahet.

Emanuel looked 'round, calling to Edric, 'Is this whar we meet ta het back?'

'Think so, but it's my first trip, too.'

'Oh, Edric Bertwald Roberts, if we live through this day, I'll...' but Edric was already crossing the muddy street to buy fruit from the costermonger cart manned by a cheery seller. Emanuel hurried to keep pace with his fare back. Overhead, above the din of millions of voices, a clock proclaimed milking was just six hours off.

By the time the clock struck one, Emanuel decided Edric could be a right likeable fellow if deceitfulness was discounted. Emanuel hadn't had the refreshment of a carefree afternoon like Edric. But here, where they scratched their heads to study the magician hiding a pea under a thimble or to figure which streets and bakeries to explore while navigating 'round dung piles from hundreds of horse-drawn carriages, if not by humans, Edric seemed the closest thing to a friend Emanuel had. A chum, like might of come from Sabbaths back to home. Did not Edric say they was to experience a day of 'fun'? They was, indeed.

Emanuel's ears caught phrases from new languages. His nose was drawn to new aromas, his tongue and tastebuds nibbled new flavors while sipping tart ginger root. Why, even his eyes had took off like a colt breaking fence. He gazed at London's tall struckchures, peeked inside clothing stores and he knowed he was not dressed as many, though London had its share of people in bare threads. He saw displays of craftsmanship not common to where he'd lived 'fore, and certainly he knowed he was not dressed as most.

When I'd hear Emanuel talk of the day, I'd see he could not sit still as he tolt of it, like he was right there again, running his hands over furniture smooth enough for a king, listening to dogs yelping for their lives in rook'rys for why he knowed not, and his nose finding London smelled worse than ever he'd 'magined. He also kept an eye out for a Kisbey, just in case.

But crowds there was! People jostled with rarely words of regret. Walks, streets, shops crowded with famlys, couples, individuals young to old.

Another bell chimed.

Then another.

In spite of smells, crowds, and fear their shoes would never clean up, Emanuel knowed it'd be hard to leave so much not yet discovered. That's when he heard a man hawking, 'Ye'll not be sorry boys. Bring ye tuppence and see the world's tiniest freak pig show.'

If he was going to see something not common to farming and fieldwork, perhaps a freak pig show would be sensible, educational perhaps. 'Edric, we got money fer the world's tiniest pig show?'

Edric checked his pockets. 'Tell you what, Manuel, I got enough and then some, but why don't we try to win some shillings by guessing 'bout where the pea is back at that thimble game? I think I could do it. How many times did you guess it right when we was watching?'

'I 'ardly ever got it right.'

'Ah, com'on. If we both keep an eye on the pea, I'll bet we'd win. Let's watch and work out a signal.'

'I think I'd rather see the freak show. Tha's a shore thin'. No guessing. Gist looking, for a price 'course.' 'But if we guess right, we'd take home extra shillings, or split winnings to do t'other fun stuff. Let's try.'

Edric was older. Manuel was coinless. Why not follow Edric? 'Cain we come back 'ere if we win?'

Assured they'd return to the pigs, the boys retraced steps, planning how they'd outsmart the magician. They separated so the magician wouldn't know they was together. But they wasn't the first boys in London to try that. The puff-sleeved magician 'bout twice their age shuffled the thimbles for a small crowd. Manuel and Edric signaled guesses to each other, saprizingly improving their guesses after a few minutes.

Shore enough, the magician had spotted them, shaking his head like he shore hoped they'd not play. A player or two won, but most got guesses wrong. Once Manuel couldn't help but blurt, 'The middle one, not tha' one!' The player shrugged his shoulders, saying somebody else better take his place.

Edric did.

'Now boys,' the magician warned, 'I saw ye helping each other guess and I saw ye's getting it right. I'm 'fraid you'll wipe me out in no time. If only one's gonna pay, only one's gonna play. What'll it be?' Manuel shook his head.

Edric confidently tried it alone, his six pence pulled across the box by the magician. Quickly the magician placed the pea, then covered it with a thimble and began shuffling the thimbles left, right, 'round again many times. The magician stopped. 'Watch this smart lad, gentleman, he'll get my shillin' I'm shore.'

Manuel wasn't certain, but he hoped Edric'd pick the middle thimble. Edric studied thimbles a moment. He pointed left. Empty. Edric groaned. Looking at Manuel, the magician said, 'Where'd you'd tolt him to look?' Manuel pointed to the middle thimble, and sure enough, there was the pea. 'Your friend could clean me out. Good thing he's not playin'.'

Edric tried again. And again. Each time, though he'd sworn the pea'd be under the thimble, 'twas not.

The magician asked Manuel for his guess, and Manuel'd hesitantly point to a thimble. Sure enough, the pea was there! If only he'd played. This was his game!

Manuel figured they'd better quit while they still had some coins. He motioned to Edric.

Edric crossed to Manuel and gave him six pence urging, 'Manuel, you get it every time. You try.'

Manuel hesitated, fingering the money that felt strange to his calloused hands. They and most others heard the magician's whisper, 'I hope he don't, his eye's too keen.'

Manuel couldn't resist. He put down the only six pence he'd touched since he couldn't remember when, but he did so thinking, 'Wouldn't a shilling feel even better in my fingers?' 'Sides, to his mind's calculating, didn't he need to win back what Edric'd lost?

The magician groaned, 'I'd like ye not to play, boy. We all saw ye get it right. Why don't ye take yer six pence and go home?'

'Twas the best advice the boys could get, but Manuel was determined he'd play once.

'He's already put it down, you gotta let 'im play,' another fellow spoke up. The magician shook his head, placing the pea, then covering it with a thimble. The shuffling began. Manuel was certain the left thimble covered the pea. Why, he was right! Reluctantly the magician gave him two six pence coins, begging Manuel to move on or he'd lose his day's earnings. But would he walk when earning more was so easy?

Edric and t'others urged him play again. 'Well,' Manuel thought, 'why not get another shilling back with his keen eyes?' Manuel'd not had a group cheering him on like was forming now. He put down his coin and the game began.

Shuffle, shuffle, shuffle. 'Twas easy. Middle thimble, even Edric said, 'Yes!' when Manuel pointed.

But alas, the pea was not there! How'd he lost his keen eye?

The magician asked him what his second guess would of been, and Manuel pointed to the first thimble. Sure enough, there was the pea. Didn't seem quite right to Emanuel, but who was he to take on this man? At least he had something.

Manuel decided to keep his six pence. Edric, however, wanted another chance. Manuel tripped as he stepped back, so twas logical he squat to tie his shoe. He pretended it needed a special knot as his darting eyes adjusted to the darkness under the magician's table. Hmm. He spotted a couple peas on the ground, but more importantly, his eyes was level with the boxlid. He saw it! The magician picked up the pea while shuffling! None was under any thimble!

Edric was 'bout to point. Manuel stood and grabbed Edric's arm, startling Sir's stepson. Manuel had never put a hand on anybody at that place, so Edric wondered how he dared so it now. He looked directly into Emanuel's face. 'You better explain what you're doing, grabbing me like this.'

'Edric, don't guess. Ye'll lose,' Emanuel said loudly.

'Whatcha saying, Emanuel?' Edric looked at his London companion questioningly. "Tis my turn, like we agreed.'

"e's got th' pea, Edric. It ain't on the table no matter where you guess.'

Edric's brow furrowed. 'What'd you say?'

'Oh, now young gentlemen, that's a serious charge ye's making against me,' the magician began, suddenly joined by a couple other 'bystanders' who agreed the boys was wrong to call someone a cheat.

'Then show yer 'ands, Sir,' Manuel began, but elbows connected with his body. 'Turn the thimbles, Edric!' Manuel hollered, turning an empty thimble hisself, preparing to run.

Edric turned t'other two empty thimbles up as the chap next to him slapped his hands. 'I've been robbed, give me back my money!' Edric began, but the magician's walking stick suddenly appeared and seemed likely to crack Edric's skull, scattering the crowd.

People yelled for a bobbie to stop the game swindler, but the boys found themselves scuffling with men mysteriously angry at the boys. Edric shoved the magician, causing him to lose his balance. 'Manuel, run like pigs!' Edric yelled, and he fled with a squeal and grunt, Manuel knowed not where.

Manuel hoped he'd understood Edric's intent, but regardless, he had two men trying to hold on to him, one, Manuel noted, being someone who'd supposedly also 'lost' to the magician before Edric and Manuel put down their money. Manuel squirmed and kicked and, with help from a couple others who'd likely seen the boys play, pulled himself free to cut loose, full speed. His chores payed off, his lean body weaving 'round corners and cutting through busy streets, slipping only once on some dung, but never falling completely. In no time, he'd zigzagged his way to the pig freak show the same time Edric did where Manuel slapped down his six pence, pulling Edric past the startled hawker and quickly disappearing among people beyond the entrance.

They'd been had, but they'd figured out how, and that's to their credit.

Inside, they panted, their hearts racing. Soon the magician's shills could be heard yelling and asking 'bout the where'bouts of two boys who'd ruined 'fair enterprize.' The hawker, to Emanuel and Edric's deep satisfaction, seemed unable to comprehend what stirred the pursuers so. Nodding to 'thother, they knowed the extra tuppence was well spent. The hawker tolt the pursuers his tent was full but they was welcome to spend their tuppence for the next show in ten minutes if they cared to wait. When there was more commotion, he warned the crowd he'd get a Bobby if they wasn't peaceful. Inside, 'fore he raised the show curtain for the freak show, he whispered to Manuel and Edric the men was gone.

The live tiny freak pigs turned out to be 'bout as dishonest as the thimble-rig. In a miniature pen was cork snout 'pigs' made of hollowed acorns and short wooden picks as legs, ears, and tails which slowly wiggled the 'live pigs' 'round the pigsty 'cause flies was trapped inside. 'Fore the kind hawker sent them safely on their way, Manuel learnt how such tiny pigs was made, and that horse flies was liveliest captives, but a common fly would do. Over the years he'd show people his own 'live freak pigs.' As our children grew older, I encouraged their making 'tiny freak pigs,' espeshly days I had too many flies 'round.

The pair ventured on, but not as fast as the hands of the clock. They picked their way in a fairly straight path, glancing back to remember their way through the noisy labyrinth of London. They counseled to select what to do next. They was not 'bout to waste more money on tricksters and if they'd stayed an extra day or two, you'd hardly knowed they was young men fresh from the farm. Standing in front of a noisy building, they decided to investigate.

'Is you men looking for work?' a voice called above the throbbing of machines rhythmic'ly creating yard goods for shops and eager seamstresses. 'I could use a couple more if you can start immediately. Let me show you 'round.'

Emanuel and Edric didn't know how to not follow. They came to a large room, filled with looms unlike anything they'd ever 'magined. These was not small looms or spinning wheels like mothers use. These was long horizontal looms. The air was filled with bits of fabric and Emanuel stifled his sneeze. Edric was coughing, but 'cause of the noisy machines and 'cause t'others was coughing too, the manager seemed unconcerned. He coughed, too. Running between the highly productive machines was several young girls and one young boy. Agile children, 'bout half the age of our adventurers, scooted under machines for loose cotton or dropped material scraps. Stationed above on boxes near the loom was other young ones watching for broken woof or warp threads to quickly repair as shuttles flew back and forth, weaving a perfect cloth.

'They's scavengers and piecers,' the man explained above the noisy machines. No worker was talking. All was intent 'bout their jobs. 'I don't need any more of them right now, but if I did, you'd be too old. 'Sides, I get a steady supply from orphanages if not parents, less o'course other factories get 'em first. Here, let me show you fellows 'round. We'll see if you're bright enough for working here.' And with that, he moved toward another section of his textile factory. 'Fore them was vats of material soaking in dyes, then drying rooms and folding machines.

Suddenly a yell drew the owner from them. Curious, they followed. Two workers hunched over a young girl writhing in pain. Blood spurted from where her hand now dangled. 'Wrap her up and put her outside in the fresh air,' he instructed. Looking down at the fainting child he spewed, 'Foolish little imp! You was warned to be careful. Look what you've done! How can I make profit if your blood messes things up? Don't think you'll work here, you hear? I need those that listen.' And with that, he walked to Emanuel and Edric to show them where they'd work.

Looking from the girl at each other, they knowed they'd not be employees. 'Wot'll 'appen to 'er?' Emanuel asked. 'Who'll git 'er 'ome?'

'She's not yours, is she?' His brazen comments continued. 'If she'd listened I'd maybe care. Obviously she didn't. Some children work here years and not get hurt. Then I get one who won't take instruction. Used to be, till a couple years ago, I could make them listen.'

He pointed into a room they was passing. On the wall hung several contrivances like the one Emanuel knowed was in the barn. 'These things, I'll tell you, these things worked. O'course there was times children, and for that matter, other older public nuisances, got pretty beat up, even kilt, if a person set them out to a crowd taking took matters into their own hands. But I tell you, it'd make everybody work hard 'fore a bunch of high class know-it-alls threatened to punish us operators if we put our child workforce into locks. Worst thing they ever did, taking stocks away. That girl prob'ly won't ever learn to listen. Too careless. Well, good riddance to her. She'll be hungry and sore a day or two, but whoever hires her next will likely thank me for teaching her 'bout listening. Who knows? Maybe she'll come thank me if she turns out to amount to anything.'

A whistle blew and he asked the pair to wait while he checked on something. Instead, they found the nearest door. Outside they learnt the injured girl was from an apprentice home which would refuse her now. Unclaimed, she was bleeding to death. A couple women tenderly bent over her nearly lifeless form as Emanuel and Edric hetted toward the carriage stop. Silently they dodged puddles and piles best they could. Emanuel longed for the meadow.

'Din't we turn 'ere?' The city was looking mean and uncaring and Emanuel hoped to leave it far behind as soon as he could. But where were they to go? Every street was starting to look like t'other and none was staying distinct like when they'd first stepped off the carriage.

'I thought we turned up there, but t'wont matter. Just so we get past the thimble swindlers and end up at the carriage stop,' Edric answered.

'The police's shorely closed those cheats down. 'E wos settin' us up. Good thin' we dint 'ave much money or we'd lost it and be in a fix. But let's go the way we came and if we see 'em we cain go 'nother way. It's gittin' late un we need ta git ta th' carriage. W'ere we need ta be?'

'I don't know, I was dodging dung piles and getting knocked 'round by those who knowed where to go.'

Edric studied the streets. 'I think we went in that bakery, so this street'll retrace our steps.' They went a few paces and turned to walk past the bakery.

'That's the boy! That's him! Stop him, he's a thief!' someone called. A panicked youth 'bout their size bumped sharply into Emanuel as he dashed past him with a loaf of bread under his arm. A Bobby responded quickly to the commotion and began weaving through the excited crowd. Emanuel and Edric picked up their pace, knowing they was yet a good distance from the carriage stop and wishing they'd dressed warmer against the chill settling in. From somewhere within the mob, the baker yelled again, 'Catch him. He stole bread and shillings. A reward to whoever gets him!'

The boys looked at each other. Reward? Why not?

Emanuel led the chase, struggling to clear a channel. Emanuel'd heard the Bible said, 'If ye won't work ye won't eat' and in another place not to steal. Some pursuers was in front, but most behind, including Edric. Shoppers on the muddy streets merely kept moving toward their appointments elsewhere. How could they let a thief escape? Did rewards not tempt them? Emanuel worked forward, learning to use his elbows like a Londoner. He spotted a cap ahet of him.

'I see 'im,' he called back to Edric, still clinging to his fancy hat but whose size and weight once again was a hindrance to hisself and t'others 'round him.

The boy with the bread turned to see who'd identified him just as the Bobby somewhere back yelled, 'I got the thief!'

Bewildered, Emanuel halted to consider how that could be.His eyes met the boy's ahet of him from whose ragged sleeve protruded the baker's loaf. Who, then, did the bobby holt?

Edric!

How many thoughts can a mind holt in a split second? Emanuel weighed justice as best he could. On the tip of his tongue was, 'Ye got the wrong boy,' and in the same instant he questioned the morality of catching a beggar whose hunger drove him to steal bread. Should Emanuel let that one get caught? Was it only for hisself, or was others needing that loaf? Edric was certainly not underfed. But he wasn't a thief either. What was justice? His gut tolt him to 'least clear Edric.

'Ye got ~'

'Emanuel! Tell them we're together, tell them!' Edric hollered as the baker helped the bobby drag Edric away.

Later Manuel would say, 'Justice aside, there went my carriage fare,' and he'd chastise hisself for thinking that of that fix coming for him 'fore he thought of justice, though,truth be tolt, who knowed where Justice sat on a case like this.

Emanuel had to think what was right to do. 'Wait, 'e's not the thief! 'E's with me. We was chasing the boy with the bread!' Emanuel yelled, making his way toward the trio.

'Aha, the accomplice!' the baker proclaimed. 'Good work, Bobby, two for the price o' one!' Emanuel felt two strong hands wrap 'round his upper arms which now felt incredibly boyish.

Their protests 'bout the mistake was drowned out by condemnations from the crowd. 'To the station with the likes o' you,' the Bobby yelled, motioning for help from willing bystanders. Was this whole day a nightmare? No, a fist from nowhere confirmed that. Dazed a bit, somewhere in the distance a bell tolled five times. Where had time gone? What did it matter?

Edric's skull was inches from the Bobby's stick. What'd he lose by speaking up again? 'Sir, I'm not a thief. Why don't you see if you can find any trace on me of the goods?'

'We'll see o'right. Why believe you even if you don't? You street thieves think we Bobbies is imbeciles, but we're getting on to you and we'll clear London of the likes of you!' He opened the heavy station door, announcing he'd nabbed two more thieves. Curiosity seekers clustered 'round to watch the proceedings.

'Sir,' Emanuel began, 'We's not thieves. We's walkin' by the bakery w'en the baker yelled 'bout somethin' bein' stole.'

'We didn't steal nothing,' Edric interrupted. 'In fact, we chased the thief with the black cap.' A few began mumbling and arguing 'bout the black cap. Finally the commotion settled so Edric could speak. 'Search us, we don't got the bread or the shillings,' and with that he pulled out the pockets of his coat, vest, and trousers.

Emanuel sighed. 'And ye don't got our carriage money either, do ye?'

Edric's face quickly flushed, realizing the seriousness of their situation. 'I swear, Emanuel, I did not spend our fare.' His pockets was all empty. No bread. No shillings. That was in their favor. No fare to get home was not.

Edric took a deep breath, asking to sit down. The officer behind the desk nodded. 'Sir,' Edric began, 'we did not steal. We was robbed.'

'Least twice,' Manuel put in.

'In London? You think this fair city has pick pockets and swindlers?' Edric was unsure 'bout his response, but Emanuel caught the fatherly smile. 'So boys, tell me your side of the story 'fore I lock you up for punishment befitting a thief who steals a loaf of bread.'

'Shall we separate them to see if stories match?' the Bobby wondert.

'I don't think that'll be necessary. I've heard lots o' stories but I think this one'll be fascinating. Convince me, fellas, you's not the baker's thieves.'

Emanuel wasn't sure he'd entrust his innocence to Edric who'd entertained the ladies in the carriage hours earlier. 'Sir,' Emanuel began, 'I'll swear on a holy book we's not thieves. We don't even wanna be in London, do we Edric?'

Edric nodded. 'We'd not been, Sir, if I'd not tricked Emanuel into coming this morning. You see...' And Edric spoke with such sincerity that Emanuel knowed he was watching Edric's first steps toward maturity. Not a man by far, but on his way.

After a few minutes, the baker motioned the boys was innocent and left to close his shop. After all, the bell chimed 'twas six o'clock.

Emanuel dropped his head.

'And the worst part is,' Edric was concluding, 'I convinced Emanuel he'd be back to milk by six o'clock. That may not be important to you or me, but it's extremely important to my stepfather. Whatever you do to us will not compare to what's probably waiting when we get to my stepfather's farm. That is, o'course, dependent upon our figuring how we'll get 'bout fifteen miles from London in 'bout as many minutes without carriage fare.'

'I think you young men need a miracle. And I don't do miracles. But I'll tell you what, I believe your story. I feel bad 'bout falsely accusing you, too, for if we'd not, you might of been home by chore time.' He looked at Edric, 'There's that matter of deceiving your friend, and I suspicion you deceived your stepfather as well, but that's not for me to settle. And further,' he continued, 'I regret your pockets got picked your first day in London. But I suspicion as you make your way home tonight, you'll admit you're wiser than you was this morning.' Looking to the Bobby, he asked, 'Do you want to add anything?'

'Yes, Sir, I do. I add my apologies. I hope this first day in London won't be your last.'

Then they was let go. Catching the carriage was out of the question even if they found where they'd stepped from it. London was still bustling. Best comfort was knowing if other pick pockets tried their thievery, they'd come up empty handed. Emanuel wasn't bothered in the least he was walking next to a rich man's stepson. For the next few hours, they'd be equally destitute. It matters not how much money one has if one can't access it. 'Tis a hard lesson, but a true one I learnt myself.

As they walked, Manuel could almost hear rocks splash in the stream his father had taken him to 'bout ten years ago.

Ripple. Ripple.

A NOVEL APPROACH TO BIBLE STUDY
LESSON FOUR · QUESTIONS 65-80
(INCLUDES QUESTIONS REFERENCING "CARES COWS, CARRIAGES, AND COMMOTION" /CHAPTER THREE, 1843-1845)

65)   Listed below are the behaviors that are abominations in the Lord's sight as mentioned in Proverbs 6. Note how many of those seven abominations happened in this last chapter, and note by whom and to whom. It might be helpful to note the page number. Answers will vary.

Proud look-

Lying tongue –

Hands that shed innocent blood –

Heart devising wicked imaginations-

Feet swift in running to mischief –

False witness speaking lies –

Someone sowing discord among brethren –

66)   By researching the meaning of names, the author found Gertrude's meaning was either "piercing sword" and/or "adored warrior." Emma means "whole, universal, complete." Often, we individually determine what comes to mind when people hear our name, just as others have determined how well we will like or dislike a name. We may temporarily dislike a name based on an earlier acquaintance's character, but later like the name when we meet one who brings honor to that name.

"Gertrude" could easily have been tied to Biblical references had she been one who wielded the "sword" (God's Word) with skill. But in "Leaves.." and "Unto All Generations," Aunt Gertrude's "piercing" disposition poses some difficult problems for her relatives, while Aunt Emma seems to be the relative most of us would like to claim.

A) Compare how Esther presents the two aunts in the novel.

B) Which similarities does Esther have to Aunt Gertrude?

C) Which similarities does Esther have to Aunt Emma?

D) Which actions of Aunt Gertrude do you find most detestable and why?

E)   Most of us will not get through life without encountering at least one "Aunt Gertrude." How did you handle, or how do you wish you had handled, a person like Aunt Gertrude?

F)   Are there some aspects of Gertrude's behavior you are willing to excuse or defend?

G)   Is Esther being charitable when she states Gertrude was a lost soul like a person can be after losing a child? Why do you think Esther would say that?

H)   Describe some happy people you met who still harbor bitterness.

I) What does your name mean and how can that coincide with your servanthood to the Lord?

67) Read and jot down a brief summary from the New Testament the following scriptures:

A. Ephesians, chapter 4, verses 31and 32
B. Hebrews 12, verses 14 and 15.
C. Galatians 5: 16 through 21.
D. If you were asked to counsel Gertrude biblically, using these and other verses within the Bible, what counsel might you give to Gertrude at this point in her life?

E. If you were to counsel the Kisbeys biblically after Aunt Gertrude announced their future, support the counsel you would give them.

68) Believing God's Word is always true, are there times when you might not like to hear verses like those found in Romans 8?

69) What are two of Emanuel's desires as the consequences of Aunt Gertrude's actions are being realized?

70) By the end of this chapter, we have observed how both Esther and Emanuel encounter the poor and hungry. If you lived among the hungry in London in the 1840s, which character would you say would do the most good for your immediate hunger? Which would do the most good for your future?

71) What did Esther discover about Emanuel's character, and her own, when she tried to urge him to dream of success?

72) Summarize "Sir's" life based on his conversation with Emanuel. Note or speculate on the similarities and differences for Emanuel, Edric and Sir in terms of their fatherlessness state.

a) Father-Son relationship   b) Son's Reaction/Result to absence c) Behavioral consequences

Sir

Edric

Emanuel

73) What evidence is given that tells how much Emanuel values the role of fathers and how do you think that will shape his adult life?

74) In the next chapter, we will read the imposed consequences for Edric and Emanuel, the two lads loitering too long in London. Sometimes we seem to be unable to avoid an uncomfortable or awkward situation. Occasionally those turn out to be instances that provide a humorous story, but sometimes the consequences are life-long and sobering.

Our God is an economical God, and even the "incidentals" in life are not surprises to Him. If you are willing, share a time someone talked you into participating in something that had not been totally cleared with those in authority? What do you wish would have happened instead? Do you remember both the consequences and the "take away" you carried with you as you matured?

75) What role do consequences play in this chapter?

76) What role does awareness of consequences play in your life?

77) The boys are told they are probably a lot wiser at the end of their eventful day in London. What do you think each learned, and how?

78) Any comment about the "ripples" that Emanuel might have been hearing as this portion of his story ends?

79) Why do you think the author ended this, and every other chapter, with a reference to ripples?

80) If you were writing a novel, what thought would you like to have repeated often?

Closing Thoughts   Even today, you and I probably made some ripples. We will again tomorrow. If you live with loved ones, or even ones a little hard to love, you are making ripples in each other's lives.

Looking back over this past year, are there ripples you are glad you made? Any you regret making? Any ripples perhaps might want to deal with? Has someone made ripples, intentionally or unintentionally, in your life that you appreciate more now than you did earlier?

Prayer:
Father God, it is so comforting to know that You know everything there is to know about our lives and every situation around us.

Thank You for being good and trustworthy, for being our Almighty God Who wants justice but Who knows fully the "back story" and understands the hearts of all participants in an event.

Help us to hear You clearly when other voices call to us to follow; sometimes You will be in the call and we should go; other times, if we go, we go in a direction away from honoring You.

Be with us and others who are this day too close to being carried or persuaded by evil individuals or by temptations we, or our brothers and sisters in You, feel inadequate to resist. If we are Yours, if they are Yours, You will provide a way to honor You regardless of what else is taking place. In Jesus Name, Amen.

Now do a quick read of Exodus 20:1-17 and examine the Proverbs passage as Chapter 4 'Another Man's War' begins.

CHAPTER FOUR

ANOTHER MAN'S WAR

1845

CHAPTER FOUR
ANOTHER MAN'S WAR
(1845)

My son, if thou be surety for thy friend, if thou hast stricken thy hand with a stranger, thou art snared with the words of thy mouth, thou art taken with the words of thy mouth. Do this now, my son, and deliver thyself when thou art come into the hand of thy friend: go humble thyself, and make sure thy friend. Give not sleep to thine eyes, nor slumber to thine eyelids. Deliver thyself as a roe deer from the hand of they hunter, and as a bird from the hand of the fowler.

King James' version of King Solomon's advice, Proverbs 6

Monday, March 8, 1880 A.D.

My readers, I'm eager to begin again after a cold but good weekend. O'course we took time for church. The preaching was good. I figure most sermons across the land was good if any heart's ready to listen. Good taking in's not so dependent upon the preacher as on whether people's let the Lord prepare them.

Truth be tolt, I was tempted to write on Sabbath, as this writing gives me pleasure and is not 'work' to me, but may be to some t'others, so I refrained. Let's see, where was I? Yes, Emanuel's terrible fix. Oh, my.

Seems days you'd rather forget can rise like cream unless you spend considerable energy separating them to their place. Who's to say what place they should deserve? Land sakes, some days get considerable more thought than a day deserves, seems to me. Some's particularly hard and some's chockfull of blessings, but if a body's always recounting the past, 'today' is missed.

Some days is like having your foot strike a stumbling stone that pains and festers too long. Some takes lots of years, lots of living, to begin to understand why they was assigned to you. Some days likely come just to make us move to a new path. Some's wretchedly unpleasant and might need a hearing in Eternity to understand. Most times we're wise to keep going, just taking what God allows to come without mulling much.

For Emanuel and Edric, their day in London was closing without a miracle, and in fairness to God, the Only One capable of solving the two stray's fix, requesting the Almighty's help hadn't crossed their minds yet. Like trapped or netted creatures, pausing to assess escape or appease captors seems less logical than clawing with all one's might. Sometimes panic works against a body, partly 'cause in panic, few pause to figure things.

Edric struggled to keep pace with Emanuel who'd decided the sooner the better for facing Mr. Roberts. Anger has a way of growing if unattended, and every single minute his absence was knowed was likely stoking the anger embers. Didn't mean Emanuel wasn't keeping his eyes on the muddy street for carriage fare, but coins that wasn't on the surface wasn't going to be noticed, that's for shore. 'Sides, who'd tote the light for carriage horses once 'twas dark?

But Edric, unaccustomed to earning his way, kept scheming how they'd get people's pity and then passage back to the farm. 'Why don't we,' he'd begin, only to be voiced over by 'Edric Bertwald Roberts, no more of yer id'es! Let's gist make the best o' it un walk ta the farm.'

You can 'magine Edric's response, how impossible it seemed, how hungry he was, how unsuited he was to make good time. 'I got you here, I should get us home. Listen to me. Let's find someone who'll lend us fare and food…'

'Lend? Edric, even I knowed ye don't mean 'lend.' The distance and lack of patience was increasing between the pair. 'And, Edric, 'as it crossed yer mind yer parents is likely wond'ren where ye be?'

Edric's hesitancy was deliberate. 'Mother maybe, but my stepfather'd miss his precious Devons more'n he'd miss me. Let's hope they got out and he's occupied…'

Let's 'ope they dint. 'E'd be twice vexed!' Emanuel's gut tolt him the accounting ahet would be unpleasant. He groaned,

'Oh, Edric, w'ot made ye thin' London was a good id'e even if ye 'ad approval, w'ich I doubt. Why'd I not star' walkin' the minute ye tolt the lady yer stepfather dint know we was gone?'

Edric laughed. 'You looked so funny when I said that. T'others thought so too.'

Emanuel had to grin. 'If I'd jumped out I'd prob'ly brokun a bone or got keeled by the carriage and yer stepfather'd still bean angry at us. Come on, Edric, keep up.'

They'd already passed the corner where hours 'fore Edric had bought his first of many tastes of London.

'I'm already out of breath. You go ahet. Remind me to get out more often if we're going to take excursions like this.'

Emanuel looked at his winded friend. Yes, he was the closest being to a friend Emanuel had and he doubted he should desert him with the night so quickly darkening. If he'd caused Mr. Roberts anxiety 'bout his Devons, adding anxiety 'bout arriving home without Edric would not likely set well either. 'Oh, Edric, w'ot 'm I ta do? The later we git there the worse it'll be.'

'At least there's two of us. We could just declare London our home and not go back.'

'Edric, don't waste yer scarce breath on crazy idees. Do ye want ta work where the likes of that textile man dictates yer life? Come on, keep walk'un.'

Perhaps even with aching feet Emanuel could of made the return trip 'fore last light. Judging by the carriage ride from crossing to outskirts, the road was likely 'bout a dozen miles. With Edric's pace, however, the time would be doubled. As darkness fell, Emanuel concluded that by now the milking was done and whatever punishment was in store would feel the same whether laid on him tonight or tomorrow. He'd prob'ly deserve a sound thrashing. Edric'd prob'ly be allowed time to recuperate. Emanuel was the chore boy, Edric the heir.

There'd be no discussion, least not till after judgment had been administered. He'd not expect Edric to implicate hisself. Why should he?

On they trudged, their hands chilled after scooping water from the stream they followed. Edric offered to share his gloves but Emanuel's hand was too thick. When Emanuel slid his tingling hands under his coat and into his armpits, he found it awkward walking without freedom to swing his arms and having them ready in case his foot caught something his eyes had not. Old 'Man in the Moon' was 'parently passing judgment and spent most of the night hiding behind thick clouds.

Several times the hair on the back of their necks raised when barking dogs tolt them they'd been heard. Shortcuts took them through fields allowing the dew a frosty free for all. Even so, the ground was more solid than London's sloppy streets. A fox scampered between them, eager to nestle in its warm bed.

Sometime well after midnight they reached Roberts' fence line. Edric doubted he could lift his weary foot over to set foot on 'home.' Emanuel pulled him across. 'Come on, Edric, I cain make out the 'ouse un barn from 'ere. We're 'most 'ome.' For Emanuel it wasn't home, but for better'n a year it'd been where he slept and ate. The cows, thankfully, was not in the paschure. 'I'll go to the barn w'en we git t'ere. Think ye cain git into yer 'ouse?'

'That depends on whether it's latched from inside or not. I'm reckoning it's latched inside so they know when I get back. If it's latched, I may sleep on straw next to the Devons. It's likely the safest place tonight.'

'Wot 'er ye goin' ta till yer folks?'

'Me? I'm the great storyteller, remember? No, I'll let my stepfather know I got you to go with me, if he'll let me tell him. Is you worried?'

Emanuel shrugged. 'I figger I got w'ot's comin' ta me. I've not 'ad a thrashin' like some boys git, but it won't keel me.'

They was near the barnyard now. 'Emanuel,' Edric whispered, 'my mother's tolt of things going all wrong when she was growing up, and she'll just laugh and laugh. Can you see us doing that?'

Manuel shook his head. 'I think I'd pa'fer havin' yer mother laugh 'bout this'n, too. She's prob'ly really been worried. Ye'd better git in t'ere.' Edric started to walk away. Emanuel thought of a weightier concern. "Ey, Edric, ye ever 'eard yer stepfather laugh 'bout 'is growin' up?'

Edric stopped in the moonlight now finally brave enough to watch the travelers. He cocked his head, thinking of the few conversations he'd had with his stepfather. 'No, I reckon not. Don't think I've heard him laugh 'bout anything.'

Emanuel felt his stomach flash hot. He hoped Edric was oversimplifying. Edric's raised whisper carried across the yard with some levity, 'Manny, I do hope we'll both decide today's trip's worth telling to entertain somebody some day.'

'If enyone could do that, it'd be ye, Edric. G'night.'

Edric managed to open the door and Emanuel watched him silently wave 'fore disappearing inside.

He'd gotten Edric safely home. There was some contentment in that fact. In the morning he'd learn what Mr. Roberts thought was his just punishment.

Emanuel walked 'round to the darkest side of the barn where the small door opened to the place he'd bedded down each night. His hands felt for the crude wooden block to pull and open the door. It wouldn't budge. He tried again, wond'ring if the night's moisture caused the block to swell. Had it frozen against the wooden tray that helt the block in place once it fastened?

Emanuel used more force to open the block, then jumped at the sound of milking pails laden with metal pieces crashing to the floor. His heart raced. His difficulty in opening the door had nothing to do with 'mother nature!' Next instant, the force of the swinging door struck Emanuel's right side. He was 'bout to discover the nature of 'Sir' Roberts. Blood streamed from Emanuel's eyebrow, making it hard to see. But unmistakably, he was facing a very distraught Sir.

'Where've you been?' Sir bellowed, splitting the night air. 'Answer me!'

The side wall of what Emanuel's knowed as his room now helt a freshly driven wooden peg. From the peg hung a lantern whose light fell across Emanuel's face, partially silhouetting Sir's tensed and furious body. Leather straps dangled from Sir's right fist. Sir's left grabbed the front of Emanuel's coat, roughly twisting it as he lifted Emanuel forward, placing him squarely in front of Sir. Emanuel, whose drowsiness had fled, saw the rage within Sir's eyes.

'Sir,' he began...

'Don't call me Sir, you ungrateful waif!' and with that Emanuel was shoved far enough away to allow Sir's forceful swing of the straps to come against Emanuel's left side. Emanuel's coat helped block some damage intended by the straps, but his hip and legs was stinging. 'Where've you been? Did you forget you're responsible for my Devons?'

'I 'membered, S-' Emanuel began but caught his word 'fore it left his mouth.

'I tolt you, Waif, don't call me Sir. If you thought of me as 'Sir' you'd not neglected your duties today!' Again the straps connected. And again, 'Where'ov you been?'

Emanuel breathed deeply. 'Ta London, S-.' Old habits was hard to break! But if 'Sir' was an earned title of respect, perhaps it did not fit the raging man with straps.

'London?' he shouted. 'You wanted to see London instead of tending to duties here? Well, I'll teach you what London offers,' and he lifted Emanuel off his feet, dragging him into the open area. He continued past the Devons, most nervously milling from the commotion and shouting. 'You're still ruining my cattle tonight! Production was down! You pranced off to London and carelessly left a cow to calve alone! You're worthless, you imp, but you'll pay if it's the last thing I make you do!' He cracked the straps, wrapping them 'bout a pole.

Sir stopped below the contrivance Emanuel had not understood till his visit to London's textile factory hours earlier. Emanuel regained his footing, only to see Sir's face reddening and to hear his wild breathing. Emanuel's heart pounded fiercely as he watched Sir's free arm angrily jerk the pillory from the wall. 'You, Waif, will learn respect and responsibility,' Sir's voice seethed, rising further. His words spewed so rapidly Emanuel could barely understand them. Then his jaw set and his eyes was more fiery still.

Emanuel helt Sir's stare. Never in his life had he witnessed a being so out of control, so wild. Fear for his own safety begged him pull away and run, but his body refused. Emanuel's mind raced to make sense of what he was experiencing. A trip to London had been wrong, but...

Now the attacker's voice lowered, raging in unfamiliar tones, 'Ye'll not pass yer work to me, Orphan! Ye'll learn yer lesson. I shoulda ne'er took ye in, Waif! I'll throw ye to the crowd and ye'll see w'ot comes ta boys like ye! Ye's begged yer last crumb from me!' and on he ranted, releasing Emanuel's coat to wildly search the wall for the key to open neck and limb holes of the hideous contrivance. Down he knelt, frantically pawing through straw and dirt for the key. 'Ye hid the key, did ye?' Sir needed more lantern light but 'twas too far away. He looked from the lantern to the criminal he wanted to impound, unsure of how to carry out his justice. Emanuel suspected the key no longer existed, or that 'least 'twas no longer kept in the barn. 'Don't ye move,' Sir threatened. 'I keep extra keys and ye'r goin' in this thing!'

Awkwardly he lifted his frame. His eyes caught Emanuel standing alone and in his path toward light. For an instant Sir paused, eyes bewildered. Then feeling the pillory in his hand, he grabbed the straps and snapped them, catching Emanuel's hands that'd instinctively risen in self-defence. Like an animal who'd tasted blood, he bellowed, 'I'll lock ye in so tight ye'll never git out!' He sneered, 'Ye's lucky the crowd's not here yet to torment ye, but I'm here un tormented ye'll be!' He cracked the straps, then raised them again, taking aim at Emanuel.

Bloodied, Emanuel backed slowly away. 'Mr. Roberts,' his voice calmer than he'd dared hope, 'I'm not goin' ta let ye strike me 'gin. Ye'll not do this ta me. I'll not be goin inta tha' thin'.'

'Ye is! I decide what happens to ye!' Sir's arm swung the straps.

Emanuel, half-way to his room, stopped and helt his position. 'No, Mr. Roberts, ye'll not.' His voice was firm. His eyes watched for opportunities to lock with Mr. Roberts' eyes, while safely keeping his distance.

'I will!' Mr. Roberts declared, heading toward the lantern.

Emanuel turned ever so slightly, keeping his eyes trained on Mr. Roberts as if working a roped horse circling him. 'No, Mr. Roberts, ye'll not,' he said, his voice conveying a strange threatening sound new to Emanuel. 'Mr. Roberts, 'ear me. I's sorry tha' I was not 'ere fer chores ye gave me. I deserved un expected a thrashun o' some kind. I caint 'old tha' agin ye.'

Mr. Roberts was half listening as he carried the lantern past Emanuel, holting it to inspect the wall for the key. Finding none, he set the lantern on the floor and began running his hands up and down the wallboards. Turning, he picked up the pillory and squeezed his fingers into the holes, prying with all his strength, but it refused to give. He flung the pillory to the floor and down he went to resume his pawing search for the key.

Emanuel, aware his relationship with this pitiful being was closing, felt obligated to carefully consider his words so he'd not live with regrets.

I know that part of living with no regrets 'twas a policy of Manuel's begun that day. When we was one, I strove for adhering to his policy, too, best I could.

There on the floor the man was mindlessly shifting dirt and straw and straw and dirt, side to side.

Emanuel had not pitied any one more, not even the dying girl the afternoon 'fore. What words was there to say? Tears came to Emanuel's eyes. His throat tightened. His voice quivered but it didn't matter. This pitiful man needed words.

'Mr. Roberts, wha' I did wos wrong. I ought not left yes'day 'out bein' certain I 'ad yer 'proval. Fer tha' I'm sorry, un I ask yer fergiveness...'

Mr. Roberts started to rise. 'Don't think ye'll whimper yerself out of this, orphan. Ye has this coming!' But rising took too much effort and he slumped back down.

'Mr. Roberts, I'll gather w'ots mine un be gone by mornin'.' Emanuel heard the barn door opening behind him. A quick glance tolt him Edric and his mother had come to be certain things was not out of hand. They hung back, unsure what was transpiring. Emanuel continued, feeling childhood's wings lifting to take flight. 'Mr. Roberts, ye owe me nothin' un I don't b'leve I owe ye more thin' the 'pol'gy I've give ye.'

'Ye'll stay. You'll take whatever punishment I give as many times as I give it.' The fire was gone, and monotone words came as if writ by 'nother.

'I'll not, Mr. Roberts. I don't d'serve w'ot yer bent on givin' me.'

'You do.'

'No, I don't.' Emanuel paused. He studied the heap 'fore him. 'And neither did ye, Mr. Roberts.' Emanuel swallowed, his lips pursed. Mr. Roberts looked up, his eyes fastened on Emanuel, squinting to clarify who stood 'fore him.

Emanuel began slowly, deliberately. 'I'm Emanuel. I'm not ye, un none o' us is yer uncle, Mr. Roberts.'

The motionless man's eyes studied Emanuel. He looked away to stare at the pillory lying beside him. He grasped it. Again he looked up at Emanuel, but he didn't speak. Emanuel kept his eyes locked on Mr. Roberts' and began slowly shaking his head. He didn't care his tears was plain to see. He watched the man's grip release the pillory.

Slowly Mr. Roberts pulled his knees against his chest and buried his head in his arms, releasing one long sad, lonely wail. The barn kept silent except for the flutter of a pigeon and the breathings and millings of Devons. Hesitantly Edric and his mother crept closer, saying nothing, silently appraising marks on Emanuel and seeing where blood had trickled down his exposed leg.

Emanuel compassionately studied Mr. Roberts, now rocking back and forth, face still buried in arms tightly grasping his knees. Emanuel waited. Sweat and blood from Emanuel's eyebrow stung as it seeped into his eye. Then, respecting the healing power of silence, Emanuel whispered, 'Ye dint d'serve it, Mr. Roberts. No one does.'

More silence. Mr. Roberts raised his head, the lantern catching the moistness of his eyes. He shook his head 'fore he buried it again. 'I didn't deserve it,' his voice broke. 'He had no right to hate me. Ma and Pa was dead.'

'I know. I know. They'd stopt it if they cou'd of. No one ought ta of 'hurt ye. 'Twas wrong.'

Edric looked quizzically at Emanuel and his mother. These was things 'bout his stepfather he doubted even his mother knowed.

Emanuel backed further away, unsure what else he could say. He was likely coming fourteen and 'fore him sat his employer, a crumpled heap of a man trying to reconcile a past with today. Emanuel reprimanded hisself for his own tears. He'd never seen a man cry 'fore. But if somehow he'd looked into a glass, he'd for certain seen one that night.

He turned and went to where he'd slept for over a year. He looked 'round. There'd not be much to put in order. He'd give the famly time to figure out how to get Mr. Roberts to the house. He hoped to sleep after that.

'Fore long he heard them silently usher Sir from the barn, knowing it'd be some time 'fore they spoke aloud. Whether 'twas good or not, Emanuel didn't know.

Emanuel checked the door, hoping his last hours of the night would be undisturbed. He tried to sleep but his mind kept asking, 'Where'll ye sleep when this day ends? Un w'ot 'bout th' next?'

Where indeed? Life was making many changes for Emanuel. Ripple, ripple, ripple.

A NOVEL APPROACH TO BIBLE STUDY
LESSON FIVE ·QUESTIONS 81-105
(INCLUDES QUESTIONS REFERENCING "ANOTHER MAN'S WAR"
CHAPTER FOUR, 1845

Welcome back to the "Novel Approach to Bible Study." If you've been reading the corresponding chapters in the novel, I hope you are finding them "loaded with good stuff," even when they are a bit difficult to read. This section follows the showdown in the barn.

It's likely you and I know individuals whose early years were traumatic. Some marry into abusive situations or work under an abusive overseer. Perhaps trauma is part of your story, too. This would be a good time to pray for all whose lives are scarred, whether visibly or invisibly, by the ugliness of others.

Let us begin with the questions and see where God's Word takes us during this study. God's Word is "living," and quite possibly you will be ministered to by the Lord while in His Word, but not necessarily with the exact same verses as others who will also do this study. Discussions could bring out more richness. May you be blessed in working on these questions.

81) As a quick review, picking up from the earlier assignment and with additional freshness, jot down key thoughts you have from Proverbs 6:1-15:

1-5

6-11 –

12-15-

82) In Proverbs 6:16-19, what 7 things are abominations to God?

83) In Proverbs 6:20-35, parents are instructed for shaping their children's morality. What does this passage indicate the Bible believes is immoral? What may be the consequences of immorality?

84) Esther tells her thoughts about how a sermon becomes meaningful. To what extent do you agree or disagree and why?

85) Esther tells of her struggle to observe the Sabbath by refraining from work, but states that her writing does not seem to be work to

her. In Esther's era, not only did people need rest, but rest was needed also for the animals that pulled their wagons and plows, etc. You may remember how strictly Esther's father observed Sabbath in the earlier chapters.

Perhaps you have noticed that our work load is typically a lot less physical than the workload Esther and her family would have had in the 1880s. Generally, however, often we are undisciplined about getting our rest. How and when do you refrain from work and why do you set aside that time? Do you intentionally set aside time to worship God?

86) What are your thoughts regarding the possibility that even in our day of grace, Sabbath was designed by God for our physical, mental, emotional and spiritual health? Can you see benefits from "observing Sabbath"?

87) Darkness has its own foreboding implications in scripture, and sometimes for many of us regarding life situations. What are some of your mental pictures from reading of the two young men making their way back home in the dark after an exciting, deceitful, highly emotional, and otherwise exhausting day, but also knowing Emanuel has broken a trust factor with Sir? What advantages could walking prove to be for them/for others needing to sort out one's thoughts about an experience?

88) Some people never outgrow their uncomfortable feelings about walking in the dark, even in somewhat familiar surroundings. We sometimes think a mark of bravely is one's willingness to go out into a dark night or into a dark cave, etc. Peruse the references (below) to darkness and light and, as though you were a "spiritual psychologist," analyze why being uncomfortable in darkness might have deeper roots than merely preference or childish behavior.

For starters, thoughtfully read the two sentences found in Colossians 1, verses 9-14, and fill in the blanks regarding the transfer accomplished when an individual becomes a true follower of Jesus Christ. This is exciting reality.

As a convenience, I've copied those verses from the New American Standard Version (NASB). Italics are for clarification only. You may use your favorite version to answer these or similar questions. We're reading a letter from missionary/apostle Paul to Christian believers in the city of Colossae. The Christian faith is new and he wants to help converts to Christianity understand the changes that took place in their lives spiritually at their conversion because these are automatically God-initiated consequences for individuals who submit to the Lordship of Jesus Christ. These changes did not stop with first century converts.

"For this reason also, since the day we heard of it, we have not ceased to pray for you and to ask that you may be filled with the knowledge of His will in all spiritual wisdom and understanding, so that you may walk in a manner worthy of the Lord, to please Him in all respects, bearing fruit in every good work and increasing in the knowledge of God; strengthened with all power, according to His glorious might, for the attaining of all steadfastness and patience, joyously giving thanks to the Father, who has qualified us to share in the inheritance of the saints in light. For HE delivered us from the domain of darkness, and transferred us to the kingdom of His beloved Son, in whom we have redemption, the forgiveness of sins." (Colossians 1, verses 9-14).

From the above sentences, the transfer is from the kingdom of _____ to the kingdom of _____.

89) Think for a moment on who seeks to be the ruler in each of those kingdoms. Listen to the news or read the headlines most days and answer this: Which kingdom's occupants seem to be grabbing the headlines where you live?

90) Exploring the passage further, fill in the following blanks:
Paul and Timothy ceaselessly pray for these believers to be _____ with knowledge of God's _____ in _____ wisdom and understanding. Why? So that they may walk in a manner _____ of citizenship in the "light" kingdom under their king, the _____.

91) In order to be a respectable citizen in the Lord's kingdom, Paul prays they may _____ their King in _____ respects; that they may _____ _____ in every good work; that they may _____ in their knowledge of God.

He also prays (and remember Paul/Timothy are talking to God who wants to do these things in His kingdom people) that those believers will be _____ according God's might. Why? Believers are to be _____, _____, and _____ to the Father.

92) What three actions did the Father God take that should make us joyously grateful every day of our earthly lives?
He_____;
He _____ and
He _____ of His beloved Son!

93) Almost finished: Which two citizenship benefits are guaranteed to those who take the transfer? R_____ (no longer slaves to the old master), therefore we have the forgiveness of the debts we brought from our activity in the former kingdom where we had been citizens doing either what pleased us or pleased that kingdom's ruler. That glorious benefit, in a phrase is "_____ _____ of _____."

If you responded when the Holy Spirit nudged you to take God up on the transfer He offered you, do you feel like shouting, "Hallelujah!" right now? After all, as Christ's humbled followers, we are rescued from the enemy's kingdom of darkness! We are transferred into the "Light" Kingdom!   Why/How?
God extended grace to us so we could place our faith in the complete work of Christ:
His sinless life,
His certain death which conquered death!
God's resurrection of Him which declared all the old sin debt has been paid for Christ's followers,
And, finally, let's give attention to Jesus Christ's ascension back to sit at the right hand of God. There Jesus intercedes as part of the mysterious one, but triune, God. Today the Lord Jesus Christ intercedes for citizens of the Light kingdom.

When He was on the cross, remember, the temple's veil ripped from top to bottom without any man's assistance. Why top to bottom? God was declaring Jesus Christ's followers can enter God's throne room to speak to Him directly. The curtain separated sinners from the Holiness of God. God is forever Eternal, Holy, Righteous, Just, and countless other "God-only" attributes. But, when God ripped the curtain as His Holy Son died for the sins of mankind, God was saying that all who came to Him through Jesus Christ can step past the curtain! We are welcome in God's throne room! We come into that sacred place as God's blood-bought and respectful children. We come knowing our Father God is eager to hear our requests and to accomplish His purposes through us because we are His!

So... if God has become more than your Creator, if through Jesus Christ you are now His child, is there something you would like to say to Him?

94) Please consider: Transferring "from darkness into light" was not something we could do on our own. Apart from the gracious Trinity work, we cannot reach the switch to turn on the "Light." Jesus is the Light; we are to let His light shine through us! John 8:12, quoting Jesus, "I am the light of the world; he who follows Me shall not walk in the darkness, but shall have the light of life." What are you doing about your commission in Matthew 5:14 from Jesus, "You are the light of the world. A city set on a hill cannot be hidden."?

95) I wonder what physical expression Jesus wore when He spoke about the city on a hill. Do you suppose He was, like a math teacher, simply drawing the obvious conclusion, or perhaps He was gently shaking His finger and cautioning His followers about how obvious their relationship with Him could be in their daily lives.

Quick science review from a very "unprofessional" student of God's marvelous creation: The moon does not produce light by itself. Even though the moon is always wholly there, we say the moon has phases because we cannot see parts of it. *(When we cannot see any of it, it is because we/earth block it from the sun. Hmm. Any spiritual thoughts on that?)* By the creative, perfect physical work of God, the moon can only reflect light in direct proportion to its exposure to the sun's light. By the supernatural spiritual work of God through Jesus Christ, we who have accepted the transfer are reflectors of the Son! How fully others see us reflecting "light" depends on how closely we are to the Son. Any thoughts?

96) The following scriptures speak of light and darkness. If your group splits up verses or you decide to prayerfully check only a few, pray the Holy Spirit refreshes or increases your understanding of the marvelous (carefully chosen word) offer Jesus Christ makes possible to those in darkness.

Darkness References:

- Psalm 91:6
- Psalm 107:10, 14
- Psalm 139:11
- Proverbs 2:13
- Proverbs 4:19
- Ecclesiastes 2:14
- Matthew 22:13
- Matthew 25:30
- 2 Corinthians 5:11
- Ephesians 5: 8,11
- 1 John 2:11

- **Light References:**
- Genesis 1:4
- Exodus 10:22, 23
- Psalm 18:28
- Psalm 27:1
- Psalm 139:12
- Matthew 5:14, 15
- John 8:12; 9:5
- Acts 26:15-18
- 2 Corinthians 6:14
- Ephesians 5:8,9
- 2 Peter 2:9
- 1 John 1:7
- 1 John 2:9, 10

97) Note the differences in how Edric and Emanuel consider the consequences of their behavior. By recalling the stepfather's attitude toward Edric, and given the authoritative mindset of "Sir Roberts," could or should Edric have altered the consequences that fell to Emanuel? Explain.

98) Sometimes we witness reactions to the unexpected happenings, whether that be an earthquake, a tornado, a flood, fire, etc. Often

before these events occur, specific steps are taken to warn about the possibility of the event. Some react and others ignore the warnings.

I firmly believe we believers are fully prepared beforehand for the new experiences that seem to surprise us. When we're in a situation, when we get a diagnosis or a phone call or are struck with a tragedy that floors us, it is very human to go through a range of emotional responses. However, spiritually speaking, God sees/saw that day coming and He has been shaping us so that when it comes, we will be able to draw closer to Him as we walk through the circumstance together.

How does Psalm 139 remind us of the macro-managing God does, how "all knowing" God is, while still not creating us as robots or pawns?

99) There is the very human side, the part that tends to nurture overly-established habits we had in the kingdom of darkness that asks to respond when even a simple irritation occurs.

We may surprise ourselves by our reactions in a given situation, but in reality, what lies behind us is what we bring to a new event. Some of us have kept a few things hidden for our "that's just how I am" justifications of un-Christian behavior.

What does Jesus say to explain why we act and speak the way we do? See Matthew 12:34. Jesus' words ought to cause us to guard our hearts.

100) We try to explain most of our ugliness by saying we are tired, or we've not taken our fresh dose of "anti-chaotic" medicine found only in God's Word, or we simply try to excuse ourselves by saying we were not thinking. What does Galatians 6, verse 7 indicate as a principle that invalidates our trying to get God to overlook our "slip-ups'?

101) What we excuse as our careless speaking or action is often just a naked display of who we really are as sinners still needing to pursue conformity into the likeness of Jesus Christ. Look up and jot notes about:
A. Jeremiah 17:9
B. Romans 7:18-20

C. Colossians 2:5-7

Jot down a summary of thoughts that came to you as a result of this time in the Word.

102) Do a quick sketch of the "ripples" that led to Sir's behavior in the barn and a quick sketch of the "ripples" that led to Emanuel's behavior in the barn. *(You can go back as far as their childhood, but don't get bogged down in details unless you prefer to do your tracing that way.)*

Sir's:

Emanuel's:

103) In most novels, there are some "coming of age" or "turning points" for at least one character. What are some conclusions Emanuel is making about life because of this encounter in the barn?

104) How useful to you are Emanuel's conclusions?

105) Have you experienced situations when you saw an obvious route to take, but the route required more courage than remaining where you were? If you are willing to share, that sharing could be part of the platform God has been preparing you to use, but do not share anything you do not trust the rest of the group to keep in confidence if you want it kept in confidence.

As you think about your circumstances, past or present, you may want to read 2 Corinthians 1:3-7, another New Testament letter by Apostle Paul. His daily life provided numerous challenges and difficulties as he followed through on the consequences of his transfer from darkness to light, his transformation into becoming more like his Master, Jesus Christ.

Below is the prayer that brings this portion of the study to a close. Please consider making it your prayer as well.

Prayer:

Father God, we know You can be almost a "micro-manager" of our lives, and that You always see the big picture while we become intently focused on our little pixels of the moment. Sometimes we let circumstances gush forth as an overwhelming flood, at least until we remember Whose we are and that we, as blood-bought believers, are citizens of a mighty, holy King who even commands the Hosts of Heaven, an army without equal. We praise You for who You are and we admit we are still infants in the knowledge we now have of You.

Oh, God, how grateful we are that You arranged in eternity past for our rescue as sinners captured, enslaved by the enemy.

Thank You for claiming us as believers in Jesus Christ to be transferred from the enemy's kingdom into the Kingdom of Light through the blood of Jesus Christ. You are mighty to save! Hallelujah! Some of us were bold sinners and some of us were silent sinners but we all needed to be rescued. Thank You that nothing, no redemption, no rescue, is too hard for Thee!

Help us to be aware of captives still groping for meaning out in the kingdom of darkness. Point us to the ones You marked as people You designed for us to assist in the rescuing process so they can one day be transferred into Light and fellowship with Your Son, Jesus Christ.

Lord, You know us, how quickly we question whether "nudges" are from You or ourselves. Clearly prompt us into useful bearers of Light for your glory.

We are so grateful for Your unfathomable love and mercy, not only to us to but all who will come in humility before You in reliance upon the shed blood of Your Holy Son.

In Jesus priceless and powerful name, Amen.

CHAPTER FIVE

NOTHING

BY

CHANCE

(1846-1852)

CHAPTER FIVE
NOTHING BY CHANCE
(1846-1852)

"But this thing commanded I them, saying, Obey my voice and I will be your God, and ye shall be my people: and walk ye in all the ways that I have commanded you, that it may be well unto you." My Psalter, Book of Jeremiah 7:23, King James' Bible

I hope it may please God to favour us by and by and that all will come out all right in the end, for it is a long road that has no crooks or turns.'

My Pvt. Emanuel Kisbey's letter, April 26, 1864

Wednesday, March 10, 1880 A.D.

Loved Ones,

Just so you can know where this accounting is headed, this part will cover from 'bout A.D. 1843 for me and 1845 for Manuel, on to about 1852, give or take a little. It helps me decide what to include by making myself think on life as sections in a book. I hope you can get yourself a cup of tea and join me.

How pitiful my heirs, if life brings us across 'men' who stopped along the road to manhood, 'men' who by choice settled to be less than their Creator intended. If these refuse offers to get them back on their proper path, we find these whining creatures, for I won't call whiners men, still clinging to their childish minds, selfishly expecting, and more often, demanding that others tend to their cries for attention and prominence. These is 'set asides' by choice.

Childhood has its good and right season. Then 'tis time to put away childish behaviours. I'm not denying charity and time to those needing healings.

135

But on life's many roads, 'tis important to distinguish 'tween whiners and wounded. Whiners need disciplined prodding toward manhood by famly or fellowman. Wounded deserve gracious aid. But after a time, all that needs to be done has been done, and the rest is up to the whiner or the wounded.

Is that not the choice 'bout maturing: to whine or not whine? To demand attention or lose oneself in concern for those trapped beneath obstacles on their road? To pick wounds so they fester or to let the Great Physician and those He sends help clean and heal wounds? Some get or take the shortest route to manhood and some fight each step. Such choices come to all survivors of their early years.

Tis unlikely I'd recognized Emanuel the day after his encounter with Mr. Roberts as the same boy I'd almost left unnoticed in the carriage day 'fore. I'd prob'ly not recognized Edric a few months later, for things was changing on the Roberts estate.

Edric couldn't knowed his childish plan to spend a day in London would set him so harshly on the road to manhood. The demanding days ahet was more satisfying than any he'd of instigated on his own. He'd became more his stepfather's son, and that for their mutual good. They both had so much to learn, and so much to unlearn. In time people would even covet the respect they gave t'other and from others as well.

As for Emanuel, his road to manhood had not been ideal, if ideal means a way or model others should desire. Most might of found Emanuel's journey distasteful, resenting obstacles Emanuel had to hurdle. But he did not. Nor did Emanuel envy other's paths. He'd decided that whether pauper, privleeched, or prince, each survivor of childhood, and those wise enough to loose its clutches, ought to arrive at manhood aware of his obligation to God as Giver of the Years by clarifying for his dependents what manhood is. Overnight Emanuel embraced his obligation to make his manhood honourable and knowed that decisions – everyday ones – had far reaching consequences, and that fresh reminder weighed heavy on Emanuel's heart. He knowed when other experiences arrived unexpectedly, some welcome, some not, he'd handle them with an eye on the future. Such was his thoughts 'fore sleep claimed those few hours 'fore habit woke him.

He roused, his young body aching as he felt his way 'round in early morning darkness. He needed no lantern, he'd spent nigh to four hundred mornings in those surroundings. He heard the Devons, also creatures of habit, moving to stanchions and mangers, waiting for hay and relief from the heavy milk straining their udders. He heard young calves bawling for their mothers and needing to be fed. Emanuel wondert 'bout the fresh cow and calf.

He pulled on his ragged breeches and carefully slid his arms down the cold sleeves of his coat, grateful his hands had scabbed during his rest. His left side was most tender as he walked from his quarters into the open space for Devons. He'd make up for the milking he'd missed, then, true to his word, he'd leave. Robertses needed to be famly now.

Milking required little attention and Emanuel regularly let his mind consider a thousand thoughts during the early morning stillness. This morning he resolved to control his thoughts! He'd shift thoughts, sorting which was to stay. None would take root to fester and later unexpectedly break open in ugliness. He'd not been allowed to celebrate Sabbath for many months, but his feelings and thoughts was similar to those he'd knowed after stirring sermon preaching. How deeply he longed for another Sabbath like he'd knowed with his famly. Truth is, he once tolt me that day he knowed he just missed everybody, including God.

He squatted on his own handmade wooden three legged stool and placed the pail 'tween his knees. He gently touched each cow and spoke 'fore leaning his head against her curried red side to take the milk she was eager to give. He'd fill each bucket. He thought of how awkward it'd been when he first started working for Sir, Mr. Roberts, how unfamiliar he was with the precise routine so emphatically dictated. Would routines be possible after today? Would they be necessary?

Occasionally he'd milked a cow or two to home, particularly in the morning, but evening milkings had been his mother's responsibility. He thought of his *famly*, wond'ring what this day would be for them, hoping each was still healthy and bearing honourably the Kisbey name. He wondert if things had changed 'cause of Aunt Gertrude's scheming management. He suspected he was not the only Kisbey just trying to earn a day-to-day living who'd come cross-wise with warriors trapped in their pasts. Was his people needier than he at this moment?

Emanuel moved from cow to cow, giving each a verbal farewell. Each act had finality. Purposeful. Intentional. When he left for wherever, he'd leave orderliness.

He was working with the young calves when Mrs. Roberts came into the barn. The crisp air made her breathing visible. She stopped several feet away, crossing her arms to keep herself warm although she appeared to be wearing her husband's heavy coat. This was the second time Emanuel had seen her in the barn, the first being last night. But there was lots of things he'd not seen till last night. She seemed uncomfortable being there, unaccustomed to the smell and unsure of where to stand in the presence of the Devons.

Now Emanuel wasn't sure where to stand either although the barn was espeshly familiar to him. He'd rarely been in her presence except mealtimes and those was silent at Mr. Roberts' request. He nodded acknowledgement and she cleared her throat. From things Edric had said, he knowed she could speak, but her voice would pretty much be that of a stranger's to him.

She carefully stepped across the straw, moving closer to him. 'Ah, Emanuel, I don't really know what to say. 'Bout last night I mean.'

Emanuel didn't know what to say either. He'd figured he'd leave without a conversation, unless Edric happened to be outside when he started on his way. He tried to think of what to say, to understand why she was there. A thousand thoughts came, but not a word volunteered to form.

'Well, I mean, all this that's happened. It's so...' she too was searching for words, 'so strange I reckon I'd say. Edric tolt me 'bout some of the things you two did in London yesterday. I was worried sick you two had been hurt or run off for good or something.'

'I'm sorry we caused ye concern—'

'No, it's not your fault, I know. Edric tolt me how he talked you into going, how he basically lied to get you to go with him.' She stopped again. Emanuel was ready to offer he was wrong to not make certain he could go to London for leaving with Edric, but she started again. Her eyes was moist, 'Is you alright, your hands and leg? Your eye looks pretty dark.'

'I'll be al'ight. My 'ands got a good work w'en I's doing th' mornin' milking.' Emanuel worried she'd take his words as a request for praise. Why'd those words manage to get heard? His heart knowed he'd tolt her so she'd not worry 'bout how she'd get the milking done. 'Sides, he was fulfilling a debt. He didn't tell that his leg bled when he'd squatted to milk. But she likely could see that.

'I want you to eat breakfast if you're leaving. Well, I mean, I want you to partake of breakfast either way. I don't think you has to leave if you'd rather not.'

'I thin' it's best. I tolt Mr. Roberts I'd go.'

'I know, but, well, I don't think Mr. Roberts, my husband, was in his right mind last night. He was really worked up yesterday.'

'I feel kind o' respons'ble fer 'is gettin' upset un all,' Emanuel offered. 'I thin' our bein' gone must o' really angered 'im. I'm sorry.'

'Oh, he was angry. He saprized me, the way he reacted. Here I was worried William and you was drowned or gone for good and he was stirring 'round yelling 'bout how his cows was suffering with you not tending to chores. I'd never seen him quite like that.'

'I 'pol'gize a'gin 'bout all that. We'd never gone, even wit' pa'mishun, if we'd knowed w'ot it'd do ta 'im.'

'I didn't know he had all that anger inside. He'd never talked 'bout, you know, 'bout his childhood. He'd just tolt me his uncle saw to his raising, that's all.' Her eyes left his. 'How'd you know 'bout the,' she looked round for the nameless thing and saw it lying where Mr. Roberts had left it, 'that hideous thing?'

'I dint e'en knowed w'ot it e'en was 'til yes'day. I thought it might be fer farmin' but I cou'n't figger out how 'twas ta be used. Did Edric speak 'bout th'...' Emanuel cast the bloody scene of the injured girl from his mind for this conversation with a lady like Mrs. Roberts, "bout the fact'ry we saw?"

'I don't think I heard much 'bout that. He had so much he'd seen but he mostly talked 'bout getting you to go and holting you up such that you missed milking.'

Emanuel's respect for Edric grew. He hoped he'd be able to let Edric know.

'Well, anyhow, I figger'd out thin's like tha' thin' layin' ov'r there's so awful they's outlawt now,' Emanuel said. 'Un Mr. Roberts 'ad tolt me tha' 'e'd worked in a place somethin' like w'ot we saw yes'day. Those places is not safe fer childern, espeshly if th' person runnin' th' fact'ry don't like ye, un from one conversation I 'ad with Mr. Roberts 'bout 'is uncle, I cou' tell 'e'd always felt like 'e was, w'ot ye might call, unwanted.'

'I didn't know that.'

'No, I dint thin' so. Anyhow, I'm perty shore yer 'usband either 'ad ta spend time in tha' thin' or knowed some tha' did. I'm sure there's mo' ta it thin' tha', but I dunt know tha' yer 'usband'll ever till anyone 'bout it. 'Ow's 'e this mornin'?'

'He was sleeping when I came out here. He actually slept more soundly than I expected. He was so irrational last night 'fore you boys came home.' She stopped, pulling her husband's coat tighter 'round herself. 'I, Emanuel, I was worried for your life. He tolt me he was going to the barn to wait for you, and he was fuming with hatred. 'Twas so uncharacteristic of what I'd seen from him 'fore. I tried reasoning, but he was going to the barn and I was not to interfere. I remember I said, 'But Edric's with him,' thinking maybe that'd slow him down. He said some awful things 'bout us, how we was ungrateful and never cared how he was sacrificing for us, things like that.'

'I don't' need to 'ear this...'

'I'm sorry. I just wanted you to know Mr. Roberts was not right minded, and if he'd been, then most of last night would not of happened.'

'Ye may be right, but I 'spect 'twas goin' ta hap'n sometime. That feelin' o' bein' hated must o' bean inside 'long time. 'Least now it's been let out once. Maybe 'twas w'ot was needed. I dunno.'

'The way you talked to him, I wouldn't dared do that. But you knowed exactly how to calm him. Most who'd just been attacked wouldn't likely treated him that way.'

'I could see 'e was hurt-un. 'E was like a dog ever'body's kicked. I thought maybe, I dunno, maybe 'twas time fer the dog ta get respect.'

'Well, you was a Godsend.' She looked around. 'I'm sorry your quarters has been so...'

Manuel shrugged, saying they was fine and he'd been glad for the work and place to stay. She bit her lip and Manuel saw her eyes grow moist.

'Anyway, is you sure you should leave? I'm not sure how we'd manage without you, at least till Mr., my husband is more ready to assume some of these duties.'

'Ye've Edric. 'E's ready ta do the things I've done. 'E's not used to 'em, but 'e cain git used to 'em. I thin' it'd be easier fer Mr. Roberts if I left.'

She nodded with respect for Emanuel's decisions. 'May I 'least put together some biscuits for your journey?'

'Ye make great biscuits. I'll gist finish up 'ere un if Edric or ye bring the biscuits out, I'll take 'em with me. I thank ye. Ye've been kind ta me.'

She smiled and left the barn. Emanuel had scarcely talked with adult women other'n his mother and though this conversation had been awkward, he'd survived. He finished up choring and was putting his few things together when Edric arrived.

'Edric, I've heard some good thin's 'bout ye 'ready this mornin.'

'So you're not going to spend the rest of your life going, 'Oh Edric, O Edric?'' he responded with a smile.

'I won't tell ye I'll not do that.' Emanuel grinned, joining Edric who'd sat down on the floor, being careful not to spill the warm milk and biscuits he'd brought to share with Emanuel. 'Maybe w'en thing go wrong, I cain gist say, 'O Edric! O Edric!' un my stomach knots'll dis'pear.' They smiled and began eating.

'So you're going to leave 'fore I know how to take over your jobs?'

'Ye've been watchin' me. Ye'll git on ta 'em. Do ye think yer stepfather'll be strong 'nuff ta 'elp too?'

'He was getting up for biscuits with Mother when I came out here. He looked a lot better'n last night.' Edric stopped eating and looked at Emanuel. His voice turned hoarse and softer. 'I was so scared for you, Emanuel. Mother thought he'd tear into you bad, maybe worse if we tried to stop things. She feared for your life. That's why we came and hid right here.' He cleared his throat, picking up his biscuit. 'Is you going to say farewell to him, Emanuel?'

'I'll gist let ye tell 'im fer me. I don't want ta stir things up.' Emanuel's stomach, having missed much of the previous day's meals, was getting satisfied. He stood and brushed away crumbs. 'Is there anything ye want ta know 'fore I leave?'

''Bout farming or 'bout where you'll go or 'bout ten dozen other things you mean?' Edric couldn't hide his sentiment.

'Ye'll do fine. Next time I see ye, ye'll be all lean un runnin' faster'n me.'

'If there is a next time.'

Emanuel nodded. What was those chances after today?

The barn door opened. Mrs. Roberts was holting a box. 'Emanuel, this is to keep your things in.'

'Ye don't need ta do that, I got this sack...'

'I know,' she said softly, 'but Mr. Roberts wants you to take it.'

''E said so?'

Edric smiled, 'Still wanting to be sure, eh Emanuel? My mother can be trusted.'

'And, Emanuel, Mr. Roberts requests to arrange a carriage to wherever your famly is. He claims he owes you that much. He...'

'Ye don't need ta go out o' yer way on my 'count.'

She continued, 'He claims he's had a man working for him but he'd treated him like a boy.'

Emanuel didn't know what to say. His teeth locked on his lower lip. He nodded and cleared his throat. 'I'm very 'presh'tive o' th' offer. Would ye thank 'im fer me?'

So 'twas settled.

But where was 'home' now?

Emanuel wasn't quite ready to try to sort through London for his mother on his own. He could if he had to, he figured, but why not try to set things right with Aunt Gertrude and Uncle Ned first? 'Sides, since she'd taken the famly's reins a couple years earlier, she'd likely know information on where every member was and what they was doing. He knowed how to get to that farm, and hoped they'd still be living there. He'd see little Sallie, maybe Levi, and see how Aunt Gertrude was treating his siblings. 'Twas his duty, wasn't it?

Within an hour, a neighbor's carriage came to carry Emanuel home. And behind the carriage walked Mr. Roberts' gift of a young bull and two fresh Devon cows. The newest calf had been lifted into the carriage for the first part of the ride. She'd possessed stamina to finish the last few miles, but Mr. Roberts wanted her kept in pristine condition. He hoped these animals would help Emanuel build a herd and prosperity. These, he'd said, was not a gift but payment for work completed by a respectable young man.

Now, my readers, you know that Emanuel was headed back to find his famly. And, it's charitable of me to say Aunt Gertrude was famly. Manuel felt obligated to look after his younger siblings, to see they was being treated right. And while he came in peace, hoping to fall into good graces of his elders, Aunt Gertrude saw him as fuel oil on embers she was managing. Emanuel would always remind her of the child she'd lost, and add to that, her jealousy for the affection she saw Sallie and Levi shower on Emanuel was nearly more than she could bear. She longed to be most important to them and Emanuel had unknowingly showed her the Kisbey children's loyalty to each other. She was also not keen 'bout seeing his getting ahet in the world when she saw he brought prized Devons with him.

If you know the Bible's lesson about Joseph with his brothers or the prodigal son with an older brother, you know the standing Emanuel had with Aunt Gertrude. Top o' everything else, Emanuel looked more like his father all the time.

Uncle Ned, o'course, saw the goodness of Emanuel and wisely understood the cattle was more than payment due for the schooling and, shall we say, 'sacrifice' he and Gertrude was making for the Kisbeys. If things had been different, might of been that Manuel could of even had a share in the profits that was likely to be, for that would of fit with Mr. Roberts' gift to him. I don't know the figures, but 'tis unlikely Aunt Gertrude spent a pittance more'n she wanted and I suspicion each pittance somehow worked to her advantage. As for raising a herd, Emanuel would not get that chance.

The short of the story is that against the protest of Uncle Ned and espeshly of Levi, the youngest calf was immediately slaughtered for veal and Aunt Gertrude announced there was no need to keep such animals 'cause they'd eat more, she thought, than they'd earn or produce. Truth was, she and Uncle Ned had no comparable creatures. She planned to sell them as soon as she could and, she announced to Emanuel, the income would help pay the fares for Sallie and Levi when she took them to America 'fore long.

America o'course was news to Emanuel, and frighteningly so 'cause he'd come to help re-establish the Kisbey famly. When Emanuel tried to explain how valuable the small herd could be, Aunt would not listen, but Uncle did. Top o' that, Aunt Gertrude stated loudly to Emanuel, 'Someday ye'll see I was smarter than ye. This is for the best,' just like she had when she'd split the famly up earlier.

Later in the barn, which is where Aunt declared Emanuel should stay if he was willing to be Uncle Ned's hired hand, Uncle confided he'd not knowed they was going to America and that he'd try persuading his wife to improve her finances by keeping the Devons. If it worked, he promised Emanuel he'd do what he could to get Emanuel some of the profits. But Uncle Ned had a bigger chore than most regiments could tackle in changing Aunt's mind, though in the end, they did build a herd for a few years.

Long 'fore the herd grew, though, Aunt Gertrude decided Emanuel needed to be on his own and she shooed him off, but not 'fore he and his siblings became even closer kin. Emanuel knowed at the time of his farewell there was no talk of America and that helped ease his mind 'bout leaving.

In the meantime, I'd worked as a mother's helper for the Morton famly till the children was responsible enough to not need me. The mister delivered ice the summers I helped the famly, and farmed or did any work he found to keep the famly fed and clothed. Like thousands of other respectable young ladies, I continued domestic work elsewhere, and truth be tolt, I was glad to be of the age where I could turn a head or two of young men. While cleaning someone else's home, I drempt of the home I'd keep someday. O'course I remembered Father's stipulations.

My sister Sarah was being courted by a fine gentleman who fit well my father's requirements for his two daughters. He'd not minded had Henry been a little wealthier but was satisfied Henry was hardworking and resourceful.

Often there was few employment opportunities for hard working men, even in the United Kingdom's largest city. 'Bout this time, England's neighbor, Ireland, continued in dire straits. Beginning in 'bout 1845, Ireland's potato crop failed, and with the largest part of the Irish depending upon potatoes for most meals, a terriblefamine began. Unfortunately for the

Irish, the solution to their yearly famines became part of the agenda for the politicians sitting in Parliament.

For a time, our nation's thinking was too simple. We, society I mean, understood 'work to eat, eat to work.' Why couldn't the Irish work harder and wiser, unassisted, in solving their 'problem of famine?' Wouldn't aid hinder solutions? So, without our help, more and more Irish died from starvation.

Eventually officials began seeing the hopelessness of the situation, espeshly after learning how landowners evicted tenants either too sick to work or too poor to pay rent or debts, Parliament and t'others hoped to shed light on the cause of the problem.

Still, most solutions too often stepped past the beggar and his famly. Unscrupulous individuals cast Irishmen from their homes and onto boats with promises of health and financial turn 'rounds; many Irish died long 'fore reaching destinations. Some boats was kept from shore for fear they'd bring disease and further desperation. My father saw the sorry side of man with such dilemmas. 'Bout a hundred thousand Irishmen came to London's streets to compete for work, or hope for food alongside those claiming England as their homeland.

Emanuel was among the masses venturing to London for work 'bout that time. Farming skills had taught him more than how to work. At a couple places, Emanuel had learnt ways men used home built forges, learning how to hammer metal into useful implements. He'd been tolt a time or two he could prob'ly make a living at it, but o'course he had no way to start up that work without money or partners and without being closer to where more people needed such work. Even so, that vote of confidence lodged in his mind and in London, he sought work in iron foundrys there. His work was varied as he learnt the skills that made the Mears Bell Foundry, near Whitechapel Road, a major supplier of bells of all kinds. One of his brothers with whom he shared lodging, had suggested he become part of the crew there.

Emanuel could always make friends easily and turned out he was often working alongside a fellow a few years older than hisself, which was Henry Williams. As I tolt you, Henry was courting my sister. Sometimes the three of them saw each other and became close friends, but I never knowed 'bout it and 'sides I was hoping the young men I attracted would display a higher social standing than myself, so 'tis just as well we didn't meet. The timing was not good then.

Henry's parents and siblings lived not so far from our home and their famly owned considerably more land. Their famly was large, much like Emanuel's, only more had survived the epidemics and illnesses that had struck others. Henry worked at times in the foundry and t'other times helped farm. I'm not sure if the Williams did like the Reed's famly did, for I've learnt that Reeds had two householts; the parents lived with the youngest children, and the older children, some being young adults, lived in the second house nearby. I think there was maybe nine of them working the farmland and they was respectable good people, but my dear ones, that is for much later in my letter to you for I've not talked atall 'bout the Reeds yet. Saying more now would only sidestep this part of our lives.

We Copseys took an instant liking to Henry and perhaps I would of tried to get the attention of one of his brothers if I'd not been so determined I'd only settle for young successful merchants so I could live a life more like Aunt Emma's, but with children.

Though it's unnecessary to give names, I had one young man for a time I thought would likely become my husband. He was becoming wealthier and my father was more or less supporting the courtship, though he thought I was a little too young for such a gentleman. Every time his calling card was left at the door where I worked as a domestic I was thrilled, and looking back, I think the thrill came more from being courted by someone who dressed so fine and who was so obviously successful than by feelings for the gentleman hisself. He was kind and thoughtful but no matter how much I wanted to give him my heart, which he likely thought he had, I doubted my heart felt like what I saw Sarah and Henry had.

They'd started talking of their wedding, and if they'd not, my mother would of almost planned it for them. She knowed Henry wasn't wealthy but she believed he'd make Sarah happy and care for her best he could. There was a sentimental and romantic side to Mother I seldom saw, but I learnt of it as my courtships took place. The year was 'bout 1848.

I remember I'd recently been with Aunt Emma and while trying on her hats and talking 'bout my beau, I wondert how I'd know if I was really in love. Sarah and I'd talked of this, o'course, but not as much as I did that afternoon with Aunt Emma.

I think now I wanted her thoughts 'cause while she was married, her relationship with her husband was not so obviously warm like Sarah's for Henry, and I wondert if I was more like Aunt Emma.

Aunt Emma saprized me by getting tears as we talked. She tolt me she loved her husband, that her life was good, although she knowed she'd be lonely without her charitable work and times with Sarah and me, for too often her husband was away.

Then, wiping her nose with one of her many fancy kerchiefs, she claimed some workable marriages is less warm and likely meant to be and perhaps the young gentleman courting me would allow me to live a life like hers. 'But,' she'd said, 'if you want or get a chance for t'other, don't foolishly think wealth will give you feelings. Only companionship and love like Sarah and Henry's can.'

That conversation stuck with me. I had so admired Aunt Emma and wanted to be like her, but my own version, naturally. And I wasn't sure but what I'd expect both wealth and warmth from my beau, but my problem was that I felt I had to almost pretend to be happy to be his young lady. O' course you know courting was all proper by us 'cause we wanted to remain respectable. In keeping with our parents' wishes, neither Sarah nor I was ever really alone with suitors.

When they called at our homes, we entertained them with the *family* present and got to know them better through such parlor games as checkers, puzzles, and conversations or music at our home.

I'd pretty much decided I needed to push the courtship along in my head, hoping maybe my heart would follow. I thought I needed to see myself as a young woman who'd fashionably become another Aunt Emma. I saved my earnings and decided after purchasing a new outfit piece by piece that I needed a new parasol to complete my outfit. And so when I finished responsibilities at the home where I worked, I set out to get my fancy parasol.

I found shops with good selections and became involved in deciding which one would be just right. Thinking of my new outfit and also Sarah's upcoming wedding, I debated back and forth 'bout which one to buy. I 'magined myself strolling in the parks with my beau, twirling my parasol, or standing as I'd seen ladies do, under a shade tree by the Thames with my parasol almost as a cane, looking so fashionable, or maybe shading my face which was likely to freckle more if we should ride in a boat as I'd seen couples do. I was not sure my beau could row a boat as well as he could work a ledger, but a girl dreams such outings in her head.

My, I had lofty thoughts, did I not? Truth be tolt, I never got time for that fanciful boat ride on the Thames, but 'tis likely if I had, the sun's reflection on the water would of made my freckles come out so suddenly my beau would of been frightened away! Worse if we'd tipped into the smelly Thames!

But finally there in the shop that day I found just the right fancy parasol and made my purchase. From the shop window, I was much relieved it'd begun sprinkling just for me. My next moment was the most embarrassing of my life. I'd been thanked for my purchase and being so eager to open my new fashionable parasol I poked it through the doorway and began opening the parasol as I put my foot out to step onto the walkway. At the same instant, the shopkeeper called out 'cause I'd not bothered to get my change, so I turned my head toward him. And 'fore you knowed it, my parasol slapped right into a passerby's face, I lost my balance, and I landed smack dab on my bottom for all the world to see! So much for my grand entrance into society as a lady of high fashion! I'd failed on the first step. I should of knowed that was a prediction of life ahet!

The person whose face made contact with my parasol was somewhat tangled in my mess and tried helping me up as quickly as he could. He, o'course, was not skilled at lifting ladies more concerned 'bout new parasols than injuries imposed to self and t'others. He said something like, 'Beg yer pardon, Miss. Ye've a clever way ta meet strangers, wouldn't ye say?' He wondert if I was hurt and though my ankle was killing me, I'd not let another soul know.

And truth be tolt, there was no way I, a lady breaking into high society, would be helped or escorted by someone looking two days overdue for a bath. After all, I had a fashionable successful gentleman courting me and if seen by someone who knowed me, why, what might others think? I thanked him and bid him go on his way. Quickly go, was my hope.

I don't think I bothered 'bout getting my change from the shopkeeper. Steps was going to be a chore for a few days. I hobbled home where Mother, Father, and Sarah all pitied me but saw more humor in my situation than I thought Christian.

Later, o'course, I enjoyed telling the story and thought I'd likely been a sight to see. Naturally Father tolt my beau the tale, and my beau wished he'd been there to help me home, that he'd called a carriage, and all that. But he hadn't been. My swollen ankle got me extra carriage rides for a few outings and my parasol was skillfully repaired by Mother.

My beau and I decided, out of curiosity, we'd take in a religious meeting being conducted by increasingly popular preachers in London, though these gatherings wasn't as large as they'd become in years to follow. From what I'd heard, services was both moving and entertaining. My beau's friends had humorously entertained him by imitating fast-talking perspiring preachers. My father thought we'd take in an evening of entertainment, although I think he mostly liked my spending more time with this successful beau. My mother thought we was showing poor taste and tolt me she did not approve, for, she explained, although such gatherings was not High Church, no doubt people was coming to God through them; we was treading on sacred ground. I thought we was going out to be fashionable. And so we did. I, o'course, took my new parasol. It went with me at 'least as often as my beau.

The place was crowded when we arrived. Though my attitude had been one suitable for seeing a circus performance, almost instantly hymns sung by the enthusiastic crowd stirred my soul. I was immediately ashamed of my curiosity and though my beau elbowed me, still wanting to imitate the preacher's style, I let him know we was not seeing the same thing at this meeting. When he got out a pencil and paper to sketch exaggerated pitchures of the singer and preacher, I motioned for his paper and pencil. I know he thought I'd cartoon too, but instead I penciled things the man was saying. That put him off.

Taking me home later, he apologized for his 'poor choice for our evening's entertainment.' He thought it 'an awkward waste of time.' However, for me, the evening redirected the rest of my life. Let me tell you why, for I kept the paper with notes of that night, his cartoons and all.

Many brought not fashionable parasols but Bibles, for nearly everything the preacher said seemed to be a Bible verse. I'd not considered bringing a Bible and if I had, I fear I'd not likely found verses as fast as the preacher talked of them. I marked these verses when I found them later.

Here's a few verses I heard preached that night. The preacher preached other nights but this night he was using the little book of 1 John, found near the end of the Bible: 'If we say we have no sin, we deceive ourselves, and the truth is not in us. If we confess our sins, He is faithful and just to forgive us our sins, and to cleanse us from all unrighteousness.' Also, 'Love not the world, neither the things that are in the world. If any man love the world, the love of the Father is not in him.'

Another verse, 'Behold, what manner of love the Father hath bestowed upon us, that we should be called the sons of God: therefore the world knoweth us not, because it knew Him (Jesus) not.' Another, 'And this is His commandment, That we should believe on the name of His Son, Jesus Christ, and love one another as He gave us commandment.' Another, 'Herein is love, not that we loved God, but that He loved us, and sent His Son to be the propitiation for our sins.'

In my Psalter I've marked two more places, 'Whosoever believeth that Jesus is the Christ is born of God; every one that loveth Him that begat loveth Him also that is begotten of Him...And this is the record, that God hath given to us eternal life, and this life is in his Son. He that hath the Son hath life; and he that hath not the Son of God hath not life.'

All of these o'course, the preacher explained, and there's more in these verses than I can re-say. That night sitting there I saw two things the preacher said that was true of me. First, that I'd never owned up to my own sinfulness, mostly 'cause I found it easy to compare myself to those not as good as I tended to think I was. The preacher clearly taught that I was a sinner and if I said I wasn't, I was calling God a liar. That smote me and I knowed I blushed at the thought.

Another thing I realized that night was that I did indeed love things of the world. I was sitting beside one of the things of the world that I was trying to love, but I was pursuing that gentleman partly 'cause he was a way for me to get more things of the world. I saw some of the good things I did, like tutoring and other charity work that came perhaps so from the heart of Aunt Emma, those things I did 'cause I wanted the honour and attention she got, and truth be tolt, I'd hoped through my charity work I'd meet someone with money to spare for charity but still earn plenty to spend making certain I was comfortable.

There, I tolt you. I'd not been sincere, not pure in what I did, and that night I saw with shame I was exposed 'fore God who saw clear through to my motives. "Twas shudderingly humbling.

I don't suppose the preacher needed say another word for I do believe God was busily stirring my heart. I felt like most of my goodness was a lie hiding a deceitful heart.

Till that night I thought I was simply being clever, that good was coming from what I did so it didn't matter why I did it, and if I got rewarded for the goodness I did and caused, so much the better. I'd act'ly thought I'd impressed God. But then from somewhere in the Bible the preacher said my goodness stunk to God! I knowed I blushed hard. I sat there wishing I'd not come with my beau for I wanted to be alone, just me and God. I wanted to get a clear conscience and I sat there trying to figure out how I could ever be entitled to one.

Then the preacher did some talking 'bout other verses, telling us 'bout the ways Jesus was crucified and that we was guilty of why Jesus died on the cross. I'd heard that 'fore that night, but till that moment it'd passed over my head or missed my heart or however you may explain it. But that night, those words stabbed me like a knife and I wanted to let Almighty God know I was sorry He had to lose His Son over the likes of me. What relief came when the preacher proclaimed the verses 'bout agreeing to call sin what 'tis and that our just God by His nature will forgive us confessors.

I thought of times in my church when I'd lazily or mindlessly or even eagerly confessed words written out, but how I'd rather died than be found out by those sitting in pews with me. Group sin confessing was suitable and comfortable, but that night I knowed even if no other soul was being dealt with. I wanted peace and a clear conscience between me and God, no matter what uncomfortableness it cost me. I understood my sin and peace cost God the death of His sinless son on the cross and I was willing to publicly own up to my part in Jesus' crucifixion. My heart cried to God, 'I'm guilty and I'm dreadful sorry.' 'Twas a very moving night for me.

When the preacher asked if there was even one who agreed with God we was sinners and was ready to turn our lives over to the Lordship of Jesus Christ, I didn't hesitate. I stood. I knowed my life had offended God. My eyes was closed, but I heard others rising and I knowed God was working on our hearts. I stood there hearing Bible verses telling me that I was loved by God and I whispered back with more pure love than I'd ever knowed, 'I love you, I love you, O God.'

'Twas a refreshing cleansing night for my soul and I know no other way to say it to you. I got my clear conscience. I felt like a new person. The preacher tolt us we was beginning our eternal life and I believe 'twas so. After that when I prayed I was speaking to my Father in Heaven 'cause He had adopted me proper like. He was still Mighty God, but He'd moved from being undescribeable somewhere far up beyond the depths of the darkest regions of the sky to becoming my tender Father right beside me.

Interestingly after that, I felt God directing my thoughts, and when I felt a tinge of guilt, I was grateful, for I longed to keep my conscience clear. I eagerly spent time reading to understand God more through the Bible and my Prayer Book and these became more precious to me in ways they'd not been till that time.

I tolt you my beau apologized during the carriage ride home that the evening had not been as entertaining as he'd hoped. I asked him if he felt closer to God 'cause of the evening and he said something in a mocking sort of way that offended me. As he walked me to the house, he asked, as was his manner, when he might call again, and handed me his card. His calling card had always so impressed me and I had 'fore been so delighted to take it and wave it to my famly as I walked past them to my room. But that night standing on our porch with his card in my hand, I turned up both lower corners and handed it back to him saying softly but firmly, 'Don't.' I opened the door myself and went inside. I was not what one would call a missionary candidate I reckon. Calling cards had four options which callers left when departing or if a householt was away. The corners I'd turned up meant 'Good Bye' and 'I'm sorry to learn of your sadness.' Whether he was sad or not I cannot be sure, but I knowed I'd made a step in the right direction.

In the following week, my parents was all concerned my beau was not coming 'round. I likely seemed strange to them, preoccupied with Bible reading and discussions. Sarah, Henry, and I had a long talk, and they attended preaching with me. And 'fore long, my famly began including some 'informal' meetings in their spiritual diet as well. We still attended our cathedral Sabbath days, but we grew closer to the Lord at our own services partly 'cause we'd gone to t'other meetings. I got to wond'ring if my preacher was ever going to raise his voice to get our attention, though o'course, I found God taught me without the shouting, too.

Henry and Sarah's wedding plans began in earnest. We was not rich, but my parents wanted a lovely wedding ceremony for their oldest daughter. Truth be tolt, I suspicion they thought I'd spend my days alone, either lost in charitable work in England or on some foreign field destined to be eaten by cannibals in my zeal to know God.

I was willing to be courted by a suitable candidate. I was leaving the choice up to God as best I knowed how.

Weddings 'round 1849 England, the summer Henry and Sarah married, was sometimes simple and sometimes elaborate, often depending upon famly tradition, wealth, and – tragically · health, too. 1849 was the sad year cholera raged through our country, bringing death to nearly every famly we knowed. Thousands died, thousands. Sometimes up to two thousand died a week, so planning weddings in the midst of others' sorrows was careful. But one cannot let death overshadow all things, for weddings is to be celebrated. Weddings and births can be almost a slap in death's face and so we tried to keep a corner of our lives for times of pure joy.

Some followed wedding superstitions, but mostly as a lark and not serious for us in the Christian faith. Sarah and Henry's wedding was the fanciest event our famly put together, but in many ways 'twas 'simply beautiful.' I think 'twas on a Wednesday morning as many thought Wednesdays was the best wedding day. The ceremony at our cathedral gave it a proper and lovely feel.

A couple weeks 'fore the wedding Henry and Sarah found out they could set up housekeeping near one of our Copsey relatives. The house wasn't ready for a young couple. Henry worked days at the foundry and chored at night. With others using spare time working on the wedding, I espeshly enjoyed fancying up the house for them as my wedding gift to them. I put my heart into making things cozy and presentable, being allowed extra hours there since the famly where I did domestic work knowed 'twas my gift. After working on Sarah and Henry's house, I'd sleep at the nearby Copseys. They helped some too.

Henry and Sarah would possess sparse furnishings so I wondert what we could spare from home. Sarah was better than me on the piano, but when I asked her if she'd be taking the parlor piano she insisted I keep it to home so I could play it often, which I did enjoy for I was fond of music. Sarah knowed she was more accomplished, but if truth be tolt, I s'pose she thought I needed it for companionship or knowed I needed the practice.

Mother kept busy, knowing guests would stop by to congratulate the new couple and take home little pieces of cake. Weddings was work, and money was tight for 'bout everybody. There was three cakes, o'course, one for playfully telling the future of those who got special treats inside, and one was kept by newlyweds as a wish for them to enjoy twenty-five years later. How did such a tradition get started? Had to be by somebody with good teeth! 'Magine cake that old needs lots of romantic memories, and maybe strong 'dunking tea' to swallow. Anyhow, Mother made the cakes look pretty.

I was Sarah's first bridesmaid. There was two others. Naturally Sarah's dress was becoming to her. We put flowers in her hair so Henry's breath would be taken away, but he loved her so much I'm not sure he even noticed the flowers. But others did. The morning was lovely when the wedding party walked from a certain point in the road to the church for the service. The ushers and the couple's parents had helped scatter wild flowers along the pathway we walked so 'twas a very fragrant and happy and romantic affair. I didn't know all the best men and ushers, a few I did o'course, but not all, as some was from Henry's foundry work place in London, but they was in our group walking over.

The young men looked so responsible, even though they was light-hearted walking to the wedding. O'course I hoped for conversations with them during the day, either at church or when Mother and Father would receive guests to home. One to me was espeshly interesting. Nice looking, tall, lean, and so handsome in his fancy coat. We caught each other's eye during the ceremony, but I blushed I'm sure, and quickly looked elsewhere.

As we was going back to Mother's breakfast prepared for the couple and wedding guests, that young gentleman came over to me and said, 'Is ye the gal I sat down wit' on a London street 'bout a year ago?'

At first I couldn't think what he was talking 'bout, but I wanted to keep the conversation going so I said, in my most flirtatious voice, 'Well, Sir, I'm not sure, I think I'd remember you.'

And he said, 'I'm quite shore 'twas ye, 'cause I 'member seein' the par'sol yer totin' close up,' and he laughed. He reached for my parasol, 'Shall I show ye how it 'appen't?'

Then I blushed again! We laughed as I gave him a more proper apology. He said something like, 'Fancy meetin' ye here 'gin. I'm glad I knowed 'Enry.' And instantly my heart, too, was glad he'd knowed Henry, though in my head I couldn't help remembering how shabby I'd thought he looked the day of the parasol happening. I speculated, 'cause of his fancy clothes, that time had perhaps made him wonderfully prosperous.

We found lots of opportunities for little conversations during the bridal party meal and helping make sure Sarah and Henry had everything they needed. By the end of the afternoon he asked if he could call and you know I certainly said he could. He didn't offer a calling card, but if he had, I'd not folded lower corners.

Incident'ly, I didn't go on the newlyweds' trip although 'twas the custom of the time. They said they'd consider the cozy house their honeymoon place and Sarah assured me they wouldn't need anyone else along. 'Fore they left, Henry tolt me he was glad I'd hit it off with his friend 'cause he was one of the kindest men he knowed. Sarah tolt me later Henry, bless his heart, had purposely asked my new friend to be in the wedding party so we two could at least meet. Henry was ten years older than me but he thought he knowed who I might be suited for, and I think he was wise.

The young gentleman's name was, o'course, Emanuel Kisbey. Much later we figured out the parasol happening was our second meeting. Our first had been when we both rode to London in that carriage I tolt you 'bout. Manuel tolt me too, some time 'fore we was married, he'd seen me and my parasol, and my beau, at the preaching meeting I tolt 'bout earlier. I was ever so glad I'd turned up the corners of my beau's calling card that night. I had no idea my future husband had seen me there and had made the same commitment to the Lord I had. Methodists went regularly to such things.

I s'pose I should tell you there's no such thing as love at first sight and that a good many people get into marriages finding out what they thought they saw at first is not visible after a few months of marriage. I o'course don't know how 'tis for t'others, but 'twas not love at first sight for me. Love didn't happen for me I reckon till third sight! We'd seen each for that carriage ride when we'd been almost too scared to look at each other. The next time with the parasol, I prob'ly hoped we'd never see each other again mostly 'cause of my embarrassment and my immaturity. No, real love does take time. I'll just say we was struck by each other at Sarah and Henry's wedding and by the end of that afternoon we had at least a good start toward falling in love.

But our courtship would not be easy. My parents, who'd not given up dreams of my marrying well, at first likely thought I'd prefer an easier life with the cannibals than with someone whose past had been so hard. I'll tell you just a couple events of our courtship 'fore my parents was convinced Manuel was the husband for me.

I tolt you 'fore that I liked playing the piano, though I'd by no means excelled. For proper courtship, couples spent most of their time in parlors with the girl's parents or walked together in very public places. We both wanted our courtship proper. I knowed just causing one excuse for my father to be suspicious of Emanuel and my father would put a stop to Emanuel's calling, so we was espeshly proper. We was allowed times with Henry and Sarah and those was not nearly so stiff as early counting days with my parents. But I had a lot to learn 'bout Emanuel and one incident where we did not understand each other could of ended our courtship if it'd not been for Henry and Sarah. I call this the Music Incident.

I often sang my piano pieces while Manuel sat near me admiringly listening to notes and words. O'course I practiced more during the week, knowing he'd most likely want to hear me when he called. My parents approved 'cause they thought the piano music was a good indication we was behaving proper and we could be left alone while Mother baked or father tended to other duties. And if our courtship ended, my parents figured 'least they'd age to better piano music with their spinster daughter. Now mind you, there's nothing wrong 'bout being a spinster or bachelor. Some people's meant to be such for godly purposes. But I suspicion my parents thought the music they'd go deaf on if my courtship ended would slump into being all in a slow minor key.

We'd courted several weeks. One Sunday afternoon when Manuel called, things got interesting. We visited with my parents and then I began playing piano, which was my parents' sign to leave the parlor. I smile now as I think back on those days. My father left with 'I'll be in the kitchen if you need me.' I don't s'pose he ever thought I'd plan to need him, but 'twas his way of saying they expected things to remain proper. Some homes had suitors carve spoons for the parents when couples sat in a parlor alone, but Father thought constant piano music was better. Sly suitors might carve spoons 'fore calling. Anyhow, after a few songs, we went for a public walk. Manuel made sure I had my parasol. That was always humor between us.

As we walked, I pursued his interest in music. I asked if he'd sing along with me when I played melodies he knowed. He said he wouldn't. I asked him why and he said he didn't know the words to songs I played. After a few more questions on my part, I suggested he write a song for me to put music to so we could sing his words. He was silent.

O'course if I'd knowed he couldn't read I'd not spoken such things. So I kept at it as a young gal sometimes does with a beau she's sure can do anything and everything well. I said something like, 'If you was a composer or writ lyrics, I'm sure your works would be strong musical pieces that'd move audiences to tears. Maybe even Queen Victoria would request your work be played for her.' He thought I was mocking him, but I swore I meant it, saying anything he did he'd do well.

We just walked in awkward silence for awhile. I wondert if he believed I hadn't mocked him. Then he took my hand, so I knowed he wasn't angry or hurt by me. I said something like, 'If you was to write a new song no one but me would hear, what would you call it?' His silence had me worrying he wouldn't want to write a song for me, so quickly I apologized for asking such a thing. But real softly he said if he writ a song for only me to hear, it'd be 'She Believes in Me'. We stopped and looked at each other's misty eyes. I had to be blushing. He smiled and softly touched my cheek with his hand, but we was determined to stay proper.

As we walked home more closely shouldered together, I playfully whispered, 'Will you sing it to me?' But he begged off, saying he wasn't good with words and he wasn't a singer like me. When he bid me good night I tolt him I might just write a song to sing to him sometime.

The next week I became a romantic poet and writ a love song I thought fit us. I worked out a simple tune. This was going to be our song. A girl can get so silly sometimes.

When Emanuel came to call, we had parlor games with my parents and James and then, as the evening was getting later, I quietly handed him a folded paper with the words to the song and announced I'd play a song I'd made up. I smiled at Manuel and motioned he could follow along on the paper. I tolt my audience I'd written words but I wasn't going to sing them out.

Manuel smiled. I sat at the piano, my back to my listeners. I put my heart into the song, playing it mostly for Emanuel, hoping he understood how the music and words went together. 'Twas as good a love song as I could write and I thought it fit us. O'course when I finished playing, I wondert what he thought. He said 'twas a real nice tune and that he'd better be going. I saw the paper was still folded. I was disappointed, so as I walked him to the door, I whispered, 'Did you like the words I writ?' He tolt me he wasn't too sure 'bout the words.

I was devastated. I just knowed I'd made a fool of myself! I'd fallen too fast for Emanuel. All the things a girl's tolt 'bout not forcing romance came to my head. I soaked my pillow that night and dreaded seeing him again, wond'ring what he'd think of me if we indeed ever saw each other, that is.

I knowed London was full of bold women improperly going after men. I worried people would decide I was leaning toward being a shameful lady. What I writ was not wrong words, but I'd hinted I hoped for a future with Emanuel. My stomach was knotted, wond'ring how foolish he thought I was. Oh how I hoped he'd just burn the paper. How I wanted to get the only copy of those words back so no one else would ever see them.

I moped round for a couple days, angry at myself for letting Emanuel know my feelings. Why hadn't I waited till he tolt me more how he felt? I just knowed I'd lost my chance to be courted by him. When someone spoke to me, my voice was uncertain. Mother wondert what saddened me. I wailed her I might as well find where to sign up as a missionary to cannibals. She asked whatever could I mean and I tolt her I was afraid the only man who'd ever make me want to marry wasn't interested in me.

Through Mother, or perhaps James, word traveled to Sarah and Henry. They came over and when we was alone, Henry straight out asked me how a good relationship could go sour so suddenly. So I tolt them what happened and what a fool I was to think Emanuel cared, on and on. Henry said he'd see where Emanuel stood on our courtship.

Now I was even more humiliated that Henry knowed what a foolish sister his wife had, but Sarah tolt me he cared 'bout me like I was his sister. He agreed. I made them promise no one would know my foolishness, espeshly if Emanuel had stopped courting me. I promised them and the whole world that day that I'd not write any foolish things again.

A day or so later, Sarah asked me to come for an evening with them the following night. O'course I wondert if Henry had talked to Emanuel, so Sarah tolt me Emanuel would be there 'cause he had something to say to me. I wasn't sure I wanted to be humiliated more and begged to decline Sarah's invite, but she insisted I be there to hear him out. She claimed to not know much 'bout the evening, but Henry had asked her to get me there if I thought I was adult enough to act like a lady. I finally agreed to go.

To protect myself from shame, I brought a letter I writ to give Emanuel if he was ending what I thought had been our courtship. I tolt myself I could get over Emanuel if I had to. In my head I plotted how to hunt up cannibal-surviving missionaries. If I'd knowed of cannibals in London, I likely headed to start my work with them other'n going to Sarah's! But knowing of none, I was still intact when the carriage came for me the next night.

Emanuel was already at Henry's. He stood when I entered the room, but he had good manners anyhow. As the evening moved along I thought things seemed awkward. I decided to spare us all; I'd claim I was ill and I'd retire to another room. 'Fore I could, though, Henry and Sarah decided they'd leave the two of us to talk.

There we sat in silence for what seemed the better part of Eternity, no doubt each figuring what to say. Finally Emanuel said, 'I brought back the words you writ,' and he got them from the front pocket of his coat. 'I never read them –'

I reached over to grab the paper saying I was glad he hadn't 'cause they was just silly rhymes. He kept the paper beyond my grasp, interrupting my protest, claiming he didn't think anything I'd write would be silly, that he believed I'd only put down on paper what I believed. Now I really wanted those words back 'cause if he didn't even read them I could burn them! No one would ever read how hopelessly I'd fallen for someone who hadn't fallen for me. Then he said, 'Esta, I dint read 'em un I hope ye won't thin' less o' me fer that.'

O'course I was ready to say 'twas fine he didn't, but he went on. He tolt me he didn't read them 'cause he'd never gone to school to learn reading, even though he'd hoped one day he could. His eyes was glistening and mine teared, too, as he spoke so tenderly. He said, 'Does tha' matter ta ye that I caint read?'

I wanted to show him it didn't matter, but being proper, I just assured him I liked him for who he was and not whether he could read or not. I apologized for giving him the words, but he asked me if he could hear them like I heard them when I writ them. He handed the paper to me like 'twas a special document. My, I was not sure what to do, but I knowed I'd thought I loved the man when I writ them, so I took the risk and quietly I read them to him.

Manuel tolt me he liked the words I'd writ them, but he'd change a couple lines if he could write, for he said 'twas not right I'd writ words to 'his song' to me. I felt so honoured he trusted me with his shortcoming of not being a reader and that he was humble enough to ask me to write down his words for him. So, soon I writ down what he said would be his song. When 'twas done, the poem was not atall like I'd writ.

At home that night, I throwed mine away and, o'course, the letter I'd brought. I'll put down here what he rhymed for me that night. He worked the words carefully in his head. I knowed they was for only me and they tolt me his heart.

He called it, *'She Believes in Me.'*

I knowed I'm loved by someone who believes in me. I prayed that one day I would find someone like ye. I knowed I never felt 'fore this free: Reckon that's what love has gone and done to me.

No matter where I'll go, what I say, or who I'll be, This lovely lady tells me, 'I'll believe in ye.'

I've not much to offer, who knows if we could make it go? But the one who believes in me will be the one to know.

No soul would mistake me for a prince o' royal birth, But Esta's love's just made me the happiest man on earth!

Lord God, You've showed me a girl with sparkle in her eyes And I want to see them sparkle till the day I dies.

For I've found a woman whose love has set me free -- And I'm hoping I know her answer when tonight I ask her, 'Would ye marry me?'

Oh, Manuel, he was a romantic, the way he worked to that last line! He teased he had to end it somehow.I s'pose after trusting me to know he couldn't write a word, and finding out I still wanted to be with him, he decided he'd end his little song that way.

We hummed the words off and on in our years together and they always made us smile. I o'course was ready to say I'd marry him and tolt him so, but we both knowed he had to win Father and Mother's approval and that was still ahet.

I had to tell Sarah, and o'course Henry heard Sarah's squeal and had to find what we was all excited 'bout. When they bid us farewell as Manuel prepared to take me home, they was sworn to secrecy. They agreed we four would try to convince the Copseys I should become a Kisbey 'fore too long. Who'd want a better sister and brother than mine? My parents was still up when we got to my house. Mother seemed pleased when I answered 'bout how I'd gotten home.

A few days later a flower girl who was sometimes seen in our neighborhood came to our door. 'Twas Sabbath afternoon so Father answered. She asked for me. When I came, Father watched me receive a handful of colorful primrose. O'course there was no card, so Father asked who sent them and the flower girl said, 'A fine looking workman named Emanuel.' I immediately went to the back yard to show Mother who was sitting on a bench near her own flowers. Father followed me.

I, o'course, was so pleased and proud to be sent the flowers. Mother looked at the flowers and asked, "Emanuel sent those?"

Father said 'twas anybody's reckon 'cause the flowers had no card. I reminded him he'd heard they was from Emanuel. Then father said, 'I think you need to end this courtship 'fore it goes any further.'

I was heartsick and in turmoil since I had spent days trying to prepare to convince my parents I was ready to marry Emanuel. I'm sure my words was stumbling when I said, 'End it? Why?'

And father said, 'I'm not so sure Emanuel is a proper gentleman for someone like you.'

I asked why he'd say such a thing. Father explained flowers sometimes came from, or to, un-reputable characters. How did I know 'twas Emanuel that sent them, and how'd he got them, and, 'why, pity's sakes, would a young working man,' not 'gentleman' did he say, 'be spending what little money he had on senseless things like flowers?'

Upset, I said, 'Maybe 'cause he loves me.' O'course I said he was respectable and so forth. I wanted to say Father was being mean-spirited, but I knowed a Copsey child did not speak such to a Copsey parent, so I helt my tongue, and I hope I prayed.

Somewhere here Father said he thought Emanuel was backward, that's how he put it, and I to this day think such is an insulting word! What can it mean? All I could think of was a clock going the wrong way and I knowed Manuel was not one to go the wrong way. Father said he was sure Emanuel neither read nor writ and a daughter of his ought not marry someone who'd not give them a good life. He was certain a body unable to read or write wouldn't be able to take good care of me.

I understood Father worked hard to be sure we could read and write the basics. I remember Father saying Emanuel, with the job and limitations of illiteracy he had, could not provide for me in the manner I was used to living. He claimed Manuel would often be jobless 'cause readers and writers got jobs ahet of t'others, 'least wise the best paying jobs.

I said in a tone slightly louder than Father had heard to this point, that I was grateful for the comforts he and mother had given me, but that I was old enough to make my own decisions when it came to marrying.

O'course Father said my behavior showed I was far from ready to make any such decision. I knowed then sometimes I talk a little too much. I'd never spoken up to my parents in this manner, but my heart belonged to Manuel and inside I felt I behaved like a young woman in love would do. O'course I knowed if Father forbid my seeing Manuel I'd need to comply, 'least for a long time.

I looked at Mother who reminded me that my father had worked hard to make our lives comfortable.

I started to express appreciation for father's hard work when he interrupted me again, saying I was too used to the comforts we had and that even if Emanuel and I thought we loved each other, my discontentment would become more obvious to Emanuel every day. He said I'd not be able to hide my sadness 'bout wanting fancy things I could not own and that would make life miserable for Emanuel. He said I'd be saying he didn't measure up and was not the man I dreamed of marrying. That scared me. No man wanted that, but I knowed my childish thoughts of marrying some wealthy man was no longer part of me, but was they gone for good, forever?

I asked if I could speak respectfully to them and Father said they'd listen to sense. I tolt them I respected them both but what I most wanted in a home was not furnishings, not 'things' for pity's sakes. I said, 'Emanuel loves me, and I respect him for who he is, so what he does or how much money he has is not important to me.'

Father commented, like some menfolk sometimes do, saying things loud like they want us to know how their head is working but soft like we wasn't to hear so we shouldn't be hurt when it cuts to our hearts, 'bout me not knowing what I'd think was important in a few years and that a man who spent his money on flowers was usually one who couldn't pay his bills and was looking for someone who'd pay them for him. Things like that.

I looked to Mother who slightly cocked her head as if to tell me not to say a word. There seems to be times when a woman just stays quiet till the man's had his say whether his words fit his character or not. If it's not his character, he'll bring the words 'round to being more like him in a thought or two.

He wondert why I couldn't fall in love with a wealthy man, like the one who'd been interested in me a couple years 'fore and who'd become, Father said, even more successful. I wanted to say that man had nothing to offer but money but I helt my tongue as Father continued.

He said something like, 'I'm a barger and ag labourer, why not surpass me? Marry the man who owns the docks or the farmland we work so I could live without worrying 'bout you.'

My mother took over then and her tone had a little humor in it. She said, 'Then she could provide nicely for us in our old age, right Mr. Copsey?' I never heard her call him that more than a time or two. She continued, 'Oh, Will, I think your daughter's in love and love is so mysterious. The feelings she apparently has didn't arise by her determination to make them do so. Mr. Copsey, isn't it better for Esther to marry a person who adores her rather than spend her life as though she's married to her husband's business or to fancy things he provides for her? Will, ought we be people who only find respect for wealthy men?'

She went on to remind Father 'bout times in the past when reading was thought wrong, even for men, but espeshly for girls like his daughters. 'O'course that's not your thinking now, but some Mr. Copsey in your past probably tolt his daughters not to read.'

I could see by his nod that Father thought this talk was longer than he wanted. Then my mother moved over and took his arm in hers and gave a smile I wonder if she didn't want me to remember about how to give, and she said, 'Wasn't it my good man who tolt me to make certain our children understood, 'What we can do, what we can know, what we can own, or even what we can give away, is never as important as who our character says we is?'

I could tell Father hoped Mother wasn't expecting answers to that question, too. When he thrust the flowers toward me, I knew he hoped we'd stay on the flower topic and stop expecting answers 'bout how important character was, espeshly using Father's own words.

He'd likely all ready figured up a whole list of things he'd spend a half crown on. I knowed he thought flowers was wasteful if they was cut 'cause they wilt fast whereas half crowns would not. Mother knowed his thinking too. We'd heard it 'fore on times we walked past flower costemongers. He'd say, 'Ever seen a half crown wilt?' and he'd say it loudly til Mother would shush him. That Sabbath I watched my father turn and walk away muttering, 'Women. Such irrational creatures!'

I watched Mother's gaze follow him 'fore our eyes searched each other's face. We was both quiet. I didn't know what to expect from her.

She removed her gardening gloves as she came to where I stood clutching the primroses. She put her hand on my arm, taking in their colors, 'Such beautiful primroses, Esther.' She lifted them up to sniff their fragrance. 'We mustn't waste their fragrance. I'll get you a vase, and when they start to wilt, why not press them flat in your favorite book?' She started toward the house, then turned 'round and said softly, 'I wouldn't be saprized if your children ask to see those flowers some day.'

I stood there trying to understand all she was saying and looking at her useful garden but it also had its many varieties of flowers she so tenderly cared for. I wasn't sure I was ready to go back into the house.

In a bit Mother brought out a glass jar. 'I don't think I'd find a vase no matter how long I searched this Copsey house, but if we add a ribbon from Sarah and Henry's wedding, this should do just fine.' She saprized me with a quick hug and whispered, 'I think I'll like your Emanuel,' and went inside to find Father.

I took the primroses to my room and placed them where I thought they'd get the right amount of sunshine. And where Father wouldn't see them.

I didn't know Emanuel heard most of the conversation, for when the flower girl knocked, he was out of sight but within earshot of all that happened. He'd hoped we could go out after I got the flowers, but he didn't make an appearance that Sabbath afternoon. He left quietly, knowing the only person yet to win over would be my father and he was determined to do that if he could 'fore he'd give up on courting me.

Sometime later Emanuel and I knowed we had Father's blessing. At the little gathering we had for Emanuel's birthday, Father gave him a nice ceramic Prince Albert figure, Queen Victoria's husband. Respect for Prince Albert had grown among English subjects. Father tolt Emanuel he saw Emanuel made me feel like a queen so 'twas good his daughter was happy. He respected the man who made her so.

For the rest of the time we was in England, Father and Emanuel got along fine together, even when things got really hard for us. I think Father knowed times was hard whether a person read or writ or what. Even my Copsey parents would shed tears with us in times of sadness and espeshly dockside a few years later when we boarded for America, but as long as Father lived, he never again thought I should of belonged to anyone but my beloved Manuel.

Proof is too, a few short months after the garden talk, Father asked Emanuel when he was going to ask his blessing so we two could get on with planning a wedding. Emanuel Kisbey and I set our wedding date for July 1852. I was courted 'bout three years 'fore then.

Oh, and interestingly Mother's flowers began showing up in a nice vase Father gave her shortly after that day in the garden. I knowed he thought he'd sacrificed for it for he said we'd better not break it when we dusted or he'd question his judgment all together.

Like everybody else in 1851, 'fore we was married, we had to spend a little time and money at Queen Victoria's Crystal Palace with its thousands of exhibits. O'course we mostly went on the days when entry was just a shilling. Even the building of the enormous museum structure interested espeshly men like my father and Manuel, though I liked excuses to be with Manuel so I went whenever he asked.

The remarkable exhibit had been Prince Albert's project and he made sure England looked like the best country in the world, and since it covered much of it, few contested his extravagance to look good. We also saw things from 'round the world, even from these United States. We knowed we lived in such a privleeched time with so many inventions removing some of the hardest work from living, though many labourers worried they'd be jobless if the industr'lizing continued, and sometimes rightly so.

Some people talked of seeing Queen Victoria visit the exhibits, but we didn't see her far as I knowed. I always hoped we would and she'd prob'ly 'least waved to us if we had. By this time she was a popular Queen and the early talk against Albert's project was forgotten when thousands stirred there daily.

Crowds was so large people rightly worried 'bout getting separated in crowds. 'Twas a good place to watch rainstorms for 'twas all glass covered and not a single drop would touch you. O'course Manuel always made sure I had the parasol that'd help bring us together. Henry and Sarah and us went one day together and we was able to take other family members a time or two.

A person can't 'magine how much glass was letting in the sunlight and so 'twas a good idea to build over and 'round trees for shade inside the elaborate Crystal Palace. But a person got educated just by going and when you left, if you stayed long enough and studied a bit, you pretty much knowed something 'bout most places on earth. I s'pose people thought the idea of bringing it all together was foolish at first.

One thing that was most fascinating to think 'bout in the years soon after was the toilets they had for the public to use. Later when we was married and living in Canning Town, we often wished for another day – or even an hour · at Crystal Palace espeshly for the toilets!

I liked the pitchures and statues and such, but Manuel mostly liked the machinery and even toys being showed. Working things fascinated him and, sorry to say, I s'pose leisure things more often caught my eye.

Crystal Palace was only up a few months. It'd taken 'bout as many months to assemble it as it stood to show its insides. Even those whole trees inside was still good when the exhibitions was torn down. They used some materials for smaller displays 'round London and I s'pose some exhibits, jewels and such, went back to where they'd come from. But my, how people visited London that year! You saw all kinds of people there, people living as we was and then the rich and those that talked different. Some looked like us, many didn't.

I think we knowed the world's not so big as we thought 'fore. I don't s'pose you'll go as far away as London but if you should, I believe many exhibits I saw is still there up somewhere. I s'pose, too, some things that made our mouths drop open would make you yawn. I hear 'round 'bout that Queen Victoria still wants to honour her husband's memory, so I 'magine she's kept having good displays. I don't regret the shillings we spent 'cause sometimes a body needs to take advantage of once in a lifetime events that gives a body pleasure when recollecting later. And our days spent strolling through Crystal Palace is pleasant memories to be sure.

By the way, poor Queen Victoria's still mourning Prince Albert. She tolt her people she had no one to call her simply 'Victoria.' Even Royalty has its hardships.

Manuel during this time had worked mostly at the foundry off Whitechapel where they made bells for churches. He saved for the day we'd be married and start our own famly.

I knowed he loved children as Henry and Sarah had their little girl, but sadly all of us was left to mourn her when she

passed. Later their Edward stole my heart. I knowed from my
mother's helper work, and from tending to Sarah's little
Edward, that I'd take to motherly duties. I knowed such would
happen whenever God saw fit to make me become a mother.
Sarah, I will say, showed love outright, espeshly to her
children, and truth be tolt, I worried she might be spoiling any
and all she birthed, but they turned out good, far as I know.

Preparing for our wedding celebration, even though 'twas
not a big affair, took stirring. We invited a few friends and
famly and with Manuel's famly, that meant 'twas possible
several could come.

One of those o' course was Aunt Gertrude. For several
years, Manuel's sister Sallie had pretty much lived with Aunt
and Uncle, and Levi resided there too a fair amount too. Levi
had also looked after Mrs. Kisbey and Will. Mrs. Kisbey's
health was not very good, though I knowed she wanted it to be.
Manuel and I hoped our wedding would be a simple but
pleasant time for relatives to enjoy. We wanted both famlys
together as much as possible.

We'd not counted on Aunt Gertrude's behavior.

One Saturday morning when we'd all spent time visiting
Mrs. Kisbey and Will, Levi suggested we three go to Uncle and
Aunt's so I could meet them. Manuel had some hesitation but
Levi, eighteen, went on 'bout how they'd helped get his
schooling which not likely happened if it'd been all his mother
and brothers' responsibility, so I looked forward to meeting the
charitable woman. Manuel had said little for me to think
otherwise.

I remember the train ride to the farm as Levi tolt how
Emanuel's Devonshire herd had increased, improving Uncle
and Aunt's income. O'course Manuel wouldn't hear 'bout that
from Aunt Gertrude, not ever. If you'd asked her, she'd tolt
'bout their getting out of fences and eating up paschures and
so on. But their red coats was a pretty sight as we got to the
place. And when the dog barked, out Aunt and Uncle came
with Sallie, all still dressed up likely from going to a church
meeting, though maybe they dressed that way on Sundays

even if they didn't go. Levi hollered, 'Aunt Gertrude and Uncle Ned, I want ye to meet Miss Copsey.'

Now if Aunt was always later like she was for those first few moments, I'd found her such an agreeable person. She 'parently thought I was Levi's lady friend, though I was four years older, but maybe she couldn't tell by first look. She liked Levi 'cause she fancied she'd mostly shaped him. Anyhow, she was charming, saying 'twas good to meet me and even spoke to Emanuel. She liked my hair, she liked my outfit, on she went, hoping I'd take tea in their humble home, which wasn't by most standards all that humble for 'twas 'least as nice as my parents' house and where I worked as a domestic. Manuel commented to Uncle Ned 'bout the Devons and Uncle started to boast 'bout them but Aunt cut in o'course, telling faults and claiming they was trouble since the day they arrived.

I saw how her words hurt Manuel and it didn't take me long to size Aunt up. I moved over next to Manuel and boldly put my arm in his and said, 'We came 'cause Emanuel and I wanted to be sure you heard 'bout our plans to be married later this summer.' I watched her eyebrows rise to the sky, her chin tilt down, and her whole narrowing face change.

Meantime, young Sallie was excited with emotions too robust for Aunt Gertrude, so Sallie was chided for her outburst, but not 'fore I got my 'welcome to the famly' hug. Uncle Ned shook Emanuel's hand, though Aunt's glare cut off his arm at the shoulder.

I couldn't resist talking, espeshly since no one else was as we watched Aunt Gertrude searching for words. Did she want to take back all the flattery she'd offered or would that expose her too much? Anyhow I said something like 'I know Manuel and I'd be very happy and honoured if you would come to be guests at our wedding.' I was not aristocracy, but I knowed how to say a kind thing even when your heart's not in it.

Uncle started jesting 'bout what he'd wear and Sallie o'course was begging Aunt with, 'Can we go? Can we go?' 'Twas, after all, her brother's wedding, though she'd been kept from him most of ten years. Levi tried smoothing things, such a kind person he is and so totally saprized he'd knocked down a hornet's nest.

Then ol' silent Aunt found words again. 'When's the wedding?'

So Manuel tolt her we was planning for the end of July.

And she tolt us that they'd not be able to come 'cause they was leaving for America a few days 'fore that.

Some people say Victorian middle and lower class women had no rights unless given by the males, that they was not allowed to do as they pleased. Some wives, even Queen Victoria, consulted husbands 'fore making major decisions.

And then there was Aunt Gertrude. She had established her kingdom and I'd pitied Queen Victoria herself if Aunt Gertrude somehow acquired an army. She'd take on anybody just to do as she pleased, espeshly if she'd somehow get at Emanuel. Levi was the first to find words.

'America? When did ye decide this?'

Uncle, I could tell, knowed better than to say a word. He'd surrendered speaking rights with his 'I do' years 'fore. Not sure what he really thought of marriage.

Aunt Gertrude said, 'Now don't go acting all saprized 'bout this. Ye knowed we was planning to go as soon as we could, and a bit ago I figgered out we should go early this summer.'

I saw Uncle Ned turn slightly, taking in his cattle and his place. He silently took off his hat to scratch his head. He couldn't face her. 'A bit ago' was likely just a thought or two 'fore right then.

'A bit ago?' Levi's tone said he was unconvinced 'bout the sincerity. He pressed on. 'So, Aunt Gertrude, who is the 'we' that's going to America?'

'Ned and me and Sallie for sure, and ye, if yer so inclined.'

'I'm not so inclined, Aunt Gertrude. What 'bout yer farm? Ye was making money, good money.'

'Now, Levi, ye watch yer tongue with me young man! After all I did for ye, ye best speak kindly. Ye wou'nt know nothing 'bout numbers and reading if yer Uncle and I didn't work fingers to the bone for ye.'

'We 'elped,' Manuel said, his voice strong.

'Ye didn't do the day to day work here so don't ye go saying ye knowed a thing 'bout any of it, 'cause ye don't! All ye's been more my job to care for then yer Ma's since yer Pa left ye on our doorstep to care for.' Even Uncle gasped at her remark.

"E died, fer pity's sake, Aunt Gertrude.' Emanuel's voice showed anger, but he kept it steady. Who was on whose doorstep changing things while the famly worked the farm? Manuel took a breath, 'I'm not shore Sallie should go wit' ye, Aunt Gertrude...'

'That shows what little sense ye has! I'm same as her ma and a girl like her needs a woman like me at times like she's at.'

'I agree with Emanuel,' Levi said.

'Don't matter. I made up me mind and that's how it's to be. Your mother'll agree to it. I knowed that. It's best for Sallie, and it'd be best for ye Levi too, if ye has sense to see it.'

I don't remember whether we exchanged partings or not. Aunt had stormed back to her house and those serving time with her prob'ly didn't dare say much or they'd lose their rations.

Well, twas the sum total of happenings for a pleasant countryside train ride to meet famly! Manuel's jaw was set, saying little. I saw him kind of chew the inside of his lip like he'd do when considering hard actions to be taken. It wouldn't be the last time I wanted to cry along with him. Tears rolled and he just patted my hand but he didn't make a sound. I knowed he loved his little Sallie and felt he hardly knowed her. I still get knots in my stomach thinking 'bout it.

Our ride back was so solemn. Levi, who'd planned to stay at the farm a few weeks was also eager to learn whether Mrs. Kisbey knowed anything 'bout the trip to America. I respect those boys, they was standing their ground with Aunt but they had to be sure where Mrs. Kisbey stood on it 'fore they said much more. I thought I knowed Mrs. Kisbey well enough to reckon it'd be news to her as well.

'Twas.

The news likely made Mrs. Kisbey's health even more delicate. At such times, if a person didn't possess confidence in the sovereignty of our God, what would a person do?

Manuel and I talked 'bout how different things'd be if his father had lived, but o'course then you need to think 'bout all t'others who's lost famly to diseases or disasters. God and Times don't play favorites, seems to me. Emanuel'd so hoped we'd help keep his famly near to each other, and here 'twas being torn farther apart. We felt sorry for Levi who felt duty bound to oversee Sallie's care.

Emanuel's famly was people trying to live righteous Christian lives even though they kept getting obstacle after obstacle throwed in their paths. But one has to likewise consider thousands who just don't seem to get what one might think was fair. Half of l-i-f-e is 'if.'

Sure enough, in a few days, Aunt Gertrude called on Mrs. Kisbey, toting Sallie who'd been instructed to not make the departure harder for her mother by whining. Sallie talked of it years later. Sallie admittedly liked adventure and advantage, and truth be tolt, she'd gotten comfortable figuring out how to live with Aunt Gertrude and Uncle Ned. '

Sides, Aunt Gertrude was certain it'd be unhealthy and unwise to let Sallie be left behind with ailing Mrs. Kisbey and England's epidemics. She convinced Mother Kisbey a longer, healthier life awaited Sallie in the fresh air of a prosperous, disease-free country. Aunt claimed disease 'parently couldn't cross oceans. How could Mother deny her child life?

So many good things was reported back to England 'bout the United States. Lots of people considered earning passage to see if reports was true. But famly was important to us, and at the time 'most every blood relation resided in England. After days of talk amongst the Kisbeys, and no doubt, prayers, Levi decided he best go with Aunt and Uncle to oversee Sallie, for she was becoming quite an attractive young lady and needed an older brother's guardianship, 'least as far as Aunt Gertrude would permit. Levi's always been a helpful man, wanting to do what's best for others without a selfish bone in his body. Levi's Mary once tolt me Levi had a humor bone instead of a selfish bone, and we thought 'twas true.

Anyway, as Aunt Gertrude had threatened, they left 'fore our wedding. It'd not mattered if we'd moved our wedding date, Aunt would of turned cows loose or something just to be sure she had one more way to slight Manuel. I may feel later I'm too unkind to her, but I've purposely not tolt you her full name.

As a person counseled me, some people you just decide to set on another train track and go on after you've done your part to make things right. Now, don't you pick up any bitterness toward her as you read of her, 'cause when you read this, she'll of likely been past being concerned 'bout.

I'd rather pass the warnings 'bout avoiding bitterness. I just recount what I think 'tis necessary for you to see how our lives unfolded. Truth be tolt, I didn't grieve over the miles between her and us once we was in America, though Manuel o'course on Sunday afternoons would sometimes ask, 'Wouldn't ye like ta take a drive to see Sis and Levi?' Or when our little ones did something clever, he'd get soft spoken and wish his famly could see our children. O'course, couldn't be. Some stayed in England and most others lived hundreds of miles away when we lived in Livingston County Michigan. I'll get to that soon enough.

O'course our signatures was needed for registering 'fore marriage. I teased Emanuel 'bout his strong X, but he tolt me later he'd felt ashamed. Not ashamed he had few 'nice' things, 'cause he'd worked hard. Sometimes my humble Christian man gave to needier souls. But 'twas humiliating to be claiming he was ready to marry but couldn't even put down his name so the law could read it. I'm thankful it didn't stop him from marrying.

We made our marriage promises in Poplar in a simple ceremony July 30, 1852, me wearing Sarah's dress. Mother hosted a breakfast for us and our guests and among the most jovial was Edric Bertwald Roberts since he was shirt-tail relations by Aunt Emma. By then he was both lean and married. He and Manuel did laugh 'bout their day in London many years 'fore and how he was tending Devons, but without the regiment Manuel'd knowed. His friendly wife seemed suited to country life and their generous gift helped us for a time. If we'd been able, I think we'd enjoyed friendship with them, but we was not set to venture much.

Those first months we was comfortable. Always we was careful. Later we'd be doing the best we could to survive in London's East End, in Canning Town. They didn't officially call our region East End then, but 'tis called that now.

Canning Town and London's East End you could likely read 'bout if you wanted. Poverty was an unwelcome occupant in many homes in the 1850's. Though Queen Victoria brought many good changes, hungry people was still dying. London's destitute crowded either into slums or agreed to live in poor houses along with disease.

Aunt Emma and other charitable people and organizations worked soup kitchens to help feed the starving masses. London's kindest with lively faith served those more desperate than themselves.

There was days I gave out food, but 'fore we left, there was days I feared I'd need to stand in line to take it, too. I kept details of Canning Town's horrid condishions as quiet as I could from my famly, but they knowed more than they let on I'm sure, and then, too, people of conscience writ of Canning Town in papers. In dry and warm seasons, Canning Town had some appeal, provided you was born without a sense of smell.

Canning Town was the dump sight for livelihoods London didn't want to permit within its limits. Any day a body wanted to let a stomach be turned by bad smells, you could go to Canning Town. 'Twas home to the tanning industry and if you knowed much 'bout tanning, you know the bad smell is from more than rotting meat left on the hides. Another big business in Canning Town was the fuller business. Both businesses required urine and worse, and a top o'that, Canning Town was not where any one of consequence lived according to those who judge such things. More 'bout Canning Town later, but birth records remind everyone we was putting up with Canning Town.

Love totes you through most things, but even so, 'twas hard and 'twas unhealthy, and life broke our hearts bad 'fore we left for America. I won't give you all the details but I'll call this next part 'East End and Empty Cradles.'

'Fore I continue I must take a brisk reminder walk. Life's a good and precious gift, and one for which we give account. Today's too crisp to be out long so I'll return shortly. I'll bundle up and just walk down to a small stream on this bountifully good place and quietly watch icy rippling water peacefully ripple, ripple, ripple.

To skip the Bible study, please skip ahead.

NOVEL APPROACH TO BIBLE STUDY
LESSON SIX - QUESTIONS 106-125
(INCLUDES QUESTIONS REFERENCING
"NOTHING BY CHANCE/CHAPTER FIVE/1845-1852)

Thank you for sticking with the Bible study that accompanies the novel. I hope you are being blessed both by your time in God's Word and by the story that is unfolding. In the chapter you just read, you were taken from the morning milking to the marriage of Esther to Emanuel. Let's get started. This one may be shorter.

106) Please read Isaiah 54 and jot down why you think the author chose to put this passage for those reading her novel.

107) Comment on Esther's statement and paragraph that begins: "How pitiful my heirs, if life brings us across 'men' who stopped along the road to manhood, 'men' who by choice settled to be less than their Creator intended..." What keeps sons from manliness?

108) Compare I Corinthians 13:11 (NASB: *When I was a child, I used to speak as a child, think as a child, reason as a child; when I became a man, I did away with childish things.*) with Esther's comments regarding the consequences of the trip to London for Edric and for Emanuel.

109) What were some of the consequences of the trip to London? Which had the most difficult consequences to face? Explain.

110) How did Emanuel's attitude change regarding manhood?

111) Why do you suspect Sir's wife feels so awkward talking to Emanuel?

112) Discuss Sir's gift to Emanuel and the consequences when Emanuel brings that gift to Aunt Gertrude's and Uncle Ned's.

113) Why had Emanuel opted to go to his aunt and uncle's rather than London and what does it tell us about his moving toward manhood?

114) Comment on attitudes toward the Irish famine. Are there similarities to what we hear today regarding people without food?

115) Describe the kind of marriage Aunt Emma desired for Esther and why it might have surprised Esther.

116) Esther seems eager to pursue marriage, an expectation for the Copsey household and young women in the 1840's and 1850's. While her beau meets her father's expectations, describe what broke off the relationship. Does your faith require demonstrations of sincerity? How should faith influence dating and marriage?

117) Esther's understanding about worshipping God was changing. Why? Compare her ideas to II Corinthians 5:17.

118) According to a study regarding US church attendance, it's estimated that on a given Sunday less than 20 percent of the population would be in church, though if answering a telephone survey, 40 percent would say they are regular church attenders.

A) I've heard statistics claiming 80% of those invited would go, but only 2% of church attenders invite non-attenders to church. Why do you think few invite others? Would you think it is most likely because of an unbelief in Jesus' message of the need to be born again or because of the lack of love for a neighbor's eternal destination?

B) My husband was only months from his ordination when he realized he did not have a relationship with Jesus Christ as Savior. He'd grown up going to everything his church offered except the women's meetings. Charles Wesley was a missionary and then became converted. Sacrificial living, faithful church attendance, even preaching, does not guarantee eternal life in heaven. How do you explain Esther's being able to sit in her cathedral but not having a personal relationship with Jesus Christ, a change in her eternal destination?

.
119) Read again the preacher's verses provided at the meeting Esther and her wealthier beau attended. Which of those speak most intimately to you about how to have a relationship with God the Father through faith in Jesus Christ? How does your faith in Jesus Christ as Savior and Lord make your life different?

120) Think about the story so far and answer these questions. What of Esther's past did she give up by coming into a personal relationship with Jesus Christ? What of her present? Of her future?

121) Spend time quietly conversing with the Lord and answer this – is there anything, anyone, you would not give up if the Lord "required" that of you?

Today brothers and sisters around the world are giving up everything, including their lives, their children, their spouses, their freedom, just to remain faithful as a Christ-follower. As you watch the horrific details on the news, pray for them as you would if they were your family...or as you'd want others to pray for you if it were happening to you. (Hebrews 13:3)

122) How did faith become personal for you? How do you know it's real? Share your thoughts with the group and perhaps the scriptures or the circumstances that changed your eternal destination.

123) Why did Aunt Gertrude decide to take Levi and Sallie to America? How did Esther build up Emanuel's self-esteem?

124) Read Hebrews 9:27. How does that strengthen Esther's claim, "Life's a good and precious gift, and one for which we give account"?

125) What is one thing you can do this week to help your local church reach out to those who have not yet come into a relationship with Jesus Christ? How will you hold yourself accountable for doing that one thing?

Prayer
Father God, thank You for the joys You bring into our lives, the romance, the humor, the just plain fun. It is easy to thank You for those things and it is easy to see that You are good when our lives are being lived that way.

But, Father, thank You for the things that seem bad to us, too, because sometimes we cannot realize how those uncomfortable, unwanted moments or months or years are working out something within us that will honor You in deeper ways than if we had walked always on the easy road. We know that You know what would have happened if those difficult moments had not gone the way they did and we trust You to always be loving and good toward us.

Thank You for every good person who has aided us and for every opportunity we have taken to aid others. Thank You for every person who has tried our character, and even when we have been found wanting, thank You that it was Your opportunity for us to grow in a greater likeness to Your Sinless Son.

Examine us, O Lord, to see if there is a root of bitterness within us. Help us to remove all bitterness from our minds and lives, and once bitterness is removed, to enjoy so thoroughly the new freedom we have without it that we are not tempted to wander back to look for opportunities to nurse what needed to be uprooted.

And, Most Gracious Heavenly Father, if we are still holding onto a claim to protect our stubborn pride, if we are still refusing to humbly admit our lost-ness apart from You, break our hearts until we open them to You for Your abiding presence and control. Without the blood of Jesus Christ cleansing us from all records of our unrighteousness, we are headed for an eternity without You, a literal hell.

Thank You for allowing Jesus Christ to come into our world, and for allowing me to learn about His sacrifice on the cross because I, even today, have sinned and cannot present myself spotless before You.

Please forgive me for every sin I have committed in word, in thought, in deed, and in neglecting to do what I knew You wanted me to do. May Your Spirit so live within me that my life will make a difference for You and to others for Christ's sake, not my own.

In Jesus' soul-cleansing name, my Savior, Redeemer and Master, Amen.

CHAPTER SIX

EAST END

AND

EMPTY

CRADLES

1852-1858

CHAPTER SIX
EAST END
AND
EMPTY CRADLES
(1852-1858)

Who shall separate us from the love of Christ? Shall tribulation, distress, persecution, famine, nakedness, peril, or sword? ... Nay, in all these things we are more than conquerors through Him that loved us. I am persuaded that nothing - death, life, angels, principalities, powers, things now or to come, height, depth, nor any other creature, shall be able to separate us from God's love, which is Christ Jesus our Lord.

My memorization by heart of King James' Romans 8

Thursday, March 11, 1880 A.D.

Dear Loved Ones, many plans we make for our lives do not come to pass 'cause of interruptions. Yesterday, and 1853 – 1858 A.D., had 'interruptions.' I've made peace with interruptions. Interruptions are the 'now' in life, and sometimes the 'therefore'.

Life often goes not as hoped or planned, but as interrupted. God allows interruptions and things after interruptions don't saprize God either. Most of my life's had interruptions. Perhaps that's true for you, too?

Sometimes it seems we was called to answer all Romans 8's questions ourselves. What could separate us from God's love? Can this hard time, or this? This I can say: 'Cause the Lord's walked hard times with me, though sometimes He and I both knowed I wasn't eager to leave some hardships when He bid me journey on with Him, and He knowed I'd wallowed longer had He not gently lifted me, I've seen in most things, though perhaps not all yet, that God moves to make benefit come from what we've borne. I hope my learning from what life set on our plate can help others. Hardship came not to leave me barren and unfruitful. Like I writ 'fore, disappointments, sadness, heartaches, or shame can get strangle holts, forcing us to pick at problems till they fester and grow worse. Trusting God's faithfulness more freed me to see Him offering help in difficulties.

Think with me on this: If three, no, four things, Poverty, Illness, Death, and War, was forbidden, how would life be? 'Magine. Take time to long for such. Think on it.

So, maybe I, we, need reminders that selfishness and bitterness is often nourishing roots of times and things we really ought to learn to go on without. God doesn't owe us an easy life here on earth, does He? Can't we trust Him who strew out the stars and sun at just the right places? And what does our gratitude to Him for daily blessings look like?

Won't that life be Heavenly Paradise? Believing such helps now, and helped immeasureably during sufferings. One hard time was when my beloved brother James died in 1853.

There would be other deep sorrows ahet. 'Tis good man's simple, simple understanding is not the last word 'bout things.

Hard work don't solve everything. Apart from miracles, when two ends cannot meet, they will not meet no matter how hard's the pulling. We pulled till strength was gone, and trusted Almighty God, too. Two may live cheaper than one, but surviving costs something. Top o' that, soon I was carrying our child. 'Bout the time Sarah and Henry, also making hard decisions, up and left to farmlands near Henry's kin in Michigan, US (United States), we knowed we was likely headed for Canning Town's cheap quarters. First though, 'bout Sarah's famly.

Through this time, French, Scots, and some Englishmen was settling in Her Majesty's Canadian and Maritime Provinces. More and more Brits instead chose the independent US, leaving monarchy rule and all.

Henry's US people writ of nearby farming opportunities. For sure, Henry preferred farming over foundry work. He'd saved a little and they broke free to go. Our famlys felt lonely heartsickness, but we hoped for them, like being glad 'least somebody got out 'live from fire or flood. Sister Sarah was my dearest friend, apart from Manuel, o'course, and, outside famly, Henry was Manuel's best friend. Oh, the good times we'd shared when we had scarcely anything else to share! They hoped we'd go, too. We was pulled that way, but o'course we had neither money nor circumstances permitting such.

Sarah appreciated my saying I'd tend her daughter's gravesite. Leaving children buried faraway from parents would be, I thought, the hardest part of going. I cautioned Sarah 'bout spoiling Thomas Edward, 'Edward' to us, but Sarah tolt me, 'Esther, a mother's not spoiling or worshiping children when she's loving them. She's acknowledging God's gift. Only God knows how long 'fore He takes one or t'other to be with Him, so I'll love my children along as I can.' Sarah had ways of saying things that fit just right into my heart.

My parents was aging and couldn't go along if they'd wanted. They no longer saw those States as prideful rebels. Englanders 'parently liked places freer from poverty and disease. Father knowed US cotton helped England's textile factories. Years later, though, Father refused dock work when slavery's tobacco and cotton products was shipped. Just remember that.

Tobacco. I 'most forgot tobacco, likely 'cause I'd like to. Somewhere Manuel started using a little, not often, but tobacco could make him want more. His famly prob'ly never knowed he used it. My family detested tobacco as much as Queen Victoria did. Tobacco users at Westminster was sent to a far off room in her palace.

For us, tobacco was the weed curse if ever there was one! We'd be watering down food, scrimping to pay shelter, and Manuel'd get his 'tobacco pull.' Only real arguments we had was over tobacco. 'Twasn't really much argument 'cause he hated tobacco's hard pull on him. I can't really say the smell bothered me, 'cause truth be tolt, London had so many worse smells. But I to this day think tobacco gave us earaches and colds and gave Manuel his little cough I'd hear. Someways his cough sounded like mine workers' coughs. But lots of Londoners had coughs. Manuel didn't use tobacco much. If he couldn't get it or I argued against it, he'd holt off smokings. Manuel was good, but if there's one thing I'd change, it'd be that he'd never tasted tobacco. I s'pose he'd change things so he'd read and write.

Well, I've put off telling life's hard parts in England. I'll get this down and move forward. Would I wish our lives unfolded differently? My heart knows lessons was prepared properly, coming as I was ready even though I thought I couldn't be. Does joy or sorrow weigh less in a fancy house than in a poor house? When a child's hungry, does the plate's fineness matter? Slowly I'd be learning life's more than joy or sorrow, poverty or wealth. We had our place to holt and far as I knowed we did that for you even when 'twas hard to keep standing.

I'll put down this part, hoping when life gives you hard times you'll know you'll get beyond them. I'd like to spare you heartaches, but life passes them 'round to 'most everybody, and likely for a greater good. Though I've had my share, I'd not wish them on others. My heartaches, once I got distance 'tween them and me, reminded me Father God gave me His special comfort. Sometimes others' comfort just isn't suitable. A broken heart's simply broken. Only God and Time fix it back to working order. We, too, likely say things that don't sit right with others, even though we'd hoped to be helpful. The lesson I take is this: Be charitable toward others; few set out to speak cruelty when they come to help with burden bearing.

When we couldn't prevent it, we put ourselves in Canning Town. 'Twas a bad place. I was ashamed to be there. Canning Town sprung up on marshland 'cause more railroads, once they agreed to use tracks the same size, was transporting products and people to London's nearby docks. Labourers swarmed in 'cause London refused tolerating urine using and animal rend'ring factories. Find one who'd think rendert animals mingled with waste was refreshing! Many of us writ our names on paper to tell Queen Victoria we was dying there. One time Parliament thought their good deed was dumping tons of something to cover cesspit smells, but could o' been more refuse for all the relief we got.

For years Canning Town went unnoticed by Queen Victoria and Prince Albert. They was busy with children, and top o'that, the Crimean War had started over arguments 'bout who'd protect the Bible's holy sites. You might as well know, I cannot tolerate such wars. Countries fighting to preserve holy places but ignoring Jesus, the Peace Maker! Someday everyone will see Him as Heaven sent Peace, but seems unlikely in my lifetime. So we live and die with wars.

The Dickens brothers did us good turns by publishing how bad Canning Town was. But change threatens contented people. I'm not fond of having misery ignored while Big-wigs gather people more interested in sipping tea and eating crumpets than hearing us poor people. I've never wanted pity, just fairness. We was taxed same as t'others. Patience is a virtue. Canning Town was one of God's workbenches for surfacing virtues – when we'd let Him.

Canning Town's 'streets' was lower than both the nearby Thames and Lee Rivers. Mud ruts went 'round our miserable little drafty lodgings. Can't call them homes. Home's a sacred word. Canning Town had little sacredness. Wheeled vehicles rarely progressed there though we knowed some tried, for the entire time we endured life there, deep ruts remained. Only crime was deeper than our ruts.

The intolerable 'town' had people crammed into horrid buildings 'round open human waste pits. Sometimes two and more *fam*lys doubled up to pay rent for one unfit hovel. Everyday the stench of death, decay, disease, dust, and everything's dung filled our nostrils. London was crowded, and a shelter's better than street living for rain and cold winds. We was better than some, but we wasn't far from the street.

We lived right at New Road and New Street, more 'new' than 'street' or 'road,' close to London Hospital and Whitechapel Road. Having a hospital nearby seemed hopeful, but it got terribly criticized for patient treatment. When carrying babies was going wrong, they was no help.

The physician tending to Canning Town sympathized with all struggling to survive. When disease took people, what with rarely having clean water and cesspits overflowing from our buckets or pipes of human waste, what hope did we dare keep for health and cleanliness? Till hope and clean water was gone, most wanted cleanliness. Food was scarce.

In Canning Town rags was worn and food was ate that ought to been throwed away, but nothing was throwed away but what ought to of been kept, things that would of helped people survive, even good will toward t'other. I think if we'd not fled for America, we'd all died there.

Faith was still important to a remnant. A few clergy tried living there, but most left 'cause of no pay. Appreciation don't fill plates. Even God-fearing people need food if 'tis not time for God's homeward call, even perhaps much as they'd like to give up and just go.

We got along best we could. Many in the area became among creation's worst of what happens when the good God intended's gone, but for the decent others, life just kept us down. We tried to live honourably, but we smelt like wet middens most of the time.

Except for dry spells, Manuel's shoes and breeches was mud to his knee and any good left in his handed down mackintosh stayed only 'cause it couldn't escape, but it faithfully kept him dry most days he wore it. He helped build the Iron Works factory, but he liked the work up Whitechapel Road best, and going there was easier most days. He worked both places 'cause he was good at working metal and better yet at taking instructions from a boss, and best at striving to provide.

But sadder than wet middens and leaky huts was that I'd bear children in Canning Town. Our precious daughter never took a breath when I delivered her. I had help but she didn't move atall. I never, ever, heard that beautiful, tiny child's voice, and oh how I wished I'd heard 'least one whimper or cry as my reward for birthing her. Silence at the wrong time speaks too loudly in the memories chambers of my mind. I s'pose she came too frail to survive. She was just 'Kisbey infant' to the record place, but in my heart she was Sarah. I missed my sister so, and espeshly that day. She'd understood how I felt. First my heart broke, which didn't frighten me. Then it, or something else, started blaming me, like we chose such condishions. But what could we of done differently?

Within hours, looking for reasons, I got angry. Mother, Father, and Aunt Emma helped us prepare her tiny body, along with their kind pastor, but words couldn't touch the ache I felt. Some things I hardly recall.

In time I saw my anger was selfish, for thousands of women had lost a child. Where we lived was no place for a delicate child. It'd been tempting to decide when life don't seem fair or easy, 'tis not worth keeping. Such thoughts is against Sovereign God. I couldn't know what He'd spared Sarah from. Many others knowed child deaths, and they'd gone on.

'Fore long we was healing up and I was expecting our son George. He came healthy and strong and we was sure if he had half a chance, he'd grow to be a good man like Manuel. His hair started out black, but he lost that in a few weeks and it turned brown like Manuel's. Manuel worked long hours but I never doubted he loved us both. When he'd come home weary and see little George's smile, why, he said 'twas the best feeling a man gets.

Little George stole my parents' lonely hearts, too. They missed Sarah's Edward who'd been 'bout school age then. Mrs. Kisbey enjoyed our visits, too, and hoped we'd birth other babies soon. The Kisbeys always smiled to hear of more babies coming and saw each as God's blessing. I think my parents thought children was a blessing, but maybe they practiced contentment with fewer blessings! No, my parents loved each of us but God for some reason kept their *famly* small.

Then in 1855 our boy got cholera as it slunk through Canning Town, or maybe 'twas some other illness. Don't matter. Oh, my poor little George! His bowels was loose one day and we knowed that was a warning. Babies get loose bowels but not like he got. And fevered! My, such fussing from one who'd been so cheerful. His little eyes begged we fix his troubles, but what could be done except keep holting him day and night, whispering and humming, and o'course praying, praying, praying?

Manuel sat up with us two nights. We both knowed 'twas going bad. I got nearly hysterical when we watched him lose his struggle for his last breath.

Manuel said later he wasn't sure whether little George was fighting death or fighting life so he could go to Heaven where he'd be done with struggles. I almost wished he'd tolt me that then, but sometimes a person don't know whether to speak his thinking. Manuel prayed a lot. Maybe that was God's words to his mind.

Neighbors heard me carry on I'm sure, but 'twas night, and 'sides that, none dared risk getting what'd brought death to our place. I know sometimes when we'd heard sad souls carry on in Canning Town's blackness, and we'd had our George, we thought prayer was the only thing we dared do, for if we went to the griever we'd likely bring back what took life. 'Twas a hard place to be.

Out of respect for little George, we watched his body two days to my parents' where their white shade showed we was grief-struck. 'Twas unlikely cholera'd skipped us if we'd had better circumstances. London had sickness all over. Now I accept we don't pick the number for our days, but for a long time, I tried figuring why a loving God would even let a life start if 'twas to be over as a vapor.

But a sad mama wants people saying right things. Someone said I was young, that we'd birth children to replace the ones we lost. Replace? We'd not broke a teacup!

Another was certain God took our children 'cause He needed them more than us. I remember wond'ring how they knowed such things. I remember Manuel firmly tolt someone illness took little George. We wasn't sure 'bout God's part.

God wants all of us to come to Him, but I thought if God wanted our little ones, why'd He bother telling someone else and not us parents? Manuel thought respect callers meant well. They didn't know how to say words sad people needed. I grew tired of listening, espeshly when the 'respect' part seemed to be thin.

O'course thoughts begged position as we rode to the burial that cold afternoon. The vicar's words 'bout resurrection and heavenly reunions brought measured comfort, but I nearly squeezed Emanuel's arm in two as the little coffin was lowered and clods of cold earth struck with thuds I'd remember no matter how determined I'd be to forget them. I knowed 'twas improper, but I wanted to open the box and put in more blankets, but o'course I didn't. At the time I thought burying my babies was the hardest thing I'd bear, but I had Manuel and our famlys to care 'bout me, 'bout us.

After the lowering, I refused to leave. Manuel helt me and gently whispered, 'My Sweet, Sweet Ester, 'tis time we go now.' I tolt him I couldn't, I was little George's Mama and I needed to stay by my baby boy. Then Manuel whispered, 'Ester, yer not the one watchin' o'er 'ur little ones now.' I sobbed out, 'But I want to be the one!' And o'course we just stood huddled, sobbing for a time.

Aunt Emma came over, standing close, putting her arm on my back. In a bit she asked if she could do anything. I tolt her I couldn't leave, that I just lacked the courage to go. Aunt Emma said in a soft stern way, 'Esther, you think you don't have what you need to go from here, but you do. You just don't want to use it.'

Seeing that written now I think others might judge her harsh to speak such, but, you know, it touched me. How many times 'fore, and in life since I've thought, 'I can't do this' or 'I don't have patience to do that' or 'I don't have strength to bear such and such' or worst, 'I don't have enough faith to believe this is good'? But Aunt Emma spoke right. And I'd tell it to you my precious ones, too. God does give what we need for the next step.

Yes, lots of steps is hard steps to take, 'cause 'parently lots of life has to be hard for our good, but He's there walking ahet of us all the way. God seems to just give us what we need for that moment, or that step. Sometimes 'tis courage we need. He'll companion us throughout life. His pity and His Word does soothe sorrows. I suspicion 'twas hard, too, for God when His own Son left Heaven, even harder when He was unjustly beaten and killed. But God got Jesus back. Now I, too, look forward to reunions there. Sorrow's just hard on a person, seems to me.

Somehow I reminded myself I'd loved little Sarah no less when we'd buried her nearly two years 'fore. George I'd just loved longer. Not more. My fierce mother love tolerated no favorites. I'd not want that guilt. I'd left Sarah, my precious firstborn. I must leave George as well. Swallowing tears burning my raw throat, I followed Emanuel's lead to a draped horse-drawn carriage for our trip back to my parents' home.

After a few hours we was back in Canning Town. Much as I'd resented it, I was relieved to be behind our door, away from some respect callers, some strangers, some distraught, some stoic. None parents to George. Some who passed cards with corners turned seemed to judge us, maybe by our clothes or after finding out where we lived, thinking we brought on death ourselves. None said that o'course, and in charity now I likely just judged them wrong, but I wanted to be just us, George's sad lonesome parents.

My tears soaked Manuel's coat. I wasn't reserved and well, English. We helt each other so closely I wondert if we'd breathe. I pushed against all the sorrow imprisoning me, and when my grip of Manuel was spent, I wailed so loudly it surely troubled Manuel, for it frightened me. My sorrow had to go somewhere or I'd die.

Manuel helped me ready for bed, so quietly tender he was. I thought I'd surely sleep. We'd kept vigil those nights of hoping for life and having it taken anyhow, then days preparing and watching 'fore burying. Manuel gently kissed me, pulling up my covering. But in carrying away the candle, it mockingly cast the shadow of little George's bed upon our wall, and the truth of never holting George again struck me hard.

Would my mind break, too? Did other mothers ache as I ached? All I'd longed to be was wife and mother and I doubted settling for one would be enough. I fought against thinking of our lonely little ones in the cold earth. I wished I'd asked if my children's souls was now in Jesus' loving arms, or would they wait years till God called all His children home? I remember begging silently, 'Call me, Lord Jesus, to care for my children.' I wondert what Manuel'd think if he knowed my prayer.

Manuel didn't know how to comfort me. Was this sorrow a plague forever plotting to ravage me? My arms was empty. Love spends us. Would I withholt love for a new child, lest it die soon? Was we to be childless? Twice we'd stood 'round small coffins and open graves.

Grief demands its time, too. The best comfort don't come from people. Pity people, I say, who don't find God's comfort.

Nights I ached, I'd turn from Manuel, hoping he'd sleep. But he'd gently tug my shoulder, and I'd turn. He'd holt me till I was sobbed out. He'd quietly tell me, 'Esta, I know 'tis hard, but I still has ta believe God cain be trusted.' I'd hear Manuel, 'cause we was in life together.

'I know 'tis hard, but I still has ta believe God cain be trusted.' That became Manuel's gift to me. I thought hard on his words, telling myself they was true even if believing was hard. Hear it again: God can be trusted. Many times in life, forced to face what I didn't want to face, I've tolt myself, 'Remember what Manuel said, Esther.' I suspicion it helps 'cause my soul knows 'tis true. It spites the adversary, too.

Burying our children tested Manuel as a husband. He hurt too. But he was my protector and he wanted to stop my pain just right. For being 'bout twenty-five, he was a good comforter. God chose Manuel for me knowing how I'd ache those years. Sometimes my good husband's warm tears fell on me, long after the burials. We had some long nights. I don't know how he worked his hard job, but he did.

Well, yes, I reckon I know. He trusted God.

One day Manuel tolt me he figured he'd only helt little George 'bout five hundred hours. He broke down that day. 'Twas my turn to comfort Manuel. I didn't know how he figured, but I realized how generous God is to mothers.

Would I risk carrying, birthing, and losing children again? A mother's sadness bears woes only mothers know. My arms, my days, ached for my babies. God has mothers loving children 'fore their first move within. Fathers can't love children into living like God designed mothers to.

I'd do that loving again. And when Manuel was with his children they'd be loved, and for a time, even more freely than I could.

When Jonathan Levi arrived the last day of February 1857, Manuel said he'd be 'round so much I'd tire of him. He worked, o'course, for Manuel took husband responsibilities to heart. He talked lots to Jonathan Levi, often saying 'Papa' and 'Mama,' but I teased him he was training for 'Papa' most. He smiled his Manuel smile.

Some nights when I nursed Jonathan, Manuel sat up, too. We'd talk softly 'bout dreams for our children and then we'd go back to bed, hoping morning wouldn't come 'fore we was ready. I s'pose you Mamas know cuddling babies and locking eyes while nursing is one of woman's tenderest feelings. Memories, too, is God's gift of comfort. God supplied love for each child, though I passed it cautiously for a time.

Truth was, Manuel dreaded twelve hours from us each day. Sometimes hard work has to cover sadness. Other times it keeps famlys 'live. But Manuel worried he was risking Jonathan and me by living in Canning Town. Some was surviving safely, some not.

If we moved, how far could we go? Was the United States as good as people claimed? Levi's letters to Mrs. Kisbey said his job suited him and he'd marry soon. But he knowed reading and numbers. Manuel's sister Sallie, now going by 'Sarah,' had up and married George Fowler, an officer from West Point, US, and military life was suiting them fine. But

Manuel wasn't likely suited for that. He might like horses, but when'd he ever helt a gun?

When we talked of that far away country, I thought of two, well, no, three obstacles for me. Some people don't venture forth 'cause of new things to learn, but that wasn't stopping us. Like money, for instance. We laughed that whether 'twas pounds or dollars, empty pockets is 'nothing.' Sometimes when we faced difficulties, Manuel'd laugh and say, 'Esta, money's the least of our problems, maybe it's the only, but it's the least!'

No, there was serious things to consider. First, I'd buried my children, and my ancestors, in England. Later I saw really they was in Heaven, not England. Another thing, I wasn't espeshly taken with crossing the Atlantic, no matter how large the boat or how many travelers risked life along with us. Some people consider adventure saying, 'If you go, I'll go,' but had they not thought of how far <u>down</u> they might go? Sometimes I wondert if the ocean even had a bottom! And finally, three parents was still part of our lives, and to them we had responsibility. Time passed. Manuel kept working foundry and taking shipments to docks, hoping his work brought home more life than death.

Something comes to mind to put here. Manuel sometimes delivered Mr. Mears' Bell Foundry's shipment dockside, waiting till 'twas properly loaded. He wasn't shy 'bout striking up conversations with people nearby. Espeshly, I s'pose, people like him in life, not fancy dressed. Manuel knowed he was worthy of air same as nice dressers, but he didn't want none thinking he took what they was 'bout to breathe. Anyhow, Manual tolt me of a time he gave his name away. That saprized me 'cause Manuel was very particular 'bout his name being kept honourable. Here's how he tolt me it came 'bout.

When he was quay, or I'll say, dockside, a troubled fellow of color was there, claiming he's 'bout to earn his way working the freighter. Manuel asked, 'Is ye afrate o' the trip acrost?' No, he wasn't afraid. (Pardon readers, I almost writ 'afrate' but I knowed the right spelling, prob'ly 'cause I've been a time or two and God tells me not to be often enough in His Word.)

Anyhow, Manuel saw he was upset, so he asked if the people or work was bothering him. Sometimes people of color had harsher things happen, and Manuel hoped 'twas unnecessary worry. But no, freighter work and people was no worry. So, what's the worry? Well, the fellow says, he wants to stay in Georgia US when he gets there. Manuel, o'course, had US thoughts, too, so Manuel's happy for the fellow.

Finally the worrier says he don't know how people's to call him. And Manuel said, 'How's ye calt now?' And he says, 'Jist George.' Manuel thought George was a good name, but the fellow says he needs more to go with it. So Manuel says, 'Well, ye wanna share my name un be th' first Kisbey in Georgia?', for the freighter was 'bout to go and Manuel wanted the fellow to board.

So the fella says 'Kisbey' a couple times. Then, o'course, he asks how to spell it, but Manuel said, as Kisbeys did, 'Like it sounds.' From the plank, the fella yells, 'Is it a good name?' And Manuel said, 'Has been. Will be if ye keep it so.' And the fella nodded and waved and got to his work on the freighter. There's no way of knowing, so I've no idea whatever came of him but hope he crossed safely and lived well. If someone put down Kisbey, hope he honoured it like Manuel wanted. Manuel thought he was more or less orphaned.

Other people was changing names, too. Emanuel's brother John, not espeshly fond of foundry labour, was a servant by 1851. Maybe he'd been widowed already, but I think he married Mary Turrell later. May not of put that exact. Perhaps Aunt Emma helped Kisbeys either with employment or with courtships one way or t'other. She thought Kisbeys was trustworthy people, so she thought they was due opportunities in life.

So, as Manuel pointed out, if we crossed, there'd be good people looking after English loved ones. I kept considering, figuring I'd likely only cross once. If we bid farewell to people and to England's shores, 'less famly joined us, I'd likely not see them again. Manuel said Christians never really say farewell in God's eternal famly, for one day we'll take time for long visits in mansions along streets of gold. Just 'magine that! Hope you'll arrange to join me there for tea some distant day so we get better acquainted.

My famly's Sarah writ my Copseys that fresh air was free in South Lyons, Michigan, and fertile homesteads was nearly so. Mother and Father rejoiced Williamses had their own farm and a growing famly. They saw how desperate our situation was and wondered if 'twas good reasoning that we'd get ahet by joining Henry and Sarah. Their question relieved us. But being poor, Manuel's earnings was simply meeting demands and Jonathan Levi's needs. He was growing well.

Mrs. Kisbey's letters that came from Illinois tolt things was good for her children, too. She asked if we ever thought it wiser to leave England's hardships and resettle there.

Such talk was encouraging since we'd not spoken our minds. But going was fanciful thinking. Dreams don't need money. Going would.

My confidence in beloved Manuel grew. If he was unsure of hisself, he seldom let me know. Sure, he regretted not reading or writing, but we figured one day Manuel'd learn right along with Jonathan. Manuel'd be busy working till then. If we crossed the Atlantic, my steady, dependable Manuel would protect me best he could. He'd make certain his famly was cared for proper like, for he was husband and father.

Manuel wasn't shy 'bout changes if changes made life better for us. I sometimes worried he worked too hard, but he always took time with Jonathan, who by now eagerly squealed for his Pa and knowed Manuel's voice meant comfort and happiness. We had Jonathan baptized after he was a few months old. On his birth record you see our residence as 2 New Road and New Street in Canning Town of West Ham. That's now quite long ago, but the paper's still good.

Manuel got in good with C. J. Mare at his Iron Works, that later became Thames Iron Works, but espeshly with Mr. Mears of Whitechapel. Manuel learnt the bell factory work 'from dung to ding dong' as he used to say when he humored people 'bout his work. I don't remember the whole process, but sand, soil, and manure from London's streets was needed for bell making, shaping the core and cover between which the metal for the bell would be poured 'fore 'twas baked. When Manuel was first shooed from Aunt's place he took 'bout any work, so he joined t'others dodging carriages to keep London's streets from being barnyards. One use for horse dung was Bell Foundry and Manuel took his cleanings there, which helped lead to his being put on there.

As I understood it, tin and copper is used for bells, and the mixture has to be just right or the bell won't ring pleasant. Every Church of England had 'least one call to worship bell, and bells was used other places too. Some was sent to other countries, even to US. The 'Liberty Bell' my children read 'bout here was made at the Whitechapel foundry, but 'twas the only Whitechapel bell to crack in 400 years which I wished Emanuel knowed during his bell tending! The Liberty Bell was hid for fear it'd be melted for English cannons trying to stop America's independence long ago. You can read that other places. Today my two countries is more famly than enemy, else we'd likely not settled here.

Anyhow, words can be hammered from bells' insides out for reading right. Manuel wouldn't place letters, but he could hammer. So hot metal's poured into molds and baked. Manuel helped there too. Then bells are buried to cool slowly for a few weeks. Finished bells is brittle and very heavy, so they're packed and crated 'fore loading onto lorries bound for docks. Each handler's careful so bells ring right when they get where they need to go.

Emanuel enjoyed the responsibility of preparing the bells Mr. Mears shipped to Canada and to churches along the US St. Lawrence River. He liked watching ships head to new places. Ships generally returned without mishap, though after we'd safely crossed, he tolt of the talk 'bout the 'Montreal' steamer losing hundreds of lives on the St. Lawrence the year 'fore we went. Emanuel stepped onto solid ships weighing tons, being so large he felt small. Whichever ship the bells was on, if 'twas his responsibility, he made certain their crates was well cushioned 'fore departure, sometimes spotting likely stowaways who'd prob'ly be found 'fore tugboats left ships to sail solo 'cross waters to America. Stowaways'd pay fines and be further from a better life. He saw rich and poor who'd found ways to go to Her Majesty's North American Colonies, now Canada, or to the United States. But he'd always stepped off ships, waved to Mr. Mears or t'others traveling with the bells, and slowly turned the team of horses 'round, having hooves on cobblestone drown out the ship's farewell whistle reminding him of his responsibilities and hardships in England.

Sometimes Manuel wondert if we could just visit family and return from America. I saw him getting pulled there more and more, and slowly I was being weaned of England, land of my ancestors, my motherland. Once I'd suggested Manuel go to see if 'twas as good as people said, but he worried Jonathan might forget him 'fore he returned. He wanted his children to know their father. So each time his body stepped off gangways to the quay, wharf to US talkers, and though his mind considered what lay across the vast body of water, he knowed he'd cross only if famly was beside him. He'd not talk me into leaving. We'd both need to agree, and if Providence kept us in England, he'd accept that. Maybe, he said once, if we didn't go, we could send money so our people could visit England. I teased they'd prob'ly get so rich they'd wear out the ships without a shilling from us. Meantime we worked to stay 'live.

I'd taken Jonathan to my parent's cottage yard the morning Father brought Henry's letter. For a brief moment Mother set aside English propriety, which she'd done more often after Manuel joined our family, and responded upon seeing post from Michigan. Father's tone startled us. There was little need to hear the letter. I could read Father's face. Sarah was his firstborn, his longest loved daughter, and he'd already buried James.

'Better read so Esther hears, too,' Father's voice quivered, trying to rein emotions. My heart sank 'fore a word was read. The letter was dreadful.

Henry's letter tolt us Sarah's health and nature was mysteriously declining. Farm was doing well. They had loyal friends. Both Thomas Edward and Adelina was growing. But Sarah's pregnancy was not going well. Doctors was puzzled and had no helpful treatments. Sarah, aware of her frailty, longed for family but travel was forbidden. She hoped we'd consider crossing with little Jonathan.

'Perhaps,' Henry writ, 'a good dose of family love would encourage her getting stronger. Seeing Esther and Emanuel's Jonathan might be good medicine.' Henry admitted 'twas unlikely Sarah's loved ones could come, but as husband, he'd pass along Sarah's request. Dear Sarah's weak writing unmistakably hoped I'd come cheer her up and bring a bit of England if I possibly could. Our little Jonathan's hand wiped at tears on his mama's cheek.

How does one make such a great decision? Sure, we prayed even more than our regular daily prayers. 'Bout three weeks we swayed back and forth with reasons to stay or resettle. I'd only considered going so I'd be near Sarah and farther from hardships. I detested Canning Town's threat to life, but I was Manuel's wife and so far we'd had to stay there. My parents' house was not set right for Manuel's working from there.

Much as Emanuel longed to hurriedly go, he stayed silent. In England he kept us without having to read. Would his not reading work against him in Michigan? Could he, too, maybe get a little farmland to feed us and get us ahet? These questions he wrestled. These and more

I talked with my famly while Manuel worked. Every danger of crossing came to my ears: storms, fires, pirates and more. But if we stayed, if, God forbid, Sarah died without us or 'cause we didn't come, what did England promise us? Many was poor during these hard years. Sure, Manuel's good work was respected by Mr. Mears's foundry and he wasn't afraid of hard work so he'd likely kept at work, but did it satisfy him?

He talked most 'bout outside days, taking shipments to docks. But like most this side of oceans or big decisions, how can a body know what's on t'other side?

Surely Michigan could grant us a better life. But if 'twas only more hardships, would, could, we return? US slavery talk was troubling since 'twas long since removed from Her Majesty's empire. Could slavery stir things up, making life there unsafe? Some place called 'Kansas' kept being writ 'bout. Where was Kansas, and why was it payed so much attention? Would life be safe without monarchy rule like we was used to having? Oh, we pondered many questions as days went by.

Manuel, o'course, could only listen to talk. He didn't like his no-reading or writing found out, but sometimes that couldn't be helped, espeshly when he had to put his X. I'd reminded him he wasn't schooled 'cause life wouldn't let him. I'd taught writing his name, but if he signed legal papers, we feared they'd think he'd read what was above his name, and that was not a thoughtful thing to do.

Another thing bothering me 'bout crossing that I tolt Manuel was, if we started out but couldn't tolerate being on ship, what then? We couldn't just get out and walk back! We was trying to live Christian, but we knowed we wasn't up to walking on water! 'Least not that far!

Oh, my dear ones, we was simple folk. We'd entrust our lives to God's hands whether we stayed or whether we went. Sometimes a body wishes the weighing was over and a person was finding out if the deciding was right. But a person seldom gets 'round weighing and praying, and when things is still foggy, just trusting our loving Heavenly Father to block us if our steps is wrong.

Manuel's eyes couldn't read God's Word, but he had ears. He remembered 'bout Old Testament Gideon. Emanuel figured God knowed Emanuel inside out, as he'd knowed Gideon. Both men was uncertain 'bout what to do. So Emanuel did a fleece prayer heard only by God till he tolt it t'others time and again later. It went something like this, and beloved, I'll write it like my Manuel spoke it so you'll know him more:

'Father God, Thou is all-wise. I'm not. I caint even read Thy book, but in it there's a man named Gideon who dint know w'ot ta do.'

'In the story I heard Gideon tried ta know Yer mind. I'm in a fix 'bout goin' ta 'Merica. But 'tis not news to Thee. Should we go or stay put? Could be we'd git there un our Sarah'll 'ready be with Thee. Then w'ot? Un I dunno which talk's true 'bout 'Merica, is it a land o' conflict or oppertun'ty?'

'I don't wanna test Thee by puttin' my famly in 'arm's way. I dunno know if Esta's up ta leavin' b'hind our little George and Sarah. So, as Thou knowest, there's lots I gist dunno. I'd do as Gideon did, but I got no fleece. So with Thy pa'mission, 'ere's my fleece: First, Esta has ta tell me she'll peacefully leave our little ones. Second, Thou'll 'ave ta pra'vide ship passage. I dunno which is the biggest mir'cle, but if we go, I'll need money fer our new life, or else fer comin' back. So, those be my fleeces un I hope I'm not affendin' Thee by askin'. Thou cainst say 'nay,' un I'll tell Esta we stay. If 'tis 'yea,' I'll find a trunk ta pack. I'm grateful fer Yer leadin' either way, Father, in Jesus' Name, Amen.'

I'd not knowed Manuel's prayer. One day I tolt Manuel God had given me peace 'bout our children not laying cold in England's soil 'cause they was with God now. When I got Manuel's tender hug, he explained his earlier prayer to me. One fleece passed its testing.

Could we afford to go? No. But God could. There was three Mr. Mears. Two asked Emanuel if he'd oversee delivery of their foundry's bells to churches on St. Lawrence River. When Manuel tolt them of Sarah's situation, they kindly bid us go, saying if we returned they'd take Manuel back on.

The trunk's top item 'fore 'twas locked and bound for America was the Williams' letter inside a box from Aunt Emma who'd whispered as she gave her farewell hug that I'd been espeshly blest when Manuel fell in love with me.

Other things we brought was the neckerchief I'd given Manuel one Christmas, o'course the Psalter from James, and the Prince Albert figurine, though we thought we'd keep it tucked away in a new country. And 'cause Manuel's famly's farm helt such good memories for him, he put in a cow's horn he'd kept since his boyhood days. It carried Mother's flower seeds as part of England Sarah'd asked us to bring her, and with enough seed for when we'd possess our own US soil. The trunk helt other things we thought necessary for us and Jonathan to begin a new life near Sarah and Henry.

We'd not miss Canning Town, but we was filled with other emotions 'fore boarding. Manuel showed his emotions more than Copsey me. Most of what was left of both famlys stood along the shore waving farewell, all of us knowing we'd not see each other again in this life. But we'd been prayed over and wished healthier, more profitable lives where we was going. We carried encouragement to Sarah and her famly, hoping we'd get there in time, and hoping 'fore long we'd visit Levi, Sallie, and their mates. When our English loved ones was out of sight, it comforted me knowing we had famly t'other side of the ocean, provided we made it all the way acrost.

Churches ordered what was to be hammered into the bells. Mr. Mears tolt us one read something like, 'Gather to worship God the Father; Depart to proclaim God's Son, Jesus Christ, and let His Holy Spirit be thy Companion withersoever ye go, until ye gather with eternal praises 'round His Holy throne.' 'Twas peaceful knowing our trustworthy God knowed all our withersoevers. The year was 1858.

Monday, if God's willing, I tell of our life in America. Tonight, as I retire, I'll recall shorelines and our hopes for new life ahet, far from all things familiar. Can you hear waves gently slapping, then rippling 'round loved ones and our freighter?

Rippling, rippling, rippling, rippling.

If you wish to skip the Bible study, please skip on ahead.

A NOVEL APPROACH TO BIBLE STUDY
LESSON SEVEN · QUESTIONS 126-148
(INCLUDES QUESTIONS REFERENCING
"EAST END & EMPTY CRADLES"/CHAPTER SIX)
You may want your favorite Bible for this lesson.

126) What was the purpose of your most recent interruption, and how is it helpful to think of interruptions as the 'now' and sometimes the 'therefore' of life?

127) Esther exposes her questioning how God can bring good out of some of life's toughest moments. Comment on these proposals Esther sets forth: "Think with me on this: If three, no, four things, Poverty, Illness, Death, and War, was forbidden, how would life be? 'Magine. Take time to long for such..." What would this week's headlines be if those four things were not a part of people's lives? What "good" do these things bring? When will we be free from those "joy slayers"?

128) Comment on this "Esther thought," "So, maybe I, we, need reminders that selfishness and bitterness put(s) down roots for things we best live without... 'Tis good man's understanding is not the last word 'bout things." What have you recently wanted that wasn't selfish?

129) Many of us relocated during our lives. Some change addresses often, others have the same address throughout their lives. Why do you think it was difficult for Esther to let her sister leave for the United States?

130) Esther made a comment here and later during the Civil War, about tobacco's hold on Emanuel and others. Discuss briefly how an addition in today's society is able to continue its grip on individuals. Rarely do we classify a good habit as an addiction. Often we are told addictions occur because something is missing in our lives or because the addiction feeds a sin that enticed us. Most of us were addiction-free at birth. How sad when not true.

A. Which addictions would you definitely not want to be a part of your life or the lives of your loved ones, and why?

B. Why are destructive addictions difficult to break?

C. Some apply 1st Corinthians 6, verses 19 and 20 to the problem of physical addictions. How would you interpret these verses for your own life?

131) Recently, after sharing about our own "poor year," a young woman said to me, "There is nothing wrong with being poor. I am glad I grew up poor because it made me more resourceful." I think my young friend and Esther could have been an encouragement to each other if they had been neighbors in the 1800s. Perhaps you, too, have harvested benefits from your own tough times. Comment on how important you think it is to share not only our victories while walking with the Lord as Christ-followers, but also the times when our lives are not covering the "happily ever after" portion of life. Do we celebrate victories and verbalize praises to God then?

132) Esther relates some of life's "hard parts." What value does Esther see in difficulties? Please give examples of how she overcame difficulties such as where she lived, loss of loved ones, unexpected benefit of poverty, etc. What role does faith play in handling life's saddest moments? What do you learn from others' examples?

133) If you have been the recipient of comments that were unwelcome during a time of loss, please help others in the group understand what you would like to have been said or left unsaid during that time. If you suffered a loss and someone's behavior, silence, or comments were particularly helpful, please share that with the group. Esther seems to be charitable in that she believes the intentions are generally to be kind, but the timing or words are not always so. Does that help in dealing with those awkward comments or actions?

134) Read 1 Peter chapter 3 in the New Testament, especially verses 8 through 12 and Proverbs 18:13. Comment on the guidelines given for being tenderhearted.

135) Read 2 Corinthians 1, verses 3 through 11, paying special attention to verses 3, 4, and 5. We touched on verses 3-7 earlier, but

have extended the reading. See also Isaiah 55:8 and 9 in the Old Testament.

If you are willing, could you share about a troublesome time you faced that seems to make more sense of it now that there is a little distance between you and that difficult time? There are, however, some "hard things" that we will not understand until we are in the presence of the Lord.

136) In this chapter, we readers are present for the burial of little George, one of Esther's hardest events to that time. Comment on the following two paragraphs:

"After the lowering, I refused to leave. Manuel helt me and gently whispered, 'My Sweet, Sweet Ester, 'tis time we go now.' I tolt him I couldn't, I was little George's Mama. Then Manuel whispered, 'Ester, yer not the one watchin' o'er ur little ones now.' I sobbed out, 'But I want to be the one!' And o'course we just stood huddled, sobbing for a time."

"Aunt Emma came over, standing close, putting her arm on my back. In a bit she asked if she could do anything. I tolt her I couldn't leave, that I just didn't have the courage to go. Aunt Emma said in a soft stern way, 'Esther, you think you don't have the courage to go from here, but you do. You just don't want to use it.'"

Please skim through Esther's conclusion about those paragraphs, then offer your comments.

137) Too frequently, one of the outcomes from the loss of a child is the estrangement of a husband and wife. Generally neither the mother or father, or the sitter they chose, etc. intentionally acted to contribute to the child's death. Even if someone's actions or neglect contributes toward the causes for the death, be careful in uttering words that cannot be pulled back. God's Sovereignty is a consolation, even when we cannot understand the "whys" of life. As for blaming and fault finding, it would be hard to find anyone who perfectly parents or cares for a child, preventing all the falls or exposures to illnesses or situations where a child could be hurt.

Children are "taken" from us in different ways, including illnesses and accidents. Genetics, exposure to chemicals or a disease, an instant of inattentiveness, freak accidents, being "in the wrong place the wrong time," curiosity of a child, and other instances can result in lifelong changes to a child, including even death. Unless the tragedy is the result of intentionally inflicting harm, implying the death is the fault of someone is careless. Before we speak, we would be wise to do unto others as we would have them do unto us (Matthew 7:12).

Words can be forgiven, but some sear so deeply they cannot be forgotten. How tragic when a couple who have loved each other and trusted each other to care for their precious child, decides to blame the other for some "if only" circumstances. Those who were blamed for something that could happen to anyone might never completely erase hasty words even when begged to do so.

Another truth: It is unsound to assume each parent has to grieve the same way in order for the grief to be genuine.

Sometimes it becomes necessary to get outside help/counselors to get through a tragedy, and it is important to take those steps if a death was not by intent. If it were by intent, there are lawyers and courts to handle that. Forgiveness does not always eliminate just, legal consequences.

Now, let's go back to the loss of Esther and Emanuel's children. How similarly/dissimilarly did Esther and Emanuel work through their loss of children in those days? How do their reactions compare to couples grieving today? To your handling of grief?

138) The author employed imagination to explain why Emanuel's last name belongs to American Africans, but the illustration not only exposes readers to the couple's feelings about the value of any other human being, but also about Emanuel's determination to have his surname spoken of honorably. How have you been encouraged, or how do you encourage family members, to bring honor to your name, and, also, to the name of the Lord Jesus Christ?

A. Your name:

B. Lord's name/Christian:

139) The author discovered no way to determine exactly which foundry employed Emanuel, but combining the information and address on Jonathan's birth certificate with an 1858 map of London that revealed their home address also showed their nearness to two foundries. One of those foundries shipped bells to the United States via the St. Lawrence River. Since the author also knew where Esther and Emanuel went their first week in the United States, it was reasonable to select that bell foundry as Emanuel's place of work.

Where we reside, where we go to school or where we work often do have roles in bringing about various circumstances in our lives. Comment on how some common circumstances in your life have been instrumental in producing a major change in your own life and, if appropriate, add advice to those younger than you about seemingly unimportant decisions. Proverbs 16 has lots of advice. Verse 9 could be helpful in reducing anxiety.

140) Is there anything in your life right now that has you uncertain whether or not you dare trust God to work things out His way? If possible, find another person to pray with as you wrestle through the illogical choice of defying an All-Wise, All-Loving and All-Knowing God. Perhaps read together and comment on these "potter" passages from the New American Standard Bible (Feel free to use your own Bible version if you prefer.):

Job 38 through 40: tells the message God spoke to Job and friends. Though this is a long passage, please read it with humility. Perhaps you may remember times you questioned why God did not do things according to the way you wanted things to happen. There are more verses in chapter 40 and other chapters, but these two chapters will give us pause for "thinking too highly" of ourselves. These verses are almost like a "thundering poet" asking a few searching questions and I encourage you to read them now for times when you might be tempted to doubt God's right and wisdom. Here they are in the New American Standard Bible:

(Job 38 through Job 40)

Then the Lord answered Job out of the whirlwind and said, "Who is this that darkens counsel by words without knowledge? Now gird up your loins like a man, and I will ask you, and you instruct Me! Where were you when I laid the foundations of the earth? Tell Me, if you have understanding, who set its measurements, since you know? Or who stretched the line on it? On what were its bases sunk? Or who laid its cornerstone, when the morning stars sang together and all the sons of God shouted for joy?

Or who enclosed the sea with doors, when, bursting forth, it went out from the womb; when I made a cloud its garment, and thick darkness its swaddling band, and I placed boundaries on it, and I set a bolt and doors, and I said, "Thus far you shall come, but no farther; and here shall your proud waves stop"?

Have you ever in your life commanded the morning, and caused the dawn to know its place; that I might take hold of the ends of the earth, and the wicked be shaken out of it? It is changed like clay under the seal' and they stand forth like a garment, and from the wicked their light is withheld, and the uplifted arm is broken.

Have you entered into the springs of the sea? Or have you walked in the recesses of the deep? Have the gates of death been revealed to you? Or have you seen the gates of deep darkness? Have you understood the expanse of the earth? Tell Me, if you know all this.

Where is the way to the dwelling of light? And darkness, where is its place that you may take it to its territory, and that you may discern the paths to its home? You know, for you were born then, and the number of your days is great! Have you entered the storehouses of the snow, or have you seen the storehouses of the hail which I have reserved fro the time of distress, for the day of war and battle? Where is the way that the light is divided, or the eat wind scattered on the earth?

Who has cleft a channel for the flood, or a way for the thunderbolt; to bring rain on a land without people, on a desert without a man in it, to satisfy the waste and desolate land, and to make the seeds of grass to spout? Has the rain a father? Or who has begotten the drops of dew? From whose womb has come the ice? And the frost of heaven, who has given it birth? Water becomes hard like stone and the surface of the deep is imprisoned.

Can you bind the chains of the Pleiades, or loose the cords of Orion? Can you lead forth a constellation in its season, and guide the Bear with her satellites? Do you know the ordinances of the heavens, or fix their rule over the earth?

Can lift up your voice to the clouds, so that an abundance of water may cover you? Can you send forth lightnings that they may go and say to you, 'Here we are'? Who has put wisdom in the innermost being, or has given understanding to the mind? Who can count the clouds by wisdom, or tip the water jars of the heavens, when the dust hardens into a mass, and the clods stick together?

Can you hunt the prey for the lion, or satisfy the appetite of the young lions, when they crouch in their dens, and lie in wait in their lair? Who prepares for the raven its nourishment, when its young cry to God, and wander about without food?

Do you know the time the mountain goats give birth? Do you observe the calving of the deer? Can you count the months they fulfill, or do you know the time they give birth? They kneel down, they bring forth their young, they get rid of their labor pains, their offspring become strong, they grow up in the open field; they leave and do not return to them.

Who sent out the wild donkey free? And who loosed the bonds of the swift donkey, to whom I gave the wilderness for home, and the salt land for his dwelling place? He scorns the tumult of the city, the shoutings of the driver he does not hear. He explores the mountains for his pasture, and he searches after every green thing. Will the wild ox consent to serve you? Or will he spend the night at your manger? Can you bind the wild ox in a furrow with ropes? Or will he harrow the valleys after you? Will you trust him because his strength is great and leave your labor to him? Will you have faith in him that he will return your grain, and gather it from your threshing floor?

The ostriches' wings flap joyously with the pinion and plumage of love, for she abandons her eggs to the earth, and warms them in the dust, and she forgets that a foot may crush them, or that a wild beast may trample them. She treats her young cruelly, as if they were not hers; though her labor be in vain, she is unconcerned; Because God has made her forget wisdom; and has not given her a share of understanding. When she lifts herself on high, she laughs at the horse and his rider.

Do you give the horse his might? Do you clothe his neck with a mane? Do you make him leap like the locust? His majestic snorting is terrible. He paws in the valley, and rejoices in his strength; He goes out to meet the weapons. He laughs at fear and is not dismayed; and he does not turn back from the sword. The quiver rattles against him, the flashing spear and javelin. With shaking and rage he races over the ground; and he does not stand still at the voice of the trump. As often as the trumpet sounds he says, 'Aha!' and he scents the battle from afar; and the thunder of the captains, and the war cry.

Is it by your understanding that the hawk soars, stretching his wings toward the south? Is it at your command that the eagle mounts up, and makes his nest on high? On the cliff he dwells and lodges, upon the rocky crag, and inaccessible place. From there he spies out food; His eyes see it from afar. His young ones also suck up blood; and where the slain are, there is he." Then the Lord said to Job, "Will the faultfinder contend with the Almighty? Let him who reproves God answer it."

Also, this from the New American Standard Bible:

Isaiah 45:9-10: *Woe to the one who quarrels with his Maker – An earthenware vessel among the vessels of the earth! Will the clay say to the potter, 'What are you doing?' Or the thing you are making say, 'He has no hands'? Woe to him who says to a father, 'What are you begetting?' Or to a woman, "To what are you giving birth?"*

Isaiah 64:8: *"But now, O Lord, Thou art our Father, We are the clay, and Thou our potter; and all of us are the work of Thy Hand."*

Jeremiah 18:1-6: *"The word which came to Jeremiah from the Lord saying, "Arise and go down to the potter's house, and there I shall announce My words to you." Then I went down to the potter's house, and there he was, making something on the wheel. But the vessel that he was making of clay was spoiled in the hand of the potter; so he remade it into another vessel, as it pleased the potter to make. Then the word of the Lord came to me saying, "Can I not, O house of Israel, deal with you as this potter does?" declares the Lord. "Behold, like the clay in the potter's hand, so are you in My hand, O house of Israel."*

Romans 9:14-24: *What shall we say then? There is no injustice with God, is there? May it never be! For he says to Moses, "I will have mercy on whom I have mercy, and I will have compassion on whom I have compassion."*

So then it does not depend on the man who wills or the man who runs, but on God who has mercy. For the Scripture says to Pharaoh, "For this very purpose I raised you up, to demonstrate My power in you, and that My name might be proclaimed throughout the whole earth."
So then He has mercy on whom he desires, and He hardens whom He desires.
You will say to me then, "Why does He still find fault? For who resists His will?"
On the contrary, who are you, O man, who answers back to God? The thing molded will not say to the molder, "Why did you make me like this," will it? Or does the potter have a right over clay to make from the same lump one vessel for honorable use, and another for common use?
What if God, although willing to demonstrate His wrath and to make His power known, endured with much patience vessels of wrath prepared for destruction? He did so in order that He might make known the riches of His glory upon vessels of mercy, which He prepared beforehand for glory, even us, whom He also called, not from among Jews only, but also from among Gentiles."

141) Comments or conclusions based on the previous scriptures?

142) Emanuel put out "a fleece" to decide about leaving England. For a quick review of Gideon's hesitancy and then his leadership in Israel, look up Judges 6: 1-16, 36-40 and chapter 7. Some Christian leaders are opposed to putting out "fleeces" in our day since we have much counsel through God's Word (and Gideon would not have had that). In the past, how have you reached a conclusion when you are at a crossroads, unsure of what the Lord would be asking of you?

143) Look up and jot down helpful information from the following verses about discerning God's will for your life:

2 Chronicles 16:9
Proverbs 2:1-8
Proverbs 9:10
Proverbs 11:2, 3
Proverbs 12:15
Matthew 18:14
James 1:5-8
James 4:13-17

A favorite set of verses for many of us is Proverbs 3:5-7 (NASB): *"Trust in the Lord with all your heart and do not lean on your own understanding. In all your ways acknowledge Him, and He will make your paths straight. Do not be wise in your own eyes; Fear the Lord and turn away from evil."*

The Bible also tells us our hearts can be deceitful and wicked and that trusting in our hearts can make us a fool. The surest way I know to have a heart that is pure, is for us to be spending time in fellowship with Christ through the Word and through prayer and through sound teachings based upon the whole counsel of God. That means studying the whole Bible, cover to cover, not just a few favorite verses. Thoughts?

144) Amazingly, God has knit each of us (Psalm 139) together for His creative purposes to live our lives in a time specified by Him. The "why am I here?" question is simple and yet creatively complicated. We were formed to glorify God through faith in Jesus Christ and taking up the tasks assigned to us by the Lord. (Ephesians 2:8-10 is an example declaring this.)

Another Esther, found in the book by her name in the Old Testament, realized she had been born "for such a time as this" after Mordecai urges her not to keep silent about an evil that is going to take place when it could be in her power to change the event.

Mordecai states, "For if you remain silent at this time, relief and deliverance will arise for the Jews from another place and you and your father's house will perish. And who knows whether you have not attained royalty for such a time as this?" (Esther 4:14)

Dear born-again Christ-follower, the blood shed for you made you a child of God, not just one of His creations. As a child of Almighty God, an adopted stray now claimed as family by King over all Creation, which includes what neither the telescope or microscope has yet discovered, you are "royalty" in the kingdom not of this world, but better and eternal, not temporal.

Your loving Father plans to gather you, His blood-bought children, home after you've had time to be His ambassador here on earth. Because of your redemption purchased by His Always Holy Son, Jesus Christ, your Heavenly Father loves to speak to you about whatever concerns you. He invites you to step away from the temporal and come right into His throne room and spend time with Him so you can return to the tasks designed for your impact as His representative.

What would motivate us to attempt to live out the hours of our lives without spending time with the One who designed us? How can you, today, not let that happen?

145) We are people who end up in relationships. Some are as casual as the interaction between us and the clerk at the retail counter. Some are as intense as those with a parent, a best friend, a spouse, a child or other family member.Others are business relationships that we rely upon to pay our bills or to channel our skills and insights. Other relationships occur because of our desire, or God's arrangement, to use our spiritual gifts.

God is preparing us and placing us to be His ambassador, His answer to someone's prayer, His display of Christlikeness to someone needing a blessing. Do we mess up? Of course we do. We're not yet perfectly obedient, but we can keep improving.

Record for someone who might read your notes, or share with others in your group, instances when you realized God had "set you up" to display obedience. Your obedience most likely brought delight to the person to whom you ministered. *Friend, this is not a "look at me or brag time." Some of us may not want to share because we think it sounds like pride, but it could be pride or fear of others' opinions of us that keeps us from sharing how God has worked in our lives. This acknowledgment of usefulness to God is a way to GLORIFY HIM, and to encourage others. It is an "old fashioned testimony time." I hope part of the schedule in Heaven will be listening to the marvelous stories of how God worked in others' lives.* So, go ahead... testify to God's work in our world today by times He prompted you to obedience.

146) How would you counsel a Christ-follower planning to enter into a relationship with a non-Christ follower? How will that relationship shackle the believer's attempts to walk in obedience to the promptings of Christ-follower's "Internal Director/Holy Spirit"? What cautions would you give about the inevitable "blisters" that

will come from unequally yoked partners? (You might like going back to the diagram following question 51.) If someone chooses to ignore God's truths about relationships, what is the source of those promptings? What emotional, spiritual, financial, legal costs might await the person ignoring God's wisdom on being equally yoked?

147) **Micah 6:8** reads: *He has told you, O man, what is good; and what does the Lord require of you but to do justice, to love kindness, and to walk humbly with your God?"*
Comment on how God can use past experiences to bless others He brings across your path. Comment on how you apply Micah 6:8 in your life.

148) Comment on the bell inscription, "Gather to worship God the Father; Depart to proclaim God's Son Jesus Christ, and His Holy Spirit as thy Companion whithersoever ye go, until ye gather with eternal praises around His Holy throne." Does it seem like a reasonable guide for worship and living the Christian life? Does your place of worship still have bells and, if so, when are they used?

Prayer *Father God, You are All-wise, All-knowing, and All-powerful. We cannot out reason You and we ask Your forgiveness when we have vainly thought we knew as much or better than You.*

Father, we confess sometimes we have not liked all the things You allow into our lives. Spare us, we pray, from nurturing bitterness and from "getting stuck" in a sorrow or disappointment.

May our lifetimes make a difference and may the heartaches we feel be useful when we come across others who have experienced similar consequences in their lives.

We love You, our trustworthy God and Father, and we thank You for taking time from Your busy eternity to tailor Your love for us, too. May we bring You honor today. In Jesus' precious name, Amen.

CHAPTER SEVEN

CONSEQUENCES
OF THE
CROSS
TO
SOUTH LYONS
1858-1863

CHAPTER SEVEN

CONSEQUENCES OF THE
CROSS
TO SOUTH LYONS
(1858-1863)

With the merciful Thou wilt shew Thyself merciful, and with the upright man Thou wilt shew Thyself upright. With the pure Thou wilt shew Thyself pure; and with the forward Thou wilt shew Thyself unsavoury. And the afflicted ... Thou wilt save... For Thou art my lamp, O Lord: and the Lord will lighten my darkness... As for God, His way is perfect; the word of the Lord is tried:... For who is God, save the Lord?And who is a rock, save our God? God is my strength and power: and He maketh my way perfect. He maketh my feet like hinds' feet: and setteth me upon my high places. He teacheth my hands to war; so that a bow of steel is broken by mine arms. Thou hast also given me the shield of thy salvation: and thy gentleness hath made me great. Thou hast enlarged my steps under me; so that my feet did not slip.

King James' Holy Bible, Book of II Samuel,
Chapter 22, most from verses 26 on to 38
Monday, March 15, 1880 A.D.

Dear Ones, the last writing took more strength and days than I'd thought. John tolt me Saturday we had a letter to consider. I've almost always welcomed letters. Most always. Anyway, as promised, it's Monday and I'm 'bout the task ahet.

Our steam-driven sailing freighter was certainly not luxury passage for it carried mostly goods to market in America, crates of everything from tea to textiles. But we gratefully made it work. God oversaw so we could go without using the little money we'd saved. We got our 'sea legs' and Manuel used his to check crates, nearly tending to bells as much as to us. Once I made him relax a little by asking him if the bell's needed more biscuits. As he reminded me, he was responsible for brittle bells and though he'd helped pack them, he'd feel relieved when they was bound for steeples and we was on the steamboat for Detroit, Michigan. He hoped for no delay in getting to Henry's.

As the trip progressed, Manuel had other anxiety, too, wond'ring if his not reading would be helt against him and if he'd find good enough work. My anxiety kept me from moving on ship much, keeping Jonathan and me far from the railing so we'd not measure the ocean's depths. Least we was not going 'round lower America like some did. Little Jonathan did well, napping as the ship rocked us back and forth. Jonathan had no seasickness. We both did. Manuel's got better by seeing lands we passed, like lush New Brunswick Province and then on in along what's now called the Dominion of Canada. Emanuel's siblings had took a different route and saw the Province of Nova Scotia, where some other Kisbeys settled if I recall. We rode in a canal or two as well, and since these didn't rock us as on the ocean, I became suspicious my seasickness might last months longer than the crossing.

What joy we felt when the crew tolt us we was nearing the port city way north, called Quebec, part of Her Majesty's province of Quebec. Then we'd travel most of another week down the river and through Lake Ontario and Lake Eric to Detroit. We'd been on the freighter nearly four weeks as I recall, long enough for water in barrels to lose appeal. I looked out toward docks and solid ground. Manuel looked up and down for marks on bell crates. He was eager to get word back to Mr. Mears that all went well. He rejoined us as the crew prepared for docking.

I had mixed emotions, sad I'd not see English loved ones, thankful we'd stayed topside of the ocean, fearful 'bout how Sarah was. I remember once whispering to Manuel, 'Within a week we'll be at...,' but I couldn't say Sarah's name. Sometimes when emotions threatened, I'd press my tongue hard against the roof of my mouth. It stops tears and sobs. Why do we 'proper' English want to act like nothing touches our hearts?

Truth be tolt, heart expressions came out more the longer I knowed Manuel. Reckon he was safe to be with that way. That trip was such a time.

Manuel put his arm 'round me. Didn't matter to him if t'others saw us. I tried thinking, 'We're not in England, so what difference does it make?' He'd seen my lip trembling. He gently wrapped me and Jonathan inside his arms and I felt his lungs pull in American air. 'Twas not Michigan air yet, but we was getting closer. He'd thought 'bout America 'least since Edric read 'bout it from *The Penny Magazine*, and more when Levi and Sarah left six years 'fore. Soon he'd step on its soil. Manuel was ready to strike out and be in open spaces. Ships was too small for the likes of him.

Manuel pecked our foreheads. He, as husband and father, wanted us to be at peace. When I asked him what he was thinking, didn't saprize me he'd just thanked God for blessing him with his little *fam*ly and for all God was going to do as we started this new life. His eyes was smiling so. The way we was standing made Jonathan try to wiggle into a new position. He'd like rocking on the ship and he wanted more of his morning nap. We was a touching picture t'others I 'magine.

I felt Manuel kind of shake his head and look away, fighting tears and not telling me what was wrong. Finally he whispered 'bout what might of been, how he could of had three little ones stepping onto this new land. Our tears fell. I knowed Manuel would stay as close to us as he could for as long as he could and that any burying we might do would pain us both. I hoped all our children would honour the love he'd holt for them and me. Aunt Emma had wisely warned me not to miss having what I found with Manuel. His tenderness 'bout famly was genuine, and the highest praise a *fam*ly can feel, to my way of thinking.

So there we huddled, Jonathan snuggled against Manuel's chest while we parents looked south toward the United States. Manuel's plain trunk and a leather sack lay to our feet, holting all but the hopes we figured we'd need in our venture. If I was a good sketcher or sculptor, like those who'd displayed at Crystal Palace in 1851 A.D. 'fore we was married, I'd display us sculptured somewhere.

Or someone could fix us praying, for that we did too. Manuel's voice was unsteady, his head uncovered. Manuel would not take another step without talking with Almighty God. I remember 'twas like Moses' prayer 'bout going no further without knowing God was taking us. Then he prayed 'cause sometimes memories of England was likely to strike us, even when having joyful times. But we had Sarah to pray 'bout, too. He thanked God again 'bout providing our crossing and God's peace when we'd started out. But right then, he requested peace again, and Manuel wanted it 'fore we stepped ashore to new life and new tasks. So we stood there waiting.

I felt other poor and crew stirring 'round us pretty much reverently. We just waited for God's presence and peace. This was our first church service in America.

And it started coming. I got the sweetest picture in my mind. 'Manuel,' I whispered, 'Can you 'magine our babies in Jesus' arms? They're safe and loved, being helt like you're holting us. Can you see them too?' Forever after when I thought of our little ones, I'd see them resting contentedly, satisfied, and at peace, or little George with his smile toddling along holting Jesus' hand. I remember I whispered, 'They don't need to be here with us, Emanuel. We're still *fam*ly, but we wouldn't want to call them back to this world, would we?'

Manuel thought 'bout how no matter how much better our new life was to be, life was just bound to expose us to pain and difficulties, 'cause as he said from time to time, 'Life's just life, and earth just isn't Heaven.' He whispered, "Member how the clergyman sed Heav'n was the reward fer God's people? Thin' on it, Esta. Quite a few loved ones is enjoyin' Heaven by now.'

We talked 'bout how Heaven had no epidemics, how weather was perfect, no troubles, no tears. Manuel figured it smelled like spring with fragrant flowers and quiet waters. We had no gold here, but we thought 'bout the gold streets there. Manuel teased wond'ring if I was sure that I'd trade Canning Town's streets for Heaven's. As we talked, Manuel said he was almost getting homesick for Heaven, espeshly if we all went together. So I said I was too, but he quickly tolt me I mustn't go 'fore him. We agreed we was to finish what God had for us 'fore either of us departed earth. Manuel tolt me he didn't think he could get along without me. He claimed I talked like a teacher when I said, 'Oh yes you could, Mr. Kisbey. God would see to it. He'd never give you more'n you could bear.' I didn't want to try to 'magine what I could bear.

'Yes, Ma'am, Mis Kisbey, I 'ear ye," he said, eyes holting a slight twinkle again. 'But, my Esta, it's w'ot He might take, more'n w'ot He'd give, that'd bother me. I don't wanna be in a place where I need ta find out 'bout losin' no more.'

Peace was settling deeper. Manuel's voice was stronger as we finished our praying, thanking God for reminders of His love and goodness and wisdom. We requested His help and guidance regardless of what was ahet for us. Manuel always talked 'bout trusting God to do what was best each day, even when we wouldn't understand. He always thought I'd taught him we couldn't see as far down the road as God could. So we finished a 'Walk with us' benediction and slowly our little statue began breaking up. By then people was lined to step ashore.

Manuel helt Jonathan till I'd stepped off. He went back and picked up the trunk and leather sack, then he planted us so he could arrange things for the bell deliveries. Jonathan woke up with all the clanging and strange voices calling to each other and started fussing. I couldn't tend to him right on the spot but I spoke firmly for him to settle down. A businessman heard us and spoke to Jonathan, telling him not to so quickly judge new lands. Jonathan looked as if he was considering that admonition. We agreed he was bright for his age.

Later when Manuel would tell of our first day ashore in North America, he'd say that he was grateful he had two things in his favor: a good memory and a good wife who could read. Manuel had Mr. Mears' papers telling who'd pick up the bell shipments, so I'd read names and information if the delivery wagons was not forthcoming. Cargo unloading took time, so we had a long anxious wait. Thankfully Mr. Mears had prepared us step by step for the process 'cause he'd worked with the company, think 'twas Russell something, several times 'fore.

I had all I could do to stay clear of carriages and nervous horses 'round the docking area. I saw greetings and handshakes. Some people seemed loud and too emotional, to my thinking. Sellers touted goods they claimed we needed to survive beyond the docks. In the busy commotion Emanuel was able to release his cargo to two wagon masters responsible for carefully getting the bells to their destinations.

Manuel'd done his job. Papers was prepared and posted for Mr. Mears after kind gentlemen briefly inspected crates and listened as Emanuel cautioned again 'bout how easily the bells could be damaged if mishandled.

Just as Mr. Mears had commented, both church committees was astounded something so heavy and so costly would be so brittle. They studied assembly instructions which worried Manuel lest they ask what words meant. I kept nearby if he needed my help, but Manuel's explanations did fine. Or maybe they wasn't readers either. At any rate, both committees gave Emanuel a few paper bills and coins. Emanuel tried refusing their offer, saying he was already payed and just doing his job. 'Take it,' they good-naturedly said, 'Money grows on trees 'round here! You'll need it in the United States. Their trees might not be as fruitful!'

Driving off they shouted, 'God bless your life in the United States!' We was closer to being 'home.' But perhaps they was right 'bout the US trees!

We made our way to book passage on the steamboat down to Detroit. We bought fresh bread and a hot meal and found a place for Jonathan to move 'round a bit 'fore we started the five-day trip to reunite us with loved ones in South Lyon, Michigan.

Those five days 'board the steamboat was far more relaxing than the crossing. Knowing the bottom of the river and lakes was lots closer than the bottom of the ocean relieved me. Maybe some day I'd consider a trip back across to see loved ones in our mother country, but I preferred they come to this side of the Atlantic.

Emanuel figured more of his famly might come if good came our way, but truth be tolt, we thought 'twas likely Ma Kisbey's health might continue failing. Plain truth, too, Kisbey famlys would expand and there'd be near blood relations whichever side of the Atlantic they was on, and that seemed good to Manuel. We didn't entirely rule out going back, espeshly if US life turned bad for us, but the further we got from the Atlantic with its seasickness, endless water, cramped condishions, and the challenge of confining a toddler, the less likely returning became.

The steamer had pleasant ways to rest and, though prices was higher than hoped, we finally enjoyed our travel. Many hours was spent helping Jonathan watch the waterwheel's working and the ship's gentle quakes in blue, blue water as we moved along at 'bout two or three miles each hour. Looking back, those days was prob'ly the easiest days and the most privleeched days Manuel and I ever had. I espeshly remember how I loved the fresh, free air. And then, oh, how we thrilled to be tolt 'twas Michigan's shores in the distance.

Punctual Henry Williams stood at the dock to welcome us. Though we was English, we embraced and he and Manuel shared hearty handshakes. Jonathan let us put his hand in his Uncle Henry's but he wasn't convinced yet that he'd found a friend. Henry asked 'bout our trip as he loaded the trunk into the farm wagon. Manuel tolt him, 'A journey's not so bad once it's over.' He and Henry was right back where they'd been in England. Henry teased that the Atlantic ages bodies so he'd worked to make his wagon as comfortable as he could. I got extra hay and blankets though Manuel thought I belonged on the seat next to Henry. But Jonathan was ready to nap and his ma and the hay worked fine for that. We sat so we could talk as we rode along.

Henry apologized 'bout not offering something more in style like he was sure we was used to. O'course he knowed we wasn't. He tolt us he'd had a hard time convincing Sarah not to ride along, she was so anxious to see us.

For 'bout two hours we rumbled along the dusty roads, so different from Canning Town's. I kept from asking 'bout Sarah, though 'twas pressing on my heart. True to Sarah's way, she'd sent food for us. Here's how I remember that ride.

Henry tolt us, 'Sarah sent these bread slices for you, and a few spice cookies you always said you liked. You better tolt the truth 'cause she's made a whole bunch of 'em.' I did, and looked forward to them. Then Henry laughed, 'If you'll keep it quiet, I only pretended to like them the first time she made them. Can't guess how many I've had these past ten years. I don't possess the heart to tell Sarah I could do without them.'

We laughed at memories of Henry's first callings for Sarah. Then we talked of how Henry'd schemed to introduce Emanuel to me. The look Manuel cast my way made me smile.

'Ye was good ta do that fer us,' Emanuel said.

Henry looked tired and worried. His voice was friendly but I knowed my brother-in-law too well to not detect the mask he was wearing. Finally I got the courage to ask, 'Henry, how's Sarah?'

Henry's lips pursed and his brow furled. He kept his eyes straight ahet, his hands tightly gripping reins. He swallowed and sadly shook his head.

'It's bad, isn't it Henry?'

'I wish I could say different, but I can't. Maybe your coming will help. The doctor thinks this baby's too much somehow, or else something else's wrong. The whole time she's carried the child things has not gone right. Doc Howe don't know what to do. He reckons he just has to let nature take its course.'

'Is he a good doctor?'

'Far's we know. Something's just not right. Some days Sarah feels pretty good, some days she can hardly move atall. Days is hard for little Adelina and Thomas Edward.'

'We've come ta 'elp 'owever we cain," Emanuel offered. 'I 'magin ye've not been able ta do as much in th' fields as ye wanted.'

'I'm torn 'bout where to be. If I'm out there, I can't help Sarah. Maybe once the baby comes things'll get better.'

O'course I offered to take over the housework if he thought that'd help.

'You can see for yourself soon enough. She's counting on good times with you both. Here's our lane, and don't be saprized if my Sarah's waiting to greet you.'

'This is yers, 'enry?'

'Yep, provided I can keep it. I make payments o'course, but it's reasonably good for allowing me to do that. Do you like this air better than London's, folks?'

We breathed deeper. 'We need ta bottle it un ship it ta my famly. They'd keep coste'monge's busy sellin' fresh air!'

We pulled up in front of the comfortable home and barnyard, complete with 'Dog' announcing our arrival. As we stepped from the wagon, Sarah opened the door and waved to us. Her two little ones almost hid in her skirts, but Thomas Edward, seeing his daddy, ran to him. I hurried to give Sarah a warm embrace. How good 'twas to see her, but I felt her frailty even though she was swollen with child. Her color was not good. Indoors, when she moved, she went chair to chair. We made over each other's little ones and in no time hers understood who we was to them. Jonathan took longer to warm up. Henry and Manuel was off looking over the farm, leaving us to just be sisters and mothers.

Sarah didn't take long to tell me her heart. She asked me how I'd felt when I carried our little Sarah, espeshly toward the end. I tolt her I'd felt the baby's weak movements until just a couple days 'fore I delivered her.

She tolt me she was almost sure the delivery was going to go bad, but she had more peace 'bout it than her doctor 'cause she trusted God's sovereignty. Then she said, 'Esther, I won't make you promise, but if I should die—' and I stopped her. I tolt her such talk wasn't good, not 'cause talking makes bad happen or 'cause such talk isn't trusting God, but 'cause she needed to be considering things would go right 'fore a baby's born just to help a woman through the painful part. But Sarah gently insisted I hear her and I saw 'twas important I listen.

Sarah hoped if she died I'd see her Henry got help with the children and householt work while he was grieving, for rightly so, she knowed he'd grieve and try to keep trusting God. She'd tolt Henry she thought God was preparing her for coming to Him. She hoped her baby would survive, but if not, and they both died, she was certain she'd done the best she could so her child could be born so God could use life or death as He saw fit. She tolt me she knew 'twasn't her goodness, but her Savior, that'd open Heaven.

I kept saying, 'But maybe things will go better, maybe it's like Abraham and Isaac and this is just a test.' And o'course she said she hoped we'd spend years as neighbors in America, and oh, I wished that was to be. But, as for Abraham's test, she assured me she loved God most.

'Fore we was done talking she made me know habits of her children and things she wanted them to know 'bout her when they got older, how she wanted Christian faith and character stressed, things like that. She'said she'd started a letter to each child so they'd know she loved being their mother, but how if 'twas God's way to take her to Heaven, she'd be getting their rooms ready there. She wanted me to see she finished letters in the next day or so. Her love for Henry made her not want him struggling 'lone, and if he remarried I was to treat his new wife like she was my sister too, and to help the children see was kind if they had a new mother.

All this o'course was hard to hear, but Sarah had a peaceful look once she'd tolt it all. We prayed, her mostly speaking 'cause my words wouldn't voice. We embraced a long moment. How I wished I'd arrived sooner, for her frailty tolt me time was running out.

I helped however I could. I tolt her Copsey news and how glad we was to leave Canning Town. I spent as much time with Sarah as I could. She talked more of Heaven. The weaker she got, the more I wanted to be sure she'd tolt me all she wanted me to know. 'Twas hard when she tolt me names for the child, boy or girl, in case she couldn't name it. Her head was pounding bad as she tolt me she thought Mother and Father would be pleased 'cause she and Henry had picked Bible names our parents would like.

We'd not been there a week when my sister, Sarah Copsey Williams, went to be with our Heavenly Father. Her leaving was hard and dreadful. The doctor helped in her struggle to deliver, but truth be tolt, her Baby Sarah had died sometime 'fore birth. Then my frail sister's pain got worse, and the doctor declared Sarah was still with child. He did his best to bring 'bout a good second delivery, but the baby was turned wrong and Sarah suffered more. When Doc tolt Sarah her boy was alive, the baby heard his mother call him James, after Henry and our good brother James. She barely had strength to holt him atall. Sarah's body suffered too much, and top o'that, a fever set on. We and cool well water couldn't bring it down.

Manuel and Henry knowed of her hoping I'd agree to overseeing the children, not 'bout Henry remarrying o'course, and the men decided Sarah should know we'd stay right there at the house helping as she'd wanted. Sarah was tolt that when fever was taking her life. 'Twas sad hearing her children's crying 'bout their Mama's sickness. They was little so we'd kept them away o'course when the delivery was happening. They tried to understand why their Mama was laying there telling them goodbye, to be good and mind Aunt Esther, and Pa o'course. 'Twas a hard time for all.

When Sarah departed, the doctor was heartbroke too. I suspicion there was no earthly skill to save her. And poor dear Henry, he loved Sarah so, but I knowed he'd almost begged God to take her to Him so her pain and suffering would be over. Then, too, he was wond'ring how he'd ever do without Sarah. Their love for each other had been tender to see, start to finish.

Henry needed time 'lone. Right off, he didn't want to sleep in their room no more, so that became our famly's bedroom, with baby James, too. The preacher helped Henry talk things out and he talked with the children in ways that helped us all.

We had adjustments to make, but life had to go on. Top o' grieving, my mind and time was taken with caring for newborn James, Adelina, Thomas Edward, and our Jonathan, plus fixing for Henry and Manuel. Those days is mostly a fog. I loved Sarah's children nearly like my own and we all comforted them, wanting them to be with Henry when they needed, but not so much as to cause him more pain. Looking back, hard as 'twas, I know 'twas God's timing for us to come to South Lyon. I can't know why 'twas Sarah's time to go, but I trust God nonetheless. Manuel always insisted we trust God no matter what we faced. I figured he'd learnt to trust in harder lessons than my own, till then 'least, and I also knowed he loved those I loved.

After a few weeks, we was certain we'd need a place of our own, for my 'sea sickness' was likely 'cause I was carrying our Emma Jane. That being so, I looked for another housekeeper to do chores I'd find difficult in months ahet. We didn't know people, and Henry wasn't much help, for the men kept busy catching up on farming and putting up winter's wood. His people couldn't take on more. What was we to do? Well, o'course we sought God's wisdom and guidance, like in all things we faced, for our busy Heavenly Father cared 'bout our big or little day-to-day needs.

At a church ladies' meeting I found so many nice women, I thought surely one of those ladies could want housekeeper work, but those with children was busy with their own and those without was fearful 'bout mothering someone else's brood.

Well, thought I, other women delivered babies and raised big famlys, so I'd best accept the necessary tasks 'for such a time as this,' like the Esther I was named after did. This I did for some time, and God supplied my strength, and added humor when needed.

While picking up items in South Lyon, Manuel learnt of a literary circle in nearby Howell, a town where we had dealings from time to time. Manuel said I should attend some afternoon meetings as he knowed I was working the hardest I'd ever worked, and being with child, he wanted me to worry less over concerns. He teased that 'twas better he spend the afternoon in the house, saying he knowed more 'bout what to do with a child making no sense than with words on a paper making no sense either.

The literary circle was like one of Aunt Emma's projects. Sometimes we took turns reading newspapers people brought, giving me more awareness of how the United States was facing situations. Other times a person brought us a letter, a person like Manuel, and we'd read it to them. And in between meetings we was to try to write something to read t'others for suggestions to improve our writing. Once I picked up Manuel's poem to take but decided 'twas just for me. Though it might make some jealous by what it said, I knowed, bless his heart, it'd not holt up to fine writing, and I'd not change his words anyhow. I rarely wrote anything so I was glad they let me just listen.

Being mostly ladies, we visited. The leader was a Scot several years older than me, but we got along well from the start. She'd crossed earlier and had long since adjusted to American ways. She had such a happy way 'bout her that I looked forward to our meetings. She helt them during the day, not 'cause of her children, 'cause she was unmarried. Naturally I'd asked 'bout wanting children and she tolt me she'd drempt of being a wife and mother but never met the right gentleman. She didn't plan to marry and was contentedly thinking she'd become a school teacher soon.

S'pose you can guess how I began working. First I gave an invite to a church doings and slowly let her know I'd appreciate being spared odd jobs so I could keep attending her meetings. I quit attending 'round Emma's birth January 10, 1859. Margaret came a few times to help with children once Emma Jane was needing my care, but all the while I sort of kept her from Henry till I saw how she did in the home and felt I knowed her. Henry was like a good brother to me and I was perticular 'bout who I'd let him meet.

O'course occasionally she'd asked what the poor widower was like who had such a busy householt and I tolt her a little 'bout Henry, just casual like, so she'd not too soon discover my plan. Turned out, I'd liked her as a friend even if nothing else happened, but it pleased me when things moved along.

Finally one day I kept Margaret busy, which wasn't hard with five needing mothering, so she'd be there when Henry and Manuel came for the evening meal. Manuel knowed right away what I was doing, but since Henry'd helped us know each other, Manuel helped my matchmaking, too. 'Fore the end of 1859, Manuel and I was renting another place 'cause we had two little ones to care for and a wedding to attend.

Life was beginning to be good in America. Margaret and I has stayed closest friends all these years and when I delivered Alfred in 1861 A.D., she was one of my midwives. T'other was cheerful Olive Hayes. Margaret and Henry was satisfied without raising more children than the three Sarah bore him. Only people like me know they's not Margaret's own. I think Sarah would be pleased with how I carried out her wishes.

Tuesday, March 16, 1880 A.D.

Loved ones, 'fore I jump ahet too far, I must tell you of Christmas 1859. Last night my householt wondert how my letter was coming and thought I'd added quite a few papers to my stack. They asked what I was including and Jonathan hoped I'd tolt of Christmases. After the house was quiet I decided I'd next write of Christmas 1859 A.D. It'll always be a special keepsake of my heart. That was the year Henry and Margaret married and the year Levi and his young wife Mary Wood Kisbey sent an invite for us and Sallie and her husband George P. Fowler to gather together and get reacquainted. O'course I wondert if Aunt and Uncle was to be there. Their coming didn't keep us from enjoying the special gathering.

Levi Kisbey had bank work in Pekin Illinois, and he and Mary had tied the knot in November 1857. Sallie, (now 'Sarah'

232

to most), and her husband George P. Fowler, married in Tazewell, Illinois, in November A.D. 1855, when she was just seventeen. Not sure but what Texas was home to Fowlers 'bout then, but they lived in Litchfield Illinois a good while, too. Levi'd likely thought his sister was awful quick to marry 'fore him, and not long after they was in the US, but when one thinks it's either a good looking dark haired adventurous soldier with tales to tell of military fighting all the way to California and back, or living with Aunt and Uncle, well, how much pondering would it take? No, Sarah got a good man in George, far as we could tell, and now all these years later, they're in Florida, 'least some *famly* was last I knowed, though I've not been in touch as much lately. I think George was General Fowler 'fore he quit the military, but he fit right in with Kisbey storytellers to be sure.

While I'm at this part I'll tell you that Christmas we was a pretty small gathering, but if you put us together now, we'd be a noisy householt. I think the Kisbeys tend to be a little noisier than us Copseys was, but I've accepted half spoke thoughts would get overtaken by t'others. 'Tis just good merriment.

We Copseys thought it proper only one talk at a time, but if you descendents kept Kisbey blood flowing, you likely know one storyteller can cut in on t'other and none seems to mind, espeshly if the story coming in is as good or better than the one going out. Most stories got better with telling, or else my memory's to be questioned. Kisbeys always had so much to talk 'bout and most had a humorous story to tell which reminded t'others of stories too. There's just lots of loud laughter when Kisbeys gather. And a few pranks too 'fore people goes to home.

But 'fore I go on, I'll name famly children, as far as I know them anyhow: Levi and Mary Kisbey later had Ellen who was born 'bout 1863 A.D., Albert born 'bout the end of the Rebellion in 1865 A.D., and Henry born ten years ago, 1870 A.D. We wasn't able to keep good contact some of the war years. Seems I heard Levi and Mary lost a youngster 'bout the time of our sadness, too. I'd like to see them, but they went to Florida, as did George and Sallie Fowler. O'course we rarely saw each other, them in Illinois and us in Michigan, but 'twas nice knowing they was closer than Florida.

Now George and Sallie had a whole lot of children. The two oldest girls had trouble you'll hear 'bout with the walking, that was Lucy, born the year 'fore we gathered together when we didn't know she'd be getting 'round on crippled legs, and then Susan who was born the same year as our Alfred, 1861. Then they had Ettie in 1866, which was an honour as that's short for Esther, and Harry in 1871 A.D., and Nellie in 1873, and as far as I knowed, the last of theirs was born five years ago, in 1875, and he goes by the name of Sherman, like the General. I'll speak of our children as I go along.

That Christmas we'd be Levi and Mary, Sallie and George with Lucy, Manuel and me with Jonathan Levi and Emma Jane. 'Fore we went to Illinois, we celebrated Christmas with Sarah's Thomas Edward, Adalina, and James, and Henry and Margaret Williams. One thing I remember 'bout that Williams gathering was Adelina's wax doll and the boys' special toys my Copseys sent so they'd be remembered, but the note tolt Henry and Margaret they could say gifts was from St. Nicolas until the children was older. I remember being saprized. St. Nicolas hadn't called on us in England. Our little ones got nice gifts from their Copsey grandparents, too.

Now back to my retelling of the Kisbey Christmas in A.D. 1859.

Manuel worked but we hadn't felt right 'bout taking Henry's money when we was living there but good friends need things fair. When we'd rented elsewhere, the two traded work and when 'twas fair, Manuel got payed like any hired hand. Henry sold some crops to pay Manuel 'fore Christmas, but dollars was still short. I writ we'd decided we'd best holt off on a Kisbey Christmas.

Levi's bank work plus some side carpenter work let him send money just for this gathering. George wanted to meet the rest of Sallie's US *fam*ly, so he sent ticket money too. First we thought we couldn't use it, but their letters said a Kisbey

Christmas wouldn't be right without us, so we decided we'd go to Tazewell County, Illinois, for Christmas with Kisbeys we'd not seen for 'bout seven years! 'Twas exciting preparing. I made gifts, mostly baked or sewed. Manuel made practical gifts and some practical jokes, too. Henry took us to the train bound for Chicago, where I got a bit homesick for London, and on down to the Pekin station where Levi met us. 'Twas good seeing Kisbeys together again!

Levi and Mary was doing fine, nice house and later more land. One thing Levi said that Christmas, 'fore Aunt and Uncle arrived, was 'bout his gratefulness for Manuel's ways of trying to keep the Kisbeys together back in England. He tolt again how Manuel's cattle helped him and Sallie with schooling and made an easier life for them and Aunt and Uncle, but o'course he knowed Manuel'd not likely hear gratefulness from Aunt Gertrude and Uncle Ned. Manuel was uncomfortable, but I could tell he appreciated Levi's nice words. Manuel got sentimental saying he'd always just wanted to stay one *famly* and 'twas so hard letting the *famly* be split, but Manuel also tolt Levi he'd learnt to let God finish what God was working on even when Manuel couldn't spot where He was at work.

Even if t'others hadn't arrived, I'd thought we'd already had a good Christmas, just being with Levi and Mary. But more good things came when George and Sallie arrived with little Lucy. We o'course let our little ones get acquainted best they could. Our two year old Jonathan got lots of attention with both the men and us ladies, trusting whoever we trusted. Emma and Lucy was too young to be walking so they got passed 'round to anyone's empty arms. 'Twas good knowing George more. He was from New York, though his people had earlier come from other eastern states. George talked more like we did than our neighbors who'd lived in the United States a long time. George seemed suited for being military with his commanding way 'bout him, though o'course he was friendly enough to us and his *famly*.

We had lots to eat and lots of talk to enjoy and I learnt more 'bout US life and situations. They talked 'bout uneasy feelings in states like Missouri and that Kansas I'd heard 'bout even 'fore we'd left England. Talk was that people was angry, arguing and even worse, 'bout whether new territories allowed slavery or not. O'course England ruled against slavery the generation 'fore. 'Twas opposed in principle: a body don't make another work for no pay, 'less agreed or paying off debts or taking punishment.

George's people had lived longer in the US so he knowed more than us. He'd schooled with a Negro back east, but his *famly* was upset 'cause the Negro got taken south in the middle of the night. 'Twas never seen again. George said people with color was feeling unsafe no matter where they lived. As long as they was dark, they feared being stolen and made to work for no pay in the southern states, even getting killed if they tried to get away.

I learnt most people in the upper US, where factories was working, had thoughts against slavery and for staying one big country together. But with the country growing after warring with Mexico, people hetted to places not states yet. Some people figured new places should not permit slavery, others thought they couldn't do crops without slavery, espeshly cotton. The men talked of what might happen, how or if a body, or country, could or ought to stop slave-holting. Some of us newer to the US wondert if there'd be strikes or trouble inside this country. Land sakes, we knowed people and countries war. We remembered troubles between England and her neighbors in past years. I hoped we'd not jumped the big puddle for even bigger troubles.

We heard 'bout the troubled Englishman, Norton, who'd writ in papers he'd be a fit emperor of the US. He was buried couple months ago out in California I believe, with the title and fanfare, but not with sincerity I suspicion.

Those living in Illinois tolt 'bout the new party called Republicans. There'd been two parties 'fore the Republicans made a party. England had parties, too, but selecting someone

236

for hetting a country was so different from England's monarchy succession, or upheavals. The Republicans wanted to find a good man for 'their ticket' they called it, hoping their man'd beat t'others to Washington D. C. Being near Springfield, they talked 'bout Abraham Lincoln that Christmas. Levi'd learnt some things 'cause banking was somehow tied to people running the country. And Sallie's George claimed he'd go to war if it'd keep evil slavery from spreading. I think George had worn the US uniform several years, and now that I think of it, maybe even in war against Mexico.

There's little reason for us women to talk 'bout such affairs, but I asked what the men thought would happen if slave holters was tolt, like Her Majesty's colonies, that those was free people, hired hands maybe, but not slaves. Would United States be un-united and become separate countries like England with Scotland or Wales where lands join but ideas don't so much? Some thought we'd fight to make to them obey US laws 'bout being one country. George said something 'bout united and un-tied was just a matter of moving letters on paper but the US best stay united or it'd lose God's blessing that'd put it together years 'fore. I was glad to hear him talk a little 'bout God, for I didn't know what his faith was, though o'course Sallie was Methodist in England. The Kisbey men at the Christmas gathering gave the blessings, so I didn't know whether George was a pray-er or not.

By and by we knowed we couldn't solve US problems in Levi's parlor, so we women started making food while the men stretched their legs, walking 'round the area. Maybe that's why we women tend to get heavier than men. Men take walks while women fix everyone something to eat, and when it's done, everyone's too full and tired to walk more until the next mealtime that makes women busy again.

Aunt and Uncle, having aged, came up to Levi's for a short visit 'fore we broke up. Seemed they wasn't as comfortable with Sallie and Levi once those Kisbeys was married. 'Parently Aunt wished they still relied on her. We was civil to each other but our conversations was few. When Uncle Ned tried talking to Manuel or our little ones, Aunt always needed him for something. George saw her ways and quietly asked how it came to be, but Manuel said the past was past, and 'sides, 'twas Christmas, so we made the best of our short time together. I don't remember why, but later as everyone was talking, George asked Aunt if she liked wars. We didn't know if he was changing a subject or sticking to it, but I got the thought he reckoned she understood 'bout waging one.

I must be charitable o'course. Sometimes when there's a hidden jest it's hard to keep from smiling too much and a body has to go get busy elsewhere. I think George was just trying to humor Aunt Gertrude, but it's hard to 'magine her ever laughing. Uncle Ned laughed a few times when he was with the men, 'bout what I don't know. It's sad to think a person decides against being joyful, but some 'parently do. Bitterness is a bad root to avoid for it poisons a whole body.

'Fore Aunt left she tolt Uncle Ned something 'bout how 'twas disappointing Emanuel's children looked so much like Emanuel, and how she hoped they'd not be 'backward' like him. Uncle Ned shushed her but she claimed she was just speaking plain truth. Mary, Sallie, and me was doing kitchen work. They saw me shake my head. Mary winked and motioned to just sit quietly. Pretty soon when Emma Jane got fussy, Mary picked her up and took her to where Aunt was in the parlor. She helt Emma Jane up and said, 'Why, Aunt Gertrude, this little doll looks so much like you! Same with Jonathan. When I saw Levi toting him I knowed Jonathan was related to you 'cause he favors you so.'

And George, whose charm stole Sallie's heart the first time she saw him, added, prayerful-like, 'Now if they'll just imitate their parents' character...' And Sallie, Mary, and Levi picked up water glasses and chimed a hearty, 'Hear, hear!'

We blushed, I'm sure, but my Manuel didn't know nothing 'bout what Aunt said earlier, and I never tolt him. When he asked on the train home if I agreed with Mary that our children looked like Aunt, I assured him they was much nicer looking. My Manuel was a nice looking man and I'm not the only one who thought so.

Our Christmas went too fast. Manuel needed to be back in Michigan, so we put things in order to board the train. Kisbeys liked our little gifts and we carried home things and memories to enjoy.

'Twas nice of Fowlers to give us the pop'lar Uncle Tom's Cabin. 'Tis a big book and later I'd read a little at each day's end to Manuel 'fore I read from the *Common Book of Prayers* James gave me years 'fore. Sallie's book was sad but we learnt from it 'bout how life was for slaves and we understood more of why George was ready to want all people to be free and payed for work. When we finally closed the book many weeks later, we let it t'other people. Some liked it and some did not. Most took a long time to get it back to us 'cause of its many pages and a busy life in Michigan.

I seldom went to the literary circle I'd met Margaret at, but Margaret read the book to Henry and the children too. To think of it, I remember George asked if we knowed the Negro lady from Michigan going by the name 'Sojourner Truth' but we hardly knowed people in our little area. People said she didn't live so far from us, and from what they said, I thought perhaps sometime she'd talk in our area. Here in Michigan most people who had any think 'bout her thought she lived farther west but traveled east far as Washington D.C. Don't know much else 'bout her.

So back to telling of leaving Illinois that Christmas.

Manuel and I made a special point of saying farewell to Aunt and Uncle. 'Tis not Christian harbouring bad feelings, so we overlooked what we could. When we was to the station, Uncle and Aunt and us four, Manuel remembered he'd borrowed a little money from Levi at a shop, pro'bly for tobacco or something, but Levi was tending his horse and wagon and our train was boarding. In good faith Manuel gave a couple dollar bills to Aunt and asked her to pass it to Levi when he came to the platform. Manuel was particular 'bout paying debts as quick as he could. We bid farewell and boarded 'fore Levi got to the platform but o'course he waved us farewell.

'Tis probably something I should forget, but later I writ Levi and Mary as Manuel wanted to thank them for such a wonderful Christmas and tolt them we hoped they got the payment from Aunt 'fore she left. Levi and Mary writ back and hadn't seen the money. They'd heard Uncle asking Aunt why we'd exchanged money and Levi heard Aunt say she'd pitied us and gave us a couple dollars! They was glad they knowed more 'bout her ways and tolt us not to send the little bit as we'd tried to repay and they'd get along without those dollars. I tolt Manuel he should quit using tobacco as it only made trouble. 'Twas good he didn't use it more.

Apart from Aunt's ways, we had a good Christmas and 'twas so good knowing more 'bout each other's famlys. I think we always regretted more peace wasn't worked out with Aunt Gertrude. Even when we writ them during those years, we never heard from them. Guess I can't be certain, but I thought they could write. Maybe not.

That Christmas was a blessing too, for in the next few years things changed so much that getting together was not possible, mostly 'cause of the War of the Rebellion, or as some say the 'Civil' War. I think 'twas a Rebellious Citizens' War. I can't see calling wars 'civil.' Sometimes even God thinks war's necessary, 'tis in the Bible, but I doubt God sees wars as civil, or else maybe 'civil' don't mean what I thought. I was taught to 'be civil,' and disciplined when I wasn't. Can't see what's polite 'bout that war. In all squabbles seems there's rebellion somewhere.

That war ended 'bout fifteen years ago now. I read at times that some cannot forget the harm done to loved ones. Some still ask if the in-country warring was necessary. Why couldn't those sent to Washington D.C. just of kept tempers and stayed seated, talking things out without breaking apart a country and bringing 'bout so much heartache?

Maybe America was too young to behave like adults. In regular homes parents made squabblers settle things without another getting hurt. For pity sakes, wasn't this country to stand together like famly? It'd warred with enemies from outside, but 'parently 'twas not ready for enemies from within. The real 'within' was prob'ly 'within hearts' selfishly wanting their own ways.

Seems to me, when men either didn't get who they wanted to lead the country, or passed up their chance to vote, rather than waiting for the next time to vote, men started picking up their puzzle pieces to make a new puzzle. Schoolmasters and parents know such things don't work. In many ways the war didn't work either. The US is one big puzzle and all pieces need to fit together. I agreed with those that thought 'civil war' was like the unpardonable sin to this country. And sin extracts a terrible price.

'Tis too bad slavery ever happened, but since it did happen even ages ago, 'tis too bad people had not seen how wrong 'twas 'fore the US became a country. If people'd understood the dignity due fellow humans, 'tis likely we could of kept the peace as new territories became a part of this nation. It'd been good if the US had at least adopted the 'no enslavement' policy when England did. But sadly this nation had to pay a big price to learn to simply be nice to each other. What a pity.

Even to Michigan ears from 'bout 1859 on, we couldn't go nowhere without hearing 'bout war. The gentleman we'd talked 'bout at Levi's, Mr. Abraham Lincoln, got most people's votes to become president. We was too new to vote ourselves. I think I cast my first vote in November 1864 to put Mr. Lincoln back in as President after I'd been in Michigan 'bout five years. 'Twas almost a sacred privleech to vote for someone pulling us back to being one Union.

Manuel'd already voted, with his actions in September and 'fore.

Anyway, we had high hopes newly elected President Lincoln and t'other leaders would quiet disputes in territories that'd had deadly commotions 'bout whether they'd join the Union as slave-permitting or not slave-permitting states. What was said or writ in one place came to other places, some things was like fuel on stirred up embers. I know we wondert what states Mr. Lincoln could say he was going to preside over, 'cause 'fore the doings that ceremonially puts him in the special house, states was threatening they'd tear away from the Union. Would his good sense get to lead or not?

We hoped the talk would die down. We was far from new territories with disputes, and we was trying to put a life together with Manuel's tenant farming. By the 1860's we'd saved some money, and Manuel wanted to own 'something' so we'd both really feel the US was our home. Croplands was going at a good price. Acres went for $1.25 and up to even $20 or more. In our area reasonable acres went from $4 to $10. Manuel kept working, saving for a small piece of land. We decided to speak for a piece owned by Mr. A. W. Olds, hoping he'd consider us a good risk. His full name was Alergo W. Olds, and he and his wife was agreeable 'bout our buying that piece. Her name was Janet. Both names was new to me. If we got money together, we'd go ahet with plans to buy Michigan land.

The US was a big country, settling farther west all the time. More arguments 'bout territories and slavery kept being talked 'bout. Talk increased 'bout likely needing soldiers from everywhere, even our Livingston County, to holt the country together, or else the lower part of the country might break away.

By the time I tolt Manuel we'd be having Alfred, states like South Carolina and Mississippi, Alabama, Georgia, and Texas and o'course Virginia, though now the part that's called West Virginia didn't go for pulling away, and Tennessee and Arkansas, and some others too, was saying they'd unite and be their own country. Those last two, Tennessee and Arkansas became part of our sadness though I couldn't of found them on a map at the time. Oh, and Florida too, I think 'twas the first state to become part of the Confederacy. That's the name for the states that rebelled against being united. Like Sallie's George had said, states got un-tied in place of being united. 'Twas mostly States growing cotton and tobacco that started

242

saying they wanted their own president. They put one in too, another man from Kentucky, Jefferson Davis.

Can't serve two kings. Can't serve two presidents.

In the end, we, Emanuel's famly, didn't help decide our new homeland should go to war. But we, and I guess you'd say most famlys, was downstream from the big War rock throwed into the Living Peaceful Stream. War's ripples changed our lives in nearly everyway it got a chance. I'll tell of that in the pages ahet.

President Lincoln wanted the whole nation to be together, like Emanuel'd wanted his famly kept together. People 'round us was willing to fight to keep east to west, north to south all be one country. Cotton and tobacco states wanted to pull from the Union. President Lincoln tried working with governors of states that said they was their own country. But Mr. Lincoln had soldiers at a fort in a southern state, and the men was running out of supplies 'cause the state wanted them to give over the fort. When supplies came, Southerners kept the supplies from the soldiers. The Southerners insisted the fort's soldiers give up and let the South keep the fort. When the soldiers said they wouldn't, the fort was attacked by cannon fire in the night. That meant the war was started. The separation was real. Now soldiers would be needed to convince those separated states to rejoin the Union.

Mr. Lincoln wanted 75,000 soldiers to make the Union holt together. My, how people throughout the northern 'Union' states responded! Rallies was like high spirited revivals, like barkers calling 'bout seeing their show, except o'course, they was officers asking men and boys to sign up for war. Speeches was given, bands played lively tunes. 'Twas like a holiday catching us all up in the enthusiasm for Mr. Lincoln and the Union.

I did, and do, my dear descendents, love this country, and am forever grateful for the life and health it permitted us to experience here compared to Canning Town. But when we was at a rally or heard of it, I thought of how Englishmen organized for a day of grand foxhunting. I heard of soldiers who thought they was off for a change, a great adventure for menfolk.

Yes, we saw those that went to holt the Union together as Michigan heroes and we prayed they'd come home safely. But did they know 'twas not a foxhunt? That at day's end, or whenever they grew tired or wounded, they'd not be warming themselves back home at the fireplace? War is a serious sad thing. Sometimes 'tis necessary. Sometimes it almost charitably spares the oppressed. But 'tis a serious sad thing.

'Fore long we was hearing of battles and deaths and wounded. By July 1861, half a million pro-Union soldiers was called for. Some states begged to send more than they was asked. We spent lots of nights praying for the whole thing to be settled soon and for people we knowed that went from here. I prayed, too, that the war would stay far from us and those we knowed. Illinois was further south and we wondered if Levi's and Sallie's was safe, and what they was doing 'bout the war.

One good joy during this time of turmoil was the birth of our son, Alfred Alvin. We thought of calling him Alfred Albert, but we was becoming Americans more and more. Margaret Williams and Olive Hays was my midwives and if delivery can be fun, they did their best. Now I know some might say his name is Alfred Alva, but we'd chosen Alfred Alvin and a mother likes having children called like she named them at their borning cry. He came to us on September 19, 1861, looking like he'd grow to be tall like his Pa if he was given half a chance. Like t'others, he soon knowed Manuel's voice. Manuel was eager for when they'd be doing things together. How I hoped the war would end soon.

Those months men folk was thin from the area with the president's secretary asking for soldiers to help restore the Union. Plenty of men was ready to go. Here we was trying to make a living, raising children, working tenant land and for others too, going to church, planting crops and the like, and nearly every talk was 'bout the war. Papers on store windows tolt of more battles Michigan men and boys was in, and sometimes of who was not coming home no more.

Sometimes when Manuel'd come in at the end of a day of farm work and tell me news he'd heard, I'd ask Manuel why the two sides couldn't just get along. He'd remind me even our famly gatherings had difficult people, though o'course we'd not war over it. Once in our Common Book reading, I was reminded that thinking evil toward another in one's heart is like taking up arms to be at war, and I repented again of how easily I could remember things I might let turn to bitterness or resentment.

Henry and Emanuel still did some work together and our famlys had pleasant times. At Alfred's birth, Jonathan Levi was four and Emma Jane was two. God gave me stamina for each addition. Margaret came one time and saw all I had to do with baby Alfred and t'other two, a house and husband to care for, and meals to fix, plus helping if Manuel called. I always welcomed her visits, she was good help, and we agreed 'twas important those children knowed their blood cousins. 'Sides, all our hearts lightened just being together. When Manuel and Henry came in 'cause their work was at a quitting spot, Margaret tolt me 'twas good the children was mine till Pa came in and then they was his, or I'd be worn out long 'fore my time.

Our children did love being with their Pa. I've seen men too busy to like small ones, but not Manuel. He liked even his babies and knowed all 'bout caring for them from their early days on. As they growed, he helped them with eating up all 'twas on their plates and tolt them tales till shut eye. If 'twas nice out, he'd take them walking to see new animals, or 'fore bedtime to watch the night sky. He taught them not to fear storms for I think they'd seen me jump a time or two.

In autumn they helt ears when he fired Henry's gun to get us a duck or goose for Thanksgiving, and he bundled them for the barn in winter when they was old enough. And like most men, Manuel liked spring and summer fishing with his famly and appreciated the Good Lord's making fishing so enjoyable in these parts.

Michigan's good crisp air made a body's lungs strong. We'd noticed right off people here was so much healthier to look at, and 'tis still true when I'm writing this to you. I still knowed children could be taken from us anytime the Lord allows, but He allowed it less by our being in Michigan. Most days I didn't even think no more 'bout how I might lose one of my three babies. Nor did I worry I'd lose my beloved Manuel.

But war talk kept going on. One thing I always wondert was how all of a sudden soldiers of both sides got uniforms to tell them apart from each other. I wonder, if no woman sewed uniforms, how long would men make war last?

Manuel and others was working farms, sometimes helping famlys whose men had gone to war, and saving money best we could. In early 1862 A.D. we decided to go ahet and buy some acres from Mr. Olds. Some farmland wasn't worked as much since men and boys had gone to fight and Mr. Olds was more willing to sell land.

Emanuel went with Mr. and Mrs. Olds to the courthouse of Livingston County to draw up papers to record our purchase so it'd be all legal. 'Twas a cold day and talk would be all business and I had children to tend. I don't think Manuel did the whole court part hisself, so I 'magine Henry went along to read. Anyways, after papers was explained to Manuel's liking, Manuel made his 'x,' payed some money, came back, and tolt me we was real farmers.

We moved from where Manuel'd been tenant into a small old wood house on the property we'd bought. Margaret, Olive, and a few other friends helped me make it home. Farming went pretty fair. The war was still on, but we wasn't citizens yet. Then in 1863 A.D., hoping the war would soon end, we took out payments to take on 'bout another 80 acres in the northwest part of section thirty-six in our county. The courthouse put the stamps needed on the papers to show what we was to pay plus interest. We put down $700. Our hopes was high. So was the interest on money we borrowed. Ten percent. We'd be obligated eight years to finish paying, beginning with $100 in February or March of 1864 and $50 each winter after that when hopefully we'd sold some grains. We'd need things to work right.

All through 1863 A.D. we heard how hard the war was. 'Twas a sobering war. That fall Kansas, which was just a young state, had pro-slavery men ride in and kill many men and boys not even in the war. Made me shudder. We'd see men and boys home from the war, some wounded, some determined to go back to be with friends who'd need them in the war. And we'd hear of famlys who'd need to get along without the soldier who'd died.

That was the time of Gettysburg and, my, how many husbands and fathers and sons and brothers of both sides died there. One would think such sadness would make people settle disagreements.

I understood from writings later that Gettysburg would not only humble our good Mr. Lincoln, but it would be where his soul was stirred so much as he looked at the crosses of men slain there, that he claimed he faced his need to submit to the Lordship of Jesus Christ far beyond his past understanding of Him. Isn't it, my children, creative of our God to tailor what must take place in our lives so that we realize the steps we must take in order to spend eternity with Him? His love searches our happenings so it may overwhelm us, seems to me. 'Tis not done, ever, without love.

I only hope years earlier those men who lay buried under that 'sacred' ground had apologized to the Lord Jesus for Him having to be slain for them before they was slain for our country's unity and freedoms. If not, no matter that Mr. Lincoln asked that they not die in vain, when they stood to give their account, won't matter whether they was Union or Confederate, church-goer or no, if their soul was not cleansed by the Savior's blood, their hope for life in Heaven will be dashed.

We can't just hope God gets lenient in His love. He already showed us He was: that's why He's 'llowed Jesus to take what all of us had due. It's just a matter of justice. If we reject the payment God provided for covering our sin, then we is stuck with the bill and we'll stand with dreadful hot feet trying to pay, but no other payment but Jesus' blood would be enough 'cause of our own impurity. Better to let The Perfect One pay cause He died loving us and hoping we'd understand.

In 1863, President Lincoln declared every slave was to be set free. The war seemed more purposeful since it'd end slavery forever in the US! We was glad Negroes knowed Northerners would fight to set them free. I heard later nearly 100,000 Southerners fought to let others be free too. But most Southern farmers thought they'd never bring in crops without slaves. Why not pay workers like the Northern farmers did? 'Sides, maybe some who'd been slaves would want to buy farms or shops. Why not?

Manuel got determined to use no more tobacco 'cause he was helping the wrong side each time he smoked. Wished the whole Union Army had thought like that start to finish. 'Twas a relief for me to hear his mind, and I know Manuel wanted to lay it down forever. I tell you these things, children, 'cause even though Manuel's use of tobacco was only a little compared to the way some used it, some habits is better never started, and tobacco would be one Manuel'd keep his famly from trying if he could. That I'm sure 'bout.

But, as for making land pay for itself without free labourers like I was writing 'bout, even northern farmers was finding that sometimes owners' work don't pay out enough. And money itself was changing, too. State's money got tight and new 'national' money was printed for national banks, supposedly used most anywhere if you had it. At first we thought 'greenback' bills was funny looking 'cause of printing on both sides. O'course we wasn't seeing much of it.

Farming wasn't going right for us atall. Weather kept us from getting crops tended right. Work animals would be sick or not work together. Manuel couldn't get done all he needed to do. We writ Levi, 'cause he was *famly*, to see if he might come and help, or if he'd loan support without the high interest for little debts we was getting. We was new to having all the responsibilities. Maybe we planted poor seed, but we didn't possess much to sell that first year. We pro'bly could of sold potatoes and turnips, but we kept them for our table. Anyhow, 'fore long I knowed Manuel was wond'ring how he'd keep us and stock fed and make payments to keep our farm. What we worked with was secondhand. The whole year seemed to work against us. We wasn't envying 'nice things' or wealth, but we was moving closer to being Canning Town poor and neither of us wanted that. We hoped for just a little more help one way or t'other so we could get on our feet again.

Manuel always wanted us to be cared for decent like, and we didn't expect 'extras,' but I think what saddened Manuel further was that we could no longer help t'others having hard times too. Often Manuel'd go out saying, 'Keep praying Esta.' Jonathan and Emma tolt their Pa they was praying too. There was so much to pray 'bout those days.

I must stop my writing to you as there's other life to live on this day too and John wants me to take a walk with him. A wife needs to hear her husband's heart in his voice, and a walk will help me do that. I'll continue tomorrow.

Wednesday, March 17, 1880 A.D.

My Dear Ones,

'Tis very early and Miss Alice's poured me tea. She's been good help. We've helped her famly by having her as our servant. On with the writing I'm doing.

'Twas another disagreeable day in 1863 A.D. when Manuel asked me not to worry 'bout him as he was going to be gone for a time. I prayed for God to give Manuel wisdom. The way he said things to me had me wond'ring what he was deciding to do. It crossed my mind that maybe somehow he'd heard Levi was coming. Henry and Margaret and the children came by, for weather was keeping Henry from work, too. When I said Manuel wasn't to home, Henry asked if he'd gone to see Mr. Olds. Turned out he had.

Manuel spoke things straight with Mr. Olds. He tolt him he was fearful he'd not be meeting the big payment due in a few months with the way farming had gone for us that summer and fall. Mr. Olds knowed farmers was having trouble, but he'd need his money or o'course he could take back the farm. Manuel wanted the farm and they talked more. When he tolt me Mr. Olds had called him 'Mr. Kisbey' I was saprized as usually he didn't even call him Emanuel. Emanuel suspicioned his not reading or writing made people think he was dull.

I wondert how 'twas Mr. Olds called him Mr. Kisbey. Manuel watched my face as he talked a little different and tolt me he'd explained to Mr. Olds he could cover our first big payment and still leave me and the children money to live on while he was gone if he got the bonus and signed up with the Federal Army for the Union. He'd find someone to help me farm till he got back to home and he'd send money each month and he'd be keeping famlys safe. After their talk Manuel tolt Mr. Olds he thought he'd be getting a few dollars by express and $10 would be for Mr. Olds so he'd know Manuel was an honest man who met obligations honourably. Mr. Olds was pleased. Then Manuel said, 'I'll git ye yer money on time Mr. Olds, or I'll die try·un.' Mr. Olds had shook Manuel's hand and said with a husky voice, 'I believe you, Mr. Kisbey,' and he'd wished Manuel well.

Manuel was still feeling good when he showed me how Mr. Olds shook his hand and looked at him like Manuel was a rich banker, calling him 'Mr. Kisbey.' 'Twas a businessman's respect Manuel felt and he liked the feeling. I knowed Manuel liked hearing what Mr. Olds said, but what I'd heard Manuel say was that he was going to leave us to join the Army.

There'd been enough talk 'bout more Michigan men signing up for the long war and wanting the bonuses, so Manuel's thinking didn't totally saprize me, but hearing of others signing wasn't the same as having Manuel sign.

Fear gripped my whole being as he tolt me of his plans. Sure, we'd read 'bout Uncle Tom and how people of color was treated bad. Papers and people in town tolt that we northerners was being insulted, being called mudsills and tinkers, speaking evil 'bout us like we was ill·mannered and not schooled, that kind of thing. I knowed they didn't wish our

Mr. Lincoln well. But I suspicioned the people south in the Rebellion was reading some bad ways we in the north talked of them too.

Seemed days to be thoughtful of others was passing by, and truth be tolt, sometimes I wanted God to take us all away from the mess people made in this world. Yes, we had good friends in the community and I've always been thankful for them and loved ones. 'Round us was beautiful land, fresh air, opportunities to be healthy.

But we had to think so much 'bout war.

We'd listen to our preacher and he'd preach being like Jesus. Then outdoors people'd talk of taking up guns to restore peace. Some quoted the Bible 'bout obedience to masters. Our church had helped both Negroes and Indians by sending missionaries and we heard slavery was wrong, but some asked 'bout Israel's slaves. Sometimes talk got rowdy. T'others would talk of righteous war and how God called for war to throw off oppression.

We was in the Methodist Episcopalian Church most Sundays. Sometimes when disagreements got too loud I wished for a Quaker house. I understood they kept church quiet and had nothing to do with wars. But war was going on.

Pretending nothing's going on don't make bad things go away. 'Tis as true for a nation as for a dilapidating house in wintry Michigan in 1863.

Jonathan was six. He didn't understand war. Other children had Papas in war and I s'pose they asked Jonathan why his Pa was not at war too. Anyhow, Jonathan was so proud his Pa was talking of becoming a soldier and he'd of signed to go along if Manuel'd let him. A six-year-old don't understand how long a Pa'd be gone if he's to war. Nor dangers either.

Emma Jane loved Papa's nighttime stories. She was upset, crying and carrying on so 'bout how she was already missing Papa though he was still right in front of her. I knowed if he went she'd take it to heart bad.

Alfred wasn't much past two so he didn't know what the talk was 'bout and 'sides, he was usually in Papa's arms getting attentions. He was Manuel's shadow much as possible.

I expect he thought his pa was with him now and 'twas all that mattered. Little ones can hardly understand there will be tomorrows unlike today.

I asked Manuel when he had to let people know his decision. He said he'd wait a few weeks, and o'course he'd not go if I said he couldn't 'cause he hadn't signed nothing yet, but we'd likely lose the farm and get deep in debt. We both thought 'twas wise to keep the fox from the chickens if we could.

I asked if he'd prayed 'bout all this and he said maybe God was answering his prayers 'bout paying his debts by giving him thoughts 'bout joining with the Union Army. He liked being a citizen of the US. He wanted it to be a good place for our children as they growed and he asked how a country could be safe for grandchildren if the peace wasn't kept by their grandfathers.

'Twas his nature to dream of better days. 'Sides, since we'd crossed in 1858, now we was citizens.

His talk 'bout all this was in drizzling October and freezing November. I understood why Manuel sowed wheat early with such determination and worked hisself so hard. Spring would come and we'd be needing money and food. I was thankful Manuel was caring for us those days for some women had husbands who'd one day just pull foot without no planning with them 'bout the whole fix the famlys'd be in. Yes, perhaps the war's purpose was good, but famlys left struggling was worth thinking on as well.

Perhaps as you read this, you'll of been so long in the United States you'll think my hesitancy 'bout Manuel's going to war is too un-American. I love this country dearly. I'm thankful God worked in our paths to lead us to come to here. But thinking ahet of what could happen if a step is taken that cannot be back stepped is worthy of consideration, seems to me, and hungry children is hard to hear. Hard to hear. Manuel wanted to do the best for us he could.

Seemed day and night, whether we was together or we was apart, we kept praying 'bout what Manuel was to do. And we kept watching snow fall and we tried to keep warm.

Jonathan schooled when days was right for getting there but other days he just tried learning reading and numbers with me. Manuel took interest in Jonathan's schooling too. I tolt him on the side that perhaps now he'd learn letters and reading with our children, and o'course he said that depended on how the war part worked out. He tolt Jonathan books was important. Jonathan didn't like books much and liked being outdoors whenever he could. He espeshly liked when we said 'twas too much snow for school. 'Twas easy to think I should resent bad weather for keeping us from likely income, but then, and in times since, I thanked God 'cause God knowed Manuel'd go to war and 'least we had some famly days 'fore he left.

Manuel cut lots of wood and stacked it near our door. We butchurt a beef and a sheep and put that meat away. I made some warmer clothes for Manuel and for us. We hadn't said he'd go, but every day we couldn't earn money I knowed we was getting our answer even if we didn't like it. I writ Levi for Manuel, telling him of Manuel's plans to enlist with the Union Army, but no reply came to help us so I knowed letters was not going through like they had 'fore the war.

Manuel spent a great amount of time making Christmas toys for the children, including a little wagon for Alfred. O'course Manuel planned to watch the children with the presents he was making. He tolt me he was a busy St. Nicholas. The Kisbeys was for St. Nicholas more than us Copseys, but that's prob'ly 'cause they was more likely to be storytellers.

Anyhow, that Christmas the gifts was to be from St. Nicholas and we knowed 'twas likely Jonathan's last Christmas to be extra good during December. O'course his pa tolt him St. Nicholas carried coal too, so later I whispered to my St. Nicholas he could leave a heap of coal in a box near the stove for me if he liked. Manuel's children wouldn't get coal.

They might get the spanking to make sure they didn't get coal at Christmas, but Kisbeys liked seeing children pleased with Christmas. We planned to make this a special holiday since things seemed more likely Manuel'd be gone the next two Christmases if he did sign up, and if the war lasted that long.

Late one night after I'd finished reading to our little famly from the Common Book of Prayers and we'd prayed and put children to bed, as we was getting ourselves ready to bed, Manuel tolt me he thought 'twas time for him to join with the Michigan volunteer army. He knowed 'twas hard for me, so he talked gentle with me. He'd be going as a good husband and Pa by providing income and taking one mouth from our table. He said he almost wished he'd gone with the first heavy snow for then he'd already sent money for us and some days would already be crossed off, making him closer to being to home again.

I wanted to argue but I saw no reason to do so, not 'cause Manuel wouldn't listen but 'cause I reckoned his thinking was sound. 'Sides, I was Manuel's wife and knowed I shouldn't argue with his decisions less they was really really wrong ones. And I knowed in my heart I didn't want my Manuel going off to risk his life on a battlefield somewhere thinking that his 'Esta,' as he'd pronounce my name, was scolding him for being there.

O'course I wanted him by me and the children. O'course I wanted the country back to peace. O'course I wanted crops to pay bills so we could keep the little farm Manuel loved.

But truth be tolt, seems to me sometimes the path ahet has no good places to walk, but a person still has to walk them.

Manuel didn't think people like Mr. Olds would call him Mr. Kisbey if we couldn't pay debts and he wanted people to know Kisbey was a good name. He knowed even if Levi had more money, which we thought he no longer did, we couldn't always be asking his help. Now if Levi and Mary wanted to move closer and live with us that was one thing, but just sending money wasn't how Manuel wanted things to be. Levi's younger and Manuel'd always wanted to do good for his famly and not need their help no matter how rich a sibling got. Unless o'course a brother was lame or gone, then a famly'd be thinking rightly 'bout helping out. As for Levi, we didn't know but what he'd become worse off than us if 'twas true some banks had lost their money. Levi and Mary had land too, but if they had tending to do for that, they had bills too. Wars take money too. Manuel wanted his children to know their Pa met his obligations even when meeting them meant hardships to bear. And Manuel believed, as he said so many times 'fore: God was trustworthy even when we don't see how or where He's working.

We hardly slept that night as Manuel had so much he thought needed saying. I reckoned he'd been doing lots of thinking so I mostly listened. Manuel wanted his *fam*ly cared for and he was hoping the war'd end soon so he could come back 'fore long. Regardless, he hoped when he returned we'd be better off than we was when he left. The farm was to be for us better than money kept in a bank, since we wasn't sure banks would escape having money problems, for already the country had too many kinds of money and 'twas unlikely all kinds would be good later. All I could think of was the battles where so many was killed and I asked if he was ready for such things. How can a man be ready for such things?

I said maybe we shouldn't of bought the farm but Manuel thought if he was not to return, if 'twas God's will he not come home he said, we'd own the farm to sell to help us till we knowed if we was to go back to England or stay near Henry's or get to his *fam*ly in Illinois when the traveling was safer. Now I wonder if he bought the farm thinking he might go in the Army and we'd need a way to go on while he was away or if we turned out to be alone. Manuel signed up expecting to come home to us, and he wanted us to be waiting for him when he came home, but I think he thought when the war came along and he was a citizen of the United States that the farm was investment for us just in case.

Most times enlisted men got the best money if they agreed to sign for three years. Some signed up for less time and I'm not sure how that worked for them, but Sallie's George and also Levi signed for less time. But George stayed in the Army a long time I think. I think somewhere in these papers it tells that Sallie's George went in 1864 A.D. after Manuel but he was to stay only a few weeks or months on that assignment and I'm not sure 'bout t'other assignments. They moved some and I think he did Army a few times 'fore and after AD 64. I know they later had unspeakable tragedy trying to survive in Texas when they was there, having their girl kidnapped by Indians. What burdens some famlys carry.

As for Levi's, he served a few months and got discharged honourable. Some men, not near us so much, but in some places, tried fooling the Army by signing up, getting bonuses, and sneaking home. They 'parently wasn't like Manuel, wanting their name kept honourable. 'Sides for those fools, where'd they find people thinking they'd be good neighbors? And if they lived a life of lying, what miserable creatures they'd find themselves to be.

I asked Manuel what things he was most fearful of and he tolt me, 'O'course I could git fearful if I forgot the Lord's hands was on us while we's apart.' I recalled that many times while he was gone. He said he was fearful the children wouldn't remember him once he was gone a spell and that he'd miss teaching them and playing with them like a pa's to do. He was fearful I'd get it in my head to work too hard and try to do work a woman couldn't do. There was not certainty the Union Army would win, then what for Union soldiers, or for us? O'course Manuel'd never planned to harm another person serious like he'd likely be ordered to do as a soldier, but he did want our country back to being peaceful and it'd come to war being the only way to bring 'bout peace and safety again.

If he didn't come home, which I didn't want to hear, and every time he said it I prayed 'Please, God, bring him home safe,' but he said it anyhow, he wanted the children tolt 'bout him just like he was, not making him better than he was and even telling them 'bout his not reading but having them know how important schooling would be for them if they could do it.

O'course he wanted them to remember his love for them and his humor. But most he wanted them to become good children by making the Christian faith personal, like he and me did, when they was of the age to be understanding more of what I read each night. He said he wanted that most, for if he did not come home he wanted to be with his children when their lives was over.

Truth is hard to hear, but some important words are reminders we must know, even you. Manuel and me want to be in eternity with you. I hope I've explained how you can make reservations to join us by trusting only Jesus Christ to get you to us one day. 'Twill be important, even more important than keeping our name good and living life with good character. Several times 'fore Manuel left, he tolt the children they was to be obedient and helpful and respectful to me and their Uncle Henry and all t'others. They was to be good Kisbeys, he said, and stick together long as they could. He tolt them to keep the name good as best they could. Even tolt Alfred that. Alfred could barely say his first name then, but he was learning more how to please Pa and Ma and seemed most times delighted to do so.

Manuel had other thoughts too. One 'twas not so much fearful as just wond'ring how much he'd hear Bible readings like we did most nights, for he couldn't read and 'sides he'd want us to keep the Bible here. Bible reading had been our way to end most days for more than ten years by then and Manuel was grateful for those readings. I didn't know if soldiers took time for Sabbaths or not, but I suspicioned wars forgot which days was Sundays.

He wondert how fearful I'd be. I feared a few things too: 1, being alone without Manuel while he was at war, with me trying to care for the children and doing more of the outside farm work. But even more fearful was 2, that the children and I might be without Manuel longer, even that we might not see him again. Though God would be with us should that happen, I feared I'd find the loss too hard to bear. I loved my Manuel.

The children loved their Papa and God planned from the beginning for children to need their Pa.

Another fear was that I wouldn't know 'bout Manuel's condishions with his not being a writer. And if I writ him, would my brave soldier be willing to ask another soldier to read my letter to him?

The war might be doing good for some people, but war is hard to welcome, seems to me. Seems a war can be many things. The one big thing's the reasons for the war in the first place, and people like Mr. Lincoln thought we needed to be in a war for good, big reasons. But a war's also lots of little things. For us 'twas a home with two young boys and a girl wanting their Papa, and a wife praying to God to bring back her husband safe and sound.

We didn't talk much else but I knowed I hardly slept for all the thinking I was doing.

Next morning we put a stake in the ground near the door for Shep, and even fixed so the dog could be in or out on a chain through a little door cut out just for him. Manuel put on more ways to fasten the door so I'd feel safer when he'd go to find out more 'bout being payed for signing in and serving in the Union Army. If some man wanted Manuel to take his place, that was legal and Manuel'd get even a bigger first payment.

Finally we heard from Levi and I can put here exactly what he writ to us. It took its time to come though it's dated November 16, 1863 from Pekin, Illinois. We hadn't heard from famly for a time so 'twas good to see a letter in the express:

Dear Brother and sister, I now take the opportunity of riting you these few lines to let you know that we are all well at Present and hope this will find you all the same I reseved your kind and welcome letter some 8 or 10 days ago and was sorry to hear the fix you are in but I hope you will come out all wright after awille You saw you wanted me to send you 50 Dollars I will in diver to do so as fast as I can get it I could have sent it right of if I had known it sooner but I dont keep any money here to amount to any thing for I dont know how long it may bee good and when its out at ten per cent Intrest its still a growing alittle and ever little helps When you get this letter you will get forty 40 Dollars with it and I will try to send you the other ten in about 2 or 3 weeks if nothing hapin before then and you need it Sarah was at my house a week ago and she haed poor little helpless Childern One of them the oldest one is lame of one foot and Deafe and the other one is 3 years old and she has to carry it round or set and holt it for it has no use in its limbs to do any thing I have no fresh news to tell you as Mary and me joine in sending our loves to you all no more at Present from you Affectionate Brother & sister, Levi & Mary Kisby

P. S. rite by return of post and let me know if you get the 40 Dollars all right. L. K.

I helt that letter in my hands a long time. I saw my little ones moving 'round so fast, using their own legs and feet, and my heart just got tears of chastisement. Manuel might be going in a few days but he was still here and already I'd started to find it easy to take pity on my being 'lone, but at least while I worked Jonathan could help some and Emma Jane could be trusted to watch Alfred when I was outdoors. They could move without my toting them. But poor Sallie, and little Lucy and Susan. I thought of all the stories we'd tolt our children, Manuel and me, and I thought of how they giggled at things we said, or how easy 'twas to correct them with a word. But that wouldn't be so for George and Sallie's girls. What would being deafe mean in a home? And lame. No, we wasn't the only ones with heartaches.   And I wiped a tear too, knowing Levi and Mary had tender hearts and they had no idea Manuel was soon off to be soldiering somewhere. They didn't know I'd be alone working the farm.

As covenanted, Manuel gave some of Levi's money to Mr. Olds as a promise of payment and t'other we used on little debts and kept for days ahet. Poor was threatening with boldness. To solve our situation, Manuel would be getting money from the Army soon. He'd help the country and he'd earn three years of good income if all went well.

A person's got to hope.

On December 20, 1863, my beloved Manuel became a private in the Union Army. I wished I could of gone along the day he signed up, but o'course I couldn't. Perhaps I'd tolt him not to put his 'x' when 'twas time to do so, but prob'ly I'd still figured 'twas right, for we had peace we was doing the next, and the best, and the right thing. But since I wasn't there, since Manuel couldn't write more than his 'x,' the Army writ his name for him. That quickly writ name caused us trouble for years to come.

At the courthouse when he put his 'x' and bought the land from Mr. Olds, his name was put as Emanuel Kisbie.

When he mortgaged the parcel of land in Green Oak a year later, 'twas still the same.

His brother Levi writ his as Kisby or Kisbey.

When Levi served in the Union Army, his name was writ down as Kishby.

When my Manuel signed in, his name was writ as both Samuel and Emanuel Keisbey and Kisbey.

Later when I tried to get his payments straightened out, we found that Kisby was on his records in Washington D.C.

A body has to write for his self 'cause those who write for you cannot spell your name the same each time. Records is not always exact.

I find in my stack of papers my children's names is wrong and dates is wrong even when I payed lawyers to listen and write down what I tolt them.

Others tell me the same 'tis true for their records. But what does it matter 'less you try to get some rights and honour for a name like I had to do for Manuel?

My dear readers and children of our blood, I writ my name as Esther Copsey Kisbey till 1867 A.D. and I hope you each decide to write it that way too, cause if you change it too much you'll cause yourself and your loved ones many hard days trying to get the good things a good name should bring to you. I know. Try to be readers and writers. Manuel would tell you to do that no matter how great the struggle. Manuel's name is confused to this day. But I say KISBEY.

And what of Christmas 1863? No Manuel Christmas Eve. No Manuel the morning when St. Nicholas had the gifts waiting. And no Manuel watched children squeal with delight at how exactly St. Nicholas had knowed what was right for each one and my, how they wanted Pa to see what St. Nicholas brought them.

We'd waited and waited. I knowed most likely their Pa was just 25 miles or so away but he might as well as been in England for they could not be with him. What a Christmas.

Manuel's love was all over the place but he was far away.

I went to bed thinking I survived one Christmas without him and there might be two more 'fore we'd face Christmas again. All night I fancied how we'd celebrate Christmas of 1866 A.D. when my Manuel would saprize the children by coming home in time for Christmas and he'd be the best gift old St. Nicholas could bring children like ours.

As it turned out o'course, there was no counting on St. Nicholas after that.

Truth be tolt, I tolt the children the next day their pa had made their gifts. I just thought I had to 'cause they was thinking their pa didn't try hard to be with them for Christmas, and I wasn't 'bout to let that stand.

I knowed they was unsettled a bit learning St. Nicholas hadn't visited, but I tolt them their Pa liked to tell them stories and he thought they'd like the St. Nicholas story for years and years, but the gifts was made by their pa with more love than they could know. I remember their holting their gifts and deciding they wished they could thank Papa, but o'course that was out of the question.

The gifts Manuel'd made them was to be given saying ole St. Nicholas was so wise, but I tolt them what their Pa had said 'bout each gift.

For Jonathan, there was a plain sizeable wood box that was to be kept full by the fire so we'd be warm any time of night or day and 'twas for Jonathan cause St. Nicholas, his Pa, knowed

Jonathan was to be more growed up while Pa was gone. The wood box was to be his responsibility 'cause Jonathan was soon turning seven. He heard what Manuel had heard from his Pa 'bout being more than half a man.

For Emma Jane, there was tied to the limb of the tree facing the road a new swing. She was young, just 'bout to turn five in a few days, and he thought the swing would last plenty good till he got home even if she shared with Jonathan and Alfred.

He hung it so if she was swinging high, she might be the first one to see her Pa coming home and she could tell the rest of us. But she was to be careful and not go too high for a couple summers 'cause going too high would cause her mother worry, and maybe more bills to pay, and she'd not be able to see her Pa for awhile anyway. Manuel'd thought he'd tell Emma Jane that St Nick left him word to tie it higher when he got back 'cause Emma'd be growed to need higher swings by then.

And for Alfred, there was the wagon just right for being pulled by a two year old, but it'd also last till Pa came home and they'd get a new one if needed then. Alfred was to load things into it and play like he was a farmer and he could even sleep in it if he crunched up a bit, but his bed with Jonathan or Ma would prob'ly be best. When Alfred was five he was to start watching by the gate too, and see if he saw Pa 'fore Emma did in her swing.

Manuel'd put up another clothesline for me, so I could watch the road by both lines.

And Shep had his door to be inside or out without disturbing us at night and where he could dash out if there was noises that I wouldn't like hearing. Manuel knowed I was not so good at being alone, but somehow with the children I thought things would be less fearful. O'course, I knowed I just had to keep my mind on God as our protector. As the Good Book says, unless the Lord watches the city, they that watch, watch in vain. God would be my companion, and Manuel's too.

The children had worked with me on saprizes to give their Pa at Christmas since he'd thought 'fore he left he could get back 'fore actual duty. Henry'd thought so, too, when he tolt me 'bout Manuel's signing in. We had cookies and candy and some warm socks and the like, plus some children's drawings. Manuel o'course didn't get them, but 'least he'd had their hugs and kisses 'fore he left on December 20th.

On January 3, 1864 A.D., according to my papers, in Pontiac Michigan, my blue eyed, brown haired, light complexioned, 5 feet 10 inch 32 year old Manuel, (or did he say that wrong, for was he not already 33?) was mustered into the active roll of Company F Third Regiment. He was to be Cavalry. Sometimes he was infantry, but cavalry was his choice. There's just something 'bout a man liking a horse.

We didn't own a real horse here in Michigan, just a mule, but he could work when he wanted to and he was a better size for me to use, though o'course even mules kick high, so a body must watch.

Also on that January day Manuel met a Godsend, Mr. E. L., or by name, Elmer, Richey of Three Oaks. E. L. was to be Manuel's best friend the whole time he was in the Union Army. They was near the same age. E. L. was thirty-five and they thought they was 'bout the oldest men in the regiment. E. L. tolt me there was only 'bout 12 in the whole regiment his age or older. Boys most of them, or men just married short time 'fore going off to war. 'Least I was thankful we'd been man and wife for twelve years 'fore Manuel went to war.

I knowed when he left we was all dreadful tearful, but that day we'd thought he'd just be gone a few days 'fore leaving for the three years. Manuel wanted the Williamses with our famly and they was good to stay 'round here when the leaving began. And that December day other neighbors kept stopping by to wish Manuel well. The preacher came and read Psalm 20 to us in the house and when we'd prayed again, Manuel was ready to give us his affectionate hugs.

Henry took Manuel in the wagon to where he had to go. Manuel said he was sure once they got him signed in he'd get home another time. That did not happen, though we kept hoping we'd see him. My Manuel, the children's Pa, was Private E. Kisbey with the 3rd Michigan Cavalry, Company F, and he was signed up for three long years, or till the Rebellion was past.

Every day I thought of a thousand things to ask or tell Manuel, but he was gone.

Later I wondert if Manuel maybe knowed he might not get back 'fore leaving but didn't want us carrying on so much, as he knowed we would if 'twas our last good bye. Or his too. Farewells is hard on all.

Seemed likely we'd all needed Aunt Emma's telling us we had courage and strength and whatever else we'd need to go on even if we didn't want to use it. God has prepared us for what His children face, even if they don't think so.

I'll write more tomorrow and I'll put down Manuel's writings to me and tell of papers in the stack aside me, but 'tis time to close for today, my dear loved ones.

I guess I'll close with this thought. Farewells to brave soldiers is hard. Watching husbands and Pa's, brothers or sons, or any brave soldier leave for war causes most hearts and eyes to feel tugs and tears. Tears come 'most like a stream at such times.

I respectfully recall those rippling tears as I put down my pencil tonight. Rippling, rippling, rippling, rippling, rippling sad tears.

To continue with the novel without doing the study questions now, please skip ahead.

A NOVEL APPROACH TO BIBLE STUDY
LESSON EIGHT · QUESTIONS 149-164
(INCLUDES QUESTIONS REFERENCING "CONSEQUENCES OF
THE CROSS TO SOUTH LYONS"/CHAPTER 7)

Change is almost another definition for "life." For those who want to control their surroundings, who want to cherry pick events, who want a certain kind of behavior from people they've permitted to wander into their lives, discover instead their lives feel chaotic any time the unusual happens. In the chapter just completed, Esther and her little family change addresses by crossing an ocean to begin life anew with Sarah's family. It is in the author's family history that Sarah died within a week of Esther's arrival.

Okay, let's work with the next questions, please!

149) If you read this chapter, you know a lot happens to Esther in these five years, beginning with a deep personal loss within the first week her feet trod Michigan soil. *(This, by the way, was verified in family notes kept about Esther and Emanuel, though another update in 2012, stated Esther and Emanuel arrived on a Wednesday, Sarah had a headache on Sunday, and by Tuesday, Sarah had died, leaving Esther to help care for the little children.)* You also know that Henry's second wife will be helping with the birth of Esther's child born in 1861 *(also a family fact)*. Henry will later testify (documented) about Emanuel's character because he knew Emanuel years before Henry and Sarah left for the United States. By the chapter's end, Emanuel and Esther are facing separation from each other and expanded roles caused by poverty and his enlistment with Michigan's Third Cavalry. Now re-read the passage that opens the chapter (II Samuel 22:26-38) and comment on how appropriate that passage is for a courageous wife during the circumstances of the chapter.

150) Perhaps, like me, you have sometimes been moved by the expressions of others, especially warm ones exhibited when a returning soldier is welcomed home or when a new baby is being seen for the first time, or when it is time for "that baby" to head off to college or into marriage.

We each develop our unwritten rules about expressing our emotions, though sometimes we might find ourselves unexpectedly teary. My oldest granddaughters, for example, have been told my tears do not necessarily mean Grandma is sad, that sometimes her tears are partly because of joy. I am sentimental and have been known to shed tears at airports when I've watched others interacting and I've not had a clue as to who they were. Can't we be thankful we feel emotions?

In this chapter, we read again Esther's tendency to restrict her emotional expressions. Comment on their dealing with their losses and dealing with changes as they prepare to step into their new world and your feelings about openly expressing your feelings. Can emotions cleanse?

151) FOR PERSONAL REFLECTION
On a recent lunch date with my husband, I could barely swallow my hamburger because of the disturbing behavior of two men at a nearby table. The elderly man, I observed later, was frail. The other trailed by a generation or two.

My first thought was, "Ah, how nice, these two, maybe father-son or grandfather-grandson, are declaring their respect and friendship by having lunch together. However, I soon observed that the younger sat in silence with an air of intolerance. He finished his meal first. Silence. Independently they emptied their trays. While choking tears, I watched as the younger man walked far ahead of the elderly man toward a shiny pickup. They drove off sharing the front seat but as though they were 5,000 miles apart.

I wonder, what is the "backstory" to that silent and apparently hostile meal? Who felt "obligated" to make it happen? Who rightly or wrongly harbored bitterness, or sorrow, or...?

I don't know their stories. Maybe one or both are scoundrels deserving to be in lockdown. Maybe they were each having a hard day. Two truths I know: first, many lonely elderly people would spend days looking forward to a lunch out with someone, and second, our actions speak louder than words to people we'll never know.

I'm not their judge, but all of us need to watch our appearances, and remember the implications of Ephesians 4, verses 31 and 32.
Perhaps you have others you simply tolerate instead of enjoying the relationship that put you together.

If abusive people are in our lives, we may need to "put them on the other train track" and move on with our own healthier, and safer, life. God did not create us to be abused, but even that horridness God will not waste as He restores you to health. See II Corinthians 1, verses 2 through 11, but especially verses 3 and 4. May God grant you complete healing soon and a ministry, even a quiet one, afterward.

If, however, you proudly deny those who deserve your nurturing care, perhaps you need to seek counsel to address what causes that to happen. If we nurture old hurts and even misunderstandings, if we refuse to forgive those who wronged us, we're typically draining the hope and joy from our lives.

Disliking, holding a grudge, hating someone requires a lot of energy to keep justifying our feelings. Hopefully those deserving legal action have received the consequences and you are away from their harm. But our bad attitudes toward someone who shamed, ridiculed, or embarrassed us, or was "snooty," are instances we would do well to dismiss quickly...for our health, if not for imitating the mind and actions of Jesus Christ.

Check yourself. Is it our selfishness that insists people do things our way, or that they think like you/I think about something that isn't, after all, going to end the world? When's the last time you/I laughed with those hard to love?

The enemy of Christ would love to have you/me grow into an old bitter woman (or man), all prickly and wrinkled with sin taking its toll on our health. Demanding someone else be perfect is unrealistic. Only Jesus Christ pulled that off and it cost Him His life. Our perfection happens in heaven.

Be eager to forgive and to take steps down the road toward the one with whom you ought to be reconciled. Don't waste earth years being uncomfortable with those God put into your life unless that relationship actually threatens your welfare or, in the case of unfaithfulness in marriage, the other person has moved a spouse into the position you used to hold. Sometimes you have to move on, expecting God's fresh grace.

Repentance for your part in failed relationships is cleansing. Even if there is no reconciliation, you will rest at night knowing you did your part, and continue to pray that God prevents bitterness from taking root in your life.

Spend a few moments asking God if you need to send a note, make a visit or a phone call, to seek forgiveness for your part in a broken relationship. Be aware of needing to be safe, however. If you think re-establishing a relationship is physically dangerous, let the Lord work out the details. However, if an old grudge is hindering relationships, and God prompts you to work toward restoration, ask the Lord for the right words and actions so that you soon experience the freedom forgiveness brings. Write out Ephesians 4,vss 31-32.

152) Which of your emotions are you most thankful for?

153) List below some of the characteristics of God, His attributes. It might be helpful to itemize as many of them as you can by listing them alphabetically. For example: A, Almighty, B, benevolent, C, creative and caring, etc. After you complete your list, spend a few moments worshipping the Lord for who He is. Then, study the list to see if there are any of those attributes you would be willing to have God withdraw from His eternal being. Discuss your thoughts with someone else today if possible.

A	B	C
D	E	F
G	H	I
J	K	L
M	N	O
P	Q	R
S	T	U
V	W	X
Y	Z	

154) I like writing letters. When I was a young woman, I wrote a "round-robin" letter to my parents and siblings, telling them how much I loved them and some of their attributes I cherished. We knew we loved each other, but we rarely verbalized that truth. None of us knows how long we'll live, so affirming others is good.

Even before our children were born, my husband and I began writing letters and prayers in blank books for them. We kept those books of letters a secret until either a need to share or the child graduated from high school. Along the way, we let significant others write in their books, too. We're glad we did because three of their four grandparents died prior to giving the books to our children. Once, my son grabbed his handwritten copy to put in the closet we used as a tornado siren blew. I'm glad they were important to him.

Earlier in our marriage, a situation arose in which I felt it was necessary to write two identical letters. One I gave to my husband and asked that one be kept in case of my death. In the letters, I explained more about my beliefs and made requests about my burial in case I would not be able to explain the spiritual side of who I am to my children.

I remember, too, when my husband and I would need to do research on other religions, I would dramatically write, "Heretical! Not what we believe!" on the books' covers. I didn't want anything I left behind to distract my children from coming to a saving faith in Jesus Christ.

I also often wrote sweet notes on my husband's sermons or tucked them into his things when he was going away, and almost daily put notes into my children's lunchboxes during their early years of elementary school. Sometimes other children waited to hear what I'd written my daughter!

Maybe my interest in letters began when I discovered a long handwritten letter from my mother in my baby book. She'd put it in to explain why my baby book was so empty, but I remember how eagerly I hoped she'd make it safely home from work that night so I could let her know a little bit more about how important she was to me. Thankfully, my mother lived to be almost 97 years old and our fellowship together was sweet.

When my hospitalized mother-in-law knew she was in her last weeks of life, a good friend offered to write letters she wanted to dictate for her two pre-school grandchildren, our daughter and son. Our family treasured those letters.

All of these situations with letters prompted me to put into the novel that Esther's sister, Sarah, wanted to create letters for her little ones when it became increasingly apparent her final earthly days were being spent. Perhaps we each ought to write more letters than we do.

We simply don't know how many days we have left on earth. Maybe we have decades. Maybe our lives will end abruptly and early by most accounts.

Is there someone you could write who would cherish your words, either long after you are gone or until that person uses up the last of her/his earth-time?

If the letter you feel prompted to write is not something you are comfortable mailing just yet, be sure to mark it so that it will be discovered and delivered after you can no longer do that. If the restoration you seek is godly and wholesome, just imagine how joyful it could be if you take steps to begin the restoration. Do pray about the restoration and let the Lord direct your thinking.

Of course, if your feelings are out of line, immoral or destructive toward someone, pray, asking the Lord to straighten out your thinking. Jot your intentions.

155) Read 1 Timothy 2:1-2 and Proverbs 21:1.
We are encouraged to pray often for those who rule over us so that our lives may be peaceful. When those doing right are punished or ridiculed, their leaders especially need God's counsel. Many world leaders may not have heard truths about Jesus Christ or about God who personally loves them and Who wants to be recognized as the leader's Heavenly Father. We all, leaders included, owe allegiance and obedience to the One from Whom we can receive wisdom. How different our world could be if we submitted to God as the Ultimate Ruler.

In this chapter, we read about President Lincoln's conversion. What changed President Lincoln from someone who knew about the God of the universe into knowing Jesus Christ as his Savior? No doubt, Christians were praying for President Lincoln.

156) What was an additional reason for Emanuel to quit using tobacco?

157) What were some of his hopes and goals as discussed this far in the book, and especially in this chapter? (Some are similar to earlier goals.) Which of these seem to fit with Emanuel's entering into military service?

158) Esther recalls fears and goals Emanuel had. As you look over those goals, how do they compare to the goals you would have for your children and which would be most important to you?

159) Discuss the fears both Emanuel and Esther had as presented on these pages. How similar are those fears for individuals and families dealing with a commitment to military service today?

160) Letters did not travel well during the war and sometimes, as Esther may say later, not all questions in a letter are addressed in future correspondence. What especially struck Esther after reading Levi and Mary's letter? Why?

161) What are some of the confusions or humiliations caused by Emanuel's "X"? What are some common judgments we make today?

162) This chapter tells of two very different Christmases. The first is in 1859 and another in 1863. Compare your favorite or most touching parts in each of the two Christmases. One is the Kisbey family reunion Esther describes. The second Christmas happens just after Emanuel and Esther wrestled through the pros and cons of his enlisting with the Union Army, which culminates on December 20, 1863. Emanuel's preparations began earlier but include the Christmas part.
  A.1859 Christmas reunion with Kisby relatives:

B.1863 Christmas without Emanuel:

163) Which of your Christmases will you always want to recall, no matter how old you become? How can you make family gatherings meaningful?

164) What are some things you and your group could do for either a soldier or the soldier's family at this time, whether or not it is Christmas? What can you do for persecuted Christians in tough situations?

Prayer
Father God, We come to You knowing that You know our hearts better than we know ourselves. We sometimes are guilty of rationalizing about relationships, sometimes unfairly blaming the brokenness on others when we know we, too, are guilty of the disharmony. We know it is Your will that we live in peace and harmony with our brothers and sisters in You and also to live, "as much as it is possible" peaceably with others. We ask Your cleansing of our sinful part in broken relationships and seek Your guidance in steps we ought to take for restoration.

Father God, we thank You for the true meaning of Christmas, the birth of Your Son, sent because we were in a "world of hurt". Help us to share Truth with those who do not yet know Jesus Christ as Savior and Lord of their lives.

I ask, Lord Jesus, that You give me the goals that fit with the work designed for me and that You be glorified through me as I serve You in the world.

In Jesus' name, Amen.

CHAPTER
EIGHT

MICHIGAN
WITHOUT MANUEL

(1864-1867)

CHAPTER EIGHT
MICHIGAN
WITHOUT
MANUEL
(1864-1867)

If thy brother be waxen poor, and fallen in decay with thee; then thou shalt relieve him; yea, though he be a stranger, or a sojourner; that he may live with thee. Thou shalt not give him thy money upon usury, nor lend him thy vituals for increase. I am the Lord you God, which brought you forth out of the land of Egypt, to give you the land of Canaan, and to be your God. Leviticus 15:35-38

Thursday, March 18, 1880 A.D.

If thy brother... Oh, my precious ones, 'tis good I'm writing this after our country's mostly healed from the awful war when states left the Union. Not all feelings is healed, but progress is happening. Some 'Northeners' moved South and some 'Southerners' moved North. East and west has moved, too. People's had to choose 'bout whether to keep living the war day-to-day or to move on after treaties was signed. I had to make that decision myself, and finally our children's made it, too.

So many choices we must make is only partly our choice, for life and circumstances can filter out some options we don't want filtered, but we don't get to choose some parts. So we look at what's on the table and pick up what we can work with, that's how I see it. To my way of thinking, there didn't seem to be much to my liking on the table for quite a spell during my time in Michigan without Manuel. But 'twas how our life was, so here I'll put down 'bout our lives and the interruption made by the Civil, or not so Civil, War.

ho is my brother? Well, praise God, now I can see many good people are 'my brother.' But what a road we walked when brothers seemed hard to find, both as a nation, and as what was our little famly from England resettled in the big warring US. Blood relation was miles, even oceans away. Yes, Williamses was like famly, and they and others was good friends. But our little Kisbey famly seemed to get lost in hard times after that December day when Manuel left to sign up for Union Army duty. 'Twas not what Manuel'd planned by going, but when he left, 'twas what happened.

Much of what I'll include here's from cherished letters we got from Manuel and his siblings during the Rebellion and after. I know our letters is not newspaper or Bible writing. Some children likely put words more properly than what's writ. But what's here is how things was for us and I think 'tis important you know who we was, and perhaps more 'bout who you are.

When I copy the letters, which I'm saving for Manuel's children so perhaps you'll holt them someday yourself, I'll put them like they came to us so more can read them if t'others get lost. I'm including information from other papers, too, so you understand our time more.

The explanations I put is from my way of seeing things, and from some callers I had. For one, Mr. Elmer Richey, who's more likely to turn his head hearing 'E. L.' instead of Elmer, is a person we feel indebted to for his patient kindness to Manuel and to us, and for his calling on us when he returned to Michigan after the Rebellion. He filled in things we wanted to know. Now E. L.'s gone back to Texas where Manuel's regiment fought after Arkansas. Things is growing more peaceful there and I don't doubt but what he and the likes of George Fowler's helped that come to be. I hope E. L.'s made a famly there and is doing well.

Back to how life in 1864 A.D. moved forward.

Manuel enlisted for three years as a private from Green Oak, Michigan on December 20, 1863 A.D. The officer there taking him in had a name ending with 'bard' but my copies of Manuel's things don't let me read the first part of the name. Records don't really keep things so right to my way o' thinking.

Like I writ 'fore, my husband's names was writ two ways from the start. What complications that began. No, complications began 'cause Manuel didn't know how to put his name. But 'Samuel' instead of Emanuel? Maybe cannon or gunshot was still ringing in the scriber's ear. Could be.

I heard tell one Michigan lady went to war. Sometimes when I was 'bout to cry over problems we had after the war 'cause of records, I thought I knowed she likely went in: just to keep names and ages straight! Couldn't be, though, 'cause she didn't use her real name to enlist. Her record's all tangled, too, but God bless her somehow.

A body 'bout gives up when a name's writ wrong and people from here to Washington D.C.'s trying to understand, or maybe to forget, about a wife and children wanting respect for their soldier and also what's due them 'cause he served. I'd give up if I'd not been so stubborn 'bout honouring my children's Papa. More 'bout that later.

Manuel couldn't leave Pontiac after he'd enlisted 'cause officers kept thinking they'd go any day. If a man signed up and wasn't there when 'twas time to go, officers might think he was hornswoggling them. If he came back or they found him, he could be shot for desertion. So 'tis likely Manuel's thoughts and heart was with us here in Green Oak, but he sat waiting as the group formed.

How was we to know if, or when, he'd been ordered onward or not? It still breaks my heart to think how on Christmas morning he was only twenty-five miles from us. He certainly couldn't change that he wasn't with us. If we'd knowed, we'd done Christmas in Pontiac somehow. Instead, we was alone without Manuel. In some ways, my memories of that day seem covered with a mask. I s'pose I tried to be more cheerful just 'cause children want Christmas to be so.

Every Christmas after requires me to sort those memories.

So, with Manuel signed in, I writ Levi. Would he take over the farm while Manuel was gone? I knew 'twas Manuel's hope I'd be spared the full responsibility and Manuel thought a brother would move heaven and earth to help if he could.

I was 'bout to find out what I was made of, and the children, too.

We went ahet and took to choring, hoping three years would pass quickly or, even better, that the Rebellion would stop. We sparingly used our staples and woodpile. Neighbors stopped to see what we heard or how we was faring, but after awhile they got busy with their life too. I've done that, so I know 'tis easy, 'most necessary, to do.

Bitter cold January went by with no word aboout Manuel, and I tolt myself I ought not hope to hear other'n what general news was 'bout Michigan soldiers. War rumors was plentiful and when they was bad, I'd tell the children, 'Well, that's only a rumor so don't go believing everything you hear."

I must of pulled something feeding stock, but I had no choice other'n to keep choring and praying. Mostly I prayed for Manuel's safety and President Lincoln's wisdom.

Finally, toward the middle of February, we had express mail. 'Twas good, but 'twas from Levi, not Manuel. I've kept his letter. 'Tis on beautiful paper showing his support for the Union. It has the eagle, two gowned ladies, and has thirteen stars with some strips. There's spelling as imperfect as mine: 'E PLURIBUS UNUM.' No, I jest. I'm tolt its meaning is 'Out of many, one.' That was Northerners' sentiment. I think Levi or Mary stamped the letter to look like this as there's an ink blob.

Looks like Levi favored quills or pens, but I still use the pencil. Anyhow, he writ this to us from Pekin, Illinois on February 7th, 1864 A.D. and you can tell he wasn't sure if Manuel had left for good or not. I guess some men enlisted and could be home just waiting. Levi didn't separate thoughts, and he schooled more'n me, so perhaps he was right to do so.

Dear Brother & sister, I take the opportunity of riting you these few lines to let you know that we is all well at present thank God for it   we receved your letter the day befor yesterday it was Dated Jan 5th   its eather been along time acoming or been wrong dated   We was glad to hare that you was all well but was sorry to hare that Emanuel had enlisted. I think I should have run the chance of the draft but as he has enlisted I hope he will stick to it and not do as maney has Done hear Desert and never dare show thire heads again I hope he will have the best of luck you said you wished me to come out to ware you are and take care of the farm I dont know what to say 'bout it for I am hare alone there is noby to take charge of the place my Boss lives in Iowa about a weeks travle from hare he will be hare the 20th of this month and then I shall get a understanding 'bout it I dont Know but the bank will stop this spring and lay up all summer if it dose maby I will come out to you this spring but if the bank keeps at work all summer I dont know what to say 'bout it but maby I will come and see you in about 6 weeks I want you to rite and tell me what route I will have to take when I get to Chicago so that I may have no truble in finding the way I have nothing more to say at present but we remain your loveing Brother & sister. Mary & Levi Kisby

My letter had been slow in reaching Levi. Manuel didn't know it sounded unlikely I'd be seeing Levi and Mary anytime soon. I had Henry help write how to get here, 'cause Henry knowed such things. It looked like I'd tend chores and children for a long time. But 'twas good knowing Mary and Levi was concerned 'bout us and would help as they could. We just had so many miles between us.

'Twas easy to feel sorry for myself as I fed stock that winter. Staying warm was not possible anymore. When I was cold I'd think 'bout Manuel. We'd had more warm socks to send with him. Where was he? What was he facing? He'd confessed 'fore he left he hoped he'd not be asked to kill another man. What'd happen if he was faced with a time either he did it or it'd be done to him? If he did it, would people benefit from his action or not? I can tell you I couldn't 'magine how losing Manuel would help the country or us. Our side was thinking right. A country ought to stay together and make it so no person was allowed to be shipped and worked without hope or pay.

Lots of days when I sparingly put the wood on the fire I wondert 'bout wives and children whose husband and Pa was not coming back. Or 'bout those fighting cold 'cause husbands had not, or now could no longer, cut enough wood? We had fire and we had milk and God was Sovereign.

Yes, my pain kept on and I had no time or money to doctor, but it'd likely go away. 'Sides, I had God, didn't I? Yes, many others trusted God too, but what I mean is I ought not think I was the worst off person. I needed to remind myself: Was we not looked after by God?

Oh how the children and I got comfort from my Common Book that night we read Psalm 34 'round the flickering fire 'fore our prayers for Manuel and t'other famlys dealing with the war. 'Twas just there for us and here's how it spoke to me:

I will always give thanks unto the Lord: (how often, Esther?}. *His praise shall ever be in my mouth. My soul shall make her* (wonderful the Bible said her this time*) boast in the Lord; the humble shall hear thereof and be glad.*

(Was I 'bout to write and complain to Manuel or to talk with people to church 'bout how hard my life was? How would God be honoured with such talk*?)*

O praise the Lord with me: and let us magnify (like glasses I saw at Crystal Palace, making things more seen and clearer, too) *his Name together. I sought the Lord, and he heard me: yea, he delivered me out of all my fear.* (And children, I was letting all kinds of fears take root again without Manuel there and also 'bout his safety. Had I trusted most in Manuel's strength for us or God's and did not God know where my Manuel was?)

The Lord quieted me more with 6 and 7: *Lo, the poor crieth, and the Lord heareth him: yea, and saveth him out of all his troubles.* (Was anything, frozen streams and water tanks, broken tines, low woodpiles, emptying cupboards, strange night sounds, bullets near Manuel, was anything that happened to Esther Copsey Kisbey more than God could help her with?)

This next I loved for 'twas just right for both us and for Manuel who was prob'ly shivering in a tent somewhere near the enemy for all I knowed: *The angel of the Lord tarrieth round about them that fear him: and delivereth them.*

But the rest is good too, sounding like Aunt Emma's way of reminding us of what stock we had: *O taste, and see, how gracious the Lord is: blessed is the man that trusteth in him. O fear the Lord, ye that are his saints: for they that fear him lack nothing. The lions do lack, and suffer hunger: but they who seek the Lord shall want no manner of thing that is good.*

Now hear our Father's invite: *Come, ye children, and hearken unto me: I will teach you the fear of the Lord. What man is he that lusteth to live: and would fain see good days?*

And here's what he's offering to teach if we be teachable: *Keep thy tongue from evil: and thy lips, that they speak no guile. Eschew evil, and do good: seek peace, and ensue it. The eyes of the Lord are over the righteous: and his ears are open unto their prayers. The countenance of the Lord is against them that do evil: to root out the remembrance of them from the earth. The righteous cry, and the Lord heareth them: and delivereth them out of all their troubles. The Lord is nigh unto them that are of a contrite heart: and will save such as be of a humble spirit. Great are the troubles of the righteous: but the Lord delivereth him out of all. He keepeth all his bones: so that not one of them is broken. But misfortune shall slay the ungodly: and they that hate the righteous shall be desolate. The Lord delivereth the souls of his servants: and all they that put their trust in him shall not be destitute.*

'Twas a good reading to consider.

I writ Aunt Gertude the next day but o' course I sent it to Levi and Mary as I'd not knowed I'd ever want her address.

The letter I writ to Aunt and Uncle was friendly and I confessed that Manuel and I had helt bitter feelings toward her, mostly me for I'd taken offense for her ways, but I writ for both of us for Manuel was hurt by her as well. I asked her forgiveness for judging her and for expecting ill treatment rather than waiting to see how she'd act. I tolt her how much more quick Manuel was to not see her ways, to forget them more easily than me, for I knowed my heart: if she'd walked through my door I'd been dreading what she'd say to us and I was convicted I needed to let her record be wiped off from our accounting.

Now maybe you'd be wond'ring how then I writ what I writ of her on pages 'fore this. I guess I tolt her part in our lives so you'd know our faults, too, for 'tis a record of how I saw her actions then and in what was yet to be, but I can plainly state, the Lord's kept dealing with any hard feelings I've let reside in me.

In my letter that February 1864 A.D., I tolt Aunt Gertrude that yes, we was often hard up for money, but maybe at the train platform she was hard up too and was too shamed to ask for help. I thanked her for the good she'd provided in seeing Levi and Sallie got schooling.

I tolt her Manuel was in the Union Army and asked they remember him in their prayers. I hoped they was safe in Illinois, for I knowed they might be closer to battles than we was in Michigan. I tolt how our children was growing and then I closed the letter with a clear conscience 'tween me and God and hopefully 'tween her and us too.

I figured I'd done what I could to make things right.

God said he'd forgive us as we forgive and after the letter I felt new forgiveness.

I writ Manuel too and tolt him of 'our' letter to them. I wasn't sure Manuel would get my letters, and if he did whether he'd ever know what they helt, but I hoped somehow he'd know. Oh, how we wished he'd been able to learn reading.

People was saying the regiment was still in Michigan, but where I did not know.

One thing I did know, we wasn't getting no money for Manuel's being in the Army. That was one reason he'd gone. But perhaps it'd come.

I kept working. And praying, o'course.

Finally in mid-February Henry and Margaret came with a letter from Manuel! How could it be? Had the Army seen he learnt to write? The letter sounded like his way of talking. I'll put it here just like it came on plain paper from faraway Memphis, Tennisee. The date is February 9, 1864 A.D.:

Dear Wife, I take my pencil in Hand to inform you that I am Well at present & hope this will Find you & the childern injoying Good health

We left Grand Rapids sooner than I Expected when I Rote you the other letter We left there on the first of this month When I got to Chicago I sent you sixty Dollars in a letter by male & I would like to know if you of received it or not. I would like to seen you & the childern before I left but I could no chance for we Dident know what Day we would leave there The morning we left we came from Chicago to Cairo on the railroad The Distance is @ 68 Miles & then we took the Steamer Hanabal & Came Down the Mississippi River 360 Miles to Memphis & were landed & Marched to this fort Pekins We wore five Days on the way Coming & we are in Camp here & have nothing to Doe & plenty to eat & it is warm & pleasant here the Roads are Dry and Dusty the winter has Not ben Cold enough to freeze the Cane on the bank of the River I Dont Expect we will leave til the Rigment gets back They have Most all Reinlisted & gone Home for thirty Days & we will stay til They get back again it's all quiet here Except alitle skermishing with the Rebel pickets I an geting fatter every Day Well I will Close for this Time hoping that you Will Rite as soon as this come to hand & give all the News Nomore But Remain your Affectionate Husband Emanuel Kisbey

I turned it over and on the back it still says what it said: *Direct your letter to the third Michigan Cavalry Memphis Tennissee*

So my Manuel was in Tennessee. Dangerous Tennessee. But he didn't sound like he'd had to fire his gun yet 'less toward Rebel pickets. He was eating good, 'least that's what he

283

wanted me to think. The children and Henry and Margaret and others rejoiced with us that we'd heard from Manuel and so far he was well. Two years and ten months to go.

Sixty dollars should be coming. How'd Manuel's letter get writ anyhow? I writ him how things was on the farm. And I writ Levi and Mary.

Bits of grass was greening and I knowed there wasn't much hope for managing the mule myself. It had even more its own mind. Wouldn't even eat food I offered. Food'd be there all day and I'd worry 'twas dying. Wouldn't eat for Jonathan neither, took a little interest in Emma Jane, but not more than a handful. Then Henry'd come to see 'bout things and he'd shake a bucket and the old carcuss'd come lopping over and 'bout eat itself to death. Guess maybe the ol' mule was missing Manuel too.

How would we do spring work without a mule? I writ that to Levi and Mary, and Levi tolt us he'd come as soon as he could but he doubted a banker'd be good at handling a mule. One letter I offered to ship the mule to Manuel since it 'parently missed him so. 'Twas not being much good to us.

O'course I tolt him it wouldn't likely arrive for him 'cause it'd be required to do what I said to get there. I hoped the mule'd humor someone and still let Manuel know the farm situation was certainly not any easier without him. The mule stubbornly managed to live but we did lose a calf Manuel had payed special tension to, thinking it'd profit or feed us while he was away. I think some clawing critter got it. 'Least it stayed clear of the house and Shep.

I kept working but my sore throat hung on with the ling'ring wintry weather and my aggervating pain would not go away. I kept the children pretty healthy, God's help o'course. At church or town we'd try to find out 'bout happenings in Tennessee. Tennessee was a state not likely throwing out a welcome party to the likes of Michigan's 3rd Cavalry. Third Cavalry had a proud reputation and in Michigan men was looking toward joining up with them in early 1864.

Michigan's 3rd Cavalry had pretty much gone 'bout everywhere 'fore Manuel's group signed with them. Best I know, for Manuel's time with them things was pretty much quiet, which suited Manuel. He was like I tolt you, a person tojust be where he was to be, holting the place for who'd come next to do more or do diffrent.

Manuel served as a guard and often marched a-foot 'cause horses was away in another state waiting to come to him. Men was off on winter furlough, they'd come back to Michigan after fulfilling their three year duty, but most signed up to go back and finish up the war. Furloughs took time.

New recruits like Manuel and E. L. waited near LaGrange Tennessee while t'others of his Cavalry was preparing to return from over at Kalamazoo, west of us. Those men went down to Saint Louis Missouri 'bout May, but they waited there for the right horses from what I understood.

When they all got reunited, the recruits like my Manuel and the re-enlisted men from 'fore, they spent their days keeping Confederate General Shelby of the Rebellion Army wanting independence from Lincoln's United States, away from where the Union Army was busy trying to end the war.

Manuel was generally somewhere near Memphis Tennessee and in Arkansas near both Little Rock and a part called DuValls Bluff. Manuel's Cavalry was responsible for getting supplies, like cattle to feed their fellow soldiers of the Union Army. If they'd come this far I'd offered the mule, and I don't s'pose they'd minded for it seemed from E. L. when we talked that the food was not perhaps as good as mule hide at times.

Sometimes I had to send Manuel money which was not our plan as you can 'magine. They had food served, but local people'd make their living finding where regiments and pockets of soldiers was posted and they'd offer kitchen cooking like cakes and whatever tasted more like famly food.

Did we miss Manuel? O'course we did and something fierce. Many a night the children'd ask how much longer Pa was to be gone. Jonathan was still proud his Pa was in the army and he liked to talk to schoolmates 'bout his Pa's important soldiering, but at home, 'twas not he tried to shirk his responsibilities or such, he just missed his Pa. And a boy should.

Emma Jane o'course was Pa's girl and she'd predicted that she'd miss him when she first heard talk of his going. She missed him every day. On days when I'd be doing something else that took my whole mind I had a few moments when I wasn't thinking of Manuel, but if Emma came 'round, I'd look at her and she'd look at me with teary eyes and a quivering lip and we'd just decide to collapse in each other's sadness.

At times I'd find my Emma outdoors just looking south. She'd go to the swing Manuel had made facing the road and I'd see her sitting in it without it going back and forth. Her toe'd be anchored in the dirt and she'd slowly be letting the swing twist 'round and 'round, or move side-to-side.

One wash day she didn't know I was hearing her. Her swing times was also her prayer times for her Pa, or she'd be pretending she was telling Pa what she was doing or how he had to be watchful. Having Manuel gone was hard on Emma Jane. Later that summer I asked Emma Jane if she wanted me to push her in it so she could go higher, but she said, 'Not today Mama, it's not time yet to go high.' And I was hoping she meant she was a little fearful of going high, but I think her heart tolt her it'd be long time 'fore she should be looking for Pa coming down the road.

Jonathan kept the wood box filled and I writ to Manuel how responsible his son was getting. I knowed he'd be satisfied to hear it. Jonathan'd make his Pa proud of him.

We kept talking to Alfred 'bout his Pa 'cause Alfred was young when Manuel left and Manuel wanted me to be sure Alfred remembered his Pa till he came home. Little ones can forget after a time, so I diligently talked of Pa in Alfred's times with me. T'other children would join me sometimes and they'd tell Alfred of how their Pa did this or that thing with them.

Jonathan'd whittle a toy or hammer together some box or insist we all take time to go fishing, all 'cause 'twas something Pa'd do with us and with Alfred if he was here. Alfred kept Pa in his mind all right, and he asked us many, many times, 'Pa come home now?' After a time, a year or so later, he'd look at men and ask us, 'Is that Pa?' and we'd gently need to explain 'twas not. But there's one story of Alfred you must know and I'll tell that in a bit 'fore I finish this part.

And o'course each night, no matter how tired we was, or how ill, our little famly circle would gather, and if my throat was too sore then Jonathan worked to read from our Book of Common Prayers or the Holy Bible and we'd all say a prayer for Papa and his fellow soldiers and for President Lincoln and for the war to end so Pa'd get safely home.

Our prayer was likely similar to prayers all across the country, north and south, for everywhere there was Pas and husbands and sons gone to war and children and wives and parents wanting them safely home. Our children's Pa'd go safely home...but not as we wanted.

I'll put down more what he wrote to me and the children. When the whole war was over I think Michigan 3ʳᵈ Cavalry had only had 24 men killed from fighting and 9 killed from warring wounds. I don't know but what the ones Manuel mentioned in his letter was two of the wounded in what had to be February 1864 A.D.

All tolt, Michigan's 3ʳᵈ Cavalry had more than 2000 serving 'tween 1861 A.D. to the end of the Rebellion, and of those 8 died amongst the Rebels in prisons they set up. Over 300 had to come home early 'cause of wounds. Disease men got while serving took 333 Pa's and beloveds and sons and brothers from their homes. But if I heard numbers right, Michigan had 'bout 90,000 trying to keep or put back the US so God could bless it once again.

Loss from this time for our nation was hard in so many famlys, and even when famlys didn't lose a member, most famlys lost a blood relation or someone from their community, their church, or their area. 'Twas 'most like epidemic years with much weeping, yet in the middle of that we'd keep to chores and tending to children, that kind of thing. And when we could, we tried to make some happy times just so's the children'd know life's to be made of such too. That's what their Pa was serving for. So here's Manuel's letter.

Fort Pickering   *March the 2, 1864 AD*

Dear Wife I take my pen in Hand to inform you That I am Well at present & Hope tese few lines will find you & the children well. I Received your kind letter yesterday & wos sorry to here that you throat was sore but hope This letter will find you better & if you Dont get better soon I would like to have you go to the Doctor I wos glad to here that The Childern wos well & I am glad to here that Levi is a coming out & would liked If he could of staid with you You can let The land to any one you are aminto but I Would like to have the one that farms it to Iron the Rails & Repair the line fence I Am sorry that my Jack Bull calf is ded & I hope that you Brryed him Deasent I am glad To here that they Raised a town Bounty for the volinteyrs

I Have Ben Informed by some of the Men that had letters from home that there Wos a bounty of $50 Coming from the state But I Dont know yet what papers will be Nessissary to get it & if you find out you Can Rite & let me know I have ben here all Except three days in this fort & then we wore Colled out to go to gard a smoll fort 25 miles East from here & while we wore there there wos Wone of our boys had his gun go off & Shot two of Our boys one threw both of the legs & he Died the Next day & the other wos shot threw the left Nee & he had to have his leg taken off & he Died in a few Days

We left here on thursday & Returned on Saturday. I have sent two Newspapers & I would like to know if you Received them. I am Detailed to leave her at one oclock this afternoon & go and gard prisoners to lewisville kentucky & Will be gon Six Days I tried to get a Surtificate but Could Not get it til the Rigment gets back again & I am Mustered into The Company to which I ama going

I Think you Had Better Take This paper & go to Dr. kenbard & try and have Him get it for me. I will send you a Few lines to give to him & if he gets it I would Like if you would let me know when you Rite again   We had quite a storm here   It Lasted 45 hours & then Cleared off & it is Plasant again   Well I will Now Close By giving my love to Henry and Margret Hoping that you will Rite as soon as Posable   I hope you wont have to put your Self To any truble about my payments forithink I will be able to Meat them as fast as they Come Due if I have good luck give my love to Mary and all the Rest of the inquiring Friends   Nomore at present But Remain you Affectionate Husband

Emanuel Kisbey

Kiss the Childern for me   Good Bye
                    And on t'other side,
Address Emanuel Kisbey   Therd Michigan Dismounted Cav Fort Pickering   Write Soon

As you can read, Henry agreed that I should let the farm to someone else. The children and I would get some payments from letting it out and hopefully that'd be enough to get along. We wasn't wanting hardship for anyone else, we just couldn't make a farm go if I was to be the head of the doings.

Good Levi came for a time too and how good 'twas for the children to know they had a Kisbey in the house for a few days. He had his own to care for to home, but Levi had a good head 'bout him and he helped me put things in order business wise and he humored the children. Henry'd helped but he thought if *famly* to Emanuel was to do things it might be better. But Henry found Levi was 'bout like Emanuel so they got along and Levi trusted Henry. Henry thought Levi's words was wise for us.

Oh how I wished Mary and their little ones could of come but how could a body think traveling's safe with war? Levi couldn't stay long but he helped us with a few bills and he understood things I wasn't sure 'bout on papers, so 'twas good having men help with decisions. They built confidence in myself though and they thought my judgement was sound for going ahet on some things. I doubted I would, but 'twas good hearing a man say so when I couldn't ask Manuel in a timely way.

I kept the letter Levi writ after he was home just to remind me of how willing Manuel's famly was to help when he was gone to war. 'Twas not easy for them. Levi, well, he was like Manuel in that he and Mary treated the children and me like we was knitted to them. We was Manuel's famly and Kisbeys stuck together. Many days I thought of how if Levi'd been older when the famly was to be split apart in England days, I think he and Manuel could of kept it going, but they was both young and as I said 'fore, a bill of sale is a bill of sale regardless of age.

Here's Levi and Mary's ink letter from 'Pekin Ill Mar 14/64.'

I liked how he started it. I use pencil but it smudges so I try write careful. John asked t'other day if I needed the pencils with the eraser inside and I asked him if he'd been reading my papers thinking I had erasing to do!

No, he's a kind man and so helpful to me. I tolt him I was used to just having the eraser by my teacup and not rubbing too hard when I see I writ wrong. Sometimes I write a word that doesn't belong atall and I wonder where it comes from. I hope I find those words 'fore you do my dear descendents. Now back to writing to you, or John will think I could go back to doing what we hired Miss Alice to do. Here's Levi's letter.

Dear Sister I now take the Opportunity of riting to you to let you know how I got home I got to Peter Mills at ½ past 11 o clock and I left there at 15 min to one o clock I got to Ann Arbor at 4 o clock it was a pritty hard walk the roads was very bad I was glad that I did not start with Williams horse for it never could got through with that big wagon. I left Ann Arbor at 8 o clock and I did not get to Chicago till late the next morning for we had abrake down our Engine broke 'bout 11 clock that night about half way between two Stations and we had to back up to the one we left and stay thire till thay got it fixed and by that we did not connect with the other train at Chicago so that I did not get home till Sunday morning about 11 clock I found Mary and the childern all well but thay had been looking for me all the last week and my Boss had been in Pekin the 2 last weeks on Saturdays with the bugy to meet me there but as it was so late he misted me boath times Give my respects to Williams and his wife and family and nevery body Else. no more at present but we remain your Affectionate Brother and Sister

Levi & Mary Kisby

As I put down for you, the Kisbeys, or as Levi put it 'Kisby famly' stuck together in trying to care for each other as much as they could. Harder times for me and the children was ahet but I'll speak to you of that later.

'Fore I put down the letter I got next from Emanuel, I must tell you 'bout a few things. I'd tolt him of things going on here just so he'd know what his children was doing. I knowed how important they was to him and some times I writ of humor things they said or did and sometimes of things I knowed would touch his heart, but he was their Pa and I wanted him to know such things.

I tolt you 'fore that Manuel had made Christmas toys and gifts for his children 'fore he left and we didn't get a Christmas like we wanted, not knowing which day we'd choose to call 'Christmas.' We'd eat a few special meals and at nights we'd sing Christmas music 'fore Manuel left.   But we saved gifts like I tolt you, hoping Manuel'd come right back 'fore his regiment left so he'd watch the children get presents. If you has to do a holiday like that, one where you move the day a little 'cause of t'other things that might or has to happen so t'others can take part, you understand somewhat. But if you move the holiday 'cause of dreading what's happening to someone you love, you understand it more. Enough 'bout that.

Manuel'd been gone away several weeks and finally we was all out of doors more. 'Twas still cold o'course and woodpiles

291

cannot get too high, seems to me. If a child needs something to do and its old enough to do it, chopping wood's a good thing to keep bodies warm and use up energy. And o'course, if children ever whine or get obstinate, well every good parent can find work for the bored or moping. Go to neighbors for doing charity work if you need to! Can't 'magine having everything done to home, though.

Henry'd sometimes take Jonathan with Sarah's oldest, Thomas Edward, who'd been special to both me and Manuel since back in the motherland. His name to us was Edward, but records likely say Thomas Edward. He was a few years older than Jonathan. Margaret and me thought 'twas good for the boys to help Henry. If we'd been really low on wood, maybe we'd thought Henry should do it hisself, but we had enough to get by if we had to. Henry was good for Jonathan, and Jonathan sure thought he was growed up by helping. When I read Jonathan Pa's letter he felt espeshly proud, but I must tell you I realized I'd given much responsibility to Henry that day for we could of been bandaging our own wounds if Henry'd not looked over them so careful. They talked 'bout making trees fall and whooped, 'Timber!' as they did. Henry tolt me the boys liked the felling part best, chopping next, but they seemed to need to run off when it came to toting and stacking. But 'twas a day filled with good memories for them.

O'course I tolt of Emma Jane but I didn't talk much of how sad she was for Papa or that'd made it a harder time for Manuel and would of been the same news each letter. I made her do other things by saying, 'Do such and such and I'll write PaPa 'bout it' and she would. Helped us all I think.

Then there's Alferd, that's how Emanuel writ it, though as you'll find out it 'twas not Manuel writing after all. Well, we'd kept talking of Pa to Alfred who'd nearly cleaved to him from his borning cry on. Manuel and us wanted to make sure the little fella didn't forget his Pa by his being gone so long. So we talked often of Pa and he'd talk of Pa too. He was getting more words all the time and I'd write them to Manuel. But one day little Alfred 'bout broke my heart and I s'pose it 'bout broke

Manuel's heart to hear of it, but I wanted Pa to know how much Alfred was remembering him, so I wrote it.

One day I was hanging washing and tending chores and Emma Jane was to be watching Alfred. Jonathan was gathering eggs I believe, for we had a few chickens, or he was maybe finishing up the early milking. Anyhow, we was all busy and we'd done this set up many times 'fore, though on colder days o'course, I kept them inside except a little fresh air. Anyhow, when I finished what I'd been doing, I saw Emma Jane but I saw not Alfred and I asked where he was. She didn't know. She'd got busy with her things and the swinging and the like and we looked, but no Alfred.

A mother's not made for such times. I called to Jonathan to check with the animals 'cause that's not where a two year old's to be. But he wasn't there. We started running here and there calling to Alfred to answer us, but either we couldn't hear or he didn't answer. Finally I kept t'others looking 'round the house and barnyard and I took to looking past our lane on the road that goes by our place. And there, off in the distance was little Alfred, and he'd been farther if he hadn't had to be pulling his little wagon his Pa had made him. I caught up with him and 'fore I spanked him I asked him what he was doing. He tolt me, 'I go to see Papa. Where is he?' I didn't know if 'twas right then to spank or not, but I tolt him Papa was too far away for a little boy to go and Alfred tolt me he'd need 'horsey to help me go.' I pulled him back in his wagon, and all the way back we talked of his Pa, but I tolt him if he ever tried to go again, he'd be spanked. But in my letter I tolt Manuel if Alfred ever tried to go to Papa again, we'd all go with him! Perhaps we'd take turns riding the stubborn mule. Like Manuel, I wanted my Kisbeys to stay together much as we could. Here's the letter I got from Manuel, only you'll realize he's not the writer. Manuel wasn't holting the quill, and if Manuel'd had to holt the quill I'd likely not heard anything. My famly is espeshly grateful to the gentleman for reading my letters and writing us for Manuel. Oh, I should tell I left the wrong spellings of names and t'other words, and that Fort Pickering is near Memphis.

Fort Pickering   April the 6th AD 1864

Dear Wife

I received your Welcom letter on the 5th & wos Happy to here that the children Wore well but I wos sorry to here That you Dont get your health better   I Dont want you to worry or give yourself any trouble about Me for I am well & injoying Myself verry well here & If it is the lords will I will come out all Right again   The time is a passing off   it wos three Months last Sunday Since I Inlisted   I am glad to here that the childern are so good   I think that Alferd Would have a long road to come after Me with his little wagon   Tel him to take good care of it so i can see it when I come hom & I will bring him a little horse to Draw it with   Tel Jonathan to be careful & Not fall any trees on him when he is falling timber   I am glad that Edward is a good boy & chops wood for his Aunt   i hope he will be careful & Not cut his feet for I know my ax is to heavy for him.   I am glad that Emma Jane is so good to help her Mother to Do the work & hope you will kiss them all for

My Dear Wif you wanted Me to Send you Some money but cant for I havent Received any sence I left the Rapids & Dont know when we will get any but as soon as i get it I will Send it to you   I have allmost give up Smoking for I have no Money to buy tobaco

I was glad that you sent me them Stamps for i had Non to put on my letters   The boys havent got back here yet that went home & we Dont know when they will   they are in St Lewis Masouri yet   You Wanted To Know if we ware Cavalry or Infantry   They are useing us for infantry Til the Rigment gets back   A Part of the boys is mounted Now & gon out on a scout

I am verry well Satisfied With the way that Henry has let place   Give my love to his wife and famly

I Will Now Close for this   Write Soon & ofteten   Nomore at present but Ever Remain your Affectionate husband

Emanuel Kisbey to Ester Kisbey

Mrs. E Kisby as you Requested To know who it was that was Riting for your husband I will tell you   My Name is Elmer L Richey & Emanuel & I have be bunk Mats sence we left the Rapids & we live verry agreeable to gather so far except a few Days when he was gon to Chicago   I am a single man with no famly yet   I Will Close, You Most humble Survent,   E L Richey Direct your letter as before

From that letter I knowed how we was hearing from Manuel. After the Rebellion and duty in Texas, E. L. returned to Three Oaks, Michigan and came to visit me and Manuel's children in late 1866 or early 1867 A.D. We talked of how Army life was for Manuel, some I'll likely say later. But 'tis very late now. Tomorrow I'll write of two things to help you better understand my letter and Manuel's life. Till then, I must get my sleep.

Friday, March 19, 1880 A.D.

Loved ones, I rested well and will press on:

In Pontiac Michigan when the men, 'the boys' as some called them when they was at war, like 'the boys is in Tennessee' or 'the boys got hit hard this week,' so when the men or boys was getting the 'issue,' they called the things they'd take to war with them 'issue,' they got clothes, their gun and the like, and Manuel took whatever they handed to him. One thing they handed was the little <u>Soldier's Prayer Book</u>. Saprizes me that they had such a thing but I was grateful to hear that from Mr. Richey and I asked him how he knowed Manuel got one. I knowed Mr. Richey knowed Manuel was not a reader. Well, here's the story of how he knowed and how they got to be good friends so that Mr. Richey wrote for Manuel to us famly.

Mr. Richey and Manuel was bunk mates as Mr. Richey had writ to me during Manuel's time with him. But earlier on when they had left Pontiac and was settling into a camp somewhere quiet in Tennessee I believe he said, they was outside by the tents and Manuel was just sitting by hisself by the fire holting that little book of prayers. Mr. Richey asked him what he had and Manuel tolt him 'cause he knowed they'd called it a Book of Prayers when they handed it to him in Pontiac and he knowed we had our Book of Prayers to home. So they started talking. Now Mr. Richey had not even picked up one 'cause I guess 'twas not his practice to read from a Book of Prayers. Manuel tolt how every night 'fore we went to bed we read from the Holy Bible or the Book of Prayers in England and in Michigan and how he was missing the reading of it. So Mr. Richey said, 'I'm sorry, Fella, I'll leave you to read it,' and E L went into the tent and to bed down for the night. But Manuel just sat there turning pages and looking away north toward home, toward us.

Then Mr. Richey said kind of rough like, 'Is your reading making you feel better or worse, Private Kisbey?' And Manuel didn't say a thing. But Mr. Richey tolt me he saw a tear streaking down Manuel's cheek, and he knowed Manuel was powerful sad.

Now Mr. Richey didn't have no wife or no children and he figured he couldn't understand how Manuel felt but they was to be fellow soldiers, so he pulled on his pants and went back out to the fire. And they just sat in silence for a time.

Next night 'twas the same thing, but that night Mr. Richey noted that Manuel just helt the book and wasn't reading it, and on top o'that, when Manuel opened it and pretended to read, he had it upside down quite awhile 'fore he turned it right. When he turned it right, he looked at Mr. Richey, who looked away at first. Then Mr. Richey asked, 'Would it go better if I read some of those words?'

And Manuel said, 'If ye cain read 'em atall it'd go better cause ye might as well know, I can't read. Never could.'

And Mr. Richey said, 'Well why didn't you say so?' And he took the book and asked where to read.

And Manuel asked, 'Don't ye read a Book of Prayers?'

And Mr. Richey said he'd never thought much 'bout praying and Manuel tolt him, 'How can ye be in a war without thinking of praying?' and Mr. Richey said he guessed reading a prayer now and then would do no harm. So he started reading the *Soldier Book* to Manuel from page one. The prayer goes like this, for I was given the book from Mr. Richey and I think 'twas a good prayer for both Mr. Richey and Manuel that night in Tennessee in the winter of 1864 A.D.:

'Almighty and most merciful Father; We have erred and strayed from thy ways like lost sheep. We have followed too much the devices and desires of our own hearts. We have offended against thy holy laws. We have left undone those things which we ought to have done; And we have done those things which we ought not to have done. And there is no health in us. But thou, O Lord, have mercy upon us, miserable offenders. Spare thou those, O God, who confess their faults. Restore thou those who are penitent; According to thy promises declared unto mankind, in Christ Jesus our Lord. And grant, O merciful Father, for his sake, that we may hereafter live a godly, righteous, and sober life; to the glory of thy holy name, Amen.'

And on they read for a lesson cause Manuel knowed 'bout how long I read at nights. The next prayer is for forgiveness and the next is the Lord's Prayer taught to the disciples. Then he read the creed Manuel knowed by heart which saprized Mr. Richey cause he had not heard it more than once or twice in his life and here 'side him was a man who couldn't read but knowed all the words that say 'I believe in God the Father Almighty' and then truths 'bout Jesus Christ how he was born of Virgin Mary and how He died and was buried and then rose again and how He is sitting with God the Father and will come to judge us one day, and then the creed part, which I am suspicioning you my readers know as well, talks of the mysterious Holy Ghost, the Church, Communion with Saints, forgiveness of sins, the resurrection of the body, and the life everlasting. And 'fore the night reading ended, the soldier's book had a prayer 'twas for President Lincoln and the country's leaders to have God's guidance. By this time, Mr. Richey said, some other enlisted men had come to the fire and they listened to the prayer book too.

Mr. Richey read some more and then when was the end of the lesson, one of the men asked him, 'Is you a preacher?' And Mr. Richey tolt me as he slapt his knee, 'I said,' and then he said something I won't put down, cause talk like that is holy only when it comes in a fire and brimstone meeting which a body needs now and again but other than that, 'tis not to come from lips that say the Lord's name too, and then he tolt the boys, 'I've not been in a church since I was knee high to a grasshopper and here you think I'm a preacher!' And they all laughed heartily. But truth be tolt, 'most every night after that Mr. Richey'd call something like, 'Gather round boys, the preacher's ready to read the bedtime story.' And the boys would. The Soldier's book had all the Psalms in it and I find that comforting too, as the Psalms was my comfort while Manuel was away as well.

Then Mr. Richey tolt me how pretty soon, he got convicted in his heart that what he was reading was God's Word. And in a few weeks, he treated the Prayer Book like 'twas holy. When Manuel was set to come home, Mr. Richey was with him 'fore he left for the field hospital and Manuel tolt Mr. Richey to hang on to the prayer book like 'twas his own 'cause he knowed we'd had ours and I'd be reading it to him soon. So Mr. Richey kept it and the boys listened to it nearly every night till they either went to home or died.

When Mr. Richey came to see me that Soldier book was the one thing of Manuel's he brought since Manuel had give it to him. But when he gave it to me, 'twas a sober moment, for Mr. Richey said maybe Manuel didn't die in the war as a hero saving somebody's life, but he'd had made sure people in his regiment knowed that their lives could be saved by learning 'bout forgiveness and Jesus Christ from their prayer book.

And Mr. Richey said he thought since 'twas a good book of God's Word, 'twas likely many who heard Mr. Richey read Manuel's book or read their own all across battlefields of the Rebellion, that soldiers got to make things right with God during the war. Mr. Richey was one of them, I know, 'cause I asked him. Maybe that was one main reason Manuel had to go to war. Wars bring 'bout strange happenings and sometimes we can see the good and sometimes maybe only God can.

Another thing seems important to tell you is that while Mr. Richey writ letters to me, since o' course Manuel started to get from us, his siblings, and some good people in our church and community, but couldn't read them hisself, E. L. offered to read his mail for him. But in doing so, he thought perhaps Manuel could of read if he'd had spectacles.

Mr. Richey said that Manuel tolt him he could see so much more detail when E. L. let him try on those spectacles. E. L. tolt that after that the boys teased Emanuel to 'holt fire' till Private Richey gave him the spectacles, which made us smile.

When they was marching and doing soldier things or when 'twas time for Manuel to be having guard duty, they'd say, 'Somebody quick send spectacles for Private Kisbey or he'll shoot the whole Union Army 'stead o' Rebels.' Sounded good Manuel was liked by his fellow soldiers. E. L. said Private Kisbey was the best friend he ever had. He also said he didn't know why, but sometimes when he and Manuel killed time and Manuel'd ask 'bout words and the alphabet for reading, Manuel'd think a letter like a 'L' would be a number like a '7,' but why we didn't know. But seeing things upside down or backward would of made reading 'most imposs'ble if you asked me. Back then, after Mr. Richey's visit I wondert if maybe Jonathan had not so excited 'bout school for the same reasons. Regardless, reading and writing is not the same as character. But if there is such mix-ups, I hope 'tis understood soon.

I might tell you more of Mr. Richey's visit if I can figure how to make this letter shorter. Days is going by and seems soon more changes will occur. My famly's been patient, knowing this is a keepsake I wish to pass along. My famly is grateful for

Mr. E. L. Richey and without his help, we'd not knowed much 'bout Manuel's life in the Army.

Not many of them in Michigan's 3rd Cavalry died of wounds. Most who died died of sickness and there was powerful lot of sickness in the war, much like in Canning Town, and for much the same reasons: Bad water mostly. When one got sick, sickness just kept going among them all. If I recall war facts, we mourned each loss on both sides no doubt but those who died of sickness was maybe three for every one who died of the conflict. Can't help but wonder how many'd died anyhow if they'd been home, knowing the Lord numbers days as He does. And death is death, so mourning would not of been easier I s'pose. But may of been easier having a body home to die than faraway in a place with no famly there to help.

Theo's been up here a couple times, which he did politely since none is to interrupt me if I'm up here. Seems he thinks I am the only one that can make the cream pies the way he likes them. He's reminded me a time or two that we have plenty of rich cream on hand and when I said Alice could do fine, he tilted that head of his and though he's past old enough to put out that lower lip, he did. How dare I resist?

Even when only all of us is around the table, 'tis a good number, but there's to be company tonight. Truth be tolt, I think Theodore wants me to make an extra he could eat on 'fore the company arrives. Otherwise he's on a mission to enlist my help discreetly 'cause someone knows they're not stirring fast enough downstairs and need help but don't want to come out and beg. Miss Alice, after I showed her how to do so some time ago, is overseeing the frying of our plump chickens and there'll be platters and platters of that with mashed potatoes. Those grow good here in Michigan.

Might as well tell you I think they're doing a saprize gathering for me, since the 20th is when I turn fifty. Seems to be lots of stirring and times when someone says, 'You'll spoil it if you don't be quiet!' All that being so, and my eyes needing a break any how, I'll set the writing aside for now and go down to see if there's anything I can do, but I'll be casual 'bout it. I could be wrong and need to do some erasing! Cream pie is good anytime.

My 50th birthday, Saturday, March 20, 1880 A.D.~ Well, I'll hope if someone reads this they don't be disappointed to know I guessed it. I was right. The gathering here was a good one. Some day when my loved ones read this, they'll discover I guessed the fussing was for my birthday. As a rule we don't fuss much over birthdays, not like over Christmas anyway.

Things looked and tasted wonderful and the people made the event enjoyable. Theo did get to eat most of one pie hisself 'cause some food was brought in. But he works it off so won't show on him. Not so for me.

Back to my work for I must finish this 'fore long.

My Manuel was quite a traveler, going from Tennessee to Chicago and back. Seems shameful to me poor soldiers was way from home with no stamps. I s'pose some famlys didn't hear atall from their soldier. I continued to send stamps and news for I knowed without stamps I'd hear less from Manuel.

But as you read, Army pay was not coming like we'd thought it would. I s'pose part of the problem was 'cause banks was working out how to give the money. States mostly had their own money and our Michigan men was in a state not likely to do banking with Michigan money.

O'course you might know when money was too scarce the leaders ordered more printed during the Rebellion, but such did us no good. Some to church talked against government printing, but I just went on home from that discussion 'cause printing didn't help or bother me one way or t'other. We was skimping much as we could. When food's scarce to home sometimes a Mother doesn't feel hungry, and it's not just her being unselfish. I heard another woman say the same thing so I knowed 'tis not my 'magination. It's just the Lord's way of making the food last longer. Just seems to be so.

We had crops let out, hoping for income. We'd used most of our meat but we had milk o'course and eggs from a few chickens so we was eating pretty fair, but Manuel boasted 'bout his meals and getting fat. Truth be tolt, I doubt he was. If

I'd seen his face I'd knowed if 'twas so. I suspicion he didn't want me worrying more 'bout him than I was. How's a wife not to worry when her husband's in a war? And how long would he just be a soldier waiting for a battle? Believe me, I didn't mind and I didn't think he minded either as I figured he was hoping he wouldn't have to fire the gun at a body. If they was supplying food, foraging they called it, that was helpful soldiering, and Manuel'd likely done fine with that, but war and facing guns against another person, well, I wasn't so sure.

The wheat Manuel planted the fall 'fore came up, looking sparse and spindly, but a little promising. Then we got another freeze and wheat was not going to amount to much for the renter or us. I suspicion the seed was just not good to start with but I don't s'pose anyone would of solt bad seed on purpose. I writ Manuel, telling community news that was cheerful and that I was getting better mostly 'cause I got warmer air to breath I s'pose. When we was to church good people'd asked after Manuel, what we heard and such.

I talked with Henry and t'others and writ Levi for advice 'bout what to do. If I remember right Manuel's first $60 finally got to us so we took that to Mr. Olds, but o'course 'twas late and short of what was owed by then. We promised to see what we could do for the remainder. O'course the Army was to be paying us each month. But Manuel wasn't being payed. We was coming near the bottom of the barrel and I kept trusting the Lord to make what we had last longer. I didn't know that we was having a banquet compared to how things would turn later.

I went to Green Oak and bought some seed for a garden and others gave me some starters too, so we'd grow healthy food if weather was right. Michigan's good for potatoes and I planted them for they can be filling. I did peas and the one who let the farm put in some corn and tolt us we could eat from that if we wanted later too. We wasn't the only ones to lose the wheat.

I'll put Manuel's next letter. Not all the letter's readable 'cause it looks like it got coffee spilt sometime 'fore it got to us. 'Parently 'twas writ when Manuel's spirits was hard to keep up. He'd been away over four months, and he'd mostly marched or sat in out of the way places, not even having horses for Cavalry soldiering for 'nother thing. One sure thing, they wasn't payed for doing nothing.

But seemed they'd prob'ly not been payed if they'd been in battles either. E. L. tolt me sometimes Manuel got to thinking that no matter how or what he did lately, 'twas profiting no one.

I s'pose Manuel felt bad 'cause his being away wasn't feeding his famly or buying his farm, and now maybe his famly was worse off than when he left and I was too often doing his work. And his children was growing up without their Pa. I bet he wondert if his being gone helping anyone.

I know Manuel tried not to worry me, but it saddens me to think how Manuel must of felt. War makes it so a loved one can't help give comfort when a soldier's sad and hurting over disappointments. They had hospitals for other hurts, but probably only God and a listener could help at times.

    Fort Pickering   *April the 26ᵗʰ A D 1864*

Dear Wife, I take my pencil in Hand to inform you that I am well at present & hope These few lines may find you And the childern well   I Received your welcom letter yesterday & I Was verry glad to here that you Was better than you had ben sense I left home   I am sorry that my wheat crop is lost & I would like to know if it winterkilled or what the trouble was with it   I have often wished that I hadent inlisted But I Dont see how i would of Met my payments if I hadent Inlisted for I Could Not have Saved Them if I had Staid at Home & our Next payment is A large one & I Dont See how I would Made it if I had Staid at home for evry thing Seams to work against our Interest for the past year or Two but My Dear Wife you must Keep good Spirits & Not let it Worry your mind for I hope it may pease God to faver us by & by & That will come out all Right in the End for is a long Road that has No Croocks or turns   My dear wife you said that you had begun making Garde   I hope you will No work so as To make youself sick again   I verry often Wonder what wold become of the Poor childern if you wos to be sick And could Not see to hom   Kiss them All for Me Once Mor

I Would like to know if you have heard from Mr. Tearl & Richard Pear Sence I Lef hom or Not   I have heard Sence I am here that William Abrems is still aliving & was Coming home & I would to know If you have heard from him   Let me know when you Rite again   I would like to know if there Is any Draft there this spring or if they can get enough with out Drafting any   Well the Fort has got 70 or 80 acres in it & it is ove a Mild long & with that many people sometimes it is not entirely peaceful even within our camp.

Give My love to Henry & his wife & His famly & hope the is all Well   also to Mr & Mrs Witeman & famly & I hope they is all Well & give My love to all Inquiring friends   I will Close For this time & as ever Remaining You affectionate husband

Emanuel Kisbey to Ester Kisbey
Good Bye

Direct to E Kisbey insted of M kisbey & I will have No bother in My Male

Maybe like me, even as I read the letter again now, you can tell that this was a low point for Manuel. I knowed he was sad but what was I to write back to him?   Manuel and I spoke truth to each other on matters of famly welfare and I didn't want him sadder and disappointed more than he was. I thought maybe Manuel's people in Illinois could cheer him up, Kisbey to Kisbey, so prayed they'd write him some encouragement. Fowlers moved 'round so I didn't have or misplaced Sallie's address. Manuel had been so protective of them when they was little, Levi and Sallie, and now I prayed they'd know a way to encourage their older brother who was homesick and discouraged.

On my next letter I addressed Manuel as Emanuel so he'd get letters faster and 'cause this time the children and I solt a few things so we could send a little money along. People in Green Oak and to church was good 'bout buying our eggs and milk and to our thinking, having less to eat a few days allowed us to be cheering up Pa. I was proud of Manuel's children.

Meantime I remember I was relieved Manuel was not in Arkansas, Virginia, or Georgia. Seemed those was the most serious places when neighbors talked. I certainly didn't want Manuel to get captured and end up in Georgia in that Andersonville prison. More was heard 'bout it as time went on and the man running the prison was found guilty of how they treated our Union boys when some was put there during the Rebellion, though as I read 'bout it,

I knowed sometimes you can't even feed your family from your plate if 'tis empty. Still, if news reports was true, even in a war, people need to remember that people from t'other side is a human, seems to me.

Sometimes when letters came from Manuel, I'd read it first to myself so I could keep things from the children if I had to, and at times I did. But when they'd ask each day if we'd heard yet from Pa again, I'd tell them to get their work done and after our Bible reading and prayers when they was tucked to bed I'd read old letters to them. Nights with new letters was best perhaps, but if too much time went by between letters, Manuel's letters was like a story their Pa was telling to them and they'd go to sleep more peaceful. 'Twas good for me, too.

The months went so slow. I wasn't as good with numbers a course as Levi, English girls didn't spend much time with numbers, but I'd figured 'bout how many days we had to go 'less the war got things patched sooner.

Battles kept going on. Men and boys came home to Michigan. We'd hear 'bout who was limping and who was a hero and who was eager to get back to farming and who was eager to get back to winning the war.

Seemed Tennessee was always talked 'bout in Green Oaks when I'd go buy what little I absolutely had to get. But other states I guess was as bad or worst. People asked how close those battles was to Manuel and our 3ʳᵈ Cavalry and sometimes we'd try to figure it out together. Virginia was another place we kept hearing 'bout. Louisiana, Alabama, and even Missouri kept coming up and I'd heard lots 'bout Missouri and Kansas 'fore the Rebellion. And Georgia too was talked 'bout when people asked news 'bout the war.

But I was so thankful Manuel wasn't in Arkansas. I learnt in that April over 800 Union famlys lost a husband or a pa or a son in Arkansas alone. The injured list was larger still, with 'bout 1500 wounded.

If God had asked me where I wanted my husband to serve, what would I say? Hopefully Manuel could stay in the wilderness of Tennessee where no Rebels would find them. Maybe he could come home without firing his gun at another man. I knowed Manuel would take his duty serious, and if he had to, he'd protect his fellow soldiers and hope by firing a shot he'd also be keeping his own famly safer and the US together. As Manuel's sister Sallie writ, a war for holting the Union and stopping slavery 'twas a good cause. But 'twas a war hard on home people, too.

Sometime after the war was all over people heard tell of a soldier who said he talked t'other soldier from t'other side and they thought they could of worked things out without all the grief to famlys. But they wasn't the ones working things out, and don't know they'd kept their word if they had been. Hard to tell what could of been, but what was the problem at the time.

'Bout this time the people in Washington started putting 'In God We Trust' on coins. I hoped they all meant it. Truth be tolt, I had more trust in God than I had coins. Somewhere 'round this time, the people in Washington also decided they needed to put in a Union cemetery for our men who'd fallen in the war. That's in Washington too, and if I heard right, the cemetery begins at the doorstep where a Confederate general lived. Least that's what we heard here. Heard it takes up a whole farm size field or more. There was so many not going back to famlys. 'Magine that General needed to find a new house or live amongst grim reminders.

I kept hoping Manuel was keeping safe in Tennessee or that the 3rd Cavalry would go to another place where the fighting wasn't so spoken of all the time. I guess you see why women don't do war much. More and more I wondert if we'd tried solving our farming problems right. But I wouldn't speak of it to Manuel 'cause he was a soldier with a responsibility there more than a responsibility to home. O'course I knowed part of the reason he went to war was to take care of debts to home.

Manuel got our letter and writ back to us in a few days. God had answered my prayer 'bout hearing from his famly. Soon I heard from Sallie too. We was both wives with husbands away to war.

I know now Lt. George P. Fowler, joined the Union Army from Litchfield Illinois June 11 AD 1864 and was out that time by September 26 AD 1864. He served in with the 143 Illinois Infantry. He was two or so years older than Manuel, born in 'bout AD 1828 but he was a strong man. He'd been building on a house 'fore he went in I believe and though I never saw Sallie's house, I think he'd made her a nice one. I think I writ earlier he was from New York, the place was something field but, oh, 'twas Penfield I believe. And he's still living far as I knowed.

In AD 1864 he could be a Lt. Fowler 'cause he'd served earlier as far away I believe I heard as California 'fore he met Sallie. Don't know but what when he quit soldiering some time after the Rebellion, may be 'fore or after that tragedy of their daughter and the Indians I tolt you 'bout. Anyhow, he took to teaching and then took up lawyering there in Florida, and I 'magine he's being a good one. Wish I'd had his help here in Michigan and if he'd knowed what was going on, he'd likely tried. Sallie was proud of him as you'll see by her letter which I'll put after Manuel's.

This is the letter we got from Manuel in May and you can see he got the money we was able to send:

Fort Pickering   May the 7ᵗʰ/64
Dear Wife I take my pencil in Hand to inform you that I Am
well at present & hope This may find you & the childern
Injoying good health   I Received your welcom letter on the 5ᵗʰ
With the Money in it but it Would ben better if it had ben

Green back for there is ten cents Discount on all other Money Here   I was glad to here that you had got that Money & Paid all my little Debts up so I will have them of ov my mind For I often thought they might Maby give you trouble & that I Expect you have enough of as it is

My Dear Wife I Received A Letter From Sister Sarrah on the 6th & her & Her Husband was well   her two Little have boat ben sick since they Live there but they wos better when She Rote the letter   She sais they is Both crippels but she thinks they will Get over it again   She sais Leve & His wife & famly are well & Uncle & aunt are well   I saw a Traiter hung on the 29th of April for Smuggling gun caps & Powder threw our lines to the Rebels in a coffin   there has be Others Caught Sence one that had two hundred Suits of Cloth & wos on his way to the Rebels to & it is supposed that he will Strech hemp to the Gallows are Right here in the Fort where we can all see them

Give My Love To Henry & His Wife & famly tel them to Kiss the childern for me   tel Him that I hope that he will Have better luck with his crops Than I have had   Give my love to Mr & Mrs Witeman & there famly & all other Inquiring friends Let me know if the Cows have come in   Well I will Now come To A Close for this time   Write Soon & Often   So Nomore But Ever Remain you Affectionate husband
Emanuel Kisbey To Ester Kisbey
Kiss The Dear Children For me Good Night

Manuel was right 'bout the money and I should of knowed 'bout it or asked Levi in a letter, but letters take time. The state banks was not secure. The government started opening banks of their own. These they printed on two sides where most state's was printed on just one side. I hadn't thought it'd be a problem for Manuel when we sent it. To get people accepting the idea to use the new national money, the money we sent was discounted the ten percent. So the three dollars we was able to send to Manuel was not three dollars when it arrived. Nowadays national money's accepted, but when the war was on, mixed money was just one more complication for soldiers and their people to home.

The Witemans Manuel talked 'bout was special friends. Mr. Witeman's wife was the closest I had to being like Aunt Emma, though her name was Sophonia, his Andrew. Sophonia was older than me but much younger than Aunt Emma. Sophonia was born A.D. 1825 and Andrew was 'bout two years older than her. Their boy John was good help to them and they was familiar with us Englishmen for they had least once took in Theodore Ward as a labourer. We figured people who took in us English people just crossing was kind to give immigrants a chance at a new and better life. Theodore was 'bout same age as Manuel and me, maybe a little younger.

In June the children heard the letter from Manuel's sister Sallie. I reminded them who she was for we'd not kept in good touch and our lives had changed since the Christmas 'fore the war. I'd knowed from Levi that Sallie's children was crippled.

Sallie's Manuel's famly and I've kept her letter so you'd know her a bit at least. Maybe you'll know her famly someday after you read this. Like I tolt you 'fore, they moved after the Rebellion to Texas and then, I think, to Ohio for a spell 'fore going south to Florida.

Seems strangely good how places that was war places 'fore can be places people up and move to, like Levi's and Sallie's famly did. Well, perhaps all of us when I think of it. That's one good thing that comes from war, places get safer to go to when the disagreement's settled. Sometimes people like Sallie's George can give a hand to help places come back to good standing. I think he was liked wherever he went so maybe his being a General 'fore he was finished was a very good thing. Maybe being General could of helped if he'd of been one earlier. But, then, maybe Generals was more the targets of Rebels than the Lts and the like. We all rejoiced he made it through the war. I think he liked military life though. He may have been in on some of the sad efforts dealing with Indians, but that's a part of history I don't know much 'bout so I cannot say much. I know God made us all. That I know.

Anyhow, here's Sallie's letter. She calls me sister just like she and I was blood and not just she and Manuel:

Litchfield Ill   *May 26ᵗʰ, 1864*
Dear Sister
I now take the opertunity of writing you afew lines to lett you know how we are   I am well but I have two little girls and both lame   one has aperarliest limb and the other a very lame foot somthin like the wite swelless   thear so that I cannot get out with them at all so you see I have   a prettie hard time George has gon to the wore   its to hard to bear but it is for a good cause and woman must make sacrafies as well as men   I have written to Emmanuel and got a letter from him   is the way that I got your address   write soon and tell me all   about your Children   thar names and how many you have got   I have two Lucy and Susan   George is Leutenent in the company he went in   I dont know that I have any think more to tell you I shold like very much to see you and the children as cant you send me your likeness and I will send ours as quick as my children get so I can take them out   if it is so that you can bring the children and come and see me   I would come and see you if I cold but I cannot now   if George stays in the army I may come this fall
So good by take good care of your self then
from your Sister Sallie E Fowler.

How good of Sallie to want us to come. How imposs'ble it'd be to go. She was still being fashionable I suspicion, and likely her girls was little dolls. I prayed they'd get better. How good, I'd thought, if we could do another Kisbey gathering once peace settled again.

We wasn't hearing from Manuel like we hoped. A mind tries to figure why. A battle? A bullet? A streak of bad fortunes to Manuel or some with him, like E. L.? Margaret was almost like a good sister and she and Henry reminded me of the verse 'bout peace to minds stayed on God. Most days I felt peace, but t'other days I felt dread.

People noted we was struggling more and helped us some. My health kept me concerned 'bout the pain I kept having. If I doctored, using what little we had, would the doctor know how to help? Some doctors was talked 'bout when they was not nearby. I s'pose 'tis clear to you that men could just tag along with a doctor and learn from his work and after a time if they took to the work, they could say they was then doctors. Doctors nowadays get some more training. Some who learnt doctoring from another doctor was natural at doctoring, just like some nurses is natural at nursing. My Anna says now she wants to be a nurse but time will tell. But she seems more natural at that than doing chores for sure.

In 1864 A.D. I kept tending children and chores and overseeing crops let to the one farming for us. And making payments when I could.

Mr. A. W. Olds was not satisfied 'bout late payments even though he tolt me he thought 'twas brave of Manuel to go to war to make the payments and help holt the Union together. His wife was nice to me too. But Mr. Olds was a businessman and I didn't know the details till later, but Mr. Olds solt the stamp notes on our place to Mr. Heath and Mr. Heath was a very kind man I'd later find out. What I did know at the time was that I wasn't being asked to pay when I didn't have the money, though o'course I knowed Manuel wanted his debts met.

Word came that President Lincoln was saying the Union needed 500,000 more soldiers. Such a number! A month 'fore the papers and people claimed the President had asked for 'bout that many too, but in later times we learnt that not all we heard was true. One wondert if there was that many men left to fight, but if a war's to be settled, then seems to me 'tis best to have enough of the right side to do the settling. I tolt you I'd hoped Manuel'd be assigned away from where so many deaths had come in Arkansas. Then we heard Michigan's 3rd Cavalry was moving out. People was guessing where they'd go. 'Bout the middle of June or early July, we found out with this letter from Manuel:

Margery Kisby Warder

Duvalls Bluff Arkansas   *June The 4th AD 1864*

Dear Wife I take my pen in hand to let you know that I am Well at present & hope those few lines May find you & the childern all well

I Received your welcom letter & was glad To here that the childern wos all injoying good Health   I was sory to here that you are still Troubled with that pane in your side   tel Emma Jane that I liked that New dress verry well & hope she will be a good girl & help her Mother do the work. Well we have Finely left the old for on the 14th of May & Camped out two Nights & then we started up here   we wos two Days & two Nights on the way   The Distence the way we came is about 300 Miles & on a strate line it is only an 100 Miles to Memphis.

I wos asined To Co D after we landed Here then I was transferred to Co F Where I think I will Remain   There is Some talk of going back to Memphis again   we haven't got any horses yet   But they say the is ready for us up to St louis Masouri

the Boys from our Neighborhood in Co G is all well at present

we haven't got any pay yet and I Dont think we will get any Now til the first of July   if I Did get my pay here it would hardly be Safe to Send it & if I Did it cost ten cents on the Doller & then I would have to Run all the Risk of loosing it

this is quite a wilderness here & we don here any News here atall so I cant Rite Much   you Must Rite us all the News you can For that is all the News we is by letters   News Papers three weeks old ar worth 25 cents

Give my love to Henry & his wife & famly & all Inquiring friends I Will Now close for this Time

Nomore but as ever Remaining your Affectionate Husband Emanuel Kisbey To Ester Kisbey   kiss the childern for Me

On the next paper I think Manuel was trying to write for there is several 'E' and 'K' letters along with his address:

E. E Kisbey 3rd Mich Cav Co F
Duvalls Bluff Arkansas
E   E   E   E   E   E   E

When I saw those E's, I just knowed Manuel was going to master the signing of his name soon! That'd made Manuel so proud of hisself. And truth be tolt, a person's never too old to learn, and remember that Manuel'd be turning 34 during 1864. Least I understood he thought so. We was near in age but as I tolt you, I was a little older. Maybe he kept from me knowing how much older. Anyhow, why quit learning? Can't 'magine how little I'd know if I'd stopped learning at 34!

Now I must tell you when I saw on the envelope and letter that Manuel was in or near the battlefields of Arkansas, it gave me concern. Praying was long and hard. 'Fore he'd seemed to just be waiting for the rest of his regiment and horses. How'd Manuel go those 300 miles in just a few days in a hot summer with enemy round? How did they get good water to drink, as I'd heard men got sick on bad water. And no horses yet. How was things for Manuel?

I don't rightly remember what Manuel meant 'bout Emma's dress but when she reads this perhaps she'll remember. I know people was being charitable to us and I also know Emma liked to draw pitchures for her Pa. T'others included lines to their Pa too but mostly they tolt me what to say to him and always they sent their love like he'd sent his to them. They weren't forgetting their Pa and I was every day missing my beloved Manuel.

We didn't hear from Manuel or his scribe for several weeks but we figured the men was cleaning out Rebels in Arkansas and if that was the way to end the war, they had to do it. So we prayed more and more, and sometimes just hoped the Rebels would repent and quit breaking our Union.

We got news of so many deaths in August, but mostly in places far from where we believed Manuel was serving. Numbers like 400 killed in Strawberry Plains Virginia. I didn't know atall where that was but I remember thinking, the name sounds so peaceful and it's filled with so much heartache and blood. We heard of men killed when they traveled by railroad, hundreds at a time killed. We heard of a big explosion of Union ammunition and our men was hurt or killed.

Then we heard of Michigan Cavalry prisoners being executed that August. My, how we wondert what we'd hear next. Six Union soldiers died in Arkansas. Was they from Michigan? From our community? Was that why we wasn't hearing from Manuel and Mr. Richey? O'course we prayed for all famlys and for peace, but mostly the children prayed for Pa to come home to them.

Then there was celebrations 'cause a big city in Georgia, Atlanta, had been captured and the hopes was then that the war would end soon. We was getting close to one year being over and I dreaded the cold weather for Manuel even in Arkansas and Tennessee.

In September we waited for letters. News came that two more died in Arkansas, but what two? Manuel and Mr. Richey maybe?

Then we heard another sad thing that hundreds of the Union soldiers died in a place with another peaceful name, a peaceful refuge ought to be. 'Twas at Sycamore Church some place, think maybe Virginia again, but I remember the sycamore and church part for I thought of the Bible story of Zaccheus and the sycamore tree he climbed so he'd least get to see Jesus.

I thought, 'I wonder how many of them that died was ready to see Jesus.' A mind can think so many thoughts. Waiting to hear is hard.

Then came the day that filled us with so much joy! Land sake's, Manuel was coming home!

'Twas a saprize to us but 'twas good news. Word spread and friends was happy 'bout it too.

The worst part was o'course that he'd been ill, but we all just knowed that if he could get away from the war and get back to his famly, he'd get well. Famly's good medicine.

Wouldn't it be the most special birthday ever for Alfred if his papa came home on his third birthday? The homecoming would be like everyone's birthday. Or Christmas!

How'd we hear he was coming? Mr. Richey writ us this much welcomed letter:

Brownsville Station Ark   *Sept the 12ᵗʰ AD 1864*

Mrs. E Kisbey I can tell you our hearts 'most stopped when we saw no usual 'My Dear Wife' or 'Dear Wife' but I excitedly read to the children the whole letter:

Mrs. E Kisbey as it wos your husbands Request this Morning when he left Me for Me to write you a few lines & let you know that he wos on his way home

You can 'magine the children's jumping for joy! I knowed he was to stay in 3 years so something was not as planned, but I'd take Manuel however he came home to us. I read quickly:

He left here this Morning at 10 oclock   he will go from here to DuValls to the post hospitto & there he will get his furlow & then he will go strait Threw home   he left in good Spirits   he has ben in the hospitto 'bout three weeks   I think the climate is to worm for him here   I Never hear or the Dr say what wos the trouble with Emanuel   I would like to here from him when he gets home   please gratify me with A few lines

Yours respectfully   E L Richey
Co F 3ʳᵈ Mich Cav Brownsville Station Ark

The letter came to us on Saturday, September 17th, two days 'fore Alfred's birthday. Henry and Margaret had been to town and brought us the letter, not knowing what it'd contain. They was as thrilled as we was. My, how we hurried to get ready for Manuel's homecoming! I quickly put Margaret in charge of helping get extra washing done so clean sheets would be on for Manuel to rest in. I think everyone warned the children 'bout not wearying Pa when he came 'cause he'd be happy, but likely needing to rest his first days. Henry and the man letting the farm spruced things up along our lane and 'round the barn, even noticing flowers the children could pick in a day or two when their Pa was back. Mrs. Witeman said she'd spend the day fixing some extra nice cakes and foods for Emanuel's return and Alfred's birthday. Mr. Witeman thought of things, mostly helpful things, to keep the children out from under foot. One project was preparing papers with pitchurs to show Manuel we was thankful for his return. Even though the next day was Sabbath, Henry thought he'd bring back the ole mule after dinner Sunday. It ate for him better than for us, though it wouldn't make most persons poor feeding it. It, like Shep, would know the master was home.

We was a whirlwind of excitement and joy, perhaps the happiest day of my life. We didn't know exactly when to expect Manuel to arrive, but I kept an eye toward the road in case he got hurried along the way. We worked near heart attack locomotion with all the excitement but we knowed 'twas worth it. By late afternoon, the place looked the best we'd ever seen it, not counting fields. I thanked the good people who helped us and watched them leave so we could all try to get some rest. Even though the next day was a Sabbath, later I heard that even our preacher thought if we'd missed church to prepare for Manuel, it'd been no sin.

I know now when I try to get ready for any special visitors if we'd not seen t'other for a long time, I try to get a pound or two off 'fore they arrive. The thought came as I prepared for my Manuel, but I knowed twas likely both he and I was far too skinny to even look healthy after what we'd been through. I did pinch my cheeks a few times, but we loved t'other no matter what we looked like, and there was comfort in that.

Henry was sure it'd be Monday 'fore Manuel could come 'cause of train schedules. At church, Mr. Heath said he'd be glad to use his wagon to meet Manuel and Henry could go along. Heath was fascinated by trains and knowed the station man and train schedules. Can't say I rested much that Sabbath, but I tried. We all tried to keep things orderly. Emma Jane chose to swing most of the afternoon and I saw no problem with that atall, espeshly if she didn't sweat doing so.

Finally on Monday morning, September 19th, Alfred's birthday, we was totally ready for Manuel. The train most likely to come from Arkansas was due in 'bout 11 o'clock and Mr. Heath said he'd get Manuel to us by one-thirty or two. Henry went along just to help.

Margaret and the children stayed with us. Emma had drawn her pitchures of her pa as a soldier and as a farmer and she circled farmer as the one she wanted Pa to be. Emma Jane was coming close to being six and for a six-year-old she was a good drawer 'cause we all knowed which was the soldier and which was the farmer.

And Alfred got his wagon out like we tolt him to for his saprise and took it to the fence. Emma Jane and Jonathan and their cousins would holt Alfred up on the fence so he could watch the road for his Papa. And we waited. Alfred fell asleep on Shep still holting the handle of his little wagon his Pa had made for him the Christmas 'fore. I remember looking out and wishing I had a way to take Alfred's likeness as ole Shep let him nap on him, for I knowed Manuel would think 'twas the most special pitchure of a little boy waiting for his Pa. There was more than one soldier in the famly standing guard, but one was only three and he'd fallen asleep.

The afternoon was like a holiday for the older children. With every wagon they'd yell and we women squealed like children, rushing into the yard, me asking o'course how I looked. Then we'd find 'twas just a neighbor or someone else passing by on the road. Once in awhile one would stop to see if Manuel was back. Then they'd tip their hats and drive on. The road seemed to be so busy that day, but I was watching it more than usual.

Later that afternoon the men came back and they tolt us Manuel hadn't been on the train, and they'd waited for another one or two with connections to where a soldier might be, but no Manuel.

'So maybe he'd come tomorrow,' I thought, 'Or another day,' t'others said, and we ate the food we had to eat and people went home.

'Fore we went to bed that night Jonathan reminded me that we should pray our prayer thanking God for Alfred, the birthday blessing prayer. 'Twas a hard prayer to pray as I'd hoped Manuel would be there to pray it for his son. We was all disappointed, but we hadn't knowed which day exactly Manuel was to come.

For three days Henry and Mr. Heath checked the station to see if trains was coming from Arkansas with Manuel. But Manuel wasn't on a train all week. We and t'others had to take off the nicer clothes to do our work. But that'd be fine for we was a farm famly. Manuel's famly.

The dreaded feeling started searching for a place to settle in. I didn't want to tell the children that things was not right. My heart started telling my head I was not ever going to hear or see or touch or talk to or laugh with my Manuel again. But I didn't want to give up hoping, for hope is such a strong part of life. 'Twas easy to imagine saying to my husband, with tears flowing, 'Oh, Manuel, we thought you was never coming!' and 'course not mean it, or say, 'We was 'bout to give up hope...' and 'course he'd say, 'I tolt you I'd git back. Nuthin' could keep me 'way.' Those and lots other sayings came to mind, mixing with hope and fighting a sinking heart.

And then some days later our preacher came with Henry and I knowed hope had to be a strong part of death too.

Turned out Manuel never left the Duvalls Hospital alive from what I've been tolt. Another person said he left and got bad water coming home somewhere in Arkansas. Maybe he started and got took back.

All I know is that papers one day along time later came and said Pvt. Kisbey died the day we was throwing his and Alfred's party, September 19, 1864. I s'pose there was a better party being throwed where he was coming.

Pvt. Manuel Kisbey likely never had to fire his gun at nobody. He did soldiering like he did life: trying to keep two small and one big family together, taking his place, keeping it safe as he could for the ones with him and those who'd be coming to the spot later. He served with honour, and people, like I tolt you, knowed he was Christian man. He lived his faith and his thinking, and both was good and I suspicion by now God's kept Manuel's name straight and given him his good reward.

To us Manuel was Papa to Sarah and George whom he was tending to in Heaven and he was the Papa who'd never to be forgotten by Jonathan Levi and Emma Jane and Alfred Alvin Kisbey, and he was the beloved husband of Esther Copsey Kisbey who without shame keeps her promise to love and respect and honour him till she dies. He had some loyal friends 'round here. In the end, it didn't really change much that we was only a small group that knowed and loved him. Those that didn't missed out, seems to me. Least they could do, though, is believe he was honourable and least believe he was once alive and good.

A person's death is so much more final when a famly has a final meeting and people come to join the burying. But for Manuel, 'twas not to be.

We waited for the body. It never came.

We waited for his, what they call 'personal effects.' Never came.

We waited for a paper declaring his death. It crept to us from Washington D.C. after I writ for it with lawyers and the war was long past.

And o'course, we waited for the payments a soldier was to get for his famly so he could provide for them while honouring his oath to his country's unity. Both in life and in death. Never came.

Manuel's little famly was trying to stay together long after the states decided they would unify again.

If we was poor 'fore, what was we now?

Well, we was Manuel's Kisbeys. But for the next years I tried to prove that was so. People that was friends thought it'd be easy 'cause they knowed us.

Henry and Margaret testified 'fore lawyers and courts that Manuel was my husband, that he'd been in the Union Army. Other people did too.

Olive Hays, her husband, and Margaret, too, tolt those two was midwives for births of our American children.

Men that knowed Manuel for six or more years went to lawyers' offices with me, Widow Kisbey, to get what was due Manuel's famly.

But in charity I will say since Manuel was not a writer, papers was slow to come. Was he Manuel or Samuel? Was it Kisby or Kisbey or Keisbey? Was it Co F or Co G? Was he Cavalry or Dismounted or Infantry?

I could say yes to all, but mostly I wanted people sitting higher than me to understand he was a soldier who went to pay debts for his children and his wife so his name could be said with respect and to prove he'd fulfill his responsibility to stand guard for his famly and his country till his time was up. He'd lived Christian and he'd died honourably. He deserved respect. Private Kisbey deserved it. His children deserved payment for having no Pa, and his widow could use the $8 a month she was owed, a soldier's half pay. But no one could help me bring him respect and his due. The adversary wanted to roar again.

Mr. Heath, God bless Him, let me know he had the note on my farm and they'd patiently make sacrifices along with us if need be. He went to court with me, too, I believe.

But how was I to get to Pontiac lawyers and to Livingston County lawyers all the time? Should I take Manuel's children and just het off for Washington D.C.? O' course not. There was war on, war taking lives. I tell you this, my dear descendents, I'd been a formal Copsey who thought a woman was to be polite, letting men do the business. But in all the encounters I had, I did not get fair answers from men behind the desks. Was I really married to Manuel? Was Manuel really an

Englishman and if he was an Englishman was he really a United States citizen? Yes, Yes, Yes. But he was not payed ever for doing what he did except for the money I tolt you that came. How long can a widow and three children live on that little bit?

Well, truth be tolt, we couldn't be alive except for God's gracious goodness to us. The Holy Bible somewhere declares it does no good to trust in horses or chariots or princes or the like. O'course I'd heard that 'fore, but in the months and years ahet I found the only wise choice all along is to trust in God.

For a long time, getting what was due Manuel became my life purpose. That, and feeding our children. The farm payed bills and made bills. We solt eggs till we had to sell the chickens for what we owed. Finally, we payed bills with the last of the milk cows. The mule was gone, o'course, for the lonesome ole thing only took up space for us most of its days. Shep had to catch his own food which he was good at doing, and in fact he brought us a rabbit and squirrel or two. But even friends and famly finally decide they have to turn t'other purposes and I fault them not. Hunger is a personal thing.

O'course I writ to Levi and Sallie and tolt them Manuel was not coming home far as we knowed. And people would sometimes tell me true stories of how a man everyone thought was dead turned up to be alive and walked right home to a *famly* that'd given up. I wanted it to be so. I drempt many nights 'twas so. First nights o'course I heard him coming I was sure. But he never came. Never. Emanuel Kisbey was dead and I was his hungry widow with three sad and hungry children.

One night, and this is God's truth I swear, we was like the widow of the Old Testament except we had not so much as a drop for the oil jar. I did what mothers do. We had eat light all week and I had no way to get more. The chickens was gone. The cow was gone. Ole Shep was past his hunting days I guess. I looked to him, but I tell you, he'd been a good and faithful dog, and a reminder of Manuel too, so how could I think of destroying him? 'Sides he stood guard at nights like a

Kisbey, and I didn't know but what he might somehow still get us a squirrel or rabbit we could share with him.

I fed my children the last we had to eat. Jonathan asked for more but I tolt him, 'Not tonight, Son.' Emma Jane, just 'fore I finished combing her hair, tolt me she was hungry and asked if she could have another bite and I tolt her, and I couldn't think at first from whence it came, 'We'll eat again later, Emma.' Then I remembered. Alayna! I was just like Alayna, except I had no Esther to bring the biscuits, for now I was Esther and I had not even flour to make biscuits. I shush't the children, for we'd taught them not to carry on or whine, but I knowed they was not misbehaving. They was hungry. I was hungry too for I o'course had not eat for a day or two. All was gone.

I put the children to bed after our prayers, for I never stopped praying. I knowed God was trustworthy sure as I knowed I was Manuel's widow. And when Jonathan asked me what we was going to do 'bout food the next days, I tolt him not to worry 'cause God knowed what a fix we was in. I did not panick. But I did think we might just waste away. But truth be tolt, I didn't care. I wanted to be with Manuel anyhow, and what child would not prefer a banquet in Heaven with Jesus and their Pa to staying here on earth for days of loneliness and empty plates? I had Shep in, but I didn't lock the door 'cause I thought if a thief came he'd either kill us and get our wait over with, or he'd look 'round and take pity and if he had any feelings of goodness left, he'd likely leave us something from his sack! We was that bad off. Either way we'd be ahet. 'Twas not a humorous time atall, but I can smile as I write this now 'cause 'tis one more testament of God and how He works.

When the children was sleeping I got out my *Common Book of Prayers* and the *Holy Bible* for more reading and I tolt God, 'I will read till Thou givest me a peace beyond understanding.' I tolt God, 'Please God, I'm hungry for Thee, even more than I'm hungry for food. And Thou knowest I'm powerful hungry for food. Seems to me it'd be a mess if Ye took me 'fore the children, but Thou canst do what Thou wants to do. I'm learning bit by bit Thou doest what Thou wantest, and Thou art wiser than me. But I'd like to say to Thee, the Kisbeys is good children and they is Thine 'least as much as they is mine. I knowed people might take pity on them just as other children's being given pity when their Pa's don't come home. I leave that to Thee. But Holy Father God, please allow me something in Thy Book that is Thy Holy Word for me, Widow Kisbey, this night. Things is such that Thou art my Husband/Provider and Manuel's children art Thy orphans. Oh Father God, I will not quit reading till Thou comforts me with Thy Word.'

And I began reading. God's Word is a comfort and if you don't know that children, you don't know the first thing 'bout what you need to know. Manuel would tell you that too. Truth be tolt, he'd insist I tolt you that. If that sounds like scolding then must be 'cause you don't know that truth yet, and with a great deal of love I'd tell you 'tis past time you learnt to know God through His Word. I cannot help you 'cause I won't be with you, but even if I was to be, I could not help in nearly the ways God can. He is trustworthy and if you only learn one thing, learn that.

So that night I read. The candle light was dim and my eyes was teary at times, but I was God's responsibility and the children was too, for I read that God is the husband to the widow and the father to the fatherless, and that was our situation and that was some comfort, but I needed more 'fore I could sleep.

And then God let candle light flicker on the precious verses of Psalm 37 for this widow and her children whose efforts to get the money had failed.

People had kept the money due us from my beloved's soldiering and his death as a soldier. The farm was not ready to provide us with more for some time. We was past hungry. And we was mostly forgotten, not unkindly so, not purposefully so, but I was not telling of our needs, for I knowed God knowed and He owned everything. But nobody was distributing God's resources for Him, 'least not to us.

And here is some of the verses the way King James thought they should be writ from the original language:

Psalm 37:

'Fret not thyself because of the ungodly: neither be thou envious against the evil doers. For they shall soon be cut down like the grass: and be withered as the green herb.' (I didn't feel that kind of anger towards them that was not letting my papers get approved so we could have food, but if I was tempted to have those feelings, God had beat me to them. Then 'twas lovely for God writ--)

'Put thou thy trust in the LORD, and be doing good: dwell in the land, and verily thou shalt be fed.' (I didn't care whether God was telling me I was to be fed on earth or in Heaven, but I was to be fed. And not just fed table food, but food from God's Word, too.)

'Delight thou in the LORD; and he shall give thee thy heart's desire.' (I at first thought perhaps those was right who said until I buried Manuel's body I couldn't be sure Manuel was gone and I wanted to say to God, Manuel is the desire of my heart, but then I was humbled and I cried softly to God, 'Thou art the desire of my heart. Thy way is the way we must go.' And when I prayed that, seemed to me to be that God had put those words, that desire in my heart, that He had just placed in me that desire just like He writ it thousands of years 'fore. So I read on.)

'Commit thy way unto the LORD, and put thy trust in him: and he shall bring it to pass.' (I talked with the LORD. I knowed we was no match for His thinking for He saw all the years 'fore and ahet and I could not understand even this one day. How what had happened was best for us I could not see, but Father God, Husband God, was asking me to rely on Him and His way of working things out.)

'He shall make thy righteousness as clear as the light: and thy just dealing as the noonday.' (This brought me hope for I thought of how people questioned whether Manuel and me was citizens and married and loyal to the United States and we

had just tried to be a Christian famly who breathed good air in a free nation willing to help others have the same opportunities we wanted. I needed judgment to go for Manuel so his name and honour could get what he served in the Union Army to get; he wanted to be a good citizen who payed his debts and fed his famly and raised them to live in Christian ways. Manuel deserved respect in life and he deserved respect in death. Was God going to get that for us? Or would Manuel get his respect and honour in Heaven and not on earth?)

Hold thee still in the LORD, and abide patiently upon Him: but grieve not thyself at him, whose way doth prosper, against the man that doeth evil counsels. Leave off from wrath, and let go displeasure: fret not thyself, else shalt thou be moved to do evil. Wicked doers shall be rooted out: and they that patiently abide the LORD, these shall inherit the land.'

(Now God was warning me not to let that evil root I talked 'bout earlier with you, bitterness, take holt of my soul. If bitterness rooted 'bout not getting what was due for Manuel's sake and ours, and anger at what was not being worked fairly in the offices that helt our papers, then I was becoming an evildoer in my mind if not in my actions. I thought of Manuel's Aunt Gertrude who could not let bitterness be yanked out and I prayed to God not to let me get pulled down by bitterness.)

I started to see more how much I must learn to trust God as my only provider and father to our orphans. I was poor as poor could be but I had the Provider of the Heavens watching over us. He would perhaps take us home where we would always be safe and satisfied which seemed to be best to my way of thinking, but I knowed not to tell God how to work things out. I knowed he could rearrange all His resources to see that we got our needs met. I was beginning to rest more in Him and my faith was growing.)

The Good Book goes on with more good verses that God and I enjoyed that long night 'fore He brought me to this part:

In verse twenty-three I thought of Manuel: *'The Lord ordereth a good man's going: and maketh his way acceptable to himself.'*

I helt that verse in my head till it passed to my heart. Manuel was a good man, and not just a good man by man's standards. Manuel had heard good preachers in England and he'd been to the same revival as me in London and we had then and many times since expressed our trust in God's Holy Son Jesus Christ as our Saviour who had tolt us in the Book that He was the only way God was permitting people into Heaven. I knowed Manuel was in Heaven or he was waiting the tap's call to go, but he was titled to go and be with the LORD God Almighty. And could I question the steps the LORD had ordered for Manuel? I didn't need to like the way the steps was ordered, or find them easy but I did need to trust that God had ordered the steps for my beloved. And whether 'twas God who was delighting or 'twas Manuel who was delighting, either way, delight was good.

I thought more of our little ones that I had such a hard time letting go from this earth, but now perhaps even our little George was walking with his Papa 'round Heaven and Papa was seeing life in our Sarah that we never saw in her on earth. Oh Manuel was delighted and I knowed a thousand years is as a day and in no time our famly would be together again as though 'twas just days or perhaps minutes apart.

I was getting refreshed and restful but I was still hungry and I read on. Verses 24 to 25 was what let me fall peacefully asleep in the middle of the night, and now as I copy it to this paper I see that I many times writ 'holt' wrong likely. I sometimes writ to you with my Holy Bible open, but if I'd done so each day I'd spelt like King James said to spell. That being so, I say, I often read my *Bible* and *Book of Prayers* and then I do the writing. But I will try to remember some of the letters better. Here, children, is the verse that meant so much to me:

'Though he fall, he shall not be cast away: for the LORD upholdeth him with His hand' (That's how I was to spell holt! But more important, that night I was reminded we was helt, upheld, by God Himself.)

'I have been young, and now am old; and yet saw I never the righteous forsaken, nor his seed begging their bread.' I

underlined that here on purpose for this was the verse I would never forget. Ah! Look at that. I should write 'have'!

The writer tolt me, and I was mid-thirtys so I was not what would be called old yet, 'least not in Michigan, that in all his years he had seen God's hand upholding, lifting those who'd fallen and that the righteous would not be forsaken nor would our children have to beg bread.

That was enough. I was satisfied, full.

I took God at His word. I layed the Bible open to Psalm 37 and put a marker on verse 25 and I said softly, 'Tis all in Thy Hands, Lord. Thou knowest I can do nothing more and that this house has not one crumb left for a new day. So be it. Thou art our God and we are Thy children through Thy Precious Son, Jesus Christ my Lord and Saviour, Amen.'

I blew out the candle and though my stomach growled, I felt fed. I layed fearless in my bed, not so much sleeping as thinking how God was at work in one way or t'other. 'Twas so good to spend the time talking on with God, my Father, my Husband, my Provider, the One who would care for my children. The adversary had been chained again!

Children, if you write my obituary some day, put that in, that I wept and prayed all night after giving my children the last food in the house but that I believed God's Word was writ just for us when I got to Psalm 37, verse 25. I have no shame in letting the world know we was hungry. We was justly hungry. But God is God.

The next morning we woke hungry and there was no food to be had.

The children started dressing, but they knowed how things had been when they had gone to sleep. And they knowed I was sitting up as they fell asleep.

'Shall I set out the plates?' one of them said.

'What harm in that,' my mind wondered. So I said, 'It's a sign of good manners to set the table without being asked.'

In my mind, I was torn. If days from then somebody checked on us and found our bodies, our table would look orderly. But another part of me felt anticipation that perhaps

God wanted me to offer Him just a wee bit of any faith that He could not only welcome us in Heaven, but that He could also provide for us on earth 'til was our time to join Him.

Then the door had a knock. The children and I looked at t'other, wondering who had come 'fore chore time.

On t'other side stood a neighbor who'd not been over to our little farm for a long time. He tolt me God had tolt him to stop to check on us that morning while he was praying. His wife was with him and he asked if they could come in.

Why would I turn away God's help? They was not high and mighty, but good humble neighbors, and they wanted to know our situation, for he was convinced he was truly God-sent. I could only offer praise to Father God and thank Him for being my provider and the biscuits He'd had the neighbor's wife make was like manna to us. They saw my tears of thankfulness and they saw the need we faced.

From that point on his household quietly helped us with food and never once made us feel like we was poor trouble, but that they was being quietly obedient to God. They feared if they was tempted to be proud they could help, they'd ruin what God was teaching them about obedience. Their joy was that they'd learned to listen and we'd spoil it if we refused their help. We was somehow part of God's plan for their knowing Him better. When I tolt them about the Bible time I'd had the night 'fore, their eyes was glistening with tears and the hugs his wife and I had that morning felt so much like a hug from a too seldom seen sister. His wife and I became good friends and I shall always treasure the friendship we shared. God was faithful to us 'cause someone else was quiet then faithful to Him.

With holy reverence I state, God used people to see that His wife and His children was fed. And my readers of this letter, if God would pay so much heed to my little famly in those years, He will pay heed to you as well. When you face big problems, think like ole Abraham, God can solve even this. Is anything too hard for Him? He slays the enemy.

I even now do as the neighbor requested. I'll not reveal his name for he said he and his wife was just obedient to God, and any praise for now goes to Provider God. Later God will give the neighbor and wife their due. Earthly praise cannot.

So be it. God knowed what He was doing when He made us neighbors...and when those living nearby now was to be my neighbors...and those near you was chosen to be your neighbors.

May the ripple my neighbor began with obedience help you, and me, see how you and I can make glorious ripples that honour our Lord God.

Ripple away, my beloved ones, bring Him praise!

If the Living Water's in you, share Him with others! Ripple away.

Oh, let God's rippling waters splash till all's tolt 'God is Provider!' Amen and amen.

To continue without working on the Bible study questions, please turn past the questions designed for this study.

A NOVEL APPROACH TO BIBLE STUDY
LESSON NINE · QUESTIONS 165-188
(INCLUDES QUESTIONS REFERENCING
"MICHIGAN WITHOUT MANUEL"/CHAPTER EIGHT)

Please read Psalm 33:18-19; Psalm 34:6-22, and Psalm 37. The testimony of God's provision in Esther's 1912 obituary inspired me to write "Leaves.../Unto All Generations" from Esther's perspective.

165) In this chapter, we read: "So many choices we (has/have) to make (is/are) only partly our choice, for life and circumstances can filter out some options we don't want filtered, but we don't have say. So we look at what's on the table and pick up what we can work with, that's how I see it."

Occasionally, most of us find ourselves in circumstances over which we have little control. Some discover their spouse is unfaithful, or struggle because a business partner makes unwise decisions. Others' lives are changed by a storm, an election, an accident, an illness or a death. Listed below are a few "disadvantages" Esther probably did not like about her life in this chapter. Look at each and try to jot down how she coped with each.
   A. Absence of Emanuel
   B. Trying to keep the farm "working" and paying for it
   C. Attitude toward Aunt Gertrude
   D. Health and raising children alone
   E. Separated from loved ones: Emanuel's Michigan Third Cavalry assignments/other relatives who kept in touch with letters
   F. Poverty
   G. Taking on role of earthly provider/protector/ disciplinarian in addition to the nurturing role of mother (entire chapter)
   H. Other

166) Consider Esther's growing empathy for others. As you read, you see her feelings softening toward Aunt Gertrude, toward others whose loved ones have been drawn into wars or separations, toward those whose loved ones did not or could not gather wood, lacked food, etc. One of the ways in which Esther and the children were

comforted was through readings in the Common Book, her version of the scriptures.

She especially communes with the God of the universe as she meditates upon Psalm 34 and Psalm 37. Please read those as presented on these pages or in your own copy of the Bible and comment on how those verses brought comfort then, and could, now.

167) Though Esther and the children had an empty place at the table, because Esther had received Jesus Christ as her Lord and Savior, there was Another Presence with them, and also with Emanuel as he went about his soldiering responsibilities. By studying these scriptures, write down the role of the Holy Spirit:

A.John 14:16: (Jesus speaking to the disciples shortly before Jesus would be illegally tried, falsely convicted, mockingly crucified, willingly dying as one condemned – but by our sin and not His on): *"And I will ask the Father, and He will give you another Helper, that He may be with you forever."*

B.John 14:25-27: (Jesus speaking) *"These things I have spoken to you while abiding with you. But the Helper, the Holy Spirit, whom the Father will send in My name, He will teach you all things, and bring to your remembrance all that I said to you. Peace I leave with you; My peace I give to you; not as the world gives, do I give to you. Let not your heart be troubled, nor let it be fearful."*

C.John 16:5-14: (Jesus speaking) *"..But now I am going to Him who sent Me; and none of you asks Me, 'Where are You going?' But because I have said these things to you, sorrow has filled your heart. But I tell you the truth, it is to your advantage that I go away; for if I do not go away, the Helper shall not come to you; but if I go, I will send Him to you. And He, when he comes, will convict the world concerning sin, and righteousness, and judgment; concerning sin, because they do not believe in Me; and concerning righteousness, because I go to the father, and you no longer behold Me; and concerning judgment, because the ruler of this world has been judged. I have many more things to say to you, but you cannot bear them now. But when He, the Spirit of truth, comes, He will guide you into all the truth; for He will not speak on His own initiative, but whatever He hears, He will speak, and He will disclose to you what is to come. He shall glorify Me..."*

D.Romans 8:26: *"And in the same way the Spirit also helps us in our weakness; for we do not know how to pray as we should, but the Spirit Himself intercedes for us with groanings too deep for words; and He who searches the hearts knows what the mind of the Spirit is, because He intercedes for the saints according to the will of God."*

E.Matthew 28:19-20: (Jesus speaking) *"Go therefore and make disciples of all the nations, baptizing them in the name of the Father and the Son and the Holy Spirit, teaching them to observe all that I commanded you; and lo, I am with you always, even to the end of the age."*

F.Acts 2:38 (This scripture answers the question of when Christians receive the indwelling Holy Spirit.) *"And Peter said to them, "Repent, and let each of you be baptized in the name of Jesus Christ for the forgiveness of your sins; and you shall receive the gift of the Holy Spirit."*

168) How do you think a household would be different, regardless of which time period or which continent, if they were indwelt by the Holy Spirit of God?

169) How might the world be different if each nation's leader was indwelt by the Holy Spirit?

170) This chapter contains nearly all of the authentic Civil War correspondence kept by Esther for her children and descendants. Some letters, as you know, are from her husband and some are from either his sister or his brother. Why do you think she kept those letters even after she remarried and moved?

171) How important is it to pass information about our own times to succeeding generations, and if important, what provisions have you made to do so? What would you most want a great-grandchild to know about you?

172) Which would you rather have from an earlier loved one: a handful of letters or a loved one's marked up, well-worn Bible? Why? What Bible verses would you like the next generation to realize were important to you?

173) Both letters and well-worn Bibles have their values. The author would have been less likely and less able to write the novel without the letters she was given permission to copy, but it was essential to the novel that she also read about Esther's faith, which was described in Esther's 1912 obituary. Discuss, too, the value of an

obituary that leaves a testimony of your personal faith for the coming generations. How could yours do so?

174) Deuteronomy 1 begins with elderly Moses' message as he prepares to transfer his leadership to his successors. He spends several chapters reviewing their history together under his leadership, times of successful endeavors where they saw God's mighty work, and times of fearfulness and disobedience. He talks to them about times they were courageous and times they were frightened. Meditate and comment upon these verses:

Deuteronomy 1:30 reads: *"The Lord your God who goes before you will Himself fight on your behalf, just as He did for you...."* and *continues up to the time Moses reminds them of their being only seventy strong when Joseph and brothers settled in Goshen, but now they are "as numerous as the stars of heaven"* (10:22).

Then consider these various verses from Deuteronomy 11:

"You shall therefore love the Lord your God, and always keep His charge, His statutes, His ordinances, and his commandments. And know this day that I am not speaking with your sons who have not known and who have not seen the discipline of the Lord you God – His greatness, His mighty hand, and His outstretched arm, and His signs, works... in the midst of Egypt....but your own eyes have seen all the great work of the Lord which He did.....You shall therefore impress these words of mine on your heart and on your soul; and you shall bind them as a sign on your hand, and they shall be as frontals on your forehead. And you shall teach them to your sons, talking of them when you sit in your house and when you walk along the road and when you lie down and when you rise up. And you shall write them on the doorposts of your house and on your gate so that your days and the days of your sons may be multiplied on the land which the Lord swore to your fathers to give them, as long as the heavens remain above the earth...See, I am setting before you today a blessing and a curse: the blessing, if you listen to the commandments of the Lord your God...and the curse if you do not listen to the commandments of the Lord you god, but turn aside from the way which I am commanding you today, by following other gods which you have not known...."

In what ways are you preserving and passing on the Christian faith from yourself to the following generations, whether your own descendants or to those younger than you?

175) Many have said Christianity is always just one generation from extinction. However, we do know God has promised He will always have a remnant. Considering how much you are already doing to pass along the faith, will you prayerfully ask the Lord to show you if there are things you need to pencil in or cross off your calendar?

176) Realistically, until a fresh revival breaks out among the followers of the Lord Jesus Christ and spills over into their circles of friends and co-workers and extended families, many people you and I encounter in our lives will not hear enough Biblical truth to come to a personal faith in Jesus Christ. Few families remain intact until the children are all grown and fewer still have second and third generations intact and living near their elderly members of the family. In II Timothy 1:5 we read of two women who helped raise one of the early influential Christian leaders. Apostle Paul writes to Timothy, a minister he has helped prepare: *"For I am mindful of the sincere faith within you, which first dwelt in your grandmother Lois, and your mother Eunice, and I am sure that it is in you as well."*

Realizing the novel has Esther writing her story to pass on facts and faith to her future generations, briefly list two or three faith teachings she has passed on to you in what has been written thus far.

177) "The Waiting" for the reunion because of Emanuel's discharge from the army covers a few pages. Ironically, factually, Emanuel's death occurred on little Alfred's third birthday. Consider and comment on these sentences from the text:

"He (Emanuel) did soldiering like he did life: trying to keep two small and one big famly together, taking his place, keeping it safe as he could for the ones with him and those who'd be coming to the spot later. He served with honour, and people, like I tolt you, knowed he was Christian...He lived his faith and his thinking, and both was good and I suspicion by now God's kept Manuel's name straight and given him his good reward."

178) Which two small and which large family did Emanuel try to keep together, and how?

179) How did he take his place in the different family situations?

180) How did he try to keep families safe for his current and future generations?

181) Which situations come to mind as honourable in Emanuel's situations?

182) Based on what you learned about Emanuel's life, would you agree or disagree Emanuel was a Christian? Why?

183) Can you think of times when people, including yourself, do not live one's thinking? Why does that happen?

184) Why do you think Esther was intent upon clearing Emanuel's name?

185) Which do you think motivated her most to clear Emanuel's name: love for her husband; determination to get what was due her and the children; determination to get what was due Emanuel? How much of her efforts were to get a government to keep its promises to some "almost unknowns"?

186) The night of resignation to starvation is based on Esther's 1912 obituary, which described the family as destitute and told that Esther spent the night without food in prayer and reading her Bible knowing they were without resources because they never received the pensions. The obituary told that a neighbor came to their rescue the next morning. The novel's version describes the period after failed attempts to get Emanuel's name cleared up so the family could have pensions to help get them enough to avoid starvation. Read again the following passage from II Corinthians 1: 3-7 and comment on how it helps those going through tough situations:

"Blessed be the God and Father of our Lord Jesus Christ, the Father of mercies and god of all comfort; who comforts us in all our affliction so that we may be able to comfort those who are in any affliction with the comfort with which we ourselves are comforted by God. For just as the sufferings of Christ are ours in abundance, so also our comfort is abundant through Christ. But if we are afflicted, it is for your comfort and salvation; or if we are comforted, it is for your comfort, which is effective in the patient enduring of the same sufferings which we also suffer; and our hope for you is firmly

grounded, knowing that as you are sharers of our sufferings, so also you are sharers of our comfort."

"Hard times" in most of our lives are situations that sometimes have shown our inadequacies and weaknesses as humans. Many Biblical characters expose us to their stories of entrapment by others or failure on their own part. Few of us will get through life without some "rain" on our "sunny" lives.

If we let God do the surgery, if we let God expose light upon our failures and even upon times when we suffered because of the sinfulness of others, we are most likely able to see His sufficiency over our vulnerabilities. While we hide in the "darkness" we can feel trapped, but if God's healing comes with His cleansing Light, we and others can come to a point of glorifying God for how triumph came after trial. Sometimes we learn more about God by suffering, though we likely plot to avoid it as long as we can.

If you were spared tough situations in your past, perhaps you might pray that God would provide hearers for those whose pasts did demonstrate how God triumphed over whatever man intended for harm.

Are you willing to spend some time in prayer reviewing your life with your loving Heavenly Father, and then in discussion with a trusted friend or two, to see if perhaps the ways God permitted your history to become part of "His story" is overdue for acknowledgement of God's sovereignty? Is it time to check to see if it's fitting for you to tell more people about how your story coincides with His story?

187)   Consider what the messages are in these verses:

Proverbs 19:17 we read: *He who is kind to the poor lends to the Lord, and He will repay him for his deed.*

In Proverbs 22:9 we read, *"He who has a bountiful eye will be blessed, for he shares his bread with the poor."*

Luke 14:13, 14: (Jesus speaking) *But when you give a feast, invite the poor, the maimed, the lame, the blind, and you will be blessed because they cannot repay you. You will be repaid at the resurrection of the just."*

II Corinthians 9:6-8: *"The point is this: he who sows sparingly will also reap sparingly, and he who sows bountifully will also reap bountifully. Each one must do as he has made up his mind, not reluctantly or under compulsion, for God loves a cheerful giver. And God is able to provide you with every blessing in abundance, so that you may always have enough of everything and may provide in abundance for every good work."*

What do the above verses tell you about caring for the poor?

188)   There are two sides to the coin of meeting another's needs: the 'needy' and those 'able to help provide'. Esther experienced a miracle and testified to its reality for the remainder of her life, speaking of it so often her descendants knew it had to be included in her obituary. We do not have a record of the blessings that came to the neighbor who provided for the family, but if that neighbor had ignored the prompting to go and check on, or to provide for the widow and her children, the story would have gone much differently. I'm grateful Esther often shared it. (As an author, it was tempting to have that neighbor be Mr. Reed, but I decided I'd leave him unnamed but still not rule out that possibility.)

Share how you have been on the receiving end of a blessing because someone listened to the Lord, and with equal intent to glorify the Lord, share of a time when you were prompted to act in someone else's life and what you did about it. Share these times so the Lord is glorified and so you hear instances of how God is still at work.

Prayer

Father God, it amazes me as I ponder upon how totally sufficient and loving You are.

I am just one person among the millions who have looked to You for help in time of need, or even for supplying much that I did not need.

Thank You that You are never far from me.

Thank You that You are always willing to help me sort through my history to see ways You can help me weave our stories together. Like other humans, I have a few years to experience earthly life, to begin knowing You, and to declare Your sufficiency and love for me in personal ways.

Father God, You created me so I would add my story to Your thrilling intergenerational, multi-millennial, eternal, and unique personalized love story of my rescue if I'm willing to testify of Your intervention and goodness. That awareness humbles me, it excites me, and to at least a small degree, it intimidates me.

Even great Biblical characters prayed for boldness to share the Good News with their contemporaries, so I ask that You embolden me as You skillfully, purposefully bring the exact people into my life who will benefit from hearing me testify to Your trustworthiness. Nudge me hard, Lord God, so I don't miss the opportunity that You have prepared me for.

And, Lord, if I still have areas and circumstances that need to be exposed to Your Light, begin that work now in my life, my Great, Mighty and Loving Physician. In the only name through which we individually can be saved, Jesus Christ our Lord, Amen.

CHAPTER NINE

GOOD

MR. REED

1867-1880

CHAPTER NINE
GOOD
MR. REED
(1867-1880)

A good name is rather to be chosen than great riches, and loving favour rather than silver and gold. The rich and poor meet together: the Lord is the maker of them all. By humility and the fear of the Lord are riches, and honour, and life. Proverbs 22:1, 2, 4

Monday, March 22, 1880 A.D.

How kind of my famly to let me spend my birthday writing that last section to you. Now, my concluding 'chapter,' my Children and Descendents, will take you from the accounting of God's special provision for us, Emanuel's Kisbey's bereaved family, to the present, March, 1880. I'm set to get this done, so if I can stay warm, I may stay up with candlelight some of these cold nights. At some point, though, I figure I'd spend as much effort staying warm as getting things to paper. If that happens, I'll put things away and rest.

At any rate, you have now my memories of Emanuel and Esther Copsey Kisbey, how we came to know each other, how the unwelcome rocks in the stream our lives such as Poverty and Disease and Death pursued us to Michigan US where we'd tend our Jonathan, Emma, and Alfred, how Poverty and the War of Rebellion coaxed Death to make me Manuel's lonely widow but how God was Victor as He watched over us Kisbeys to see we was cared for. Praises be to trustworthy God who cares for us in tough and easy times, though sometimes the measure of tough times seems larger than t'other, espeshly as we're in them.

But God was preparing streams and leveling roads we'd travel. 'Tis good to remember we cannot see what God sees; we

340

cannot know all God knows. Preachers and Bible teachers put that idea into one big word, and 'tis: Omniscient. I know 'cause I asked a good Bible teacher. He spelt it for me too.

Now, to conclude: For months after Manuel's death and even after the Rebellion was put down, I devoted time and trips to get Manuel's reputation honoured and see the Kisbey name was respected for 'twas Manuel's hope. Do you understand that such trips often meant imposing upon the graces of others since we lacked even a chicken to hook to a wagon. But, when we hitched the rides, it meant filling up law offices and countless papers. Federal payments due Union widows and children would relieve the famly seeing to our survival, for the widow's half pension was $8/month.

We'd never see my pension nor money Manuel's children's was due, though I signed so many papers 'tis a wonder Michigan still has a single stand of trees! In all these things I learnt more 'bout patience, persistence, and praising God for even little kindnesses toward us.

We had considerate Michigan friends. Heaths reduced our farm payment and was lenient 'bout when 'twas due. Henry and Margaret, nearly famly, helped as they could. The charitable famly that'd brought us 'angel food' was kind, often checking us, helping when 'twas needed. We never 'expected' their continued benevolence week after week, but God gave them abundance to share at the right times. May God bless all who opened hands to us and others in need. But would we always need charity and never be able to help others?

The Kisbeys writ to us as though we was blood. Levi and Mary hoped we'd consider settling near them in Illinois so they could give help if we needed.

If? I writ them, requesting they arrange our move at their, and the war's, convenience. I waited, expecting once I heard their thinking, we'd part with Manuel's farm, pay Michigan debts, and resettle. Letters take such waiting and never answer every question a person's asked.

Weeks later, their letter tolt us still they'd found us no suitable house.

What widow pity I let settle in. Was we being forsaken? Could we not just live a time with them, with Kisbeys for support? One room perhaps? I wasn't fair, I know. How could they know how dependent we was upon others' charity? But ol' Pride don't need much to rally! Finally it bowed and I writ again when we was nearly past pitying.

Levi sent a little money, saying perhaps they'd have more to send if he dared trust the express. The Rebellion was still on. And he likely thought we had farm and pensions income.

Pensions? Sure, friends, lawyers, and I kept people shuffling papers from Pontiac to the Potomac proclaiming we indeed was rightfully due pensions 'cause of Manuel. But officials needed Manuel standing there declaring who he was and where he'd soldiered. So did I! Without him, and with legal papers spelling his names any which way, seems dizzied 'higher ups' just put our pleas aside. How could both Samuel and Emanuel have the same children and widow? And had I sometimes said 'Manuel' instead? And was it Kisbey, Kisbee, Kishby... Lawyers' children need eats, too. Nevertheless, for Manuel's and the children's sake much as anything, I kept filling papers as I could and tending to chores and whatever cooking a pot of scarcity dictates.

Why waste stamps writing Kisbeys if I had no news? Why waste hours of gardening if a trip to Pontiac or t'other lawyers changed nothing?

Henry and t'others advised selling Manuel's farm and work out moving after we had a buyer. Most didn't understand how bad things was for us. Buyers wasn't rushing to us either and the less seed we could plant, for seed costs, too, the less productive our farm appeared. Seemed nothing growed well on the farm except disappointment.

I grew weary. Truth be tolt, at times I could of growed fond of widow pity. But God's Sovereign. 'Bout the time I'd start clutching pity and thinking it justified, He'd acquaint me with someone needing my pity instead o' me. 'Twas good of Him, most likely. I didn't have much but 'least I could give pity.

I remember one late afternoon, just as the sun was taking its early leave and night was readying to rush in to send in its chill so another freeze could hold things in place like it had the night 'fore, I was wandering along a grove of trees by the little stream not far from our house, looking for loose wood or bark or a ness if fallen leaves to burn. Fire was hard to start without the small pieces and I was fretting a bit, thinking leaves would help rather'n try to find twigs. The children had colds or I'd had them out gathering for 'twas usually their chore to have fire fixings. But I was digging at a piece of wood with my shabby heel and the stubborn piece layed there like it'd made a promise to Mother Nature it'd stay put. Kicking only made me scold myself, lest I'd ruin what shoes I had.

The snow around the base of the tree had melted away some, though I wondered how it dared in the winter we was having. I'd of sat down and cried if reasoning hadn't tolt me I'd freeze long 'fore I was cried out. My fingers was numb and my skirt was not keeping my body warm atall. I was cold all over and I knowed I needed to get the fire fixings or we'd all be cold to the bone the next morning. I pushed away snow with one of the sticks I had found, using it to help me look for leaves that might be taken in to dry 'fore morning fire.

I was having a running talk with the Lord, partly to be sure He was aware of how things was and what it was I was looking for out in His big world that was growing uncomfortably dark with each moment that passed. As I pushed at the snow, I had trouble finding leaves, just bare ground. I looked up at the sky to ask God why this was so hard, and there I saw why I wasn't finding more leaves. Some of the leaves on that tree had refused to let go when fall had come. Oh, they was brown and they was as cold as I was I was sure, but a handful of them that would have started my fire was clinging here and there to the tree for life.

My mind has kept that likeness. I had snowy ground all around me and I'm sure it was still just as cold as it had been the moment before, but for a few moments, I forgot winter and just pondered what I was seeing. Those leaves, they was going to lose what little bit of life they had left. Spring would come. A wind or too much heat from the sun, something would happen and they'd either give up or be pushed off to make way for the new crop of leaves, that's just how the time has to be. But they was in no hurry for what was next. Other leaves had quit life, and likely looked good as they did, all colored and all. But these, and they wasn't many, but these had chosen to hang on for as long as they could. Or maybe hanging on hadn't been entirely they're choice, maybe there was a reason for their hanging on. I'd heard winter's winds. I'd seen limbs, I was picking up limbs stronger than those with the clinging leaves, but somehow those frail leaves helt on. They'd withered some of course, but not completely, and they'd lost the way they used to look before they rode out the winter, but they was declaring 'twas not yet their time to be no more a part of the tree's life. 'Parently they hoped to believe they'd still see another summer, another fall, if they could just make it till spring. Maybe they'd tell tales to their next generation. If they had to give, they'd do it, but not 'fore their time. I think the Lord knowed they had to be still on the tree that night. Looking at them, and to Him, was more important than finding a few wet leaves at my feet.

If they could of heard me, they'd heard me say to the Lord, 'Let me be like those faithful leaves, Lord. You hear me whimper too much 'bout hard days and You know if it wasn't for the children, I'd probably find it'd be easy to just give up sometimes. You are more than a tree, Lord, so much more, but let my children, and any t'others You choose, see me cling to You like those leaves clung to this tree, hanging on with something to encourage the next generation. You've been faithful, Lord God, in generations past, and You will be faithful to generations after my bones has turned to dust, which You might let happen soon. Even so, forbid me from giving up and being willing to wither till You say 'tis time. Yes, Lord, keep me from withering 'fore my time.'

I soon found enough fire fixings to get the place warm in the morning. But that night I hunted in my Bible till I found

Psalm 1 and I read it to the children, telling them of what I saw in the woods that night.

I was going to go on, but I find myself prompted to writ down the Psalm here from my Psalter. I cannot say whether I do it for you, or only for me, but I'm trying to learn that if I'm prompted, 'tis best to obey:

Psalm 1 from my Psalter:

Blessed is the man that hath not walked in the counsel of the ungodly, nor stood in the way of sinner: and hath not sat in the seat of the scornful. But his delight is in the law of the Lord: and in his law will he exercise himself day and night. And he shall be like a tree planted by the water-side: that will bring forth his fruit in due season. (God's timing, Esther, I hear my Lord whisper to my heart). *His leaf also shall not wither* (My Manuel fits that to me. His season here was short, too short I feared, but truth be tolt, 'tis not over for him or for the way his ways keeps working in our lives and likely my children will pass to theirs Manuel's ways.) *and look, whatsover he doeth, it shall prosper.* (We can not measure like God does.) *As for the ungodly, it is not so with them: but they are like the chaff, which the wind scattereth away from the face of the earth.* (I might as well tell you here since it comes to mind, I scolt my children the day they came from school and said somebody was 'chaff.' Such words is not 'llowed here and such judgement is left to God who will do the separating. No child of mine ought judge so harshly.) *Therefore the ungoldly shall not be able to stand in the judgement: neither the sinners in the congregation of the righteous. But the Lord kneweth the way of the righteous: and the way of the ungodly shall perish.'*

There, I put it down and it helped me to writ it ~ hopefully 'tis more in my soul than 'twas 'fore.

Life kept going day-to-day, threatening to leave if I thought on 'tomorrow.' At long last, Levi's letter came, still considering me sister. It's from Pekin, Illinois, dated March 23, 1865 A.D.:

Dear Sister   I now take the opportunity of riting you a few lines to let you know that we is all in good helth hoping this *will find you all injoying the same blessing   I received A letter from Geo & Sallie Some time since and they sent me 2 Notes wich thay helt aganest Ned: one for $15.00 & one for 27.00 Dollars & told me that if I could get the money to send it to you and I have been trying to get it ever since I got the Notes to get it till I got tired of trying and now I guess that I will send them back to George and let him try it him self. I could get it out of Ned if it was not for the old woman and she is Neds boss and I dont think that thay will ever get the money out of her ~~~~~~~~~~~~~*

Levi put in the line, and like the Kisbey gentleman that he is, he did not say all 'twas on his mind. Hmm.   Had you noticed, like me, when my beloved Manuel writ once that Uncle and Aunt was well, 'I saw a traitor hanged' was the next think he thought? Did even Manuel's charitable mind find it easy to skip from Aunt Gertrude to thinking 'bout traitors? I can tell you that if Aunt and Uncle had let the $42.00 owed George and Sallie come to us, we'd fared far better. If she'd remembered t'other $2 from the platform, why that'd made over 6 months widow pensions. We widows was to live on $8/month. After awhile a person remembers Who sends help.

Levi continued this way:

I have been agreat many times to the Postoffice thinking thear would bee aletter thear from you but have allways been Disapointed I should not have rote this till I saw Ned again if I could have got aletter from you but I thought you maby took it hard because I did not send for you last fall but what I told you was the trouth   I could not find a place to put you in and I dont know that I can this spring   I have spoke for a house but I cannot tell any thing a bout it till the first of May but you must not get mad at me if I dont get it for ill do my best to get you out hear for I' often think and wonder how you are geting along I wish you was hear now that is if you want to come so that I could help you a little as I think it is my Duty so to do but any how if you is any ways hard up send me word and I will send you 5 or 10 Dollars any time I can spare it

Send me word wether you have sold your farm yet or not
or wether it done you any good or not last year or wether you
entend to sell it or not   I have nothing more to say at Present
Kiss your childern for me and Give our love to Mr & Mrs
Williams and rember me to Mr. Roper and Mr. Hill and your
nerast nabor   I for got there name but rember me to every
body   So good Night   We remain you brother & sister
    Levi & Mary Kisby

I appreciated their concern and I know 'twas impossible for
them to know how hard our life was. I say to God's credit, we
never was starving again, we never ever begged bread, nor was
we naked, though we might o'been thread bare at times.

I writ Kisbeys again o'course, but I decided I could not rely
upon their help, for even if they got us a simple house, at what
cost or safety could we go there? So I helped neighbors when I
could and I solt from our land what I could. And God proved
cap'ble of tending to our daily needs.

The War Between the States was still going on. Most
battles we heard 'bout was in Virginia, Georgia, Louisiana and
Alabama. Maybe Florida too. Everywhere the Union was
pushing rebels back home. But lots of blood was spilt on both
sides and it seemed like I'd be testing God to set out knowing a
picket might think we was on t'other side cause spies and fools
was likely the ones traveling most often.

My, the whole North was saddened with the steamboat
explosion that April. Here they was coming back to their
people and they was killed not by war but by the explosion.
Some of them was released prisoners from the terrible prison
at Andersonville. God seems to have our days numbered. You
can be safely out of a war and then your number comes and
what can you do?

Our beloved President Lincoln was killed in April and we
mourned like he was *family* to us. The war was so close to the
end, though it took a few months more to settle it all. S'pose
you know a woman by the name of Mary Surratt and some
other rebels got found out and was hanged that summer for
planning ways to kidnap and kill Mr. Lincoln and Johnson and

Seward. The hanging was in the papers. 'Fore that, Union soldiers killed John Wilkes Booth a few days after he'd shot Mr. Lincoln. Now I don't want you thinking long on this as it won't likely ever be true again, but the Mr. Johnson put after Mr. Lincoln was like Manuel. He'd had no schooling and didn't read or write, not till his wife taught him. 'Magine what Manuel would of become if I'd taught him reading and writing! No, Manuel did as Manuel was to do, and the Lord knows I'd taught Manuel to read and write if we'd had time for such things. But we did not.

Just 'fore the death of Mr. Lincoln, General Lee signed a paper to say the South was done fighting to be a separate country. That was in Virginia where soldiers had fought so much. He gave the paper to the man who was just recently our president, Ulysses Grant. I s'pose I need to say that a month or so after President Lincoln's death, the Union capchurt Jeff Davis and fighting was 'bout all finished by then. The big disagreements ended but it took months to bring quiet and years to fix lands and heal hearts after the Rebellion.

Some Confederate leader or Lincoln's assassin or some such person was capchurt in a tobacco barn. Tobacco's no place to hide. That capchure may of been the only good thing I ever heard 'bout tobacco. Enough said.

Well, Children and Descendents, time went on. We never moved to Illinois 'cause travel was expensive and what we saved for moving was spent on debts and staying alive. I thought little of going back across the Atlantic for famlys was mostly gone and 'sides we could not buy fares. England had money problems of its own with banks and businesses closing. If we'd had a hard time 'fore, what would England be for us now? Only good thing I heard from London was 'bout religious people doing more work where we'd lived and worked, Whitechapel and East End. A crowd preacher named William Booth, no relation or temperament I'd likely think to John Wilkes Booth, got people help and coming to the Lord. Also a good soul who preached some in America, too, was Mr. Mueller, who'd likely seen my children was fed if they'd been orphaned in his part of England. Think his orphanages was from where Mr. Roberts' herd was from, so hope Edric's famly heard him 'least once.

But we was in the US. None of us knowed enough 'bout swimming to do us any good when it comes to crossing 'tween here and England! 'Sides, America had promises to keep for us. Finally I took stock of my situation and decided I'd just make Michigan work 'cause we had friends here too. A body can't always think the place they is is not the right place to be. Sometimes the only thing missing is the decision to make it the right place and espeshly when the Lord's not opening t'other doors. A door pryed open isn't much use afterward, and in forcing a door your fingers can get caught bad. And then there was Aunt Emma's saying, 'You have what you need, you just need to use it.' And Manuel's talk 'bout God was to be trusted even when we don't understand or see where how He's working. Can make a mind puzzle some to think that God's always working, but He has to work in so many heads to get things even close to the way He and we think they should go.

So, I'd be a Michigan woman, 'least till I got someone to give me what Manuel had coming. O'course I was a poor Michigan woman, but lots of women was widows after the war. Lots of children got took in by others. Mostly relatives took fatherless children but 'twas impolite to ask if a new addition was a blood relation or a neighbor or what. A body didn't need to know. If you could give charity, you did, and you was likely blest by giving it.

I was Widow Kisbey. I was somewhat proud to be so, not that I didn't miss my beloved every day, but I wasn't Widow Nobody, I was Widow Kisbey. I preferred being called Widow Kisbey instead of Mrs. Kisbey. I thought Mrs. Kisbey was just stating fact: I was one who misses Kisbey, misses my Manuel Kisbey. Daily I dealt with what life had handed me. Every widow misses her husband dreadfully, so why keep reminding us at every greeting? Just call us Widow such and such. That reminds us to, but different somehow. 'Least to me. I knowed God knowed all 'bout us and He'd allowed it for some reason beyond what my mind could holt, but I kept deciding God was trustworthy.

In 1866, Manuel's Michigan 3rd Cavalry, finished the Civil War's last battles in Texas. Soldiers came back to Michigan. One looked me up as he'd been with Manuel for his last days.

The children and I wanted to know what he could tell us for we'd not heard from Mr. Richey for some time although I'd writ him late fall 1864 to say Manuel never got home in any fashion, except o'course to his eternal reward. O'course we didn't see that, we just knowed that.

The Company F gentleman tolt us that when Manuel was brought in from the field doctors to Duvalls Bluff Army Hospital, least I thought he meant Army hospital, but to some hospital, Manuel was fevered, likely from bad water, and they tolt him to stay. But Manuel was eager to continue home. He'd just walk home if they wouldn't help him go. I wondert what it all meant 'cause Mr. Richey writ Manuel was in high spirits when he saw him last and he was to het straight home, but some things remains not part of my understanding. Maybe for some reason this was a few days after Mr. Richey saw him. Finally they calmed Manuel down, with medicine the gentleman thought, to keep him and get him healthier. But the doctors didn't have what they needed and Manuel got worse instead of better. Finally a nurse was put with him, for they knowed he'd likely not be leaving atall.

This gentleman who called on us was bedded nearby, healing up from a wound and he tolt us how the nurse talked to Manuel and asked him what he wanted her to read or if he needed to write to someone. He said he wanted to write but he couldn't, and she just thought he was too tired or too sad, so she got him some paper and a pencil. Oh when the man tolt me I so wished Manuel could of writ, but like the man tolt me, the nurse came back in a bit and she figured why Manuel didn't write down nothing. I guess he drawed our big tree with the swing, the little wagon by the road, and both the wood box and clothes lines was full. All these had stick people nearby. I wished I had his paper to put with t'other letters and papers, but I never got nothing from Arkansas atall except the *Soldier's Prayer Book* I'll tell you more 'bout.

Anyhow, the nurse was good, the man said, and she just sat down and patted Emanuel's hand while he wept without more than a whimper or two. He said Manuel was weak but he tolt her to draw up a letter to his wife and children and he got started, but he couldn't say what he wanted for he seemed so disappointed he was not getting home to us as he'd tolt us he would. I knowed Manuel was a man always determined to keep his word, even to his dying day.

The man tolt us the kind nurse tolt Manuel he could just talk to her 'bout his famly. So he did. He named us all and tolt of us to her, but he was having a hard time. He asked her what day 'twas and she said 'twas turning September 19, and he said, 'That's my boy's birthday and I wanted to be there to kiss him as he turns three.' Then Manuel tolt the nurse how going to war had not gone right atall for him, how he wanted to help his *famly* 'least as much as he wanted to help the US famly, and how every time he tried to holt a *famly* together it never worked right, 'least not like he'd planned. And he was worried 'bout how we'd get along without his help and all. Then Manuel'd said sorrowfully, 'I never was able to give them what they should of had.'

And the nurse said, 'Did you love them?' And the man watched Manuel nod with tears rolling down his cheeks. The man said he hisself had tears just listening, and I suspicion he did 'cause he had them again as he tolt us of Manuel's passing. We did, too. And the nurse said, 'Did you live honourably?'

And Manuel said he lived best he knowed how to live, but he did nothing special and even the regular things he wanted to do, he couldn't 'cause now he was dying.

And the nurse I wish I could meet asked Manuel, 'Maybe Private Kisbey you's leaving this world 'fore any planned for you to go, but did you tell your *famly* how to meet you again?'

And he said, 'Esta'll tell 'em fer me 'cause we both wanted the children to know. I know she'll make efforts to get us together over there.'

And the nurse said, 'Private Kisbey, you gave your *famly* love. You showed how to live honourably so there'll be respect of your name and memory. Top o'that, you Kisbeys'll have a reunion ahet better'n any birthday saprize a famly can plan. I think your *famly* is blest by both you and God.' I'm so glad she tolt Manuel we was blessed by him, for his ways of being Manuel has blessed us. And, then, till he died the nurse who was truly Godsent, read from the Bible, and toward the end she took a soldier's book like I have from Mr. Richey and she turned to the end pages and she sang softly holding the book in one hand, and holding Manuel's hand in t'other.

The soldier tolt us Manuel was a good man who most times just stood guard while soldiering and the world could benefit from being guarded by men like Manuel. I think the world did. And still does.

The man could sing pretty fair so I asked if he knowed the songs writ in the soldier's book.

He took his from his pocket and sang two songs to us. 'Twas like a memorial to Manuel as if we was at our church or at a gravesite. The children and I just sat holding each other. 'Twas a sad but comforting time for us who belonged to Manuel.

I s'pose since I writ this long I could put the words down of two of the soldier's songs. The print is so small 'tis hard to read but I'll write it normal for you.

All the songs became special to me, espeshly those first years when I had to be without Manuel, but I'll just put down two for you and if you want to know t'others maybe another soldier famly will let you read them:

First one he sang was just numbered as '26' and 'tis just called 'Another' but that's the name of most of them, 'Another.' Whoever thought up the words didn't put their name there, likely not wanting special notice, and espeshly not if 'twas sung when 'twas time to bury a soldier.

Soldiers need the honour, not the one who writ something for the people to sing while the soldier's layed to rest:

'Servant of God, well done!
Go forth from earth's employ.

352

The battle fought, the victory won,
Enter thy Master's joy.
At midnight came the cry,
"To meet thy God prepare!"
He woke – and caught his captain's eye,
Still strong in faith and prayer.
Soldier of Christ, well done,
Praise be thy new employ;
And while eternal ages run
Rest in thy Savior's joy.'

I couldn't help but think of how Manuel and I'd stood on the freighter to step into America and how we waited till God let us pitchure our Sarah and George with our Saviour Jesus, and how that'd comforted us then. I know the nurse's song to Manuel comforted him as he prepared to go be with Jesus and Kisbeys already in Heaven.

Another one the soldier sang to us that day was this one, writ as a title '23 For a Funeral' and that was as close as we had come to a funeral so we asked him to sing that to us:

'Hear what the voice from heaven declares
To those who in Christ die!
Released from all their earthly cares,
They'll reign with Him on high."
Then why lament departed friends,
Or shake at death's alarms?
Death's but the servant Jesus sends
To call us to His arms.
If sin be pardoned, we're secure,
Death hath no sting beside;
The law gave sin its strength and power;
But Christ, our ransom, died!
Then, joyfully, while life we have,
To Christ our life, we'll sing,
"Where is thy victory, O grave?
And where, O death, thy sting?"

I asked him if Manuel was still breathing when these was sung for I wanted to push forth those last lines to tell ole Death myself that it'd not be victor and no grave would give us so bad a sting as to keep us held down, for our Jesus is the Resurrection!

He tolt me, and I don't know if 'twas 'cause he thought I had to think it or if 'twas true, but he said Manuel whispered, 'Esta'd like that one too,' and then Manuel was past talking. True or not, I knowed Manuel'd knowed if I had a piano and knowed the tune, keys'd be hit hard for those last lines! Those words brought from me my 'Declaration of Independence' from the holt ole Death had helt on me. Now let me put it right and readable for certain: I was released from the hold ole Death had held on me! Slay the adversary!

Songs by strangers, scriptures we read, and the very presence of God helped us in our getting beyond Manuel's death. And I often tolt my children how to make certain they'd see their Pa again.

Life's full of rippling waters, some good and some seem not so good. Some seemed to cross their boundaries or came as torrents attempting to wash us from our foundations. But they did not, for our foundation was certain. Truth be tolt, if one can lift her eyes and cast them toward a distant shore where crystal clear water's peaceful and soul refreshing, then one can take up work and know, 'Better is ahet.' I could honour both Manuel and God by doing that, and so I did. There was children to raise, decisions to make, and life to be finished as God would place it 'fore me.

So to you I say, 'When life is hard, listen to the distant shoreline with its peaceful ripples. Ripple. Ripple. Ripple. Have peace. Find rest in Him. God wills it so. Ripple. Ripple. Ripple.'

So now what's happened to us? Like I tolt you many papers ago, my name is Esther Copsey Kisbey Reed. By the way, I kept petition papers for widow's and children' pay with signatures of Michigan lawyers and Washington officers, but what good is they now? What good was they then? We never thought paper was food when we was hungry. But they record my efforts to claim what was rightly our due, so I kept mine from morning fires, though I sometimes suspicion higher-ups started morning fires with the ones I sent them. God supplied our aid those days.

Then God took care of us another way. I'll make this brief as other changes are coming again.

Mr. Richey came to see me, like I tolt you 'fore, and he was a nice enough man and still single. He felt like he knowed us, but to spare you details, he went back to Texas and got involved in humoring and changing the world there, even holding offices I heard. We'll always be grateful for his kindness in helping us hear from Manuel and I wish him well. I reckon he's a famly man now and we think he deserves to be happy and live a long and peaceful life.

I one day did again what I'd done when sister Sarah's death left a famly needing care. A neighbor, whose wife was a wonderful Christian woman, passed in giving birth but her baby lived. The househoilt, household, needed help. I think 'twas God prompted me to offer tending the newborn being called Theodore George, like our George now with Manuel in Heaven.

Caring for the baby seemed a healing for me as well. The older child, William, needed looking after too, as the farmer had plenty to do. I rarely saw the man except when he'd bring Theo to my house in the mornings where I'd keep him till my children and his William walked to William's house for the evening where I'd come to prepare a meal while Emma tended to Theo and the boys did their school work. We ate 'fore my children and I left, leaving a portion for the farmer for when he came in after chores. Often I took baby Theo with me to spare the man night feedings. I kept my children from spoiling the little thing so he'd not make life more troublesome for the widower. 'Twas the Christian neighborly thing we did, and earning our evening meals and money for our work helped us, too.

Seems in every community the devil places one idler thriving on making guesses 'bout other lives. Hardly ever knowed a man to be that, but a woman can be that way with such little provoking. She saw the comings and goings and 'fore long her mind got to mixing together things that was was neither together nor fact. The Bible calls people like her a gossip. The charity we Kisbeys thought we was doing for a nice Christian famly became the town's whispers, saying we was not being separate enough.

Neither the farmer nor I knowed what was being said for we was both minding our own and separate chores. He was a Bible teacher at the church we all attended. But one day the preacher separately asked us to stay after services. We didn't think nothing of it really. I thought maybe the preacher had another person to tend to little Theo George, or he wanted help on a church doings, that kind of thing. The preacher asked our assorted children to go outside. Then he tolt us he heard we was improperly keeping company together!

We was both so angry. We stood up and in raised voices we tolt the pastor one after t'other there was no shred o'truth in such a thought. We hardly was ever at a house the same time, how we knowed each other's children much more'n we knowed each other, and that in fact it'd never ever crossed our minds to even think of t'other in a romantic way. That was God's truth.

Then the farmer asked who the gossip was and the pastor tolt us and the farmer loudly asked permission to talk face to face with her. Such was granted, but the farmer said he was too mad to talk civil to her right then. But he left no question he'd be talking to her. I was glad I'd not be her, but I couldn't feel sorry for her then cause I knowed she deserved more'n words to get her cruel thinking straight.

As for me, I never wanted to talk to her again. She wasn't going to miss my speaking to her as I'd not really knowed her 'fore anyhow. If I'd been rich, I'd bought us tickets to England or to somewhere faraway.

I thought I should stop caring for baby Theo and I knowed I could not step foot near that house again whether the farmer was there or not. None of my famly could go near that house no more, even if the children was friends by now. The pastor approved our ideas, obligating his wife to help with Theo and William temporarily. We'd be without that bit of tending income, but God was still my husband and the father to my half-orphaned children.

O'course all the children wondert why our lives got disrupted, but I was at a loss of how to say why, so I just said, "Things change."

I thought how Joseph was falsely accused by Potipher's wife and I felt so badly for the kind farmer. But more'n that, I thought how I'd trudged Michigan to protect Manuel's good name and if the gossip wasn't stopped, even the good name of Manuel would be ruined by me, his wife, who'd only done Christian work for a famly with a new baby boy 'cause Manuel couldn't be there to help us find enough to eat.

Where does a poor widow's famly find a church without gossips, or 'least with people less likely to hear it? I'd try.

However, the next Sunday, Henry and Margaret came, insisting we ride with them in their wagon. Yes, they'd heard the gossip, but they knowed 'twas not true. They's friends like blood to us, and o'course their children is blood. I tolt them I'd write Levi again so we could move soon. They thought the gossip should not win, but maybe if Levi found a house, we ought to go there.

I didn't even look at the farmer who was always early to church. Our famlys often sat on the church's same side but pews apart, and we'd not even thought of that being so till that Sabbath. I led my family so we sat on the opposite side of the church.

Gossip was there too o'course, figuring, I feared, she'd righteously broke up a sinful relationship and earned stars in her crown by telling the pastor her thoughts. But I hoped and prayed she'd come over and apologize to me if the farmer'd set the record right with her. I could feel if things was not soon made right, I'd have to hoe hard to prevent bitterness from planting itself in me.

The farmer hadn't talked to her yet, and if I'd knowed that neither the Williams or the Witemans or the Heaths or their teams of horses could of got me there that Sunday. Even if they was hooked together! I'd worshipped at a church as far away as I could go if I'd knowed he'd not set the gossip straight. I found out when the farmer stood to his feet and said he had something to say to Gossip.

I doubt I'd blushed in years, but I'm sure I was beet red for I realized he was going to talk to her in public and I thought things was only going to get worse. My children just knowed we was not tending to the farmer's famly, but they was too young I thought to be tolt the whys when the gossip was all false.

The farmer started in by standing up on his side and looking squarely at Gossip. He said something like, well, a lot like, for humiliating days is hard to forget, but I'll not reveal her name,

'Miss ____, last Sunday I learnt you tolt the pastor a lie 'bout me and Widow Kisbey. I was too angry when I heard 'bout the lie to come see you then. I'd of behaved toward you in a most unchristian manner, and your words is not worth that.' in a most unchristian manner, and your words is not worth that.'

Miss ____ was looking shocked, my Jonathan tolt me, 'cause I was not looking anywhere but at my lap. Jonathan hadn't knowed who the gossip was, but her face gave her away for even young children. O'course all this was news to the children and I sat there questioning whether the farmer had forgot that.

Then the farmer said, 'Your tongue is described in the book of James. I'll be teaching that book for the next five weeks, and if you don't come to my class, I'm Christian bound to come to your house and personally make certain you understand the book. Now that could ruin your reputation, couldn't it Miss ____? But I'll park my wagon or walk to and from your house as many times as it takes for you to understand what your tongue does to people. Your tongue is like a fire that wants to destroy whatever's in its path and you, my sister, if indeed you is my sister but I'll leave that between you and the pastor to determine, need to repent of your evil ways.'

He was good. I looked up a bit to see how people was taking things in. The pastor stood by his pulpit but he recognized a Holy Spirit fire when it fell. The farmer continued,

'Now Miss _____, what you said 'bout two Christians in this congregation was evil and totally unfounded. Widow Kisbey was kind enough to care for my newborn son at the death of my wife who was as wonderful a woman as I hope to ever know. I'll love her till I die just like I promised to do when we married. And you know Widow Kisbey was married many years to the late Emanuel Kisbey who served the Union honourably 'fore being taken in death by disease in Arkansas. I've no reason to think other'n that Widow Kisbey made the same promise to her husband when they married years ago. He's been in the Lord's presence no doubt now for close to three years. By the way, Miss _____, should you ever see some gentleman call on Widow Kisbey, you can rest ashirt he'd be doing so in a proper fashion. She's a Christian woman. All know that except perhaps you. With your tongue you sought to dishonour that fine gentleman's reputation and the fine reputation of my beloved wife, as well as dishonouring the reputations of Widow Kisbey and me.'

Like I said, the farmer was a good talker, and I heard several say 'Amen,' which made me proud Manuel and me had been defended in public this way.

Someone started to say, 'Her tongue's hurt more than just you sir,' and another said, 'If your tongue causes you to sin, you ought to cut it out rather'n go to hell because of it,' but the farmer said 'twas wise advice but not quite exact, and he kept the floor.

Then he said, 'Miss _____, like in Joseph's day, when his brothers brought evil upon him, they meant it for evil, but God changed things 'round and brought good from it.' The farmer got gentler, and he stood there, like he was still thinking. 'This week I've been dumbfounded trying to see how even God could bring good from the way your tongue slays reputations.'

I thought he was done but then he opened his Bible and started again. 'Then a couple nights ago when I was reading for this morning's class, something happened. I saw something 'bout myself I'd not seen 'fore and I want to thank you for what you taught me.'

I worried he was to say he'd been convicted of a sin. Later Henry and t'others said they thought this humble man was going to give a little beneficial scripture. But he started walking to the front, then back and acrosst, with his finger marking his place in his Bible as his fingers grasped it closed, like I'd once saw a tent preacher do. Walking, not standing pole-like as I'd growed up seeing.

And then he said to Gossip, 'You got me thinking. I've been so wrapped up in my grief and farming that I couldn't even tell you what color eyes Widow Kisbey has, or what color dress she's wore to my place. I didn't know what name she had but Widow Kisbey, though I think her employer should know her name. I now know she's Esther Kisbey. I don't know what she likes or what she hopes for her children or what makes her laugh, none of that. I just know she's good for my children and that she'd of cared for my newborn without pay if I'd let her. She took my Theodore to her home nights so I'd not be up to do the feedings babies need, Miss _____. She didn't have to do that, but I think she's the type of woman who can love babies whether they's hers or not.'

He pointed towards Henry. 'I remember my wife claiming how kindly Widow Kisbey cared for Henry's babies years ago.'

Henry and Margaret said 'twas true. The farmer moved toward the middle of the church's front, eyeing Miss Gossip.

'So, Miss ___, for the latter part of the week, I've been thinking. Maybe I should see what else there's to know 'bout Widow Kisbey, that is, if she'll let me. Perhaps God's given me a special neighbor I should get to know.'

He was still some distance away, but I felt his eyes resting on me, though I wasn't sure where to look again. 'So,' the farmer continued as he moved toward our side, 'If no one objects, this morning in front of all of you, I'm asking Widow Kisbey, will you let me take you to the next community doings? I believe there's a doings out to Heath's farm this Friday night, and I'd be honoured to be your escort.'

I know I blushed all the way to my ole hat, but mostly I kept my head down wondring what to do. Emma said he smiled when he looked away at the congregation. 'Could be none of the rest of you knowed there was a doings at Heath's place Friday night, but there is to be 'cause this morning I asked him to prepare one.'

I remember the congregation chuckled and then they clapped and I was so fluttered I didn't know how to answer. He said, 'Well, maybe I'll have to ask the Heath's to keep holding doings till I can convince Widow Kisbey to be my guest 'least once. Maybe we'll just end up being good neighbors, but Miss _____, maybe God let your tongue wag so I'd look up and find out He wanted me to know Widow Kisbey as more than a neighbor.'

Well, the farmer's name was John Reed, so you can put together whether or not I finally let him escort me to a Heath's doings.

Truth be tolt, I wasn't sure I could or wanted to make room for any husband 'sides Manuel. I took some time. 'Twas a new thought to me. I writ Levi and Mr. Richey, which was a little difficult, but they both writ back and said that far as they could think, Manuel wanted his famly taken care of and the children would benefit from having a good father, so if I could have feelings for another man, I should go ahet, for I'd still be honouring Manuel's hopes even if I married.

John is an honourable man and we combined our famlys on December 4, 1867, with Rev. Thomas Nichols officiating and our witnesses was Henry and Marjotte Davis of Brighton. They too became wonderful friends. And, in time, I found I easily found feelings for John Reed. He's an Englishman, and we talk lots of England and how his famly's farm set them well there. He's takes on new ventures after careful consideration. He had to be that way for he worked hard to become a father to my brood and his.

We was young enough to add to our combined famly. Now we have my three, Jonathan Levi Kisbey who has since married Francis Elliott, loved one of Miss Alice who's been lately our household servant.

Emma Jane Kisbey whose eyeing George Marshall who earlier, along with his sister Maria lived with the Hopkins family not far from us in Washtenaw County, eventually brought about their wedding that took place the sixth of last September, ·· I hope my daughter and her husband will remain happy, and how grateful I'd be if God allowed us to continue living close enough to have our special visits.

Alfred Alvin who's moved 'round a few years now.

Harry Reed, born to John Reed and his wife Sophia in AD 1857 like my Jonathan, Theodore George Reed born March of 1867, whose birth you could say got this whole Copsey Kisbey Reed combination together following the sad death of his mother Sophia when us Kisbeys responded to the mothering need for little Theodore George.

Then o'course, there's my husband John and our young Anna J Reed, born ten years ago in December AD 1869.

We lost Lewis in infancy. That's three babies I buried. Two in England, one here. Seems no matter where one lives, there's ole Death lurking 'round somewhere waiting its turn, or just barging in when no one's noticing its coming.

John's a skillful farmer who's provided very comfortably for me and the children beyond our biggest dreams. I now have a beautiful home with tall white pillars and out buildings holding amply supplies. We've never asked t'other to lessen the love we helt, held, for our first mates, for their memories deserve remembrance with honour and will be spoken of in that fashion by both of us. But we've become most happy together as well. John has treated memories of Manuel with respect and my children as his own, though by agreement mine kept the Kisbey name to honour, and when I solt Emanuel's farm, our children received their fair shares. I thought Manuel'd be pleased with how I'd kept our promises to each other. John's children are as my own as well.

But we've had a few times of adjustment that tested this mother's heart.

One very kind thing John did for me and my children happened one Sunday afternoon, and 'twas a saprize to me. 'Twas a lovely day and John had the children gather flowers and asked us all to ride with him to the cemetery where Sophia was buried. He o'course asked if I was offended, and I was not, for children ought to honour parents whether living or dead. On the way we talked of their mother and I thought 'twas a good thing for the famly to do. And the cemetery time seemed right for all.

Then John said to me and my children, 'Now, let's honour Emanuel Kisbey.' I was unsure how we could do that, but John took us a few steps to a new stone, and there was 'Emanuel Kisbey' chiseled on a nice stone. I remember my first thought was of how few times I'd seen Emanuel's name writ out.

John had ordered and placed that stone out of respect for Manuel and love for us, who was now both Manuel and his famly. Manuel's body never returned to Michigan, but it doesn't matter for he is with the Lord.

How did John think to do that? He's just a good man. But perhaps also, one reason came 'bout several weeks after our Anna tolt John, her father, how Emma and Alfred talked 'bout their Pa, feeling lonely. Anna, so much younger, asked why their Pa died. Alfred tolt her us folks said 'twas 'cause doctors couldn't figure how to heal him up so he'd get home like he'd set out to do. Emma tolt Anna of the kind nurse who'd made her Pa's dying easier for him and them. That afternoon Anna tolt her father, 'I think I'll be a nurse to sit with people when they're dying, or get them well so they go home so people won't have to be so sad.' I think Anna just may.

Theo's taken Anna under his wing much like James took me. He's been saving money to give her a gift 'fore long, and I suspicion what 'tis, but I won't tell as my children might read these pages 'fore they should.

While we was at the cemetery, John read a couple verses he thought right for such a gathering. He had talked to our preacher and writ down things preachers say at such times, like 'bout 'it hath pleased Almighty God of His great mercy to take unto Himself the soul of our dear brother here departed and we commit his body to the ground: earth to earth, ashes to ashes, dust to dust, in sure and certain hope of the Resurrection to eternal life, though our Lord Jesus Chirst,' and the verses 'bout Jesus being the Resurrection and the Life and knowing that our Redeemer lives (it is in the Old Testament and I can't seem to find it in the candle light as I work now), and the part 'bout bringing nothing into the world and taking nothing out.

Another thing that's happening as I finish has to do with my Alfred. Alfred broke my heart with how he longed for his Pa, always missing him.

Once I showed Alfred, AA, things we brought from England and tolt him someday he'd likely get a few of those if he was so inclined. O'course I'd consider t'other children, too. But Manuel's and my things should one day go to our children.

At times Alfred almost resented John's goodness to him, and even to me. A pa's son is hard to figure sometimes.

A couple times John heard AA speak disrespectfully to me. Such words stirred John. Whether the disgust rose from John's love for me or his intolerance of disrespect, I don't know, but AA, and all children, should know to speak kindly.

Alfred was 'bout thirteen. That's often a hard year. Somehow AA had got to thinking I'd made his Pa join the Union Army where o'course he died, and that by marrying John Reed, I'd forgotten all 'bout Alfred's Pa.

My child's cruel words put me in tears, making me ache for Alfred, for Manuel's memory, for John, and for myself. I had sense to not reply. Instead I silently prayed.

John, I think, dismissed what I thought might cause of AA's anger. John is often tender. But as you can 'magine, he felt obligated to deal with disrespect regardless of why's.

John rarely raised his voice. But it was raised when he asked AA to come with him to out by the barn. My mother's heart was a bit fearful, but then I remember I'd chosen to marry a man I could entrust my children to if I'd not lived, for many women left children for husbands to raise because of hard days that was common to us all. Sarah and Sofia were close proof of that.

There by the barn, John spoke straight with AA, tolt him the facts 'bout how good Manuel was, but that Manuel decided to enlist 'cause soldier pay would help meet farm payments when Michigan's crops was failing and how it'd feed his famly. John explained Union bountys and bonuses. John tolt AA some day AA'd be wise to have gratitude toward his parents and toward John, and that while he knowed he wasn't taking Alfred's Pa's place, John'd do his best to be a father for Alfred, but he wouldn't make Alfred take what was offered. Some of this I heard as I watched. The rest John tolt me later.

During that talk by the barn I know John tolt Alfred 'twas time they dealt man to man. I think AA said something 'bout John not being his Pa so he didn't have to listen. I suspicion that not all John's ways with my three was identical to how Manuel would of done things, but I honestly can't say which would train children best. A blood Pa and boy can have strained relations at that age too. And I know a Ma can err, though in my heart I wanted to do all 'twas right to do to prevent losing closeness with my child.

Manhood takes time. I've concluded AA kept dreams of how he thought home would be if Pa had come home. But I conclude, too, God is Sovereign, totally trustworthy. Won't work for me to say God looked away when our lives unfolded like they did. God knows not just earth life, but eternity too, and His eyesight's clearer than ours for sure. But sometimes hearts aren't open to hearing such thoughts, espeshly if the heart's bent on keeping a wound festering that the Great Physician offered to heal.

AA was in his teens when he whisked past me to pack his things, shouting harsh words to us 'bout our not caring 'bout him like we should and how t'other children got more minding after. I didn't raise my voice, but we talked eye to eye.

I'd prayed hard while he was upstairs packing. I slipped out and tolt John. He met Alfred on our porch and asked Alfred to reconsider, but AA wasn't of that temperament at the time. As he left without looking back, I asked John, 'What can we do?' 'Course I was hoping John would call out something that would bring sense to my child. My 'We love you, Alfred' seemed to just hang in the air without a heart to take it. As tears spilled, again I whispered, 'John, what can we do to make him come back?' John said, 'Make the road home as easy and as welcome as we can, that's all.' I couldn't bear that AA didn't even look back. 'Twas like he was saying he'd already seen us more than he wanted. My own son that I'd of given my life for just walked out. For a time both John and I kept on eye on the road, hoping we'd see Alfred.

A Sunday back our preacher talked of God turning His back to us when we sin ~ His holiness prevents His looking at sin.

'Tis easier to think of turning from God, but 'tis hard to think of God turning from us. If 'twas only love, God wouldn't turn from us. 'Tis not so much God turning 'cause He's disgusted, preacher said, but turning so His holy eyes don't have to behold sin. He said God can't let sin be in His presence and He can't let His eyes take in sin, or let His mind study sin.

So same was true when my Lord, God's precious sinless Son was on the cross becoming sin. God could not watch. Mary could and John could, their love likely made them keep looking. God's not looking didn't mean His heart wasn't broken when He severed His relationship with His Son. To think my sin, and sins of my loved ones is what put Jesus on the cross. God's heart had to breaking when He looked away. And Jesus' heart felt so forsaken by God.

I often wondert if my AA felt forsaken by Pa. Someday I hope it gets to AA that his Pa was trying to make it so he could spend even more time with AA.

I never purposefully shorted AA. He had my heart same as t'others I birthed, and on top o'that, I've a God-given capasty to love some not born to me. I don't think that's wrong. We all tolt AA here was his home. I tolt him not a day'd go by but what his Ma'd be praying for him. And that was true.

Why did things go that hard way? AA just missed his Pa. Maybe some day he needed attention I didn't give, or we heard each other wrong without knowing it. Was we wrong to keep his Pa's memory so fresh when Manuel was away to war? Maybe AA'd accepted John more if AA hadn't heard so much 'bout his Pa. But we'd hoped Manuel was coming back and 'twas what Manuel asked me to do. How was we to know Manuel'd not come home? I doubt I'd do that different.

I've worried much 'bout young Alfred. Then God reminds me, AA's Manuel's son and Manuel was early on his own too. And look how Manuel turned out. So prob'ly like Manuel's mother, I've prayed that AA's warm and well and coming to realize he's loved by us and Sovereign God.

Sometimes John's reminded me that if AA's to only understand one of those loves, 'twill be best he understands God loves him. Still, my heart tells me Alfred can't have any idea how a mother's heart aches when her child chooses to go away in anger, not letting her know if he's alive or not.

When you mourn a child you've buried, 'tis one thing. But when life you hoped you'd share with a living child ~ and the child don't want to stay 'round to share his life with people who love him, well, that's a quiet sorrow awful hard to carry too. 'Course if 'tis God's way for a child to go, a mother honours both God and the child in letting that be, too. If that was how 'twas, God would give me peace in the child's going. He offered me rest in Him. And patience. I wasn't eager to take either at first.

But lately God's added a new hope.

A person's got to hope.

Perhaps Alfred's reasoning is coming into manhood.

His letter came from Kansas, of all places, while I writ this to you. 'Kansas' kept shaping the world even 'fore we crossed the Atlantic. Kansas was part of what took Manuel from us. Maybe Kansas owes us something in God's eyes, for once again Kansas may help determine what happens in our lives....

Here's what AA writ to us:

Sheridan Township, Kansas February, 1880

Dear Ma, I take my pen in hand to write these few lines to you to tell you that I am well at present and that I hope you and the rest of the famly is well too. I've been in Kansas a few months and thought I'd write since I've been gone from Michigan 'bout five years now.

When I threw my temper tantrums and left home I headed west. I guess I headed west like my Pa did when he went out on his own. I'm glad Pa and you tolt of his life, for now I've his stories to tell children if the Lord should so bless me some day. Don't worry Ma, I don't have my cap set for any girl yet. I don't think many young women'd be thrillt to live as I live, but I intend to change my situation in time with hard and honest work.

I worked a few places and for farmers here and there in a few states. Some of the time I was befriended by a young man 'bout my age. Even heard of a Kisby a time or two, but was never close enough to establish a tie. Time came when I decided to take on Kansas as I heard talk of its farmland and adventures.

I'm not the only bachelor who's dug myself a home, though I'm young to call myself a bachelor I suppose. My dugout's in Sheridan Township in central Kansas near towns somewhat like Green Oak. One is called Clifton and people in these parts seem kind enough. Some is from England, Germany and some is Scots. Even Swedes is in these parts that's still being settled. And we've not been scalpt yet though I hear.... No, Ma, even if 'twas true I know not to speak of such dangers to you.

I do find farming satisfying and though it'll take considerable time, I'm eyeing a place that suits me if I can convince banks to let me become a real farmer. I'm saving most I earn to convince more people I have learnt from experiences.

I've done lots of thinking since the last time we talked.

I do hope this finds you well, and John too, for you two did not deserve how I was with you. I guess I'm asking your forgiveness as your son, and I guess I'd let that go for John too, if he has a mind to be forgiving toward me. My tongue and my way of thinking likely hurt you both and I want us to have no bad feelings towart each other. For the most part I can see you was treating me fair and doing what'd been good for me if I'd been less stubborn and more respectful to all my 'parents.' I want you to pass on to John that we have our differences 'bout a few things but I' finally realize John's a good man who sacrificed to care for us. John cannot take the place I have for my Pa, but John deserves my respect as I should respect a Pa, for he's cared and provided for us Kisbey children and he's been a good husband for our mother.

So, with that in mind, I extend to you and John and any t'others a 'Kansas Welcome' if you is so inclint to take me up on it. If you don't want a dugout, there's houses a distance away too, and there's lots of timber in these parts here. Not like Michigan's timber, but I 'magine generations to come will have to clear it for fields.

If you'd like to see me, I'd be honoured to have you come. I can't leave here to go to Michigan for we homesteters keep on our land so people know we is serious and not just squatting now then going. I'll check the Clifton Post Office weekly for your kind reply.

Ma and John, I don't have a fatted calf but I think I could catch good catfish from the crick if you come. We can test whether Kansas has room for both Kisbys and Reeds.

I Remain, Your Affectionate Son, Alfred A. Kisby.

Ma, you'll likely be upset I droppt the 'e' but it's shorter and Pa's was written so many different ways I thought it couldn't hurt.

PS And if you do come, I do know I'd appreciate things you and Pa brought from England that you said could one day be mine if I was so inclint. I'm now inclint, but could you holt them for me till I have a woodframe rather than a dugout?
Alfred

John's saw the letter first. He thought a week, but he does lots of thinking in a week, as we know. He's talked to blood relations and friends 'bout his place. Now our plans is we'll leave for Sheridan Township in Kansas by mid-April. Some Reeds and some Kisbeys is staying in Michigan, but some's talking of maybe joining the Kansas adventure ahet of us.

It'll be good to see Alfred.

Surely I won't write of that adventure for I'm now past fifty! (Two days!) But then, far as I knowed, I still have considerable life left in me. Therefore, don't write my obituary yet.

I'll not quit life till God wills. If He so wills, I hope you'll judge I've stood in the gap for you, or like Manuel, responsibly guarded my portion of life till you take your place in your time. We Copseys Kisbeys Reeds lived to pass to you what makes life workable. Seems 'twas God's will we simply be His common people and I purposed so He could trust us to be just that. I know to trust Him and His ways, even when I don't understand all He's 'bout. As His Word says, His way's and thoughts is higher than mine. He's trustworthy, that I know, and that's sufficient.

So I'll put down my pencils after these last words for you:

May God's mercy and grace surround you. May your life be useful to Him and to those who come after you. May you keep our name, and the Lord's name, with honour. We'd expect no less, precious ones, no less.

Esther Copsey Kisbey Reed
(Finished: Monday, March 22, 1880 A.D.)

370

As Manuel'd say, Kiss all the children for me, for us, for children must know they is loved by you, faults and all, cause faults don't last forever.

P.S. Some people's putting 'Reed' as Read, and also Reid. And Alfred's writ Kisby. I've seen Esther as Ester on some records.

Soon 'twill be your turn to keep spellings straight.

Truth be tolt, spelling don't matter as much as people's thoughts when they hear a name, so make it pleasant to the ears for generations to come, whether born to you, brought in by you to your home, or just pleasant to think on 'cause you was the neighbor God knowed they needed. So be it.

Now, dear ones, whether my blood descendants or brought into ours and God's expanding famly one way or t'other, but all through the blood of the Savior, when you find this to read somewhere, I leave you this bit of counsel: Don't stew over another's ripples, you just make the ripples Our Creator's planned for you. That's all He asks.

If I don't meet you in this life, we'll keep watch for you along Heaven's rippling shore till we greet you some good and distant day.

You'll be there, won't you?

'Til then, you set your mind to ripple, Loved Ones, ripple.

The End

A NOVEL APPROACH TO BIBLE STUDY
LESSON TEN - QUESTIONS 189-216
(INCLUDES QUESTIONS REFERENCING
"GOOD MR. REED"/CHAPTER NINE AND THE NOVEL.)

THANK YOU ... *for doing a "novel approach to Bible study." This is the last assignment for this novel. The author's other novels will likely also have discussion guides and Bible studies, but most will probably be shorter. If you'd like her to minister to your group, please contact her at* <u>author.speaker4Him@gmail.com</u>
Last assignment for "Unto All Generations/formerly Leaves that Did Not Wither" . . .

Please read Psalm 1, 145, Proverbs 22, and the warnings about gossip from James (New Testament).

189) Esther jumps right in and tells her readers about the "unwelcome rocks in the stream" that were part of the life she shared with Emanuel. She is referring back to the lesson Emanuel's father taught when the son and father splashed rocks in a stream and talked about consequences in the early chapters. What are the rocks Esther identifies as "unwelcome" in these last chapters, and are they prevalent today in your community?

190) One of Emanuel's goals had been to live his name with honor among his fellowmen and before God. In this chapter, we see different ways Esther tried to ensure "Kisbey" was an honorable name. List a few of the ways Esther sought to help honor her husband and her children's surname.

191) There are instances throughout the book of Esther's humor, and it's included in this chapter as well. What does she say about "widow pity" and what opportunity happened when she was ready to justify feeling sorry for herself. When have you experienced God bringing into your awareness a need you can meet just when you might have found it easy to pity yourself? What summation of the Ten Commandments in the New Testament indicates God knew

we'd benefit from loving our neighbor, especially when the neighbor is in need?

192) Review the incident when Esther's hunting for kindling to start her stove's fire. She ends up taking us quickly through Psalm 1. Perhaps you, too, have seen spring come and noticed leaves holding on until the new growth pushed the leaves from the tree. The leaves were wrinkled and looked useless, but they still served a purpose in Esther's time of need. If lives of earlier Christians encourage us, they are like leaves that outlive their season, leaves that do not wither beyond their usefulness. How do you think Esther's character might provide enlightenment or encouragement to you when you face uncomfortable situations?

193) Many times we relatives or friends or neighbors do not provide much tangible help, partly because our lives are busy or we do not cross paths with the other people very meaningfully or very often. When Levi and Mary's letter comes in 1865, about a month before President Lincoln is assassinated, circumstances make it unlikely Esther can let them know, in a timely manner, just how difficult life has become for her and the Kisbey children. Besides the war, there was the expense of travel and communication and the bleakness of circumstances. What are the usual reasons we are not assisting others sacrificially?

194) What was the only good thing Esther ever had to say about tobacco, and why was she so opposed to its use? It has to do with the capture that helped end the war.

195) Though we've read a couple of these verses before, how might the following verses apply to a form of stewardship regarding our bodies:

"Do you not know that you are God's temple and that God's Spirit dwells in you? If anyone destroys God's temple God will destroy him. For God's temple is holy, and that temple you are...do you not know that your body is a temple of the Holy Spirit within you, which you have from God? You are not your own; you were brought with a price. So glorify God in your body." (I Corinthians 3:16; 6:19-20)
    and

"...We are the temple of the living God: as God said, 'I will live in them and move among them, and I will be their God, and they shall be my people..." (II Corinthians 6:16)

196) How practical is Esther's decision to remain in Michigan and what do you think of her statements: (Remember this is written as though her education is limited and took place in England.)

"Finally I took stock of my situation and decided I'd just make Michigan work 'cause we had friends here too. A body can't always think the place they is is not the right place to be. Sometimes the only thing missing is the decision to make it the right place and espeshly when the Lord's not opening t'other doors. A door pryed open isn't much use afterward, and in forcing a door your fingers can get caught bad. And then there was Aunt Emma's saying, 'You have what you need, you just need to use it.' And Manuel's talk about God was to be trusted even when we don't understand or see where how He's working."

197) What do Esther and the children learn about Emanuel's honorable death and how might they have more closure since they had never received the body or personal effects? How important are "closures" to you when someone dies?

198) Esther again speaks about rippling waters, an image she has used in every chapter. In this instance, the rippling water she focuses upon becomes her encouragement which she passes on to her readers because it helped her begin afresh in tackling responsibilities. What was her focus and advice?

199) What were the circumstances that brought "Good Mr. Reed" into her life and how would you speculate God had prepared her for this situation when you consider a few earlier sorrows she had known? Esther sometimes gets a bit close to "Gossip" when she relates her encounters with one particular woman. How do you think Esther will need to continue working on handling gossip and its consequences that can occur both inwardly and for its victims? Why is it easiest to see another's faults?

200) In the book of James, a whole portion is about the evil nature of the tongue. What tips did you harvest about your own tongue from the little book of James?

201) God became Esther's "husband" before she remarried. He became the "father" to her "orphaned" children. Widows and orphans are tenderly watched over by the Lord God in different passages within the Bible (Hagar, Naomi, the widow Jesus cares for, etc.) and God's presence is with several 'orphaned' youth within the scriptures (Moses, Joseph, Daniel, etc). God sets the pattern of caring for widows and orphans and reiterates that in James 1:27, which you read earlier.

In Isaiah 54, God tenderly tells Israel, *"Fear not...for your Maker is your husband, the Lord of hosts is His name; and the Holy One of Israel is your Redeemer, the God of the whole earth he is called. For the Lord has called you like a wife forsaken and grieved in spirit, like a wife of youth when she is cast off, says your God."*

Husbands are to be providers, protectors, and defenders of their wives and children. That is part of the role assigned to them by God in the Bible. In what ways did Mr. Reed serve in those roles even before he and Esther ever spent time getting acquainted?

202) How does James 1:26 apply to John's little speech at the church? How does James 1:27 apply to John's behavior before and after he met Esther?

203) Sometimes when couples marry who both have been widowed, there is a sensitivity toward the other's first spouse. Widows and widowers generally enter into a second marriage differently than those who chose to divorce. Understandably, those who have gone through a divorce are likely to be more hesitant to trust the "goodness" of another person since their earlier marriage did not last. Widows and widowers may remarry with different "baggage," and may come into a remarriage with a great deal of trust and joyful expectation, or perhaps with measured contentment even if the other person is not "perfect." What advantages did these two have in their marriage, even when it did not start with a strong fascination for each other?

204) How did John express his tenderness toward Esther and yet maintain his love for his first wife? Consider his actions not only in this chapter but how he was earlier introduced to readers.

205) How did Esther express her tenderness toward John and keep her two promises, which included loving God and Emanuel until her death?

206) As the book ends, another heartache is revealed with the encouraging possibility of restoration. Esther realizes how similar generational stories can become: Emanuel's father died when Emanuel was young; Emanuel died when Alfred was young; both Emanuel and Alfred were out on their own early though by somewhat different circumstances. Both Emanuel and Alfred desired to keep their families together, but in Alfred's case, his actions do some of the fracturing. As you might guess, the author has now written the sequel though she's altered the names a bit so she's no longer writing about people in her family's graves. When, and why, did Esther's young son leave Michigan?

207) Note that throughout the novel, we see Esther maturing in her faith and personality. By the last chapter, she applies II Corinthians 1:3-4, regarding comforting others with the comfort with which she was comforted. Rightfully so, it took time for her to accept the sadness that came with losing her own children (two in England and one in Michigan). God had her tender heart enabled to care for others' children, including her sister's children and later, the widower's children. In God's economy, Esther's needs are met and her faith becomes stronger and, interestingly, when the book ends, she has to acknowledge she is a woman blessed. She discovers God is actively still faithful, good, and loving, even when life is hard. How have you discovered that truth? When you re-read James one, what maturing benefits did you note from verses 2-4?

208) Esther's closing thoughts offer a few questions for her readers to evaluate. Has she "stood in the gap," responsibly guarding her portion of life until the next generation takes her place? Can you apply Psalm 145 to her, and consider it for your own life direction as well?

209) Esther lived partly to pass on what was "workable." What sage advice did she impart throughout the novel and now in her summary statements?

210) Esther says if she doesn't meet you in this life, she's counting on seeing you along Heaven's rippling shore some good and distant day. Obviously, since Esther died in 1912, meeting her, or other loved ones who have died as believers in Jesus Christ, in heaven is your only real option. How are you certain you will be there? Which of these scriptures are most useful to you in proclaiming that "know so" certainty to someone who is unsure about where he or she will spend eternity?

A. John 14:6 (Jesus): *"I am the way, and the truth, and the life; no one comes to the Father, but through Me."*

B. John 3:36 *He who believes in the Son has eternal life; but he who does not obey the Son shall not see life, but the wrath of God abides on him.*

C. John 3:16, 17 *For God so loved the world, that He gave His only begotten Son, that whoever believes in Him should not perish, but have eternal life. For God did not send the Son into the world to judge the world, but that the world should be saved through Him.*

D. John 1:11-12 *He (Jesus) came to His own, and those who were His own did not receive Him. But as many as received Him to them He gave the right to become children of God, even to those who believe on His name...* (This is the 'believe, receive, become' passage many like to use to explain salvation through Jesus Christ.)

E. Romans 3:23 *...for all have sinned and fall short of the glory of God.*

F. First John 1:8-10 *If we say that we have no sin, we are deceiving ourselves, and the truth is not in us. If we confess our sins, He is faithful and righteous to forgive us our sins and to cleanse us from all unrighteousness. If we say that we have not sinned, we make Him a liar, and His word is not in us.*

G.   Romans 6:23 *For the wages of sin is death, but the free gift of God is eternal life in Christ Jesus our Lord.*

H.   Ephesians 2:8-9 *For by grace you have been saved through faith; and that not of yourselves, it is the gift of God; not as a result of works* (my own goodness acted out to please God), *that no one should boast.*

I.   Romans 10: 9-10 *...if you confess with your mouth Jesus as Lord, and believe in your heart that God raised Him from the dead, you shall be saved; for with the heart man believes, resulting in righteousness, and with the mouth he confesses resulting in salvation.*

J.   Romans 8:1 *There is therefore now no condemnation for those who are in Christ Jesus.*

K.   First John 3:1 *See how great a love the Father has bestowed upon us, that we should be called children of God, and such we are...*

211) Esther's goals included honoring vows she made to both Emanuel and to God. Even when Emanuel failed to return from the war, she kept her vows to love and honor him, incorporating his goals into her life as much as she could. Beyond her immense loyalty to loved ones, her faith and trust in God grew. She increasingly learned to dismiss the unimportant things by prioritizing. She kept her humor despite when life was hard and the family was hungry, but she also legitimized real sorrow while acknowledging that God was still in charge. She was confident heaven was ahead for her.

Emanuel's desires focused on holding family together, whether that be his first or second family or the country that was splitting apart shortly after his arrival, and secondly, to live a Christian life so the name of His Lord and his family name would be honored.

In taking up the task of writing about their lives, Esther was attempting to help bring honor to her husband's name and character because she worried both the government and her runaway son had questioned the motivation and the genuineness of Emanuel's desire to serve the United States of America. The government's bungling of his name probably caused the legal issues that arose, which denied

Esther and the children the pensions they were due, as well as the army payments while Emanuel served. The son, however, built resentment toward John, so he's not listening to Esther's verbal explanations about Emanuel's time in the service.

How closely did Esther fulfill her vows to the Lord and to Emanuel, and did she help prove that Emanuel had sacrificially attempted to fulfill his goals? If her runaway son were to ever read Esther's writings, do you think most of his resentment toward John would end? Why or why not? How did marrying John, or anyone, fit with faithfulness to Emanuel's goals... or did it?

212) I first entitled the novel, "Leaves That Did Not Wither" and retitled it, "Unto All Generations," because I felt that part of the reason my father became a Christian man was because Esther's faith had outlived her. Becoming a Christian is an individual decision, but we can influence the atmosphere in which our children and grandchildren will be raised. I do believe my father's parents and grandparents influenced my father's willingness to explore the Christian faith, but coming to faith in Jesus Christ had to be his, and later, my own decision. As others have said, there are no grandchildren of God, we have to become children of God by a new birth. Christianity is an option. The "faith of our fathers" cannot save us, but it can lovingly demonstrate faith in action.

My mother, too, was an exemplary Christian woman who actively nurtured our faith, and her grandchildren's faith, in word and deed. I am indebted to both of them for the values they instilled in each of us children.

Their desire to pass on the Christian faith, to "work the soil," made us more receptive to hearing about Jesus Christ. Their example helped us want to have a personal intimacy with Jesus, too. Esther and Emanuel's faith, and their descendants' faith, became like leaves that did not wither, influencing generation after generation. A good example increases the likelihood of a future generation becoming interested in Jesus Christ.

I realized, as I sought to live my Christian life in front of my children, that day-to-day schedules exposed just how much control I yielded to the Holy Spirit. Of course, I sometimes failed miserably in imitating Jesus Christ. I do hope, though, that my children and grandchildren will also conclude that I, too, was a leaf that did not wither when it comes to living my faith in Jesus Christ as Savior and Lord, and that they want to become those kinds of leaves, too, so the Christian influence continues to be lived out for future generations.

That faith legacy is more important than any financial gift I could give them. The china in the cabinet, the old pitcher, the ancient mantel clock, an odd silver dollar or two, these all lose their value in a disaster or, at most, bring pleasure for a brief time. However, if I can encourage my family and friends to trust Jesus Christ as their own Savior and Lord, well, that legacy has eternal results for them.

We all will leave a legacy, a reputation, a character attribute that is associated with who we were. What are you doing about your legacy that outlives you and will benefit someone for eternity? Read I Corinthians 11:1, Matthew 5:14-16, and John 13:15.

213) You've completed the Bible study and are ready to set aside the novel. Why would a loving God ever dismantle our comfort zones? What insights were reinforced or introduced to help you hold on to faith and humor when God seems to be dismantling your comfort zones?

214) Which verses or concepts made you more equipped and encouraged about moving on with life when it brings some hardships, sorrows, or challenges your way?

215) Esther referred to spiritual faithfulness as "standing in the gap" until the next person comes to take her place. How are you being/becoming intentional about doing that? Where are the "open places" in your surroundings that need a Christian's voice and action, that without it, the fence line will deteriorate and evil will gain more territory?

216) Are you willing to gather with others to pray for guidance so Christ's followers will "man" the "gaps" and the culture will make that turn that spares the faith for future generations?

If so, whom can you enlist to help you "make ripples"? It's never been popular to live one's Christian faith and it seems the Bible indicates the enemy will work with more brutality as the last days begin arriving. Who will you enlist to stand with you until every knee bows before the King of Kings and Lord of Lords?

Blessings upon you as you seek to remain faithful to the Lord until you see Him face to face. I'm looking forward to an eternity in heaven, how about you?

Thank you for completing these lessons. I hope this study blessed you. You didn't dig in scriptures alone, for I had to dig there first and the digging blessed me. I keep working on Bible studies, stories, articles, and/or presentations to help introduce or nurture those walking in faith in Jesus Christ. Please visit my page on Amazon to see what new works are available.

You might be interested in knowing a fictional account of the "runaway" has been completed. It's entitled, "Elizabeth's Prodigal," and though the names are altered, I think you'll easily pick up where this novel concluded.

I suppose no author says, "I've written everything I ever wanted to write…." So, watch for updates about more writings just waiting to get onto paper.

Thank you!
Margery Kisby Warder
Author.speaker4Him@gmail.com

Other comments from the author . . . .

How would we have reacted if we'd walked in Esther or Emanuel's shoes? What kept young Esther from wanting to know the love of her life? Esther made changes she hadn't planned to make, but did she believe they were worth it?

I've observed our default reasoning wants to excuse our own imperfection more easily than to overlook the imperfection in others. We come into the world ready to be self-centered, giving little concern that our lives can inconvenience others.

381

Have you ever thought about the fact that if circumstances were "right," we'd sit on thrones with servants and insist our fairytale life come true? Is there even one kernel of decency in our longing for a perfectly wonderful life?

A perfect earthly life is unrealistic. We all mess that up. But, take heart. The good news is that there is at least one kernel of decency in our longing for a perfectly wonderful life. The problem, the bad news is that there are a thousand other less noble kernels eager to overpower the one kernel and shove it to the bottom of the bin.

That one kernel knows this: God has put a longing for our home in eternity, where everything exists in perfection, in our hearts and minds (Ecclesiastes 3:11). We look around at circumstances and headlines and we know we were created for more than this! We know we were made for more than chasing after a now when there's a forever to be had.

Our problem of not living that perfect life here on earth is universal.

Our first parents chose to destroy our unhindered entrance into living a life of ease, of perfect communion with our Holy Creator, of being thoroughly mesmerized by the beauty of vibrant life around us, of seeing nothing working its way toward death.

The indisputable fact is that ever since the garden, we've familiarized ourselves with the "It's not my fault" chant. True, our first parents started it, but if we had been in the garden, there would have been a day when we would have set out for the tree, touched it, and decided no one, not even our Creator, could tell us to get along without what we wanted. We can blame our earliest parents, but we know we would have done the same thing. We can't always turn down things we should in our lives now, so what's the difference? We'd have bit into the forbidden fruit, too.

As long as we're on earth, we're physically bound to living with the consequences of existing in a fallen world, but our hearts long for what was to have been and what our Creator has prepared for His children.

How will we have the right to gain heaven instead of reaping the consequences of our selfish living?

Thankfully none of us can earn our entrance into heaven. That's the good news. It makes things fair.

The worst possible news is that unless we intentionally change where we're headed, we'll miss eternity in God's presence and instead spend our forever cast away from God's mercy.

If we reject Jesus Christ, we'll spend our eternity where evil is unharnessed, unrestrained. All those horrible things we've wanted to avoid in this life will pale in comparison to an eternity coming to those who reject God's only offer of escape.

The God of heaven tells us that unless we believe in Jesus Christ as our only Savior from sin's consequences, we are doomed, but at least He tell us. Jesus sometimes told his listeners, "He who has ears to hear, hear."

And, besides warning us, God prompts us to realize He loves us and is asking us to come to Him. He planned for us to spend eternity with Him. That's why Jesus Christ went to the cross: to die for mankind's sins, to take those sins upon Himself, bearing their punishment.

Prayerfully consider this, speaking about Jesus Christ:

He was in the world, and the world was made by him, and the world knew Him not. He came unto His own, and His own received Him not. But as many as received Him, to them gave He power to become the sons of God, even to them that believe on His name: Which were born, not of blood, nor of the will of the flesh, nor of the will of man, but of God. (John 1:10-13, King James Version)

Jesus said, "I am the way, the truth, and the life, and no man comes to the Father but by Me" (John 14:6)

I'd dare say there's little point in arguing with the Creator who loves us!

(from my blog ...)

Website/Blog:http://margerywarder.com

Appendix

Nearly all scripture within Leaves That Did Not Wither/Unto All Generations are from "The Book of Common Prayer... , later versions of the King James Bible, and from the non-copyrighted "The Soldier's Prayer Book. duplicate of the 1861 Union Soldier's Prayer Book, as noted on the copyright page.

Research was conducted via internet and family members to discover facts and understand documents about both Esther and Emanuel in England and from their United States land purchases and, after Emanuel's death, documented appeals for funds due a widow and children of a Union soldier. Marriage, births, deaths, and military records and wills were resources to supplement family information. Military records were found for Emanuel and Levi Kisbey/Kisby and for George Fowler. Fowler's obituary and family research provided most of the facts for this character, the husband of Emanuel's sister. Both Levi and Sallie/Sarah came to America after their father's death, likely coming with and later settling near the aunt and uncle referred to in their letters. Rightly or wrongly, a reference to Ned's difficult unnamed and stingy wife who refuses to help Esther was the basis for Aunt Gertrude.

Copies of the 1863-1865 letters from Emanuel (E. L. Richey as 'scribe'), Levi Kisby, and Sarah Kisbey Fowler and E. L. Richey are owned by the author of Leaves That Did Not Wither through estate distribution to descendents of Esther Copsey Kisbey Reed and are quoted precisely within the manuscript with the exception of one letter's fictional and non-significant, but more suitable ending. Richey's letter of Emanuel's homecoming is word for word.

Esther Copsey Kisbey (Kisby) Reed's obituary (died December, 1912, in Clifton Kansas) tells that Esther became a Christian at an early age, received *The Book of Common Prayer* from her brother James for her tenth birthday, her marriage to both Emanuel and John, the children born to them and their deaths in infancy, and included the account of God's provision when she was destitute and suffered deprivations because of Emanuel's death during his service with Michigan's Third Cavalry in 1864 and not receiving pension money due his widow and children. She had fed the children the last of what she had in the house and had put the children to bed while she spent the night in prayer and weeping and, the obituary states, Esther always believed that God who fed the ravens and who never let His children go begging bread (Quotes Psalm 37:25) brought the neighbor to Esther's door the next morning who subsequently brought them their needed food. Esther Copsey Kisby Reed is buried north of Clifton, Kansas, as are some members and descendents of her family.

Michigan Third Cavalry and Emanuel's military life were researched for accuracy to the best of the author's ability as were military and other records for Levi Kisby and family and George Fowler and family. Census records were of assistance for all family members.

John Reed's obituary, also from Clifton, Kansas, in the 1890's, tells that he was a Bible teacher and died in his home one Sunday after church while visiting with his family and would be buried the following day. He was a successful farmer in both Michigan and Kansas. The author has been in the comfortable, pillared Reed home that the family believes was where Esther and John Reed resided before leaving for Kansas in April, 1880, to relocate near son Alfred Kisby.

Alfred Kisby did leave home at about age thirteen because, the family understands, he and John Reed were having difficulties with each other at that point. Alfred reportedly lived in various states before living in his dugout in Kansas. When Esther and John and their younger children moved to Kansas in April 1880, Alfred apparently re-united with them. We know Alfred devoted time tending to the needs of his mother, step-father, sister Emma and step-sister Anna's until death parted them. Alfred married Grace Campbell and became a well-to-do and charitable farmer in Kansas. They raised four sons and three daughters on the farm near the author's childhood home. Her father, Earl, was one of those sons. Alfred's will gave information about items brought to America.

Copies of several notes from the Kisby/Reed family Bible were given to the author to help identify family members and facts, including the information about Esther's sister's death. Other family researchers, in the USA and England, gave information to the author which helped develop character information. Not all our conclusions were identical. The author asks for grace in our differences, especially as she wove together the facts with speculation to create this story. Some family timelines on both sides of the 'pond'/Atlantic do not exactly reconcile. Sometimes it appeared several relatives liked using the same names over and over and based on the best conclusions at the time, the author constructed this historical and fictional blending to create a story for others to enjoy. Many facts are exact according to records and the rest is fictionl.

Research about Livingston County, Michigan, its residents, and legal documents regarding Esther after Emanuel's death were helpful sources. Margaret, for example, was both Esther's brother-in-law's new wife and Esther's midwife. Relatives doing family research contributed their facts for consideration for which the author is grateful.

A few characters are purely fictional and many historical/actual individual characteristics, conversations, and incidents within the novel are entirely fictional. 'O'course' some of the same blood runs through the author's veins as did in the two main characters, and if patterns of thinking and other personality traits are passed from generation to generation, perhaps not all 'speculation' is entirely 'fictional' after all.

Respectfully,

Esther and Emanuel Kisbey's Grateful Great-Granddaughter,
Alfred and Grace Campbell Kisby's Granddaughter,
Earl and Astrid Kisby's daughter,
Margery Kisby Warder, Author, writer, speaker, Family/their times researcher,
'Civil War letters' transcriber, and Keeper of papers for projects to remember common people living lives that honour the Lord Jesus Christ.

Author's Contact Information

Margery Kisby Warder's latest writings can be found at her website (http://margerywarder.com) or on her author page on Amazon:(http://www.amazon.com/Margery-Kisby-Warder/e/B00GPELE7I/ ref=ntt_athr_dp_pel_1)

Titles *from* Parson's Creek Press

Christmas in Our Hearts* in Christmas Musings(2013)
Christmas Musings – Contains 3*(2013)
Elizabeth's Prodigal (Includes abbreviated "Novel Approach to Bible Study) (2015)
Last Christmas* in Christmas Musings (2013)
Mary, Meet Dr. Luke* in Christmas Musings (2013)
Twelve Times Through: Daily Directions for Life from the Book of Proverbs (2014)
Unto All Generations & A Novel Approach to Bible Study: Holding onto Faith and Humor When God Dismantles Our Comfort Zones (2015)

Other Titles by Margery Kisby Warder

Leaves That Did Not Wither (same story as "Unto All Generations," without Bible study); Xulon Press, 2009.

Essays in both "Seasons of Life" and "Seasons Remembered"
"Wings Against the Storm,"
"The Scoop on Leadership Development," "Marveling at Gracious Love," and "My Tribute to a Gracefully Aging Lady"

(Articles by the author appeared in both Villisca Viking and Red Oak Express, weekly newspapers in Iowa, from about 2000-2011. Letters to the Editor have appeared in various newspapers. Her earliest published magazine article was in the early 1970's.)

Website/Blog:http://margerywarder.com
Facebook: https://www.facebook.com/margerykisbywarder

Note to Bible Study Leaders:

When I began this combination of a novel and a Bible study, I had every intention of keying pages to the questions. However, as I revised and reformatted the manuscript, the page numbers became all jumbled and I knew each electronic reading device would scramble them more! Thus, I ended up deleting them because an incorrect number could be more frustrating than no number.

If you are stymied about the point of a question, or would like my insights, please feel free to email me if you do not see the answers when I blog about the Bible study questions for a span of time after this novel is published.

Note to those who have "Writing a Book" as part of your ministry, I like to encourage others who want to get the Word out through both fiction and nonfiction. I am holding a "Missional Christian Writers Retreat" in 2015, and may decide to hold others if there is sufficient interest. I see a Christian author's words as missionaries to a reading world.

One "sequel" to 'Unto All Generations" is "Elizabeth's Prodigal." The runaway is Albert instead of Alfred, and the mother and step-father are Elizabeth and Matthew rather than Esther and John. I chose not to tie myself to total accuracy when writing about people in my family's graves. "Elizabeth's Prodigal" is fiction, but it contains many truths and has a very abbreviated Bible study included.

Thank you.

Preview of "Elizabeth's Prodigal" on the following pages... The story picks up a few pages in.... (Albert might well be Alfred...)

The Storm Breaks Forth

LORD, *you have examined me and you know me. You know everything I do; from far away you understand all my thoughts. You see me, whether I am working or resting; you know all my actions. Psalm 139:1-3*

1875, Michigan

One glance at the two dog-eared books resting alongside Matthew Redding's smooth-armed oak rocker proved the King James Holy Bible narrowly outranked The Old Farmer's Almanac. However, as good as the almanac was for predicting weather for a farmer's planting season, it completely missed the life-altering storm that fell upon that Michigan farm on a muggy Wednesday afternoon in the late spring of 1875.

For weeks that spring Albert had spent his spare time planning how to make his mark in the world.

He was a quick thinker, a reader, and a listener who mulled over ideas others shared. He would not duplicate their efforts; he'd devise ingenious ways to surpass them. If their simple ideas were successful, wouldn't better ideas mean greater success?

His interest in school had not always been as keen. There had been days, and quiet conversations between his ma and his teachers, to discuss Albert's supposedly bleak future. That was before his interest in school had been sparked by a most unusual paragraph in a newspaper. Now, years later, Albert had big plans.

Albert longed to hold onto any morsel of memory he had of his father, and he mentally catalogued any information others had added. Obviously, his father had been a horseman, so it seemed unavoidably natural to Albert that he, like his father Emanuel, had a fascination for horses. He wanted to be like Pa in as many ways as he could because Albert never forgot he was a Kelsey. He never let others forget that important part of his identification, too. Albert knew Pa had signed up near Christmas in 1863 because the cavalry needed men. Before Albert was old enough to continuously pull his own weight in farm chores, his favorite pastime was watching horses. He especially watched colts and yearlings as they reared and raced across pastures on the Redding farm. They had freedom to live out who they were created to be.

His love of horses, therefore, made it inevitable that, when Albert was nine, he would notice a horse sketched in ink on the front page of Matthew's weekly newspaper. He consumed the article about Kingfisher and his already active imagination kicked into a gallop. He even desired to talk about it at school.

Miss Gilkey noted his demeanor with surprise. Devoted to teaching, she routinely studied Albert intently to see if she could somehow entice him toward learning. She tried topics from anteaters to zebras, but Albert had only sighed and looked out the window. He had only raised his hand once, and that was to ask how long until recess. Miss Gilkey spent evenings thinking about quitting her profession, but knew that other students did well under her tutelage. Besides, what else could she do?

The very night before Albert's demeanor changed, Miss Gilkey shed tears over another "F" on Albert's illegible spelling test. What should she do? He'd not be the only Albert she would teach. If she couldn't teach him, should she quit? The board was sure to want a reason. Young women taught until some man proposed marriage. Dare she risk discouraging any interest a certain young farmer had shown by buying her boxed supper a week earlier?

And then, Albert came to school a bit more excited.

Miss Gilkey liked challenging her students in any way she could. Was there finally something that might draw her despondent third grade student out of his aloofness and into his studies? She was certain he was capable of excelling, but equally certain she could not spur him on to become an eager learner unless she encouraged his pursuit of some topic that interested him.

She watched quiet Albert that recess as he timidly told the boys about the article he'd read in Matthew's newspaper. He had read? Miss Gilkey hadn't even been certain Albert recognized his alphabet. She had edged closer to eavesdrop, and to observe a transformation.

Once the boys heard Albert tell how quickly a man's fortune changed by making a wise purchase, shy Albert had listeners. Though Miss Gilkey feared the school board would severely criticize her if anything she taught dared suggest horseracing was an honorable way to earn a living, she did let the enthusiastic boys learn how to do any math Albert needed help deciphering.

Once Albert figured that some man named Swigert invested four hundred and ninety dollars that grew to nearly one thousand percent profit, he bolted through the academic starting gate. He loved working with numbers. He wrote imperfect poems rhyming Albert with Swigert. He began using words like "speculation" and "strategy" in sentences where other boys opted for "guess" or kept silent. Almost immediately, Albert volunteered to read and write stories for extra credit, which soon, he did not need.

Miss Gilkey had allowed his mind to gallop, and since Albert's high marks consistently won the school countywide recognition, the school board only raised eyebrows when they finally realized horseracing stories had started it. Albert's educators continued to refer to him as someone "gifted" and "exceptional" in calculations and problem solving. Miss Gilkey kept teaching, even postponing her answer to Richard Hultgren's marriage proposal until she was sure Albert could sail through his last exams with perfection.

Receiving the county's highest score on the eighth grade examination earned him a nice letter of commendation from the county superintendent, nodding approval from Ma, and a silver dollar from Matthew Redding. Most importantly to Albert, the score confirmed he could trust the value of his thoughts and rely upon the reasoning congregating in his head.

Those who sat around the Redding supper table were not as impressed with Albert's mind as he was. He understood why. They were people who worked slow and steady. They were skeptical about new ideas and untested methods. They liked old ruts.

Though Matthew could afford to buy the new, he saw little logic in risking the purchase price of something that "might work" for what already worked, even if the "new" boasted about saving time or money. Oh, Matthew looked through advertisements posted at farm implement businesses in nearby towns.

Matthew even took his older boys along to visit manufacturing plants in Ann Arbor. However, Matthew was strongly opposed to, even feared, idleness for his boys. Most excursions brought home a new scythe or hand tool rather than a piece of equipment for his teams of horses to pull. After all, he had lots of young men to train for manhood and sweat was good for cleansing the body of impurities.

What was so wrong about wanting to find an easy route to reach one's goals? What was so horrid about wanting to end up with a more comfortable life?

Many in the community would say the Reddings' lives were comfortable. Albert knew that. But the buildings, the herds and flocks, and the seemingly endless acres all required long hours and hard work. Year 'round. Daily. Weekly, except on Sabbath. When would the comfortable life require less effort?

At least Albert wasn't afraid to make plans for change.

Every time Albert thought about Swigert's luck in turning fast profits with Kingfisher, he could almost hear prize money jingling in his pocket. Of course, he didn't yet own a fast three-year-old racehorse, and though Matthew had a couple nice horses his family could ride, and ride at a good pace occasionally, neither of them were sure bets in a race. He needed a real horse. A fast one.

If Matthew Redding were to release much cash for horses, he'd purchase another good workhorse team. There was no sense in asking him to consider a racehorse instead.

Albert certainly didn't have four hundred and ninety dollars to buy a fast horse. He didn't have but a half-dozen silver dollars, and as Ma and Matthew pointed out, those wouldn't buy much since gold had replaced silver in "the crime of '73."

So far, when he asked about earning money elsewhere, Ma and Mr. Redding reminded him he needed to work on the farm that provided for his daily needs. After one discussion, Matthew commented that when Albert turned eighteen, he'd "settle up" with him for any extra work he did if Albert chose not to remain as part of the Redding farms.

Now, at thirteen, eighteen seemed eons away. Albert figured he'd be long gone before then.

So, as Albert pitched hay to livestock or drove sheep back to their shed at the end of day, or sat astride Starlight when she wasn't about to foal, or Chester, but still not yet astride Gideon, Albert let his imagination spend and re-spend the prize money he'd someday have from a racehorse like Kingfisher.

First, though, he'd have to break loose from the confines of the Redding farm. Then his best plan would be to cleverly purchase the next unnoticed great racehorse. In his mind, there was nothing he could not do; or a place he could not go, if he had money. In fact, if his own pa was alive somewhere, money would certainly help Albert find him, and oh, how they'd make up for the years they had missed.

In fairness, racehorses were Albert's most entertaining ideas, but they weren't his only. Albert quickly saw solutions and shortcuts to reduce work on the farm.

Albert wasn't opposed to having partners if they became his shortcut to wealth. Finding partners who recognized his logic was more difficult than expected.

He tentatively tested the waters to see if his own Kelseys might come on board with any number of his plans. Shortsightedness cost them their opportunities.

It took him a few days of rehearsal, but one afternoon he managed to have enough courage to propose two of his best ideas to Mr. Redding. He was uncomfortable around the man, and when Mr. Redding said he thought Albert better think on the idea a bit more, he bolted without any further explanation. He casually hinted about ideas with the Redding boys. He concluded his closest audiences were either only half-heartedly interested or entirely disinterested.

The barn became his refuge. There he mulled over imaginations and new concepts, tossing some and tailoring others for success. Restlessness plagued him. Patience ebbed. Change begged to offer him the reins to set him free.

Then one day, in an unanticipated moment, a couple randomly dismissive remarks clashed with restraints that had bound Albert to civility, and for far too long people would remember the tone and words of that day in the barn and on the back porch that exposed the ugliness of festering wounds and plaguing questions.

Jonathan Kelsey, now twenty-years-old, impatiently waited to step from the chilly barn into the sunny barnyard to tackle some odd jobs waiting there. Albert was into one of his nonstop talking sprees and mistakenly thought the two "real" brothers were having a meaningful conversation.

Suddenly, Jonathan interrupted, "Albert, stop. Don't tap that nail! You're not paying attention to what you're doing! Honestly, Albert, sometimes you just jabber away, lost in your dream world of making fast money, talking about some racehorse when the horse depending upon you right now is about to suffer because you're not concentrating. Albert…"

"Hold on! What's your gripe? I've shoed horses for over a year and Chester trusts me."

Jonathan now bent down to be face-to-face with Albert who had placed Chester's right front hoof between his knees. "First," Jonathan said, trying to drive home a point but aware his brother was just thirteen, "I don't think you spent enough time preparing Chester's foot to put on a shoe, and second, look at what you have in your hands. It's not even Chester's shoe."

"Oops, didn't notice that. Thanks for catching it." Albert knew as soon as the casual words were out that Jonathan wanted greater remorse on Albert's part.

"Catching it? Come on, Albert. It's careless. Your mind's a million miles from the hoof you're supposed to be trimming to shoe. If I weren't here watching you, we'd have a lame horse in no time. Honestly, you need to learn…"

"Need to learn? I know how to do this; I've shoed horses lots of times. Calm down, big brother! I just grabbed the wrong shoe, but I only started to put in the nail. You talk like I don't care about horses. I wouldn't intentionally put the wrong shoe on him. Give me a break. It's not like I don't ever see things you do wrong."

"Albert, this wouldn't happen if you were more realistic instead of coming up with all the wishful thinking you keep jabbering about." Jonathan picked up the correct horseshoe and handed it to Albert. "Do you think you can do this or should I finish up here and you go in the corral and hammer nails in a few places that are loose? At least there you wouldn't be hurting anyone but yourself if you do it wrong."

Albert set Chester's foot down. He quickly untied his leather apron, roughly letting it and the tools fall at Jonathan's feet "You're like the others. You don't want to hear my ideas. Some brother you are!" Albert felt his face reddening as he grabbed the claw hammer from its place on the wall and headed toward the door.

William Redding, fifteen, had overheard them. "What'd ya do now, Albert?" he asked as he pitched another forkful of dry hay into the mangers for the evening milking.

"Leave me alone, all of you, hear? I get sick of all you thinking just because you're older you're all so much wiser than me!" he yelled as he headed into the corral.

"Calm down, Albert," Jonathan called after him. "Sometimes we all have to realize we don't know as much as we think we do."

William watched Jonathan begin refiling Chester's front hoof. "Was he that lost in his daydreams?"

Jonathan looked up at William without commenting and went back to his filing. Jonathan saw a lot of potential in William, but one of William's shortcomings was his unbridled tongue. Another was his eagerness to drive a wedge between the Kelsey brothers. Jonathan wasn't going to gang up on Albert and Albert didn't need a nosey peer correcting him.

William climbed out of the haymow to watch Jonathan's work before strolling to the narrow opening in the barn door. He liked checking on other people's work more than working, but he felt most comfortable checking on Albert's work. He'd been around Albert for years, even before spending the last seven in the same house since his pa married Albert's ma.

William competed for his busy father's attention, especially when Matthew had to spend time trying to talk sense into Albert. When Albert was in a good mood, the two boys had fun together, but when he was in a rotten mood, or when he paraded his smarts in front of others, both of which happened regularly, William had little patience with him.

Albert's back was to William, the hammer dangling in his hand.

"Looks like ole Albert is still looking for his pa to come walking through the creek," William said loud enough for Albert to look his way. He raised his voice. "Albert, if you ask me, ten years is about as long as it ought to take for even a man on stumps to make it back if he was coming. It's time you gave up…"

William didn't finish his thought. Jonathan's firm grip swung him back inside the barn, one fist above his face. "William Redding, don't you ever, ever talk like that again, you hear? I'm so close to knocking sense into your head that when I count to ten you better be out there making things right with Albert or I'll be figuring out how to apologize to your pa for the mess I'll have made of you, hear?" He shoved William through the door toward Albert.

William untangled his feet and headed slowly toward Albert, glancing over his shoulder to be certain he would go unassisted. He disliked when Jonathan got bossy and threw his weight around.

However, William knew Matthew respected Jonathan's opinion about most things, even though William was Matthew's son. Now he'd been ordered to make things right with Albert. What should he say? Could he let his words come so they kept Jonathan inside the barn, yet spared him total humiliation in front of a whiner several months younger than he was?

Albert waited, fists clenched, seething at the disrespect not only shown to his Pa, but also toward him. Albert's fights had taught him a few holds that triumphed over his opponents, so fear wasn't a factor as William cautiously approached. He eyed William. "You have something to say to me?"

"Yeah, I do, Albert. I will apologize for saying that about 'stumps'..." The movement of four Kelsey feet confirmed William had not yet offered a fit apology.

Abruptly raising his hands to keep the Kelseys at bay, William rushed to continue. "Okay, so even if my words weren't the right ones, Albert, can't you agree you spend way too much time feeling 'sad' about not having your pa?"

William heard Jonathan widening the barn door as it rolled on its hangers. He looked back to see Jonathan standing, feet apart, arms crossed. William needed to rapidly water down what he'd implied. "I chose the wrong words," he said quickly, turning to see if he would have a two-way or a three-way conversation. "Let me explain...by telling you what I ought to have said instead."

"Go on," Albert said, sizing up the difference William's sixteen months and twenty pounds would mean in a fight. Matthew would punish physical fights among family members, but it'd be worth it.

William's mocking tone, as though he had counseled scores of troubled youth, began. "Well, I just mean, look at facts, Albert. Most of us here don't have the parents we started out having. Hugh, me, and Charley, that's three, we don't have the ma we started out with. Theo don't have either the ma or pa he started out with, so if you wanna feel sorry for someone, you oughta choose him. He's about your age and you don't see him gazing off toward heaven wondering if either of his parents are about to come back and improve his life. You three Kelseys don't have the pa you had. Of the, what's it? Eight? Of the eight unmarried people here on Pa's farm, just one has both her parents. Did you ever think of that?"

Albert hadn't actually tallied up this household in the manner William was offering, but he said, "Your point?"

"Face it, the rest of us was strong enough to get over it…"

"Over 'it'?" Albert interrupted, spitting. "That's a very cavalier way to speak of losing a parent!"

"Cav-a what?"

"You know what I mean. You're disrespectful to your ma's memory, William."

"Then say that instead of all those big words you throw around acting like you are so high and mighty compared to the rest of us. You think you're the only one who ever lost a parent, but besides those of us here on Pa's farm, I can name at least two other boys living with families that aren't the ones they started with. You're not even the youngest kid here who's missing a parent, so what gives you the right to go 'round acting like a…"

A sudden thought stopped William. Did he really want to discover the impact one, maybe two, Kelseys could inflict upon his body?

William didn't like even imagining pain. When he had been young enough to be in school, he'd endured taunts about how quickly he could high tail it for his desk if boys started shoving each other around. He'd never learned to fight, partly because he knew his pa enacted punishments for fighting.

As a child, he'd received a few physical consequences for behavior Matthew found intolerable, and those had been severe enough not to want any more. Now, most likely Matthew's punishment for family fighting would be more creative, but unwelcome just the same.

"I'm just saying you need to get to the place where you realize moping around prevents you from doing even the, shall we say, the mindless things we less brilliant people have to do, like shoeing Chester. It's not fair for you to hide behind your sadness to get out of work, if I can speak it plainly. You need to, as the Bible says, 'let the dead bury the dead.' That's all I want to say, really. I mean, face it, Albert. All the rest of us know your pa is not coming back. People think you're not that far from crazy, if you want to know the truth."

Yep. That was William. He didn't know when he'd said one sentence too much. Jonathan knew William's harsh words only mimicked brotherly compassion, but his assessment of Albert's need to get past the grief that bound him had been part of Jonathan's conversations with Albert, too. William habitually failed to sift what wandered through his mind. Matthew's most frequent reprimand of William was about William's brashness. Jonathan chose, again, to ignore William's careless words.

Albert, however, had not. His eyes blazed, "And just who around here has said I'm crazy? Tell me that, big mouth!"

From where Jonathan stood, William rather timidly shrugged his shoulders. From where Albert stood, however, William's facial contortions and his fingers' enumerations thrust another jab, and Albert exploded.

"That's it!" he said, throwing the second hammer in about as many minutes. "I hate this place and I'm outta here once and for all!" He stomped off toward the house, hoping the tears threatening to spill would not humiliate him further. He needed to find a place where he could scream his lungs out. Though Matthew Redding's acreage was vast, Albert had not found a spot where he felt he was away from everyone's scrutiny. He crossed the yard to the back porch in seconds, passing Ma and Matthew who were working with Hugh, Matthew's oldest son. He had begun building his own house on a nearby half-section of Redding land and had come by to help with the summer kitchen project.

Matthew and Ma saw Albert's face as he passed. His whole body proclaimed his fury and in near unison, they called, "Albert, what's the matter?"

Albert bounded up the steps as he yelled, "Don't talk to me. Leave me alone! I've hated this place ever since you made me set foot on it, and I hate all of you! Give me my Kelsey money and you can be rid of me once and for all!" He let the door slam behind him. .... Read more: Elizabeth's Prodigal...

Margery Kisby Warder

Made in the USA
Columbia, SC
08 October 2018